UNDER CARIBBEAN SKIES

A Novel

by

Aisha Banks

Godfolks Media Group
godfolks@aol.com
www.UnderCaribbeanSkies.com

ISBN 0-7414-4441-0

Published by:

1094 New DeHaven Street, Suite 100
West Conshohocken, PA 19428-2713
Info@buybooksontheweb.com
www.buybooksontheweb.com
Toll-free (877) BUY BOOK
Local Phone (610) 941-9999
Fax (610) 941-9959

Printed in the United States of America

Printed on Recycled Paper

Published February 2009

This book is dedicated to
John M. Banks, Jr., the love of my life. I praise God for sending you to me. You are my earthly king, my best friend, and a true example of what God means when He commands us to be a light in a dark world.

ACKNOWLEDGMENTS

I am eternally grateful to my Lord and Savior, Jesus Christ who is truly the strength of my life. Special thanks to my editor, Ann Freud, and to my editor-and-unexpected-blessing, Sharon Cole. Thanks also to Cheryl Boston, Pat Green and Joan Sibilly for their valuable feedback on drafts for this book. Much love to my sister-friends Ayana Pittman, Sandra Jenkins, Cynthia Jones, Solange Destouche, Eleanor Garcia, Dancella Hillman, Hasaana Watson, Veronica Davis-Shivers, Khadijah Jones-Calloway, Beverly Potter and Avis Harrell. Finally, thanks to my sons, Ajamu and Simeon; my grandchildren, Kamari, Ajoni, Adjoa, Asha and Amira, all my family and friends for their encouragement in making this book a reality.

Chapter 1

St. John, U.S. Virgin Islands, is one of the most breathtaking places in God's universe. About three months ago, my best friend since childhood, Lisa Walker, left Los Angeles after a failed marriage and headed for the Caribbean in search of paradise. She settled on St. John, the smallest of the three U.S. Virgin Islands. Everyday she blew up my phone asking me to join her,

"Faith, girl, there are real men out here, pack your stuff and come on!"

Real men in the islands?? Now, I like my men well-groomed. I want them to smell good, have clean nails, preferably manicured, and no little nappy peas all over their heads. I will consider dreadlocks, but they have to be salon finished, not those big clunky buzzard-nest-looking ones. Only God knows what's growing up in those things! Let's face it, with all the new beauty enhancement products on the market, there is no reason for anyone to step outside of their front door in the morning looking rough. Even 7-11 sells hair gel.

Anyway, I decided to take Lisa up on her offer. I had absolutely nothing to lose. There was definitely a dry spell going on in my life. I went to work, I went to church, and I came home. The biggest highlight of my life was watching Home and Garden TV and waiting for the brother I'd been dating for four years to put his key in my door. Lord, that was one relationship that didn't seem like it was moving forward no matter how hard I tried. Our relationship was as stagnant as a cesspool, and the sad part was he was just as happy as a pig in sunshine. I guess you could say I was partly to blame. I cooked some lip-smacking, suck your fingers, and lick-your-plate-when-nobody-was-looking dinners for him like he was my husband. I'm talking about oxtails smothered in gravy, collard greens, bar-be-que ribs in my smoker out back, peach cobbler, black forest cake and sweet potato pie just like my grandma. And did I tell you I let the man stay the night at my house? Yeah, he stayed at least five nights out of the week. On most Friday and Saturday nights, he wanted to hang out with his boys. I told myself that was cool. I'd use Friday night to do our laundry and Saturday to shop for our groceries for the week and study my cookbooks so I could come up with some more interesting and exotic meals to cook for him during the week. My mother used to ask me all the time,

"Faith, when's that man going to do the right thing and marry you?"

My dad is the pastor and my mother is the "first lady" of Christ the Solid Rock Pentecostal Church in Atlanta, Georgia. Praise God they live in Atlanta, so they aren't seeing my indiscretions right up in their faces.

About six months ago, my father decided to do something about this life of fornication I was leading. He gave Daemon a call while he was in Los Angeles for his annual pastor's conference. When Daddy called me to ask for Daemon's number, he said he wanted to take the young man out to dinner and get to know him better. I thought it was a great idea. Little did I know. My daddy told Daemon,

"My daughter that you're sleeping with...I made her, and if you think you're going to continue to take advantage of her, I'm here to tell you I'll hurt you and ask God to forgive me."

Daemon got so mad at him! He came in my door pacing back and forth, ranting and raving about how he's a man and doesn't need anyone talking to him like that. Right before my eyes, the man turned into a monster. He really lost his mind when he told me I should be happy and grateful for all the stuff he does for me. It was sad when I asked him exactly what it was that he does for me that I should be so grateful for. The fool could not come up with a thing. Well, he did come up with one thing, but I'm ashamed to tell anybody what that was. My daddy's words really put a serious chill on our relationship. Daemon stopped coming around. I could not believe it! All the time we spent with each other. Who would think a threat from my daddy would put an end to our relationship? I mean not even a "let's work this thing out." Just gone! I felt so hurt and betrayed! How could this man just drop me like that? I prayed and asked God to keep me from doing something stupid. One night I laid in bed and thought of a bunch of mean things to do to this man. I went so far as to put sugar from my pantry in a measuring cup and headed over to his house to put it in his gas tank, but he wasn't home. I just came back to my house sad, ate a half-gallon of ice cream and cried. The next morning, I changed the lock on my door, trashed Daemon's toothbrush, and donated the clothes he left in my closet to the Salvation Army. Daddy sure did know how to put an end to a going nowhere relationship. He and Momma had spent a lot of time teaching me right from wrong and instilling godly values in me. I guess he thought if I didn't have enough sense to realize I was allowing this man to disrespect me, he would make it plain for both of us.

I told my parents I was going to the Virgin Islands to visit Lisa for a few weeks. I didn't tell them I'd rented out my townhouse to one of the Sunday school teachers at my church for a year so I could see first hand what was going on under Caribbean skies. I also didn't tell them I'd quit my $150,000 a year job as Director of Information Systems at Raytheon. I can still remember the day Raytheon recruited me from college. Daddy was so proud of me. "You know,

Faith," he said, "this is a great day for our race." My whole family came to the house and gave me a send-off like a queen. I definitely can't let them know anything about me leaving California and moving to the Virgin Islands until I'm settled into my own place and working. That way it wouldn't appear I was acting irresponsibly and letting everyone who believed in me down.

The first day Lisa arrived on the island she met Trevor, a building contractor. Trevor is a strong muscular man, probably from swinging a hammer and lifting sacks of concrete all day. His skin is very dark and smooth, and he has pretty white teeth. Other than a little bit of a belly he's carrying around, he's not too bad looking. Besides, whatever he lacks in looks, he makes up for it in the beautiful luxurious houses he builds.

A taxi driver told Lisa about a house for rent in a section of St. John called "Chocolate Hole." The house belongs to a judge who lives in Ohio. He used to come down to the islands once a year for a few weeks, but health problems made him put the house up for rent. The taxi driver told Lisa she needed to speak to a man named Trevor about the house. Trevor and the judge became close friends when he contracted him to build the house. Trevor had invested so much time and love into building the house that the owner asked him to look after it, and manage the rental.

Lisa had the taxi driver take her to find this man named Trevor. They found him on top of a second story stone building under construction, reading blueprints. The driver called up to Trevor to come down. He told him a Yankee woman in his taxi was interested in renting the house in Chocolate Hole. Trevor allowed Lisa to move in that same day and has been coming over to visit ever since. Lisa, a nurse by trade, landed a job as soon as she applied at the local clinic and fell right into the island style of living. Trevor taught her how to cook West Indian style food. I laughed when she told me about boiled fish and fried bananas, called 'plantains'. The only way I'd ever eaten bananas was cut up in my cereal; fish was always fried and topped off with lots of Louisiana hot sauce.

I've been on the island a little over two weeks now, and it's everything Lisa said. The men are out there! And, they certainly do know how to serenade a sister. One man has been leaving mangoes on the porch for me everyday since he gave me directions to the health club at the Coconut Palm Resort. Now, the man must be seventy years old. Some of these older sisters need to step up to the plate and help the brother out. Then there's Fitzroy, the police officer who's married. I've seen him, his wife and children riding around town in his car, and he has the nerve to wave at me with the woman sitting right next to him. I told him I don't go out with married men but he continually tries to convince me he's not married. Half the time I can't understand what in the world these men are saying, so I just look and smile. I don't want to say yes to anything and find myself in a compromising position.

Now, if you ever want to find out who's married to whom, just drop by the local beach on any Sunday afternoon after church. I wasn't trying to spy or anything. As a matter of fact, I was hanging out with Lisa and Trevor, relaxing and enjoying the beautiful blue sea before the interviews started on Monday, and guess who I ran into? Fitzroy and his family. I made it a point to sashay past the picnic table at Hawksnest beach where Fitzroy, his wife and five children were having a birthday celebration for one of the kids. Do you know that man had the audacity to introduce me to his wife, asked me to join the party, and then started to fix me a plate of peas and rice and goat meat! I politely declined and left the picnic area as fast as I could. You should have seen the way that woman stared me down. Now, where I'm from, women don't play when it comes to their husbands. I've known many women who got their weaves snatched off, leaving bald spots in their heads from fooling with somebody's husband. My auntie Dot once caught Miss Sadie, a sister from the church messing with her husband and she threw hot grits on both of them. Uncle George's left eye doesn't completely open to this day from that burn. I guess he won't be looking out of that eye at any more women. All I could think about was this woman pouring hot goat water on me because she thinks I want her man. Trevor thought it was funny when I shared with him and Lisa what had just happened. Then he told me Fitzroy was from his village in Nevis and they used to play cricket together, and he's not married to Lucinda, that's her name.

"And I guess those aren't his children either," I said sarcastically.

"The two little ones are his. They're twins. But the three older ones are by a dead fireman," Trevor said.

"Then he should do the proper thing and marry her."

"What if he doesn't love her?" Trevor retorted.

"Then he should have thought about that before making babies."

"That's right," Lisa chimed in.

"So every person you have sex with you should love?" Trevor asked.

Lisa and I answered at the same time, "Yes!"

Trevor got a big hearty laugh from our response. "Then, Lisa, I guess that means you love me," he said. At that point, I excused myself, telling the love birds I had to get an early start in the morning, and I'd check them later.

I could hear Lisa giggling like a schoolgirl as I climbed into my jeep and headed towards Chocolate Hole.

My first interview was with the cable station on St. Thomas, located high on top of a mountain in a section called Iguana Hill. The grounds were expansive and well-manicured. I sat in the executive office suite, impressed. A lot of money has gone into this facility; there are four television studios and four master control rooms, five editing suites, eight conference rooms and a plethora of executive offices with a view that is spectacular. This is truly a first class operation. After a few minutes, a short woman with blonde hair, who looks like she's Spanish, French or something, greets me. She smiles a lot and talks like a sister with a slight West Indian accent. Her name is Janna and she takes me on a tour of the station. I continue to be impressed. There are three employee lounges. Each office or cubicle is furnished exquisitely and enhanced with magnificent artifacts. Janna, is the station's Operations Manager. Immediately I like her style. She's personable, professional and neatly dressed. Her nails are well manicured and the girl's perfume smells good. She's wearing Dolce & Gabbana, my favorite! I must remember to ask her where she gets her nails done. I can't say I've met her type since I've been on the island. Most of the women, unlike the men, are not friendly at all. They begin interrogating you right after you say "hello" or "isn't it a lovely day." Most of them want to know where you're from and what brought you to "their" island, which is a joke because half the population migrated from some little non-American island in search of jobs. After being quizzed by so many people about where I was from, I decided to tell them I was from St. Croix and that I left the islands when I was young. That explains my Yankee accent and why I don't know a lot of families on St. Croix. Bingo, it worked. I was accepted as an equal because all that's important to islanders is that you are "bawn here" and not an outsider. Lisa thought that was clever and said she would try it too.

Janna gives me a little history and background about Mr. Atkins, the owner of the station. He's rich... and why doesn't that surprise me? She tells me that he came from Puerto Rico to St. Thomas a few years ago and bought the telephone company, the power company, and all the television stations except one. The locals got a little suspicious when he tried to purchase a major chain of banks. Now they think he's trying to take over the whole island. What would ever give them an idea like that...duh!

The position I'm interviewing for is Director of Information Systems and surprisingly, it's paying six figures. My second interview is at Chase Bank. It appears they are still operating equipment from the early 90's. That position is only paying upper 80's. The benefits would have to be out of this world before I'd even think about going down that low.

I thought my interview at Chase Bank was a disaster. When you hear people say, "the islands is small," believe it. As I entered the bank's business office, guess who the receptionist was? Lucinda, Fitzroy's woman, and if looks could kill, I'd be dead. Since I don't want her man, I found it easy to be polite and ask her how the children were doing. I expressed how surprised I was to run into her. I tried to engage her in small talk while I waited to be interviewed, but she wasn't having it. Lucinda left her ringing-off-the-hook phones a few times to go and chat with a couple of her female co-workers a few cubicles away and all eyes turned towards me. I felt a few fiery darts being thrown my way with their stares and the sound of teeth sucking. I decided not to succumb to their pettiness. As a matter of fact, they'd better be careful because if I got this job, I'd probably be all of their bosses. Finally after the phone rang about 15 times, Lucinda returned to her desk, answering multiple lines with an attitude as if the customers were annoying her. I just smiled as I read a copy of last year's Forbes Magazine I spotted on the waiting room coffee table. Finally I heard my name being called by Lucinda. The bank manager was ready to see me. As I stood at the counter waiting for Lucinda to lead me to the back office, I noticed that her nameplate read "Lucinda Bramble." I guess Fitzroy wasn't lying when he said he was not married to her, because his last name was Brown.

Lucinda introduced me to Everett Bramble, the bank manager. Either this was her big brother or her father. They looked just alike. Mr. Bramble and I talked for what seemed like eternity. He was quite impressed with the skills I could bring to the bank. I found myself also impressed with how focused he was about what the bank's needs were, and what type of communication devices were needed to bring them up to date. Mr. Bramble knew exactly what was needed to drive on the information technology highway and to be competitive with the mainland banks. I also learned during the course of our conversation, that Lucinda is his daughter. There were pictures of her children on his credenza. We shook hands and as I was about to leave he assured me that I would be hearing from him soon. Just when I turned to exit, Mr. Bramble called me back. He said he had one more question he wanted to ask me that was not related to work. I was a bit nervous and certainly hoped it wasn't about his daughter and Fitzroy. I was beginning to feel like I was being pulled into a relationship against my will, one that was growing by osmosis.

"I just want to let you know you are a beautiful woman and I find myself attracted to you...Would it be possible for me to take the boat over one Saturday or Sunday to visit you on St. John's?" Mr. Bramble said.

I know my mouth was open because I could feel air going in, however nothing would come out. Finally, I managed to say, "Have a good day," and left.

Chapter 2

If the truth be told, I was a little flattered with all the attention I'd been getting since my plane touched down on the runway at Hamilton Airport. Let's face it, the brothers in the states have a different game. These men here are kind of primitive. It's almost like, "me Tarzan, you Jane." Whenever they see a woman they like, they step up and claim her. They don't ask you if you want to go to the movies; they ask questions like, "what kind of house do you want me to build you." Hello! Now I don't know about you, but I have never had a brother ask me what kind of house I wanted him to build for me after only dating a few weeks. My girl Lisa already picked out the land where Trevor is going to build a house for her and their future babies. He's made it clear that he wants plenty of children. I told her to get married first before she started talking about breeding babies for that Mandingo warrior and to make sure the house and the land are in her name. We're almost 32 years old, and too seasoned to be making foolish mistakes. Besides, her ex-husband back in Los Angeles took her to the cleaners, but we won't go there. Well, maybe for a minute.

Jason was a trifling man, and he hated me, because I saw right through him from the start. First, he claimed to be an actor and was always going on auditions, but never got any parts. I mean the man wasn't even getting any extra's parts, and all you had to do to get one of those was show up at the Hollywood Unemployment Office on any morning before 9:30 and sign up to be in a crowd scene. Even though it only paid $75.00 a day, that was enough to buy a little groceries or put some gas in the car. Lisa loved the man's last-week boxers, and all I can say is "that thing must have been good." Now, I am not one to talk about anybody behind his or her back, especially my best girlfriend, so what I'm saying, I already said it to Lisa, too. I think Jason had a little "sugar in his tank." He giggled too much like a little woman and was always in our conversation, pecking like a hen. He talked with a little lisp, like his tongue had to slide under his teeth before he could get his words out. Lisa justified it by saying some men are just sensitive, and Jason fit into that category. Like I said, it must have been good because my girl was blind! She couldn't see the forest for the trees. Lisa was married to a *down low brother.*

A co-worker of mine, who was trying to make it in the comedy world, invited me to hear him at a little club in West Hollywood. I told him I would come and support him, even though I don't do clubs. They're too smoky. He was so happy to hear I would come. He told me a few of the people from the office promised they were coming when he performed at this club last month, but no one showed up. I'm not sure if that was to make me feel obligated to come or not, but hey, Brian was my boy and if coming to his show would help him work his way out of the mailroom at the office, then I was willing to be uncomfortable for a minute. I managed to hang through the first set. Brian's act consisted of satire, both secular and Christian. The boy was good! He had the audience in stitches! I especially enjoyed when he imitated black ushers in the church marching into service singing "We are Soldiers of the Army." He did a dip and a pivot when the ushers turned the corner that folks only did in our churches. When his set was over, I went back into the dressing room and told him how fabulous he was and then slipped out the side door.

I was so sad to leave but my lungs just couldn't take any more smoke. The club shared parking lots with a well-known gay club next door. As I headed to my car, two men had apparently been smoking marijuana, because the smell lingering in the air took me aback. Now they were kissing! "How sick," I thought. This certainly would have given my daddy, a heart attack. Daddy preached from his pulpit that homosexuality is an abomination. "Love the sinner, but hate the sin," he'd say. Then I reminded myself I'm in West Hollywood, nicknamed "Sodom City." To see a man and a *woman* kissing around these parts is odd. As I opened my car door and was about to slide in, I heard that laugh followed by a little lisp. Lord, have mercy! Please don't let it be him! I turned to have a closer look, starting at the shoes and working my way up. I didn't need to go any further. Once I saw he was wearing the shoes Lisa bought him when we were out shopping at Nordstrom's the previous Saturday, it was confirmed. This was Jason kissing another man in the parking lot of a gay club. I hollered his name. I'm not quite sure, but I think the man wet his pants. There appeared to be a wet spot on the ground. But only God knows for certain what that was. You could tell from the expression on his face I was the last person he anticipated calling his name. I think he would have expected to see Satan before he saw me that night. There was absolutely nothing he could say, he was cold busted!

Now you know how our people get sometimes when they are wrong. They try and make it seem like it's your fault. The sissy had the nerve to say I was spying on him and trying to set him up. Can you believe that? If I tried, I couldn't have come up with anything like that. I told him to have a nice day in hell and I got into my car and drove off.

Lisa was working four days on and three days off at Children's Hospital only a few blocks up the street and would be home in a couple of days. This was not something you laid on your best friend at work. So I decided to wait until she got home and I had time to pray about how to tell her something like that. However, "demon" Jason had other plans. He moved everything he thought belonged to him out of their house before the girl got off work. Now mind you, he had no job the whole time they were married. Please tell me what made him think he was entitled to the plasma television, DVD player, stereo system and their king-size bedroom set? There's no telling who he's got sleeping on that bed as we speak. To tell the truth and shame the devil, I wonder who he had sleeping on it when it was at Lisa's house. Needless to say, my girl was a wreck when she walked into the house and discovered what had happened. And to add insult to injury he had the temerity to leave a note saying he couldn't take it anymore and if she had any questions, ask Faith. "Ask Faith?" No, he didn't go there, was all I could say. Now, it looked like I was the reason for them breaking up. This definitely put a temporary strain on our friendship, because as I said before, people always want to blame other folks when things go wrong, especially when it concerns the relationship between a man and a woman. Lisa and I exchanged a few choice words or should I say she called me a few choice words in between her rivers of tears.

This went on for weeks. The first couple of days I cried with her. Then I'd had enough of her pity party and decided I was not going to let Jason do this to both of us. Somebody had to have some sense. Finally, I told her "the man was not interested in women. I tried to tell you this two years ago, but you wouldn't listen."

There wasn't any need to pour salt into the wound, so I'll take it to my grave with me what I saw that night on Santa Monica Boulevard. The main thing now was, and I made it very clear: she was *going* to have an AIDS test! Lisa agreed. We both were on pins and needles waiting for the test results. Praise God she was given a clean bill of health! It was then that she decided she had had enough of Sodom City and was leaving for the Virgin Islands where she heard they had real men.

Chapter 3

Now if I could just back this jeep up on this barge without hitting someone's car. I decided to bring my car over to St. Thomas instead of taking the commuter ferry. I figured I'd have more flexibility and not be at the mercy of cab drivers when I was shuttling between interviews. This worked out well. The commuter ferry departs just a few feet from where the barge is positioned. I could see it was packed with people just getting off work, waiting to get over to St. John. The last thing I felt like today was being part of that cattle call. Besides, it's some kind of hot out there. Once I get this jeep on the boat, I'm going to roll down the windows, catch the Caribbean breeze and take a nap until we get to the other side. At least that's what I thought was going to happen.

One of the crewmen on the boat directed me to park on the starboard side of the deck, sandwiched between two very large garbage trucks. In my thirty-something years of life, I had never smelled anything that foul before. The sad part was I'd parked so close to the two trucks, neither of my doors would open wide enough to let me get out and go to the observation deck for some fresh air. I thought of rolling up the windows and turning on the air conditioner, but there were several signs around the deck which read in bold red letters *"Virgin Island Penal Code 659190 requires that all car engines are turned off while the boat is in motion."* Between the stench and the barge rocking with the waves, I got so sick! I had to stick my head out of the window and puke on the deck in the little bit of space available between the garbage trucks and me. When we arrived on St. John it took every bit of energy I could muster to drive that car off the barge. I was too sick to file a complaint. I prayed I would see Lisa or Trevor in town so they could drive me home. No such luck. I decided to just park and hope relief would come soon. I turned on the air conditioner, reclined the seat and closed my eyes.

Someone tapping on the window startled me. There was Fitzroy, grinning like a Cheshire cat. Did this man have some kind of radar or was he stalking me? He continued to tap on the glass until I rolled it down. I must have looked sick.

"What's wrong?" Fitzroy said.

Before I could answer, I was pushing the door open and spitting up on his shoes. Fortunately, not much came up. I realized I hadn't eaten all day. Fitzroy helped me move to the passenger side of the car, reclining my seat gently. My tired brain was saying, "What is the man doing here, and thank God!" After securing my seat belt, Fitzroy climbed in the driver's seat and pointed the car in a direction other than Chocolate Hole. I could barely lift my head up to see where we were going. However, as he stopped to let the debarking boat passengers cross the road I saw a familiar face staring into the jeep. It was Lucinda getting off the commuter boat with the crowd of workers coming from St. Thomas. Suddenly, I felt sicker.

"Don't worry, she has her own ride...you just relax, I've got something to make you feel better," he said, as if reading my mind.

Neat, neat, neat is all I can say to describe his house. Fitzroy lived just above town in a section called Gift Hill. He had a spectacular view of the Cruz Bay harbor. His house was furnished like a stateside home. The living room was adorned with a nice leather love seat and sofa accessorized with beautiful coffee and end tables. The corner of the room sported a large plasma television. The floors were finished with large Mexican terra cotta tiles. His bedroom layout included a king-size four-poster bed in the center, and what looked like a Broyhill matching highboy and dresser along the sidewalls. Another large screen television stood in the corner. There were lots of plants in each of the rooms. Healthy large plants, housed in beautiful vases. In the second bedroom was a set of bunk beds. The room décor had a western theme. This must be his sons' room. Then there was a third bedroom, which appeared to be the combined guest room and library. A queen-size rattan sleigh bed accompanied by a lovely bed treatment and matching nightstands was positioned on an angle in the corner of the room. Several floor to ceiling bookshelves embellished the other walls. His master bathroom boasted a double-sized bathtub with Jacuzzi jets. And get this, the man had a bidet opposite the toilet. There was a center island in the kitchen and a replica of an old-fashioned O'Keefe stove and refrigerator. The kind my grandmother had when I was a little girl. Hanging from the walls was beautiful West Indian art. The paintings were originals signed by local artists. Most of the scenes in the pictures depicted life around the island of St. John.

Fitzroy changed out of his police uniform into a pair of blue jeans and a colorful T-shirt. I noticed he took time to place his gun in a locked cabinet over the kitchen sink as if it was a ritual he went through each evening. It dawned on me that I had never seen him dressed in civilian clothing other than the swim shorts he wore when I ran into him on the beach. Correction, when I ran *from* him on the beach. He unquestionably looked like a different man. There was something pleasantly puzzling about him. My stomach was still doing summersaults. I settled down on the leather sofa while Fitzroy served me some "bush" tea from his yard. He said it was from the sour sop tree and it would calm my stomach and give me rest. Maybe I should have been drinking this at home, but I was so comfortable right there on this man's couch. I sipped the tea sweetened with honey he boasted came from his dad's honey farm in Nevis. Before I knew it, I was dozing off to sleep. I could faintly hear Fitzroy talking on the phone. He was talking to either Lisa or Trevor because he told them not to worry about me. He would make sure I was feeling better before he allowed me to drive home.

The next morning I woke up in the guest bedroom with a sheet over me. I was still wearing the clothes I'd worn at my interviews. Fitzroy was standing over me as my eyes focused on the room and my brain adjusted to the fact that I was in a strange place. He was holding a breakfast tray. On the tray was a porcelain teapot with matching cup, a bowl of oatmeal and a piece of toast along with a new toothbrush. I must have looked a wreck, even though he said otherwise. Fitzroy was dressed in his police uniform. He asked if I wanted to shower at his place and then drop him off at work. It dawned on me then that he had driven my car to his house. His car must still be in town. I decided to put the new toothbrush into action, wash my face, eat the oatmeal and pass on the bush tea. I needed to be alert today. I had another interview scheduled for two o'clock this afternoon. I thanked Fitzroy for all his help as I dropped him in front of the police station. Of course, every officer was either coming on duty or going off duty and took the opportunity to gawk at us as Fitzroy got out of the car. At one point, I thought he was going to kiss me, but I turned my head like I was watching out for the traffic on my side of the jeep. Trust me, I was not ready for him to kiss me right there in front of God and everybody. It was bad enough that I was dropping him at work like I was his woman. He caught my drift, smiled and told me he would see me later. "Oh," is all Jane could say to Tarzan.

When I got back to Lisa's place she had already left for work. She left me a note on the refrigerator saying she needed to talk with me. She wanted me to meet her in the clinic's cafeteria at 11:00 AM. It was just eight-thirty. I decided to commit one of the biggest sins on the island and take a hot, *long* stateside shower. People don't play when it comes to their water around these parts. You can eat all their food, but don't waste the water! Can you imagine going to the sink and nothing comes out when you turn on the faucet? Or, God forbid, what if the toilet won't flush after you use it? Most people on the island have cisterns and they depend on rainwater, which collects on the roof and drains down a pipe into the cistern. The cistern is like a large swimming pool under your house. When there is no rain, there is no water. Many water companies offer desalinated water. Trucks will come and fill your cistern up for a hefty fee. However, sometimes it doesn't matter how much money you have. When there's a drought you can wait almost a week before the truck can get to you. The water companies are so swamped with calls that people wait on the road to offer them a few extra dollars to move their names up on the waiting list. Of course, that could still be a while because they have to service their mother, sisters, brothers and cousins first. Thank God, the man who had this house built thought like a statesider. There are four cisterns built under it. One services only the pool and the garden. We are blessed with so much water that we could easily sell a truckload and still have enough to live like we're in the states.

As I stepped out of the shower, the telephone was ringing. As soon as I picked it up, the person hung up. This is a regular occurrence. It really burns me up when they call around three o'clock in the morning and don't say anything. Lisa says this has been going on ever since she moved in. As soon as I turn to go back into the bathroom to blow-dry my hair the phone rings again. I answer it a little crudely, immediately regretting it. It's Janna from the cable station. I quickly apologized telling her I keep getting hang-ups. I'm surprised by her response.

"It's probably some jealous woman trying to get your man to answer, so she can find out why he hasn't been over lately," Janna says.

"Oh," I say.

I mean what else do you say to something like that. Sounds like there might be a little bit of wisdom there. Janna tells me they'd like me to come in for a second interview this afternoon. However, the interview will be on St. Croix and they will fly me over in the company's plane. It appears that the owner is going to be at their affiliate sister station and would like to meet me and make a decision on the position today.

"Great, what time should I meet with you?" I ask.

Janna instructs me to meet her at the freight and cargo section of Hamilton Airport at one o'clock. She tells me I'll see that entrance as soon as I turn onto Airport Road. We hang up and I think about Lisa. Maybe I could go and meet with her now. Eleven o'clock won't give me enough time to talk, take the barge, and get down to the airport, which is on the other end of the island from where I disembark. I know one thing: hell is going to break loose if they ever ask me to park anywhere near a garbage truck when I get on that barge!

Lisa was just coming out of a staff meeting when I arrived at the clinic. She got right to the point. One of her co-workers told her they saw Trevor with a white woman sitting at the bar at a restaurant called Shipwreck out in Coral Bay. Coral Bay is located on the far end of the island. Not many people live out there. However, it has its own little sense of community. I asked her if she told Trevor and she said no. She didn't want to get into any petty he-say-she-say business.

"Obviously it isn't that petty if you're talking to me about it," I tell her.

I then reflected on what Janna said about the telephone hang-ups. I ask Lisa if she had ever gotten any jealous woman phone calls.

"Yes," she hangs her head and whispers.

Here we go again, *déjà vu.* My girl had managed to get her nose opened again. Lisa was so vulnerable.

"OK Lisa, let's look at this with an open mind. Let's say Trevor is cheating. He's not going to admit it if you ask him. And whatever cheating he's doing it can't be all that much, because he's always up in your grill," I say.

"Take it slow. I mean, don't forget you came down to these islands to clear your head from your last mistake. Heck, you're jumping from the frying pan into the fire. You haven't let the reality of your divorce marinate yet. If Trevor is the man God has for you then there isn't any white woman, Chinese woman, Pakistani woman or African woman going to stand in your way. Besides, I bet he ain't building a house for her."

"That's another thing I've been asking him when are we going to closing on the land and he keeps saying 'any day now'," Lisa says with doubt in her voice.

"You know between that inheritance you got from your parents and your salary, you have more than enough money to buy your own land, have a house built and still have a nice little chunk of change left in the bank. You don't need Trevor to give you anything! Your daddy made sure of that before he died. Us sisters need to stop validating who we are by what a man is doing for us! Get your own land in your own name and hire him to build the house for you! Men appreciate you better when you let them know you aren't stupid first, and secondly you ain't up for any crap!"

Lisa began to look a little relieved. I made her laugh when I told her I generally charge people for this kind of wisdom, but I would give it to her for free if she promised to listen.

We chatted a little longer about my getting sick on the barge and about Lucinda, her daddy and Fitzroy. We were laughing so loudly folks in the cafeteria were starting to stare. Lisa wished me well with my interview; we hugged and promised to go dancing this weekend at a local place in town called Fred's. It would be a "girls only" night out. I waved and raced to catch the barge.

Chapter 4

When I arrived on St. Thomas it was around twelve o'clock. I decided to stop in Red Hook, the area where the boat docks, grab a sandwich and check my e-mail at a little cyber café. I didn't want to risk getting sick today for any reason. I also needed to make sure I cancelled the interview I'd scheduled several days ago with the University of the Virgin Islands. God willing, I wouldn't have to reschedule. I feel like today someone is going to make me an offer. My e-mail in-box is full. I haven't been online since I got to St. John. I can't believe it. The things that are so important to us in the states seem to take a back seat in the order of priorities down here.

There were about 75 messages. A lot of them were junk mail. Well, Lord have mercy, there are four e-mails from Daemon. I thought he'd forgotten my name. What could he possibly want? He writes:

"I went past your house the other day to pick up the few things I left there and someone else had moved in. She wouldn't give me your forwarding address. Where are you staying?"

None of your big-eyed business! I didn't write that, I just thought it. Next e-mail from Daemon reads:

"This is my second e-mail. I wrote you a week ago. I hope you got it. I was wondering if we could do lunch."

You must be crazy! I'm doing lunch right now, and guess what? It isn't with you! Maybe I should send this one. Let's see what the next one says.

"Faith, I went back over to your old place and begged the woman living there for a forwarding address. She still won't give it up. I'm going to stop by your church tomorrow, maybe I might find you there, or get information from your pastor on where you moved to."

And hell will freeze over before he tells you anything. My pastor never did like you. Just like my daddy and momma, he, too, wanted to know when you were going to marry me. Yeah, go on by the church. Maybe the Holy Ghost will jump on you and make you new. I might seem bitter if I send this one.

Last e-mail from Daemon.

"I went to your church yesterday. They were having revival services. The Holy Ghost was all up in that place. You'll never believe this in a million years. I went down and got saved. I saw the woman who lives in your townhouse at service. Still no one would give me your address or phone number. I'm glad I came, though. The Spirit convicted me to write an apology letter to your parents and ask them to forgive me for all the years I disrespected them and their daughter. Well, Faith, I hope you get this e-mail. Thanks for all you did for me." Signed, Daemon.

To God be the glory! I'll drop him a post card to congratulate him on becoming a new creature in Christ. But know this, I am not trying to go backwards.

Have mercy! My daddy has e-mail now!

"Hi, Pudding. Yes, it's Dad. Your mother bought me a computer for my birthday, the one you missed. Don't fret over it, I am not mad, I just assumed you're having so much fun down in those islands with Lisa you forgot about your old dad. Just be careful and remember to keep God first. E-mail me back with some photographs of those pretty islands so I can practice downloading pictures. Oh, we got the strangest letter from that old boyfriend of yours... love, Daddy."

I can't believe I forgot his birthday! I guess I was avoiding calling since I wasn't exactly honest about my living situation. As I look at the clock, I'm reminded that I need to get going. Lisa showed me a short way to get to the airport via Skyline Drive. Lord, please help me not to get lost. I know there is a funny little turn you make down in the bushes somewhere near Mountain Top where they boast of having the best banana daiquiris. There are usually a lot of tours going there so I'll remember to make a quick right into the bush as soon as I see the safari buses.

Janna was waiting for me in the hanger. She was wearing a cute fuchsia silk suit with a white blouse. Her long curly hair was pinned up with a few little curls dangling on each side of her face. Let the record show I looked good, too. I was wearing a beige Anne Klein linen business suit and beige Joan & David pumps with a matching purse. Janna greeted me with a big smile and a hug. She has a way of making you feel like you've known her a long time. Janna, the pilot and I boarded the six-passenger plane. I had never been in a plane so small. Janna sat in the co-pilot's seat next to Junnis. Junnis, a big African warrior-looking man seemed very nice except he smiled a little bit too much for me. It was like he was a bit superficial. He, too, like Trevor, had a mouth full of beautiful pearly-white teeth, a complete contrast to his dark skin. After strapping in, Junnis guided the little prop plane onto the runway where we sat until the tower cleared us for takeoff. The flight was about 25 minutes and I prayed the whole time until we landed. Every little clang or ping or what sounded like an irregular hum of the engine sent my mind tripping. I imagined us going down in this little plane, and being attacked by sharks on impact. Then I immediately hated myself for letting the power of fear take over. In my next scenario I pictured the plane going down and I was the only survivor. That gave me a little more comfort. The landing was smooth and not a moment too soon.

We touched down at Henry Rohlsen Airport. A black Lincoln Navigator SUV was waiting for us as we deplaned. Janna and I climbed into the back seat as the driver held the door open for us. Junnis came over to the car and exchanged a few words with Janna who was all smiles. O.K., now I see what's up; Junnis is Janna's man. As we pulled out onto the airport road Janna was still smiling.

"I guess you figured it out, huh?" Janna said.

"Figured what out?" I replied.

"Junnis, he's my boo."

I thought I'd choke when I heard this woman call that black giant her "boo." Now Lisa would be proud of me...I was cool. I replied, "You *go* girl." Janna continued smiling as the Lincoln merged onto the highway and picked up speed. The station was not far from the airport. It was located inside a little shopping mall called Sunny Isle.

Once in the office of Channel 18, Janna introduced me to everyone we came in contact with. The people seemed very friendly. Janna led us into a conference room where an island girl with a heavy accent asked if we wanted something to drink. I was definitely parched.

"Would you like some of our local soda pop that's manufactured right here in Frederiksted, St. Croix?" she politely asked.

How could I say no? Janna was familiar with what they called Brow Soda. She requested the banana flavor and suggested I try the coconut, which is a favorite of most people. The young girl returned with the drinks in old-fashioned glass bottles. My soda was really good. I was afraid to check for the number of calories. The rule of thumb is if it's good, it's fattening.

Finally, a short bald-headed Spanish man came into the conference room wearing tennis shorts, white sneakers and a golf T-shirt. He smiled and shook my hand. We made small talk about Los Angeles. He knew a lot about the company I had worked for the past three years and even dropped the names of some of the executives. I was impressed. He told me he'd spoken with my previous supervisor and they had nothing but great things to say about me. However, they were a little sad to see me leave. Then he asked Janna if she thought I would be a match for the company. He certainly wasn't one to beat around the bush. I thought they would at least excuse themselves and talk about me behind my back.

"Absolutely!" Janna said without hesitation.

"Make it so!" Mr. Atkins replied.

"All right, Captain Jean-Luc," was all I could think to say, to myself, of course. Mr. Atkins again shook my hand and welcomed me aboard.

"I'd like for you come out to my little castle, and meet the Mrs. when you get settled," he said before leaving the conference room.

"I look forward to it," I replied. I felt like singing "The Hallelujah Chorus!" Finally I could call Daddy, wish him a happy belated birthday, and tell him and Momma "I'm an island girl now!"

The flight back to St. Thomas was uneventful, thank God. We landed around five o'clock. Junnis said good-bye and told Janna he'd stop by later tonight. As human nature would have it, I felt a little jealous. Even though Daemon was using me, I did miss male companionship. Now what's wrong with that picture? If any of the sisters from my church heard me say something like that, hands would be flying in the air trying to get to my body to lay hands on me. I'd be anointed with so much olive oil you could fry chicken on me. Can we be real for a moment? The flesh gets weak. However, I made a promise to God and myself that the next man who gets this will be my husband. I'm going to put all that stuff I learned at the thousands of women's retreats I've gone to since I was five years old into practice. You know, stuff like "Woman of Purpose," "Love Yourself First," "Woman Thou Are Loosed" and my favorite, "Rebuke That Jezebel Spirit."

Janna asked if I could drop her at the station to pick up her car. She had ridden to the airport with Junnis. We talked all the way to the station. I learned that Janna has two children, Nyla and Chloe, and she's in the midst of an ugly divorce. She married Eric, her high school sweetheart, who over the years became an abusive alcoholic. A year ago, she had the police remove him from the house. The problem is they built their house on his family's land and it's sandwiched on a dead end road between her mother-in-law's and her sister-in-law's houses and they both hated her and want her off their family's land. Eric said he would kill her if she weren't the mother of his kids. Janna tells me that she has a little piece of family land her daddy gave each of his children, but she isn't moving from where she lives until she gets her half of what Eric owes her, and his family can go to hell if they don't like it!

The television station was very quiet when we got there. The only people still around were the newsman who was busy getting ready for the six o'clock broadcast, and Jay Stewart, the workaholic Chief Financial Officer. Janna showed me my office and told me to feel free to get rid of whatever I didn't want and to order any new stuff I needed. The office was beautiful. On one side of the room is an out-of-sight view of the airport runway and the beautiful blue sea next to it. From the opposite side of the room, looking out of the floor to ceiling window, I could see a picture perfect view of Water Island and sea planes landing and taking off. Janna asked when I wanted to officially start working. I asked if next week Monday would be good.

"Officially, you're my boss, so why are you asking me?" she laughed.

"Send out a memo that the new Director of Information Systems will join the staff of WVIR on Monday, August 18th," I say very authoritatively.

"Yes, sir, I mean ma'am. I'll make sure my secretary takes care of it first thing in the morning," Janna salutes and we both laugh.

Janna invites me to her house for dinner. I remind her she already has a guest coming.

"Oh, Junnis," she said, "he probably won't show up until midnight. We try and wait until all eyes are asleep. You know, my neighbors."

I thought she was talking about her kids. I figured I wouldn't comment. I didn't want to come off holier than thou just yet, so I said "Yes, I'd love to have dinner at your house. Is there a nail shop on the way? I'm badly in need of a fill, a pedicure, and waxing. I'm starting to feel like Chewbacca, the ape in Star Wars."

Janna lets out a big hearty laugh, pulls out her cell phone and calls the nail shop. "Ling, I need you to hook me and my girl friend up. We are on our way and I don't want to have to wait when we get there! Girl, don't go there. I'm on my way now," Janna hangs up the phone. She then tells me to follow her. Janna lives near the Tutu Park Mall where the shop is located.

When we arrived, I noticed that the operators were of Vietnamese descent. I could not help but wonder whether they dominated the industry here in the islands, as they seemed to do in Los Angeles. Janna got a pedicure and waited while I got the works.

Afterward, we went to her house for a dinner of leftover boiled fish, fungi and dumplings. Her kids, Nyla and Chloe, took turns showing me their photo albums. Chloe had many pictures of her standing next to a horse where she had won ribbons for her performance. Nyla, a drama queen showed me pictures of her competing for the title of Carnival Princess, which she'd won last year. Both girls had a lot of questions about California. They wanted to know if I knew Denzel Washington, Brittany Spears, Beyonce or any stars?

"You two are the only stars I know," I say, to their delight.

Chloe shows me a few calypso moves and Nyla laughs when I try them. She thinks I dance like a Yankee with very little rhythm. I break out my old school moves on them. This leads the way for lots of amusement and laughter.

Chapter 5

Ooh, doggie! I was some kind of tired with a capital "T" when I got off that barge and put my key in the door. Lisa was still at work and I didn't expect her until tomorrow. Trevor never came by unless she was home so I decided to get naked, slip into the jacuzzi, take a shower and crash hard in my bed. As soon as I got comfortable under the jacuzzi jets the phone rang. This time I was prepared; I had the cordless phone nearby, ready for the hang-up. However, the call caught me by surprise. It was my mother, just the person I wanted to talk to. "Momma is that you?" She sounded a little strange.

"Yes, baby. You need to come home. Your daddy has gone to be with the Lord; he had a heart attack this morning."

Everything else was a blur from that point until I reached my parent's house in Atlanta the next afternoon. There were so many people at the house; the cab driver couldn't get into the driveway. He had to drop my things and me at the curb. My mother looked tired. There was no sparkle in her eyes. I held on to her and cried for what seemed like an eternity. My aunties were there along with many of the church sisters who were in the kitchen cooking, along with my cousin Debbie. I spotted Alma right away. She served as President of the Bereavement Committee. If there ever was a faithful servant in the church, it is Alma. She never missed a funeral and made sure all her team members were there to help. You never heard of them running out of food, especially fried chicken. My cousin Debbie was the second in charge in the kitchen. She was being groomed to take over when 90-year-old Alma died or decided to hang up her apron; whichever came first. Debbie was my girl! As kids we were inseparable. She lived next door to us. Her mother and my mother are sisters. When I was in first grade, Debbie's father moved them across town to be closer to his job. They still came to my daddy's church on Wednesdays for Bible study and on Sunday for service, but it wasn't the same. I missed being with my cousin everyday and sharing my secrets with her. When Debbie moved, Lisa was glad not to have to share me with my cousin anymore, at least not on a regular basis.

Debbie got married to one of the young deacons in our church right after high school. I think she got pregnant on her wedding night. They had five girls in a row. Talk about being fruitful and multiplying! God had my cousin in mind when He said that! Every time I'd call her from college, or see her at family gatherings, the first thing she would say was "Girl, guess what? I'm pregnant!"

Her oldest daughter is named Faith, after me. The other four children's names all begin with an "F." Faren, Farrah, Freda and Fuisha. Debbie whispered in my ear that her husband Byron might be the new pastor of my daddy's church if all goes well, followed by "guess what?" Only, this time it's twin boys! I had to holler. "Finally, boys!" I shared with her how pleased I knew my daddy would be if Byron took over his pulpit! Byron cut his teeth on the Bible, just like his father and grandfather. He's a man who not only talks the Word, but also walks the Word. The way he feels about God shows up in the way he treats his wife and five girls. Debbie and Byron have raised their children to love God and not be ashamed to share the gospel with their friends. I only pray that the people at Solid Rock Church know that they will truly be blessed if they accept Brother Byron as their new Pastor.

Momma led me upstairs to her and Daddy's room. We hugged and cried some more. Then she shared with me how peacefully he passed. Daddy woke her up around three o'clock in the morning to ask her what that light was in the room and who were those people calling his name. She thought he was having a dream, but saw that his eyes were opened and he was smiling. "He's O.K. now, my child. It's us standing in need of healing right now," she said.

I told Momma how bad I felt about missing his birthday. She immediately dismissed it with a wave of the hand. "Girl, your daddy knows you loved him. He didn't need a birthday greeting to validate that," she says while hugging me.

In the corner sat Daddy's new computer. I smiled and tried to picture him sitting there sending me an e-mail. I loved him so much. God help us to get through this!

Lisa arrived the day of the funeral. I was so glad to see her. We didn't get to talk much because of all the relatives, friends and well-wishers stopping by. Lisa asked if she could sing a song at the service. She sang one of Daddy's favorites, "Balm in Gilead." There wasn't a dry eye in the church when she finished. Both Lisa and I grew up in my daddy's church and sang in the choir as long as I could remember. Lisa lost both her mother and father to cancer about eight years ago. They were heavy smokers. Her mother passed first, then her dad a few years later. When Lisa's dad passed, we both were in our last year of graduate school. It was a difficult time for her. She was just coming to grips with losing her mother and then cancer took her father. It was only by the grace of God that she graduated. My parents became her parents. Daddy took care of all the funeral arrangements. Both he and Momma helped Lisa sort through her parents' personal things and put the house on the market.

Lisa has a half brother named Bubba and only God knows where he is. A few days after her father's funeral Bubba showed up looking like life had beaten him down. His momma must have driven him over there straight from a crack house when she found out Mr. Walker had passed. She waited in the car while he stepped up on the front porch ringing the doorbell, ready to claim his piece of the pie. My daddy warned Lisa that Bubba would be showing up. However, we at least expected him to come to the funeral. Thank God, Lisa's daddy was very explicit in his Last Will and Testament. He stated that his son was not entitled to one penny of his insurance, his estate or any of his holdings. For 18 years he paid his child support on time to a woman he never loved and offered to pay college tuition if the boy would show some initiative, which he never did. Mr. Walker bought Bubba a new car when he graduated from high school. Bubba wrecked it the first week driving drunk. Mr. Walker paid for numerous attorneys every time Bubba was in trouble. Finally, he decided he was aiding and abetting and it was time for Bubba to stand up and be a man. My daddy made a copy of the Last Will and Testament and when Bubba rang the doorbell he opened it and handed it to him. He told him if he had any questions to contact the Executor of the estate whose number was on the document and closed the door. I had not seen Bubba since we met at a restaurant in Los Angeles for dinner several years before and he stole my wallet out of my purse when I went to the ladies room. I later found out he was strung out on crack.

And now my best friend was there for me. Lisa had contacted the television station to let them know what happened. Janna must have gotten my parents' address and phone number from Lisa because they sent the biggest floral arrangement I'd ever seen. And Janna called too. She told me not to rush getting back. My desk would be there waiting for me when I got there and she would have her secretary send out a memo. We both laughed. Lisa stayed a week and helped Momma, the aunties and me sort through things. Then it was time for her to head back home to her Trevor who had been calling every day saying how much he missed her. Even Fitzroy sent his condolences by way of a telegram with flowers. How sweet, I thought. Momma's sisters, Aunt Dot and Aunt Lucille assured me that they, along with all the cousins and the church family, would be there for Momma, and that everything would be fine. They gave me the green light to leave and told me to get back down to those islands so they could start making plans to come visit for Thanksgiving. It was hard leaving my mother. Praise God, I saw a hint of a sparkle in her eyes as I boarded the plane for the Virgin Islands.

Chapter 6

Once back on the island, I immediately went to work, which was the best therapy for me. Some days I worked from seven in the morning to well past nine at night. I decided to look for an apartment on St. Thomas. Taking the barge every day was becoming a bit expensive. It was either that or purchase a little boat of my own and row over each day, which was unheard of. Janna offered to rent me the downstairs unit in her house. I went to look at it and found it to be just what I needed, a two bedroom apartment with a fantastic view. Janna assured me that her ex-husband would not be an issue because the judge had given her permission to stay in the house until her ten-year-old daughter Chloe turned 18. Needless to say, Lisa had a hissy fit when I told her I was moving over to St. Thomas until I promised I would come over every weekend. Then she gave in. She also took the advice that I didn't charge her for and purchased a piece of land in her own name on Bordeaux Mountain.

We must have walked up and down that mountain scouting out land for a month every Saturday from sunup to sundown and every Sunday after church. She finally found a piece of land in the nosebleed section of the mountain with the most awesome view I had ever seen. It looked out onto Little Thatch, Big Thatch, Peter Island, Jost Van Dyke, Tortola, Virgin Gorda and a few other little islands I'm not sure have names. A native guy who owned the little market in town was selling a few acres he had inherited from his grandfather. He needed the money so he could move to Florida. I thought he must be crazy to leave here and go to Florida. Florida doesn't have anything on this island. All I could say was, "I hope you don't sell it all, my brother, because when you get to Florida and find out all that glitters ain't gold you'll be back." He was asking $40,000 for a quarter acre. I don't know if it was the Holy Spirit talking to me but I started negotiating. I said, "If we brought two acres could we get it for $80,000?" I'm not sure if the $80,000 dollars was all he could hear because he said, "Yes," not realizing that he was giving us much more land for $40,000 dollars. Lisa looked at me like I was crazy.

"You don't think you're going to live up here and enjoy God's handiwork all by yourself, do you? We're going to be neighbors, child. Now what side of this mountain do you want, the east or the west? Do you want to see the sunrise or the sunset?" I said.

"I want both because the way I'm going to build my house I'll see the sun rise from my great room and I'll see it set from my wrap-around veranda," Lisa replied.

We laughed so hard that I know Mr. Balthrope, the seller, must have thought we'd lost our minds. Before he could change his, we had him meet us in town at our attorney's office. They ran a title search and we went to settlement the very next week. Trevor pretended to be happy for Lisa, but we knew better. He tried to tell her she should have consulted him before she bought the land. He said the Balthropes were famous for taking advantage of people. Lisa just smiled. Trevor told her he could have gotten her an acre of land in the same area for $75,000. He really got mad when she calmly said, "I paid much less than that."

The job was all I expected and then some. What a laid back atmosphere. No one rushed for anything, and by the grace of God, things got done. My new landlord and employee, Janna, and I became great friends and had a wonderful working relationship. However, Janna was one strange sister. The girl was either crazy or stupid. Janna was French West Indian. Her family came from St. Barts, short for

Saint Barthhélemy, a tiny island in the French Antilles. In St. Thomas, the "Frenchies," as they are called, have their own district known as French Town. Most of the men are fishermen, love their children and drink a lot. The Frenchies tend to stick with their own people. Well, my dear, Janna broke all the rules. Maybe it was because she was born a St. Thomian, nothing like her ancestors from St. Barts. I could not believe she had her Mandingo "Boo" Junnis coming right up in the yard where her in-laws lived on both sides of us, to spend the night. I mean the divorce papers had not reached the judge's desk yet. Janna thought she was being respectful because Junnis always came after the neighbors were asleep, like nobody could hear his raggedy car bumping down the unpaved road leading to her front door. Every time he turned in off the main road you could hear his muffler scrape the large rock at the top of the hill. It woke me up and I'm a hard sleeper. But hey, I didn't come to these islands to be telling people how to run their lives. I have my hands full trying to fight Officer Fitzroy off.

Do you know that fool had the nerve to send the Chief of Police to my job with sirens blasting at high noon? The Chief came into my office and said he had a warrant for me. He said I had outstanding tickets and needed me to come down to the station. I should have known there was something wrong because I'd never seen anyone get a ticket on these island's streets. I mean people double park, triple park, stop in the middle of the road to talk to their friends, and please don't blow the horn or you will get cussed. But I was so frightened and embarrassed by all the attention, I held my head down as I passed my co-workers and I went with him as quickly as my feet would move. Once outside, the sounds of a local brass band could be heard playing "A Lover's Concerto" West Indian style. Then out of the back of the police car steps Fitzroy carrying flowers and balloons. Of course the music brought everyone inside the building out to the parking lot to see what was going on. My mouth was open so wide.

"Girl, close your mouth for the cameras; your tonsils are showing," I heard Janna whisper in my ear.

Someone at the station had the bright idea of videotaping the whole thing for the 6 o'clock news. And if that wasn't bad enough, the Daily News showed up just as Fitzroy handed me a bouquet of flowers with imprinted balloons attached saying "I love you," just before gently kissing me on the cheek. Fitzroy smiled for the cameras and asked if I would meet him for dinner at Bluebeard's Castle. He promised no more sirens. My brain was in park. I still could not believe all this was happening. My girl Janna was still at my side and I guess she felt the need to answer for me since no words would come out of my mouth. I heard her say, "She'll be there at 7:30.

" OK, that would be great," Fitzroy, answered.

Fitzroy and Janna were making plans for me. Just as I came out of my trance and was about to speak, I saw him throw me a kiss as he climbed into the police car and drove away grinning like a Cheshire cat once again. Janna had an even bigger grin on her face. Needless to say, I was the talk of the station for the rest of the day. I decided to shut my office door and have my secretary hold my calls. I needed to talk to my mother.

Momma was hysterical with laughter. That was the last reaction I expected from her. I thought by giving Momma a little background about Fitzroy and drawing a vivid picture of the mentality of West Indian men, and how they believe in multiple women, Momma would feel a little guilty for laughing about my embarrassing situation. Not! She said men have been acting like that since the beginning of time. And stupid, desperate women allow them to get away with it. Momma shared that when she first married Daddy, several of the single women in the church were infatuated with him. They were constantly calling with their concerns, day and night. They were still in denial and could not believe he married someone from another congregation, especially when they had been in competition among themselves to see who would get "Rev" for quite a number of years. Mother put her foot down and told daddy she wasn't having it and those little hussies better move on and get a life! She restructured the deacon and deaconess ministry, making it a standard rule that women in need called on the deaconesses, and men called the deacons. Momma told Daddy if he had a problem with that he could talk to the Lord. No more was said and she and Daddy had a wonderful marriage, free of drama. Momma told me I was too uptight. Fitzroy sounded like a good man and besides, time was ticking and she wanted some grandchildren. She was tired of her sister showing off her grandchildren's pictures and bragging about what they did that was so cute! Then she had to remind me that after I'd wasted all those years with that deadbeat, Daemon, surely I could give Fitzroy a chance.

I had never heard Momma talk like that. She sounded more like a girlfriend who'd known me all my life than my mother. It was a refreshing feeling. We talked a little bit about the land on Bordeaux Mountain. I explained what a cistern was and how much it was costing to have it built. Momma assured me if I needed any money all I had to do was ask. Daddy made sure Momma had everything she needed and then some, before he went home to be with the Lord. I thanked her and told her I was looking forward to her and the aunties coming down next month for

Thanksgiving. After I hung up from Momma, I thought about my father, smiling as I played back the vivid scenes running through my head of great times we shared together. I prayed that God would bless me with a man like my daddy. Then I said a prayer for my mother that God would help her heal and give her peace. Momma did seem to be slowly adjusting. Thank God for her sisters who kept her busy. I know going through Daddy's things and deciding what to keep and what to give away was hard for her. She finally decided to get rid of everything except the pictures of the two of them and the many cards he had given her over the years that she kept in several keepsake boxes. Momma encouraged me to go out to dinner with Fitzroy and at least hear what he had to say. She and I prayed together that God would give me wisdom before we hung up, and somehow, I felt better. I even found myself chuckling at the events of the day.

Janna tried to talk me into wearing a red hoochie momma dress I had in my closet left over from my partying days. I told her I was not trying to send the wrong signals to this man. The dress was screaming "harlot." Since Janna liked the dress so much, I decided to bless her with it. I'm sure Junnis will love seeing her in it. I don't know where she'll wear it other than in the bedroom, because that seems like the only place he takes her. But hey, I'm not trying to run nobody's business in these islands. I settled on a stunning floor length floral dress. Janna said I looked like I was going to church. "Good, that's the image I want to project," I yelled at her as I slid into my jeep, leaving her standing on the dirt road in front of the house, and headed to Bluebeard's Castle to try and talk some sense into this overly zealous man.

The hotel-restaurant was housed in a renovated sugar mill and abounded with elegance. The sound of steel pans pounding softly could be heard as I entered the restaurant foyer. A gentle evening breeze was blowing and with each step I took across the elegantly tiled floor my dress moved ever so graciously as if it was keeping rhythm with the steel pans. The maitre d', grinning from ear to ear, greeted me as I approached the podium. You must be Miss Davis. Please allow me to show you to your table. Officer Fitzroy is waiting for you. Everything seemed fine so far, I kept reassuring myself. No sirens went off and I didn't see any television cameras. Today I had had enough excitement to last me for a while. Sitting in a far corner of the restaurant next to a window with an out-of-this-world view, I saw Fitzroy examining the wine list. He looked different. Maybe it was the navy blue sports jacket with a beautiful teal colored linen shirt. He got up from his seat as I approached the table and ran around to pull my chair out. Points for manners, I thought, as our eyes met and we both smiled.

"You look stunning, Faith," he said.

I settled into my chair and placed my purse on the vacant seat next to me. "Thank you. You look quite handsome yourself," I said, smiling.

Why was I feeling like a schoolgirl on her first date? I couldn't stop grinning. I don't know if it was the atmosphere, the music, Momma's prayers or the champagne that Fitzroy ordered, but I saw this man in a very different light. We talked for what seemed like hours.

Fitzroy shared his life story with me. I learned he was from a little island called Nevis in the British West Indies. He lost his mother about a year ago to diabetes. His dad, like mine, is a pastor. He serves a small church in a section of Nevis called Charlestown. He also operates a honey farm. Fitzroy plans to return to Nevis soon, run for political office and help build the economy.

I noticed that I had no problem understanding what he was saying. He spoke with a proper British accent. He was educated in London before moving to St. John where he became a U.S. citizen, later joined the U.S. Marines and served in the Gulf War. I avoided asking any questions about Lucinda and the twins. I wanted him to be the one to initiate that conversation. I felt it would show me he was honest and had nothing to hide in every aspect of his life.

As I've probably said before, the islands are small. I'd just finished taking a bite of prime rib and I almost choked as Lucinda's father, Mr. Bramble from the bank, approached our table. With him were several of his colleagues gawking at us as if we were the special on the menu. Mr. Bramble shook Fitzroy's hand and flashed me a sexual smile that made me feel like I had just been violated.

"Great choice, Fitzroy, my boy. I can't say I'm not jealous. I was trying to get that for myself," he said as he and his group continued to their table across the room.

Once again today, my mouth was stuck in the open position. Fitzroy obviously felt my anger and embarrassment. He then reached his giant hands across the table, placed mine into his, looked into my eyes and said as gently and as sincerely as he could, "He's as ignorant as his daughter. I'm sorry."

We both burst out into laughter, causing eyes from across the room to stare in envy. Fitzroy gave me the option of leaving if I felt uncomfortable. I declined and told him I wasn't going to let ignorant people run me away. He was glad to hear that. "Are you sure?" he asked.

I replied with a smile.

We did talk about Lucinda. Somebody needs to come down to these islands and film a soap opera! It appears that Fitzroy had a twin brother named Wilroy who died in a boating accident and Lucinda used to date him. What is it with these "Roy" names? The guy in the programming department at the station is named Iroy. During Lucinda's grieving period over the loss of Wilroy, late one night she paid a visit to Fitzroy, saying she was having trouble sleeping. He prepared her some bush tea and offered her his guestroom. This certainly sounds familiar. Later that night, he woke up and found Lucinda in his bed, and the rest is the story of how he made the biggest mistake of his life.

Almost nine months exactly, brace yourself for this - she gave birth to the twins Wilroy and Fitzroy!

"Are you sure they're your children and not your twin brothers? Please forgive me," I quickly recanted.

Fitzroy was quiet for a few very uncomfortable minutes then replied. "That was one of the last things my mother and I talked about before she passed. I've never shared this with anyone before, but I've had my doubts. It's just that they both look so much like me, which is expected since Wilroy and I were identical twins. However, their personalities are nothing like mine. Wilroy acts exactly like my brother and Fitzroy is a male version of his mother, God help him. Even though we were identical twins our personalities were as different as night and day. Daddy always said I was him after he found the Lord and Wilroy was him when he was a lost soul.

The night my brother died I was on duty and a call came in to the station from the Coast Guard saying they were in high pursuit of a speedboat believed to be carrying illegal drugs from Tortola and heading towards the east end of St. John. It's not often that we get any action on these islands, so every officer from near and far, on duty and off duty, headed out east to Coral Bay to capture this drug smuggler. The Coast Guard boat had him cornered but he thought his little speedboat was fast enough to jump the reef and break the holding pattern they had him trapped in. As I reached the shore I heard the crashing of the boat breaking up in the barrier reef. Of course no one dared to go into the reef to recover the boat or the bodies. Everyone just waited until the tide washed everything ashore. A few days later, on the shoreline of Coral Bay, my brother's body was found tangled in seaweed. Attached to his body were several pounds of crack cocaine."

Fitzroy quickly wiped a tear away that was about to roll down his cheek. This time I placed my hands on top of his giant hands and comforted him. Fitzroy paid the check and we left, ignoring tacky, loudmouth Mr. Bramble as he hollered across the restaurant to us. "Don't do nothing I wouldn't do," he said laughing.

Fitzroy paused for a moment and turned in that direction to go and confront him. I repeated his words quickly and quietly, "He's as ignorant as his daughter."

We laughed and stepped out into the Caribbean evening breeze.

Chapter 7

When I got to work the next morning there were at least 20 messages on my desk and as many e-mails, along with a copy of the Daily News. Of all people, two messages were from Lucinda. Fitzroy and I made the front page. The caption read, "Romeo Meets Juliet." The first call I returned was to Lisa who was at home. I had so much to tell her and there was no way I could tell it all on the phone. We decided to meet for lunch. She suggested the Green House, but we needed some place a little quieter. We settled on Megan's Bay Hotel. That would cut down on the possibility of running into any of the locals since it catered mainly to tourists. I wanted to minimize the chance of any drama since my face was now posted on the front page of the newspaper.

Tourist season wasn't in full swing yet so things were pretty sedate at the hotel restaurant. Lisa and I were seated beside a large picture window with a view of the golf course. We decided to sample the "all you can eat" buffet. The food looked as good as it tasted. Lisa had clipped a copy of the front page article about Fitzroy and me. She retrieved it from her purse, placing it on the table as we settled down to take the first bites of our decadent lunches.

"Just so you know, this is going in the mail today to your momma," she said.

"Girl, don't make me have to throw you out this window onto that golf course below," I hollered.

"And don't make me have to call Officer Fitzroy to come with sirens squealing to arrest you," she responded.

I laughed so hard, I had to excuse myself and run to the ladies room. I shared with Lisa my romantic evening with Fitzroy and how determined I am to take this relationship slow in spite of all the fanfare. I reminded her of the promise I made to God and myself after breaking up with Daemon. I said I was going to wait on Him to send me the man He has for me.

"How will you know when he's the one?" Lisa asked.

"I'll know, and it won't be based on sex because the brother ain't getting none until we say, I do! I don't even know where Fitzroy stands with the Lord yet. He said his father is a pastor, but so was mine and I was fornicating with Daemon for years. I tried to justify it under the pretense that it was going to develop into marriage. The next time Fitzroy asks me to go out with him, which I'm sure will be soon, I'm going to say, 'Let's go to church'," I proudly say.

"Then you might as well consider yourself married because as soon as you walk into one of these little island churches with a man, especially one that's shared the front cover of the Daily News with you, folks are going to pronounce you husband and wife!" Lisa responded.

"I'm not going to worry about every little thing these people think. I'm going to concentrate on doing the right thing. Then I know it will be blessed. Momma told me to give him a chance and that's what I'm going to do. If the man has a problem with God then we can eliminate this relationship before it gets started," I say.

We talked a little about Lucinda and the twins. I told her about Fitzroy's twin brother Wilroy. She was shocked and called St. John a little "All My Children." Lisa said she was ready to move to St. Thomas as soon as possible. Trevor was still mad at her because she wouldn't fire her building contractor. And he hadn't been over to see her in more than a week. She said she wanted to leave herself open for God to bless her too. Lisa didn't want me to get all the blessings and leave her out. I told her I would ask Janna's permission for us to share my two-bedroom apartment until our houses were built.

"Now, about that article?" I say, in a joking fashion.

"Federal Express picks up at three o'clock," Lisa boldly states.

Janna agreed that Lisa could move downstairs, as I knew she would. It was set that Lisa would move in on Saturday. Thankfully, neither one of us had furniture to move. Fitzroy volunteered to help Lisa load her boxes on the barge since Trevor had a burr in his behind. Lisa had ended their affair, and he refused to help. I was called over to St. Croix that same morning for an important meeting of all the directors. "What on earth could this be about?" I wondered. The company plane was waiting for me as I arrived at the St. Thomas airport. However, Junnis was not the pilot. "Maybe he had the day off," I thought. A very handsome man, who looked to be mixed Puerto Rican and African American, introduced himself as Billy Vanzego. Billy had a New York accent.

During the smooth flight over I learned that Billy had been living in New York for the past 10 years but is originally from Puerto Rico. His cousin, Rosalinda, is married to the owner of the station. When Billy got laid off from U.S. Air last week, he made a phone call home and his cousin hooked him up. It must be nice, I thought.

"When one door closes, another opens. Or, should I say, 'Ask and it shall be given unto you,'" Billy says as if reading my mind. We both laughed.

"So I trust you're a Christian?" I say.

"Washed by the blood of the Lamb!" he replies with a smile.

I like this man. He's intelligent, looks good, smells good, and loves the Lord. We continued talking until our little plane touched down at St. Croix's airport and pulled in front of the designated hanger. Billy is single, praise the Lord, has no children, praise Him again, and will be taking over Junnis's position as Chief Pilot for the company. He could not say what happened to Junnis but assured me many questions would be answered at the meeting.

Before we reached the office my cell phone rang. It was Lisa. The drama had started. Trevor dropped by as Fitzroy was loading Lisa's boxes into her car. The two men got into a big argument because Fitzroy was helping Lisa move her things down to the barge. Trevor accused him of trying to take his woman. Lisa tried to talk some sense into Trevor but he was not listening. Fitzroy told him he was crazy and if he knew what was good for him he would get back into his truck and go find a roof to fix or cistern to dig. This really angered Trevor. He turned as if to leave, spun around and threw a punch at Fitzroy who blocked it just before it landed on his face. Lisa tried to break the fight up but was no match for two strong angry men. Trevor pushed her out of the way and she slipped down the gravel driveway. Now she thinks her arm is broken. Fitzroy, after breaking Trevor's nose, managed to handcuff him and called for someone from the police station to come and arrest him. Lisa sounded hysterical. I told her to put Fitzroy on the phone. From the tone of his voice when he came on the phone and said, "hello," you would never think this bushman warrior just finished beating another man down to the ground and breaking his nose.

"Hello Faith. I miss you. Go to your meeting and don't worry about anything. I'll see that Lisa's things get on the barge and I'll get her over to St. Thomas safely," he says.

"OK," I say, sounding like a little girl talking to her father.

After he put Lisa back on the phone there was nothing else to say. Fitzroy definitely had it under control.

As we pulled into the reserved parking space at the station I took a quick glance at Billy and, somehow, he didn't look as good as he did on the plane. He looked small compared to Fitzroy. Now don't get me wrong, the man was still fine, but he just wasn't, as Janna would say, *my* "boo."

The atmosphere in the station was a little tense. As I entered the reception area, once again I was directed to the conference room where all the station directors were seated around the table. Mr. Atkins greeted everyone and, staying true to his character, he got right to the point.

"I'd like to thank each of you for taking time on your day off to meet with me. Let me start with the not-so-good news. Many of you have been asking the question, "Where is Junnis?" Well, he's no longer with the company. My cousin-in-law Billy has taken over that position. Junnis was using the company's plane for illegal personal business, and it was only by the grace of God that customs didn't seize the aircraft and close us down. I won't go into all of the details of that dreadful situation. However, might I suggest to any of you who call Junnis your friend, be careful that you don't find yourself in trouble with the law because of his indiscretions. Starting next week each employee will be subjected to mandatory drug testing. I have arranged for the testing to take place on-site by a company hired by the station. Testing will take place on a quarterly basis. If you or any of your staff has a problem with this drug testing, rest assured that I will pay unemployment benefits when you are released from the company."

"Moving on to a brighter subject, we will soon launch a new television station. Its call letters will be WVIT Channel 2. This channel's main purpose will be to promote the Virgin Islands. We will highlight shows that focus on the history and culture of the Virgin Islands, including the British Virgin Islands. Many of these segments will be aired on travel networks around the world. It's time someone stepped in and gave our tourism director, Linda Brown, a little help in getting more tourists down to these islands. I've got just the plan that can help spark this economy. Now, when I say "I," I'm talking about "us." This project is going to take a lot of team effort in order to be a success. It might mean working late hours in the infancy stages, however the rewards for the Islands will be great, as will be the bonuses for you and your staff."

Everyone seemed to perk up when Mr. Atkins mentioned bonuses.

"I've hired a gentleman by the name of Bob Lever to come and join our management team. Bob is from an affiliate station in Los Angeles, and he will be our new Vice President of Operations. Bob will help us accomplish our goal of making Channel 2 the best it can be, but he can only do it with your help. He's a sharp guy and he comes with years of experience."

My mind was still parked on Junnis. Mr. Atkins didn't have to tell all the details. I had a clear picture in my head of Junnis running drugs from island to island using the company's plane. I wondered if Janna knew what he was up to. Lord, I pray she isn't part of this mess. Mr. Atkins pulled me out of my daydream when I heard him call my name.

"Yes sir," I replied.

"I've been hearing nothing but good things about you since you joined us and I'd like you to head the Channel 2 initiative as Director of Production. I want you to work closely with Bob Lever and Jay Stewart, our CFO."

That was the last thing I expected to hear. I was an IT person. Computers, websites, databases, network security, programming, software; these were my areas of expertise, not television production.

"I look forward to the challenge," I say smiling. Where on earth did that come from? It must have been a Holy Ghost thing, is all I could surmise!

"Great. I like that! We all should welcome new challenges in our lives. Lastly, I'd like to take this opportunity to invite all of my directors and their families out to my house for Thanksgiving dinner. Now, don't feel obligated to come, I know many of you want to be at home with your own families or have travel plans. But for those of you who can make it, please join us for an evening of fun, fellowship and an opportunity to bond as a working family. Let my assistant Shonda know if you plan to attend as soon as possible and whether you'll require transportation. If there are no questions, I'll let you get on with your day," he says.

The flight back was uneventful. Billy and I shared small talk. He gave me an inside tip on Mr. Atkins. It appears that he really likes having a close relationship with his employees. Mr. Atkins was raised in an orphanage in Puerto Rico, and ran away from it at age 16. A storeowner in downtown San Juan found him sleeping in the back of the store one morning, felt sorry for him and offered him a job. George Atkins always had a thirst for learning. Within a year he became manager of the little shop and encouraged the owner to open another store in a newly built mall. This investment proved to be a lucrative one. Within three years, Atkins and his guardian angel opened several more stores. After a buying trip to New York, Atkins came back home and convinced his now partner to purchase the first K-Mart franchise in the Caribbean. A few years later Atkins' partner died of lung cancer, leaving all his assets to Atkins. It was then that he learned his partner had been an orphan just like himself. What a touching story, I thought.

"He's a great guy," Billy said, as we touched down on the St. Thomas runway.

I reflected on the events of the afternoon as Billy and I walked together to the parking lot. When we reached the place I'd parked, my car was not there. Billy kept asking me if I was sure this was where I had parked the jeep. For the third time I said, "yes." I guess he could tell by the tone in my voice not to ask me again, so he offered to take me to the police station to make a report and give me a ride home. Suddenly I felt violated. Someone had stolen my car. This is the Virgin Islands, not New York! As we exited Airport Road I spotted "big girl," that's the nickname I gave my jeep, parked in front of the Washboard Laundromat.

"Pull over," I yelled, "there's my jeep!" I know I frightened Billy with my sudden outburst, but he quickly responded to my cry, crossing two lanes and swerving into the laundry parking lot. There was a note attached to the windshield, which read, "take your Yankee ass home if you know what's good for you." Oh my God! Fear suddenly enveloped me. Billy took the note out of my hand and read it.

"Get back in my car Faith, "while I examine the car and make sure the brakes, transmission etc. have not been tampered with," Billy said.

I obeyed. While watching Billy check and recheck the car, I sat there in fear and then the strangest thing happened. I heard my daddy's voice. It was like he was in the car with me. He said, "God has not given us the spirit of fear, Faith." When Billy came back to the car he found me laughing and crying at the same time. I shared with him what had just happened. He prayed with me and we rebuked the enemy together. Billy believed the car had not been tampered with. Someone was just trying to scare me. However, he suggested I drive his car home and he would follow behind in my car just to make sure everything was all right. All the way home I kept thinking, "who could this person be?"

As we pulled onto the road leading to Janna's place I spotted Lisa's car. Fitzroy was unloading the last of her boxes as she looked on, wearing a sling on her arm. Junnis's car was parked in front of Janna's door. So much for him coming by only at night when everyone was asleep. I never thought I would be so happy to see Fitzroy. When he spotted me getting out of Billy's car and Billy following behind in mine I could see the confusion on his face. However, my smile put all questions aside for the moment, as he walked up to me and gave me a hug. I held on to his embrace and would not let him go. He broke the embrace after hearing me sob.

"What's wrong with her?" he blurted out at Billy who quickly answered to avoid any misunderstanding.

"Someone stole her car and when we found it there was a threatening note on the windshield," he said.

Fitzroy was outraged. We all decided to go inside the apartment and try to sort through this issue. Lisa cooked her famous spaghetti, in spite of her handicap, and I made a salad. Lisa was clearly enamored of Billy, and it appeared as if the feeling was mutual. We talked and laughed long into the night until Fitzroy announced that he had to leave in order to catch the last boat over to St. John. I was sad that the night had to come to an end. Billy volunteered to drop Fitzroy at the boat. Lisa and I walked the men out to the car. Fitzroy kissed me on the forehead and told me to ring his cell phone anytime I felt frightened or just wanted to talk. Lisa and Billy both agreed it was nice meeting each other, smiled, and shook hands. We both felt like schoolgirls as we waved to the men as they pulled out of the driveway. Praise God, He had allowed us to be in the company of two real gentlemen.

Chapter 8

Not everyone at the station was happy. The word was spreading like locusts about my new position and there were a lot of ankle biters. Before long I started to hear the "Damn Yankee" words again. The general consensus of folks in the islands is Americans come down to our territory and take jobs from us. Well, hello, I didn't ask for the position. Mr. Atkins chose me and if anybody had a problem with that then they needed to see him. Besides, if I ain't mistaken, the Virgin Islands *is* America! So don't give me that Yankee crap! I decided to pray for my enemies and move on. I learned a long time ago that everyone is not going to share in your joy and everyone isn't going to like you. So, they can just get over it. No matter what everybody felt, they still respected me.

Jay Stewart, our station's CFO, was happy for me. He and I shared a "Yankee" thing in common. Jay was a great guy and made it a point not to mingle with the local people. He somehow was under the impression that Yankee white people and locals didn't mix well. He wasn't prejudiced, he just preferred to fraternize with his own people and I'm sure his uppity wife wanted it that way.

Janna seemed a little sad because it meant we would be working in different departments. Nonetheless, she was happy for me. I asked her if we could get together for lunch and talk about a few things, including our strategy for moving her to my department as my assistant. She liked that but told me she already had a lunch date with Junnis. We decided to hook up on Saturday after she took Chloe for her horseback riding lessons. It was agreed we would go for a manicure, pedicure and then check out the new Chinese restaurant in town. Janna wasn't looking good. She had bags around her eyes and her clothes looked like she had slept in them.

Shortly after Lisa and I moved in Janna's downstairs apartment, we would hear Janna and Junnis fussing some late nights. Once it got so bad they were out in the parking lot yelling at the top of their lungs. I cautiously climbed the stairs to the parking lot to see what was going on. Thank God Lisa was working a double shift at the hospital because this would have freaked her out. It was very obvious that Junnis was high. He was holding Janna's purse, and she was fighting him, trying to get it back. When Junnis saw me standing at the top of the stairs wearing my sleep shirt, he started to cuss at me, telling me to mind my "damn business and go back downstairs." Junnis was so angry. When I didn't obey him, he approached me, still holding Janna's purse and started yelling louder in my face. Janna then picked up a rock from the ground and knocked Junnis in the head with it so hard some of his blood splattered on my shirt. Blood came gushing out of his head and running down his face. Janna finally got his attention. Junnis dropped her purse and she ran to pick it up. I was frozen. I wasn't sure if I should turn and run back downstairs and lock the door, call an ambulance, or call the police. So I just stood there watching as Junnis staggered to his car and drove off.

Janna was in tears. I watched as she stood in the parking lot clutching her purse, crying. It was clear she needed a friend to talk to, so I invited her downstairs for a cup of tea. We drank tea until the sun came up, then we cooked breakfast and talked some more. Janna confessed things to me that she said she was too ashamed to speak out loud, even to herself. Apparently her husband, Eric, had paid Janna over three hundred thousand dollars as the settlement for her half of the house, and Junnis had managed to smoke more than half of it up in crack cocaine.

Before we knew it, both of us were asleep on the sofa. We awoke from a deep sleep when we heard Chloe and Nyla knocking at the door, wondering if I'd seen their mother. It was 11:00 am, time for Chloe's horseback riding lessons. I was happy it was Saturday. I kissed the girls and told Janna we'd talk more later. I unplugged the phone, locked the door, climbed in my bed and went back to sleep.

Janna had gotten herself into a bad situation with Junnis. Not only was he putting a hole in her savings account and robbing her blind, she also found out he was stealing from the company and using their plane to run drugs between St. Thomas and Santa Domingo. Janna smiled when she told me the story of how they first got together. She said Junnis gave her the world and treated her like a queen, something no one had ever done before. Her smile was nowhere to be found when she told me about him owing a lot of people in Santa Domingo money and that he was trying to get her help to rob Mr. Atkins so he could pay his debts. Janna told him he must be out of his mind. Mr. Atkins was like a father to her and she would never do anything like that. Junnis threatened to go to Mr. Atkins, tell him Janna was his partner *and* she was part of the drug runs from Santa Domingo to St. Thomas. Janna had had no idea Junnis was picking up drugs in Santa Domingo; she had only gone with him to keep him company, not to purchase drugs.

Junnis refused to let Janna alone. He told her the relationship would end when *he* said it was over. I asked her why she didn't just go to Mr. Atkins and tell him the truth.

"I don't think he will believe me," she said after a long silence.

Mr. Atkins tried to tell Janna not to get involved with Junnis from the beginning of the relationship. He told her to wait until her divorce was final and most importantly not to have him visiting at her home. He stressed that it didn't look good and she was setting a bad example for the girls. Janna said she cussed him out.

"You might be Chloe and Nyla's godfather but you're not my daddy! I'm a grown ass woman and I know what I'm doing," she said.

Janna told me what Mr. Atkins didn't mention at the staff meeting. Drugs were found in the luggage compartment of the plane and Junnis was arrested. He told Mr. Atkins if he didn't use his connections to get the charges dropped he would tell the police Janna was his partner. He also told Mr. Atkins to check Janna's passport. It was stamped in Santa Domingo every time his was. To add insult to injury Junnis even told Mr. Atkins Janna was hooked on crack and plotting to rob him and Mrs. Rosalinda. It was no surprise in this island community that Mr. Atkins got the charges against Junnis dropped. Nevertheless, Janna was fired and Mr. Atkins didn't want to hear a word she had to say, even though she was willing to take a drug test. I felt so sorry for my friend. This drug-addicted man had managed to turn her life into a living nightmare.

At least four times a week Junnis would force his way into Janna's house, causing chaos. Once he came when Chloe and Nyla were home alone. He left after loading the food from the freezer and pantry into large trash bags. The girls were petrified. Yet, Janna still would not call the police. She was too afraid of what Junnis might do. I tried to give her some advice, but it became apparent this man had a serious stronghold on her. What she really needed was Holy Ghost intervention. Finally, I realized all I could do was pray for my friend that God would remove the blinders so she could see clearly and move forward.

A few days later I decided it was the better part of wisdom to remove all our valuables from the house, in case Junnis decided to venture downstairs. Just as I was leaving the office to head home at lunch time, Fitzroy called. He wanted me to know he would be working on an undercover assignment for the next two days and his cell phone would be on pulse if I needed him. He thinks he knows who stole my car and would talk about it when he saw me and he wanted to know if the new Channel 2 Director of Productions would be available to celebrate on Friday. Fitzroy had tickets to the Reichhold Center for the Arts where a West Indian play, "Dream on Monkey Mountain," was opening. We agreed he should catch the six o'clock boat from St. John that would take him to downtown Charlotte Amalie. I would pick him up on the waterfront and that would give us time to grab a quick bite before heading to the theatre. Our plans were in place for Friday, and I was looking forward to seeing him.

Lisa was home when I arrived. She had transferred her job from the Myrah Keating Smith Clinic on St. John to Roy Schneider Hospital in St. Thomas. Lisa was staying clear of St. John until Trevor had time to cool off. She found out through the grapevine or "melee," as the island folks call it, that Trevor lives with a white woman who bartends at Fred's on the weekend, and they have three children. "I bet she was the same woman with a bad attitude who served us when we went there for Girls' Night Out." Lisa has clearly moved on. Trevor was nothing but a moment of weakness and a mistake, or so she says.

"God first and the rest will follow," Lisa says is her new motto.
This was easy enough for her to live up to especially since Billy had been ringing her phone. Last night they went to Bible study together. You should have seen home girl getting ready. She must have changed in and out of 20 different outfits, trying to acquire that *holier* look.

I shared with Lisa the reason I had come home and a brief synopsis of what's been going on between Junnis and Janna. She helped me gather up our valuables and suggested that maybe we should be looking for another place to live. I couldn't believe she said that.

"You just got here and your boxes aren't unpacked yet," I said.

"Isn't that wonderful? And I'm not unpacking until I'm sure it's safe to live here!" she says.

Janna's condition continued to deteriorate to the point of depression. She missed her job so much and couldn't fathom the thought of looking for another one. She had worked for Mr. Atkins since high school. How could Junnis mess up her life like that? Now that he wasn't working, Junnis had more time to harass Janna and the girls. Mr. Atkins was grieved like a father who had lost one of his children.

"How are Janna and the girls doing?" he'd sometimes ask when I would run into him at the television station.

"As well as can be expected," I'd smile and say.

I didn't know what else to say without over stepping my boundaries. However, I did suggest he invite her to lunch. He cleared his throat and continued down the hallway.

Chloe and Nyla really suffered as they watched their mother slip further and further into depression. Their little hearts became callous. Chloe cursed at her mother and told her to get up and do something with her life. She reprimanded her like she was the child. Janna could care less. Lisa and I took the girls to church with us on Sundays where they cried their hearts out at the altar. Janna refused to come. She believed God had turned His back on her. Nyla finally came to the conclusion that there was no God because her mother only seemed to be getting more depressed. She didn't want to hear anything we had to say about God; she hated Him for what He allowed to happen to her family.

Chloe became the little woman of the house, always cooking and cleaning. Lisa caught her one Saturday morning trying to back the car out the driveway. Chloe said she was going to pick up some groceries for her family. Lisa gently scolded her, took her to the Pueblo Market and made her promise not to drive her mother's car again. Lisa asked why she didn't ask her aunt or grandmother who lived in the same "yard" to take her to the store. She said they called her and her sister little bastards just like their mother and didn't have anything to do with them. Lisa sat in the car and sobbed as Chloe went into the store.

Mr. Atkins finally decided to stop by and check on his goddaughters. We know it was Janna he was really concerned about. Word had gotten to his wife by way of Chloe and Nyla that their mother wasn't feeling well. Mrs. Rosalinda told Mr. Atkins she didn't care what he and Janna's problem was, he needed to go and see what he could do to help her! As soon as Mr. Atkins walked into Janna's house and saw her he cried. He knew he had made a mistake in judging her. Janna was not on crack; she was depressed. He blamed himself. Lisa and I had been taking turns helping the girls clean up, so by God's grace, Mr. Atkins did not walk into a nasty house. He and Janna sat and talked a long time. Mr. Atkins said he would make arrangements for Janna to get therapy and, when she felt she was ready, her job would be waiting for her. He begged her to please forgive him. And she did.

Billy and Lisa had quickly become an item. They spent much of their time together at church. It was no surprise when Billy announced that the Lord had called him to preach. He continued to fly for the company while he took online divinity classes at the University of the Virgin Islands.

I was excited when Momma called to confirm that she and the aunties would be coming for Thanksgiving. They had their plane tickets and were looking forward to some fun in the sun. I told Momma that sounds like something a young girl would say. She reminded me that she was only sixty and not as old as Methuselah. I continue to marvel at this new side of my mother. She almost seems like someone I've never met before; a real *person*, and not my mom. I told her about the job changes and about my boss inviting us to his castle for Thanksgiving dinner. Momma was ecstatic about going to a castle for Thanksgiving. I think that's all she heard me say because she kept repeating, "What do we wear to a castle?" I told her, "The same thing you wear to anybody's house for Thanksgiving." Momma said I must be crazy, then added insult to injury by saying I never did know how to dress, so why was she asking me. She rushed me off the phone so she could call her sisters to let them know they were going to be dining at a castle for Thanksgiving. I don't know why Momma thought I couldn't dress. Maybe she was thinking about the days when it was cool to wear jeans with holes in them. That drove her crazy.

Fitzroy was working quite a bit. We didn't have a lot of time to spend together, which was OK because I had my hands full with my new position. I really enjoyed television production. It was so different from my Information Technology background. I welcomed the change in my life and embraced the challenge. The Lord blessed me with a wonderful production crew. Praise God, He got rid of the bad apples. The ones who had a problem with the fact that I was a Yankee and a woman moved on to other departments, and a few left the company. My crew and I spent our days videotaping and some late nights editing. Lisa was rarely home. Between church and working swing shifts at the hospital, she sometimes only came home to shower and change. Many nights I just stayed at the station and slept in the guest cottage on the property. I smile when I look back at where my life was just a few months ago...sitting at home in my Los Angeles townhouse, waiting for Daemon to put his key in my door.

"You've come a long way, baby!"

Chapter 9

Lisa was sleeping hard, snoring in "other tongues." She had pulled a double shift at the hospital so I didn't bother to wake her to let her know I was leaving and would be home late tonight. I raced out the door to make a 9:30 dental appointment before going to work. As I walked to my car, Chloe and Nyla greeted me.

"What are you two doing home from school? I asked.

"Junnis is in the house with Mommy and he won't let her out of the room to take us to school. We called our dad and he's coming to get us," Nyla replied.

I wasn't sure if I should call the police. I knew Junnis was out of Janna's life...but what was he doing here? I could hear the undercarriage of Janna's husband's car scraping the ground as he turned off the main road. Lord, things are about to get ugly. I excused myself from the girls and went back down stairs to give Lisa a heads up. She was so sleepy; when I tried to wake her she wasn't making sense. "The doctor will be in to see you soon," she said.

Things did get ugly. Shots were fired, and before I got back up the stairs Janna and Junnis were both dead. There are several different stories going around about what happened. It's alleged that her husband, Eric, did it after he asked Junnis to leave his house and Junnis laughed in his face. Eric says he didn't kill them. Most locals believe he is innocent. Another story says Junnis shot Janna and then turned the gun on himself. He was depressed about losing his job and owing a lot of money to some drug suppliers in Santa Domingo. Junnis became belligerent when Janna tried to break off their relationship and refused to give him any more money. Nyla told the police that Junnis had forced his way into their house. Her mother kept asking him to leave, but he wouldn't relent.

Nyla later shared with me that Janna told her and Chloe she made a big mistake making Mr. Junnis her friend. She told them she was sorry for showing such a bad example of how a woman should look for a man. Janna made them promise they would not make the same mistake when they became women. When I heard this version of the story, I decided that's the one that sounded like the Janna I knew.

Mr. Atkins didn't spare any cost putting Janna to rest in grand style. Janna's parents and siblings were most appreciative. The large Catholic Church was packed to overflowing. Limousines lined the curb from Mafolie Hill to the entrance to North Star Village. Large screen televisions were placed outside on the lawn of the church for those who could not fit inside for the ceremony. And for those who stayed at home Mr. Atkins made sure the services were broadcast on all of the stations he owned. I had never seen so many people at a funeral before. It looked like a president's funeral. Every "Frenchie" in St. Thomas was there including Eric's family. Chloe and Nyla sat on the front row looking like little doll babies. Janna's family was given temporary custody of the girls. Mr. Atkins and his wife were also petitioning for custody. Eric had been arrested and charged with the murder of Janna and Junnis. However, the locals were placing bets that even if found guilty, he probably wouldn't do any time in prison. He would plead temporary insanity. I'm sure the fact that his grandfather is a senator would work in his favor.

Two women came from Dominica to claim Junnis' remains. One was his mother and the other woman said she was his wife and the mother of his three children. People in the office took up an offering to help them get his body home. Mr. Atkins made it clear he was not helping because he felt Junnis was responsible for Janna's death. I made my donation and decided to leave that comment alone.

A crowd of local West Indian people were congregated in front of the ordering window of Violet's Front Porch, a roadside food stand located at the bottom of the hill from the television station. I often stop there on the way to work to pick up a cup of lemon grass tea. Today, I wished I hadn't. The customers were all abuzz about Janna's death. Everyone had a theory about what happened, as if they'd been there. Most believed Eric was innocent. It was really hard for me to stand there and listen to them talk about my friend as I waited an extremely long time for just a cup of tea. Island people are certainly a strange group of folks. Janna was one of their own. She and her husband Eric "was bawn here" and townspeople would make sure Junnis would take the fall for her death since he was a "foreigner."

A construction worker who was toward the back of the crowd suddenly hollers,"How long a man got to wait for a johnnycake and goat water?"

"If you in a hurry, take you backside over to *Mickie D's*!" Violet shouts from the kitchen.

All the customers get a good laugh from Violet's response, and moved on to another topic of conversation. To protect his macho image, the construction worker responds, "I love that woman. I know she back dere putting she foot in de' pot"!

The crowd responds with roaring laughter. The sound of a dump truck can be heard bouncing down Iguana Hill. The truck, loaded with laborers, came to a screeching halt in front of Violet's place. The driver hollers out of the window to one of his workers, "Lee-Roy, man, if you planning on working today, you best move it, man! And tell Violet to throw me a piece of dumb bread and some bush tea in de' bag."

Violet sticks her head out from the back, yelling to the truck driver, "Hey, sweetie! How's Mommy"?

All the customers are concerned and wait for his response. The truck driver proudly responds, "She good, girl! Doctor say dey want me to take she over to Puerto Rico, for check-up, to make sure all de gout gone."

Violet responds, still yelling out to the road from the ordering window of the little stand, "Yeah, man, take she over Puerto Rico; these damn doctors in St. Thomas don't know nothing! Tell Mommy I'll stop by later with some salt fish and dumplings."

Violet ducks her head back into the kitchen. Salt fish and dumplings - just what the woman needs for her gout - I think to myself as the construction worker jumps on back of the awaiting truck after giving the driver his dumb bread and bush tea. The sound of the big dump truck continues up the road.

Things at the station were not the same without Janna. I could not walk past her office without weeping. Though I'd only known her for a short time, she was my girl. Janna had such a wonderful spirit. She knew how to love people. I'm not sure if Eric killed her or if Junnis did it. In a way, both of them took a part of her life, Eric with his abusiveness, and Junnis with his addiction and lies.

After the shooting, Fitzroy offered his house to Lisa and me. It was tempting, but I declined. Lisa thought of taking Billy up on his offer to share his one bedroom apartment in Estate Contant, but she, too, declined. God certainly was molding us and making us into different women. We clearly were not the same two who had left Los Angeles just a few months ago. We were learning to consult God before making any decisions; thinking with our heads instead of our vaginas; giving God the reigns to guide us. We had finally learned what it means to "let go and let God."

Mr. Atkins came through for us without our even asking. He had the office maintenance crew to move our things from Janna's to one of his houses on Skyline Drive. He said we were welcome to stay there as long as we needed. I told Lisa I had never moved so much in one year in all my life. We both agreed that the next time we moved, we prayed it will be into one of our own houses. The builder was on schedule but even that was moving too slow for me. However, I'm not complaining, because Mr. Atkins' house on Skyline was "the bomb!" It looked like something out of a magazine, and it came with maid service. God is good! Momma and the aunties are scheduled to arrive next month and I know this place is going to blow their minds.

Fitzroy was a jewel; I don't know what I'd do without him. We've only managed to spend a little time together these past few weeks because of the demands of our jobs. However, he still sent love my way via telephone calls and little "thinking of you" e-mails. He met me one Sunday afternoon at Trunk Bay. While relaxing on the beach after snorkeling, he informed me it was Lucinda who stole my car from the airport. I was relieved to know who it was but at the same time sad and a little frightened when I realized the measures Lucinda was willing to go through to come between us. Fitzroy promised me that he had handled the situation and I felt safe knowing that. He also said it was time to have the paternity tests done on the twins.

Chapter 10

Our new Vice President of Operations, Bob Lever, seems sharp, just like Mr. Atkins said, and he really does know the business, but I get this bad taste in my mouth every time I'm around him. He certainly has Jay jumping. Jay thinks Bob is trying to get rid of him and bring his own people onboard from the states. I've never seen anyone "brown nose" as hard as Jay. You almost need a crane to pull him out of Bob's butt!

Things were changing around the television station so quickly since Janna went home to be with the Lord. Last month I hired a high school senior by the name of Linda Peters as my intern, part of an Upward Bound program. Linda is a rare find as far as today's youth are concerned. She set goals for herself, and everyday she made sure she was on target. Linda has her heart set on attending Harvard University's political science department, and she's saving every penny she makes for when it happens. Scholarships even for the brightest students on these islands are rare. Linda made it clear; boys were definitely not a priority in her life. She believed they would only sidetrack her from her goals. It saddened her that so many of her girlfriends had fallen into the, "baby I love you, baby I want you to be mine" trap that the boys were setting. Linda knew all that meant was your man wanted you to stay at home and wait for him, while *he* did everything and everybody he wanted to do. She thought it was stupid the way her girlfriends fell for that game. Some of them were so desperate to have a man they were willing to give up their freedom and dreams of going to college for a "boy" who was playing "man." They were so consumed with the feeling sex gave them that their visions of a better life became cloudy. No one thought of the consequences of unprotected sex. To them HIV and AIDS were things that happened to *other* people.

Linda's best friend, Temecula, took stupid behavior a step further and got pregnant, thinking it would ensure her a closer place in her man's heart over the other girl. After her man found out she was pregnant, he denied the child was his and stopped coming around. Now "Tee" is stuck with a baby and she has dropped out of school to work at Pizza Hut. Linda continually tries to encourage her to get her GED and enroll in college. She even went so far as to show her on paper how every dime she was making was going to the babysitter and to buy baby food and diapers. She'd do better on welfare. "I presented a four year plan to her, which included getting on welfare, just temporarily; staying at home with the child during the day and going to night school. Then after she got her degree, get a good paying job and get off public assistance," Linda explains.

When Linda visited Government House on a field trip while in grade school, she decided then that she would become the first woman Governor of the Virgin Islands. Her vision was becoming even clearer as she matured and became more and more discontent with the way the government of the Virgin Islands was being run. She felt her Virgin Islands were being raped by excess tourism. The cruise ships were polluting the harbor and tourists were littering the roads and destroying the coral reefs with their suntan lotion, standing on the natural wonders with their fins and bumping them with their scuba tanks. The Island had no resources to bring in money except tourism, which only created minimum wage jobs for immigrants and illegal aliens. The natives were selling the land they inherited from their great-great-grandparents at an alarming rate to outside building developers. Many, after receiving much less than the land was worth, fled to the continental United States, in search of "pie in the sky," only to return home as renters instead of land owners within a year, with nothing left but broken dreams.

White people from the United States and other countries owned more than half the Island. The Arabs dominated the clothing, furniture and food industry and employed only people from their own countries to work in their stores. Linda did not like the way her island was being developed. The future did not look good for Virgin Island natives. If things did not change soon, they would become foreigners in their own land. The future depended on her. She had to stay focused on her goal by any means necessary. While in high school, Linda founded the Future Leaders of the Virgin Islands Club. Her group wrote proposals and presented ideas to the governor and the legislators, many of which were passed into law. Linda even went toe-to-toe with our boss, Mr. Atkins, on several occasions concerning issues she had with his views on tourism. She even asked to serve on his planning committee so she could better understand his rationale for bringing more tourists to her islands. Mr. Atkins loved and respected her, and knew she was a force to reckon with. He immediately realized it would be better to have her working for him and on his side.

Chapter 11

I am so excited I can hardly contain myself. I've been buzzing all morning and can't seem to stay at my desk long enough to get anything done. My intern, Linda, peeks her head into my office and asks me why I bothered to come in this morning, assuring me she has everything under control. I tell her I came in because Momma and the aunties' plane won't arrive until two o'clock and I thought I would be able to get some work done before I went on vacation.

"Girl, I got dis; you need to take a chill pill and go enjoy time with your family," Linda says.

"You're not trying to rush me out of here so you can take my job, are you?" I say.

"Miss Faith, if anyting, I want your boss's job!" Linda replies.

"Girl you are such an old soul!" I say.

"Dat's what me grandmudda say! She tinks I've been 'ere before," Linda says laughing.

"Well, I don't know about all that, but I do know you are a blessing, and I appreciate you," I say.

"Tanks, Miss Faith...now dat we both agree I can handle tings, go and get ready for your visitors," Linda says, pushing Faith out of her office.

"Well, since I'm being kicked out of my office, I guess I'll stop by the mall and pick up an outfit to wear to Mr. Atkins' for Thanksgiving dinner. Are you going?"

"As much as me would like to go, me family would be disappointed. Yah see me grandfadda lives on Water Island. Look der, you can see his house from your window."

Linda and I both look out the window in my office and confirm where the house is located.

"All me aunts, uncles, cousins and grandparents always get together this time of year and have a pig roast and lobster feast. We partay from Thursday until Sunday night. It's a lot of fun! Maybe you could bring you mudda and aunties over sometime this weekend?" She says.

"Hey, they would love it. How in the world do you get over to that little island?" I ask.

"Der's a little shuttle boat, it looks like a tug boat," she says.

"Oh, I've seen it, right next to the seaplane."

"Yes, dat's de one. Me uncle Nanno and me cousin Hilton are de boat captains. It leaves every hour on de hour. Just let dem know you're me guest and you can come over anytime. Bring your bath suit, der's a really nice private beach on me grandfadda's property," she says.

"Great, I'm looking forward to meeting your family and having a good time. We'll probably come over on Saturday. I'll give Momma and the aunties a day or so to rest after having Thanksgiving at Mr. Atkins. I know it's going to take them at least a day to come down from the excitement of flying in his private plane and dining at his castle. Oh, I've been meaning to ask you, what's up with the castle thing? The aunties are driving me crazy wondering what to wear to a castle for dinner!"

Linda lets out a big hearty laugh.

"What's so funny?" I ask.

"Nottin.' Gil, I feel yah. Mr. Atkins and he wife Mrs. Rosalinda invited me and de Future Leaders Club over to der castle last year fa dinner. All of us was wonderin' de same ting, what to wear!' Miss Faith, we spent more time with dat den we did de agenda. Finally, we decided to wear we church clothes."

"Well, was that appropriate?" I ask.

"Let's just say, Mrs. Rosalinda made us feel so at home, we could have been wearin' we birth suits. First let me tell ya dis...Mrs. Rosalinda is the nicest lady you ever goanna meet. She was wearing jeans and a T-shirt when she greeted all of us. Me son, we all felt so overdressed, but immediately, she put dat to rest. Mrs. Rosalinda told each and every one of us how beautiful we looked and hugged us. Even dough dey live in a castle, it don't feel cold or any ting like dat. Mrs. Rosalinda really hooked dat place up! You know de woman's an interior designer?"

"No, I don't know anything about her," I say.

"Well, me dear, someone should write a book about she. She mudda was actually a princess from Spain and she fadda is the governor of Puerto Rico."

"Wow, real royalty, huh? Is that why they live in a castle?"

"No, dat's anudder story. You see, Mr. Atkins meet Mrs. Rosalinda a few years ago in Puerto Rico. Dey only been married tree years now."

"Wait, how do you know all these folks' business?"

"Miss Faith, come on! Dees islands is small. Look at you, don't you tink everybody knows your business an' you only been on our island for six months."

"Excuse me! What business of mine could anybody know?"

"Wasn't it yer face dat everybody seen on de front of de Daily News with dat officer from St. John? Miss Faith people know you from here to Trinidad! "Romeo Meets Juliet!" Everybody's watin' to see what he does to propose to yah! Da island people like melee, haven't you notice we got we own live soap opera round here?"

"What in the world is 'melee'?" I ask.

"Gossip," Linda replies.

"Well, I didn't realize my life was such an open book."

"Don't worry your head, it's all good. Anyway, Mr. Atkins and Mrs. Rosalinda meet in Puerto Rico. You know he was an orphan?"

"Yes, I did hear that."

"Well, Mrs. Rosalinda every year host a big, big fund-raiser for the Los Ninos Village in San Juan, and a few years ago she raised enough money for a brand new school for de orphan chirin. The Board of Directors thought it would be a good idear to name de school for Mr. Atkins, since he was one of der biggest donors, and a former resident of Los Ninos. Dey invited him to the dedication ceremony, he meet Mrs. Rosalinda and fell in love with she at first sight!"

"Linda, were you there?"

"No, but it was in the San Juan News, the Daily News and St. Croix Avis! And Mrs. Rosalinda told us the story."

"So, what does that have to do with why they live in a castle?" I ask.

"Oh, me God, me forget dat part! Ya see, Mrs. Rosalinda's fadda always call she "Princess," so when Mr. Atkins went to ask for she hand in marriage, she fadda agreed only if he would always treat she like a princess. Mr. Atkins said he would do even better, he would treat she like a queen. So, he surprised Mrs. Rosalinda and had a castle built for dem to get married an' live in."

"Wow, what a wonderful love story," I say.

"So, Miss Faith, to answer your question, I would wear whatever feels comfortable to dinner at der house."

"Thank you for your insightful information, Linda, and I'll see you this weekend at your family's pig roast."

As I picked up my purse and cell phone to leave, Linda asked me to give the Atkins' her love and remind Mr. Atkins they have a meeting next week with the governor to discuss establishing some kind of ordinance instituting a fine for tourists who stand on the coral or remove souvenirs from the water. It appears the tourists have been taking the brain coral and sea fans home with them.

The Tutu Park Mall isn't exactly the greatest place to go if you want to do some serious shopping, but hey, this is what we got on this island to work with. There are some nice designer stores on Main Street and in the Passages, where the tourists shop for their duty free perfume, gold, diamonds, fancy table cloths, crystal, clothes and liquor. When I first moved here, I was impressed with Louis Vuitton, Gucci, Cartier, Channel and all the other expensive shops, but now, those things don't seem so important anymore. Don't get me wrong, I still enjoy fine shopping but I'm not trying to spend half a week's paycheck on a dress or a purse! Using my money to get my house built is my number one priority, not expensive clothes.

I was able to get a parking spot close to K-mart, thank God, because the heat outside was repressive. I kept the air conditioner on high in the car and did not want to turn it off while I ran into the mall, because I knew it would feel like an inferno inside when I got back in the car. I cracked all the windows and walked very quickly into the mall, so my body would not have to endure the brutal heat too long. Outside the mall there were older local island women, who set up tables to sell their island treats. Some were selling guava and coconut tarts, beef, salt fish or conch pates. Another table sold maube, an island drink made from anise and the bark from a local tree. The drink has a very bitter licorice taste to it. They also had ginger beer that was stored in an old liquor bottle with the ginger froth overflowing out of the top of the bottle. I love the local ginger beer; I'll stop and get a big cup of it with plenty of ice on my way back to the hot car. As I reached to open the door to the mall, an old woman, holding a clipboard with lottery tickets attached, greeted me. "Take a chance, me dear?" She cried.

"No thank you," I said, as I stepped inside the air-conditioned mall.

Once inside, there were vendor carts positioned in the center where you could purchase giant silver chains with humongous blingage attached to it, cell phones with fancy cases, gold rings, and purses that were knockoffs of the real ones found on Main Street. Another cart was selling pots and pans and giving demonstrations, showing how spectacular their products were. A man wearing a chef's hat was cooking "cow heel soup" and fried plantains. People were lined up to get a taste while his assistant, a beautiful young girl, passed out brochures about the cookware and rang up sales at the cash register.

I still had a few hours before Momma and the aunties would arrive, however I didn't want to push it because I know time just seems to fly when you're shopping. I went into Marian's Dress Shop and first browsed the sale racks. I found a cute white Capri pant suit and a floral wrap skirt with a matching tank top. I'd wear the floral wrap to Linda's family beach party and show off the white Capri pant suit the next time I got together with Fitzroy. Fitzroy wanted to go with me to the airport to help Momma and the aunties with their luggage. I told him we could handle it. He said he didn't like the idea of us scrambling around trying to get someone to help us. He reminded me that a lot of people would be coming in this weekend for the holiday and it would be difficult maneuvering around the airport, especially with Momma and the aunties in this heat. I told him that I plan to put them in the car after they identified their luggage and then I would find someone to help load the luggage into the car. Oh, my! It just occurred to me that my jeep might not hold everybody and their luggage! The aunties and Momma over packed, I'm sure. When we used to go to weekend retreats with the church just 30 miles away from home, they each used to travel with two suitcases, and that was just for a two-night stay. Lord have mercy, they might bring ten suitcases each, since they're going to be here for two weeks! I'd better call Lisa and see if she can meet me at the airport. I was too ashamed to call Fitzroy after I came off like "super woman."

Lisa wasn't picking up on her cell phone. It just dawned on me, Lisa was off today, and Billy was flying her over to a little British island just east of St. John called Tortola, to spend the day snorkeling and windsurfing. It seems they could not get enough of each other. Whenever they were not working they were together, either at Bible study, some other church activity, or out on a date. Lisa was standing by her promise not to give it up until marriage. At first I had a little trouble believing her, then she blasted me out!

"Hell, Faith, what makes you think your vagina is the only one that can obey God's law?" she said.

I had to laugh and agree that I didn't have a monopoly on celibacy. Billy's commitment to God's word did make it easier for Lisa to be strong. I know there was a time when...well, we won't go there. Like the Bible says: "He who is without sin, let him cast the first stone," and I sure don't have any stones to throw! I'm not going to lie; it's been a struggle for me lately, trying not to give it up. Every time I'm with Fitzroy I get weak, especially when he holds me in his arms and says sweet things like, "Faith you are so beautiful...I know God made you especially for me," in that sexy British accent! The other night, we went to dinner at Chateau Bordeaux and I had a few glasses of wine. The view was spectacular and the full moon wasn't helping at all.

After dinner, I suggested we drive up the mountain road just above the restaurant and see how the building of my house was coming along. Once up there, Fitzroy and I stood on top of the cistern among the construction debris, looking out onto the water with the full moon lighting the sky so we could see several other islands. It was so romantic! And then, he kissed me. I'm not talking about a little peck; I'm talking "tongue hockey," along with heavy panting around my ear. I got so hot, I had to run to the car and turn the air conditioner on. I know he thought I was insane, until I told him about the promise I made to God and myself. He said he understood, and would work hard at not making it so difficult for me to keep my word.

Lord, I think I see the outfit I'm going to wear to the Atkins' for Thanksgiving! I spotted a lime green chiffon pantsuit with a long flowing coat. I tried it on and it looked good! Not too dressy, but not too everyday either. Bingo! Now I need to head to the airport and figure out how to get Momma, the aunties and their plethora of suitcases up to Skyline Drive.

I had never seen the airport so busy. You would have thought there was some kind of convention going on. I circled the parking lot twice to find a spot and there was not one to be found. Even all the rental car spaces were taken. The police had booted several cars that tried to park illegally or stayed too long in the loading zone. "This doesn't look good." I decided I would park a half a mile down the road at the Beachcomber Hotel, walk back to the airport, meet Momma and the aunties, and we all would take a van taxi up to the house, and I'd get a ride back to my car with Lisa or Billy later that evening. Walking from the Beachcomber Hotel towards the airport felt like walking through the flames of hell! It was so hot, my feet were burning on the bottom from the heat of the pavement and I was sweating like a pig! "Lord, please don't let me pass out on this airport road," was my prayer. I'd underestimated the distance from the hotel to the airport. It seemed so short when I was driving, but now, the airport seemed like a little speck in the faraway distance. Thank God I had a bottle of water in my big purse that was now weighing me down. I stopped along the road to take a drink, only to discover it had turned so hot there were little bubbles in the bottle. There just wasn't any relief in sight. I decided I would turn back, go get my car and just sit on the airport parking lot until someone moved out of a parking spot. Surely, everyone couldn't be waiting for the same plane. The down side to that logic was that I only had 30 more minutes before their plane would touch down. Lord, help me! Be careful what you ask for.

A fifteen-passenger van pulled up to the curb, blowing its horn. The window turned down and I heard a familiar voice.

"Faith, get in," he said.

Thank you, Jesus! I said.

It was Fitzroy, driving the van. I felt so dumb and relieved at the same time.

"You know you're hard-headed, don't you?" He said.

"Yes," I said.

Fitzroy entered the parking lot, found a spot along the curb where the other cars had been booted, and placed a sign that read "Official Police Business" in the window. As we sit in the van, the air-conditioner blows deliverance from the heat in my direction. Fitzroy turns to me with a very serious look in his eyes and says,

"I loved you Faith from the first time I saw you." "Oh," I reply, hoping I didn't sound dumb, because didn't know what else to say. I was stuck on the "L" word!

Fitzroy continues, "Now I'm not sure how the brothers in the states operate when they love someone, but where I'm from, we look out for our lady."

I felt goose bumps and chills all over my body.

"Now, I'd like it very much if you would allow me to be the man that God has created me to be," he says.

Here came the "oh" again.

"You see, it makes me sad to know that you're out here in this blistering heat worrying your pretty head about parking and who's going to help you and your family with their luggage. And what would your mother and aunts think about me if they knew I'd let you come out here to harass yourself like this dealing with heavy luggage and things?"

Finally, I was able to say something other than "oh."

"I'm sorry, you see I'm so used to doing things myself, and I thought I would be taking you away from your work, not to mention you having to take the barge over from St. John to help," I sadly say.

"You don't think you're worth my doing that?" he says.

"Of course, I do!" I reply.

"So what exactly is the problem?" Fitzroy says.

"I never met anyone like you before," I confess.

"So, is that a problem?" Fitzroy replies.

"Not at all," I say in a very defeated tone.

"So, are you going to let me do my job?" he asked.

I reply, "Most definitely. Now turn off this van and let's get on out there so you can meet my mother and aunties and do your job!"

We both laughed as he gets out of the van and opens the door for me.

Steel pans played festive Caribbean music for passengers as they entered the terminal. As each passenger walks past the airport welcome booth located directly next to the arrival gate, a man and woman passed out rum punch and welcomes everyone to St. Thomas. Every few feet that we walked among the crowd, people were greeting Fitzroy, like he was a celebrity.

"How do you know all these people?" I finally ask him.

"I help keep them safe," he says with a smile.

The goose bumps return again, along with a big smile across my face. Fitzroy takes my hand as we walk closer to the gate.

I spotted Aunt Dot right away. She was wearing a big sun hat with a gigantic silk flower in the front. The hat looked like it weighed a ton. Walking next to her was Aunt Lucille, wearing a soft sleeveless scoop neck floral blouse with matching big leg pants that created its own breeze with each step she took and teal sandals that matched her toenail polish. Walking behind them was Momma, wearing a yellow and white flowered sundress. I almost didn't recognize her because she had her hair corn-rowed! It was styled in an upward sweep that culminated in a French roll. Momma looked 20 years younger. Both she and the aunties were each pulling a small suitcase behind them. "There they are!" I yelled. It suddenly dawned on me how much I missed my family. Momma and I embraced like we hadn't seen each other in years and then I cried. Fitzroy stood there with a strange look on his face. Almost like he'd seen a ghost. He was mesmerized watching Momma and me. Maybe he's stricken by the similarity in our features, I thought. Aunt Dot kissed me and wiped away my tears.

"If somebody don't introduce me to this fine man, I'm going to assume he's the island man I've been asking the Lord to send my way," Aunt Lucile says.

"And what exactly would your half-a-century-plus self, do with this young man?" Aunt Dot teases her.

"I'm not so old that I don't remember what to do with a man!" Lucille says.

"Calm them hormones down Lucille!" Momma interjects.

"Fitzroy, meet my Aunt Dot, Aunt Lucille and my mother, Gloria Davis."

"It's a pleasure to meet each of you," he says.

"You still haven't told us *who* he is," Aunt Lucille presses.

"He's my, he's my...," I stutter.

"I'm her knight in shining armor," Fitzroy interjects. Everyone's mouth is opened in surprise. Fitzroy heads towards the baggage area after taking Momma's carry-on. I smile and quickly catch up with him. Momma and the aunties are still chatting as they follow behind us.

As Fitzroy predicted, there were so many people in the baggage area you could hardly move without stepping on someone's toes. He suggested putting the carry-on luggage in the van while we waited for the other luggage. Aunt Lucille asked Aunt Dot if she wanted to put the luggage that was on her head in the car, so she wouldn't hurt someone with that weapon of a hat. Everyone laughed and Aunt Dot agreed her head was burning up underneath it. As soon as Fitzroy left for the van, I was bombarded with questions. First, from Momma. "Is it serious, honey?"

Then, Aunt Dot. "Girl, how long have you known him? Does he treat you nice?"

Next was Aunt Lucille. "He sure is fine, does he have an older brother?"

"I've known him as long as I've been on the island, and, yes, he does treat me nice. He's a perfect gentleman.

And, no, he doesn't have an older brother. Momma, he's the one I told you about.

"Oh, the one who was in the newspaper kissing you?" asked Aunt Lucille.

"Yeah, Lisa mailed us a copy of the newspaper "Romeo Meets Juliet" and your mother showed it to everyone at church. She even copied it and put it on the bulletin board in the ladies restroom," says Aunt Dot.

"He looks more handsome than the picture in the newspaper," Aunt Lucille says.

"It looks like the islands are agreeing with you, Faith," Aunt Dot remarks.

"Thank you. It's been quite an adventure so far," I say.

"So, I understand you and Lisa are living in a mansion on the top of the mountain," Aunt Lucille says.

"It's my boss's house; he's letting us stay there until our houses are built," I respond.

The belt starts up and the luggage begins to come around.

"Lord, have mercy, there are so many folks, we won't be able to see our luggage and this heat is brutal!" Momma says while fanning herself with a "*What To Do In St. Thomas Guide.*"

"You aren't lying. I thought I was having an extended senior moment; this place is burning up!" says Aunt Lucille.

Fitzroy returns and suggests that we all go and sit in the van under the air conditioner and come back in about 30 minutes after the crowd thins out. We all agree, and just about race to get to the air-conditioned van. Once in the van, Fitzroy offers everyone cold drinks from a small cooler stored under the back seat.

"So are we all here on official police business?" Aunt Lucille says, pointing to the police sign in the window.

"We're not picking up any prisoners are we?" Aunt Dot chimes in.

"No, putting this sign in the window was the only way I could park here without getting booted or towed," Fitzroy responds.

"We're not doing anything illegal are we?" Momma inquires.

"No Mother. I mean Mrs. Davis. In my line of work, I'm always on duty, so it's ok. I trust you ladies had a pleasant flight?" Fitzroy says.

"Everything was great until we got to Puerto Rico then all hell broke loose!" Lucille says.

"Lucille, watch your mouth," Momma says.

"Well, all hell did break loose! It was crazy. Fitzroy, in case you haven't noticed, Gloria and Dot aren't exactly spring chickens any more."

"I beg your pardon!" hollers Aunt Dot.

"Anyway, when we got off the plane from Atlanta in Puerto Rico, they told us our connecting flight would be leaving from gate H, as in "hell." Well, we started walking looking for gate H and after walking about 10 minutes, I finally found someone who spoke English and he told us that "gate H" was on the other end of the terminal. By now, Dot's gout in her knees had started acting up and my feet were killing me; not to mention that a certain person in this van, I won't call any names, was walking slow as molasses."

"I'll have you to know, I was checking out the sights," says Momma.

Aunt Lucille continues. "What sights? Wasn't nothing to see in the airport but a bunch of people trying to get to their gates. Anyway, I saw one of them golf cart-looking cars that handicapped people ride to get around the airport.

Well, I stopped it and asked the driver to take us to gate H. He had the nerve to tell us we needed a reservation to ride on his cart, and took off. The next cart that came our way, I stood in front of it and refused to move until they let us get on."

"I was never so embarrassed in all my life," Aunt Dot says.

"Uh-huh, but you were the first one to climb your big butt in the front seat! Not to mention, there was no way we would have made our flight if we didn't get that ride, especially with Ms. Molasses trailing a zip code behind us," Lucille continue to tease.

"Fitzroy, I wish I could tell you all our problems were over when we got that ride, but I can't. You see the driver dropped us off at Gate A and told us that's as far as he could go. So we had to walk from gate A to gate H, and let me tell you, they were not close together like they are in the alphabet. My bladder was about to bust, Dot's gas was killing us, and I think Gloria's feet had given out, because by now, she was only taking small baby steps. I looked back at her at one point and I didn't think she was moving at all."

"Now you know you need to stop with your foolishness, Lucille! My feet might have been hurting, but after I took my shoes off, I left your bunion, hammer-toe feet behind in the dust!"

Everyone burst out laughing!

"Momma you walked in the terminal without shoes on?" I asked.

"It was that or crawl, and don't be telling these people I had gas!" Aunt Dot says.

"I am so sorry you had to go through all of that. I'm going to change your return tickets and make sure you have a direct flight from St. Thomas to Atlanta when you leave here," Fitzroy says, feeling the burden of their troubles.

"That's so sweet of you!" Momma says.

"Thank you, Fitzroy, how kind," replies Aunt Dot.

"Does anyone want to hear the rest of my story?" Aunt Lucille says.

"No!" Replies Aunt Dot.

"Well, I know why you don't want me to tell it, because you don't want anybody to know how scared you were to get on that little bitty plane! Faith and Fitzroy, I almost had to take her to the bathroom and beat her down, when she said she wasn't getting on that little plane that brought us here from Puerto Rico! After I walked through hell to get to that gate, we were getting on that plane by any means necessary!" Aunt Lucille says, like an army sergeant.

"Well, thank God for prayer. I prayed with my sister and reminded her that God didn't give us a spirit of fear. I told her that God was the pilot of that plane and we had nothing to be afraid of! We prayed and asked God to comfort us and get us to Faith safely and that was that," Momma says.

I'm sorry you had to go through so much to get here. I didn't think to ask if your flight was a direct one," I say.

"Well, it will be a direct one going back home!" Fitzroy reiterates and then suggests we head back into the terminal to claim their luggage. The crowd had thinned out, just as Fitzroy said it would. We were able to claim Momma's and the aunties' luggage in no time, load it into the van, retrieve my jeep at the Beachcomber Hotel, and head up to Skyline Drive.

Chapter 12

When we arrived at the house we saw that Zipporah, our maid, had prepared a feast fit for kings and queens. Fitzroy helped everyone out of the van and then took the luggage into the house. Momma and Aunt Dot were in awe. They kept saying over and over again, "Faith, this is beautiful." Aunt Lucille paused outside, examining all the fragrant flowers, the fruit trees and the view of the harbor, where five cruise ships were lined up at Havensight Dock. The house was so high up on the mountain she said it was like being in the heavenly clouds.

Fitzroy didn't stay to have lunch with us. After making sure everyone was comfortable he said he needed to get back to work. He was still working on the Janna murder case. Fitzroy didn't believe Junnis killed Janna and committed suicide, despite the fact that this was the most frequently repeated version of the story. He was determined that justice would prevail and if Eric killed Janna and Junnis, he would pay for the crime, no matter who his family was. I walked him to the car and thanked him for everything. I also told him I was going to learn to let men take care of men's business. We both laughed. I asked him what he was doing for Thanksgiving, and invited him to join us in St. Croix at the Atkins' for dinner. He said he would be honored to spend the holiday with my family and me. He kissed me on the cheek and climbed into the van and drove off heading toward town. Aunt Lucille was standing near the mango tree witnessing our good-byes.

"Girl, if you don't hurry up and marry that man, I might have to stab you in the back and take him for myself!"

We both laughed. "He's been a blessing in my life, Auntie, I'm just being prayerful and waiting for God to work this one out," I say.

"Looks like He's already worked it out to me!" she says as we hug and enter the house where Zipporah is waiting to serve us West Indian cuisine.

Since the house has five bedrooms and six baths, Momma and the aunties were able to have their own bedroom and bath, with a to-die-for view. After we ate, everyone unpacked and continued to talk about how beautiful the island was and how they were looking forward to getting to know it better. Lisa and Billy got home at seven o'clock, just as *Wheel of Fortune* came on. This time it was her turn to be on the hot seat with Billy.

"Lord have mercy, Gloria, they got men down here; come look at what Lisa just walked in with!" Aunt Lucille hollers. Lisa introduces Billy. Billy greets everyone and then excuses himself, saying he has an early start tomorrow. Billy waves good-bye and Lisa walks him to the door.

I can tell Lisa is exhausted, but I also sense something else. I begin to wonder if there was any problem with her and Billy today. She seems a little sad to have just returned from such a wonderful outing. Momma asks Lisa how her day was and Lisa tells her and the aunties about Billy flying her over to Tortola for the day.

"He flew you on his plane to where?" Aunt Lucille wanted to know.

"To Tortola. It's an island that is very close to St. Thomas," Lisa says.

"It wasn't in one of those little bitty planes was it?" Aunt Dot wants to know.

"What do you think, chicken Dot? You know it wasn't no 747!"

"I'm just trying to visualize the thing Lucille!"

"Well, all of us are going to get to ride in the same plane on Thursday when we go over to Mr. Atkins' for Thanksgiving," I say.

"We weren't in the company's plane. When Billy picked me up, he said he had a surprise for me and when I got to the hanger, he showed me his new plane. Faith, it's beautiful! Oh, my God, I'm so happy for him. That's all he's been talking about is getting his own plane! He's going to have it blessed on Thanksgiving morning before we leave to go over to St. Croix," Lisa happily informs us.

"Now he isn't some kind of drug dealer, is he?" Aunt Lucille asked.

Momma, Aunt Dot, Lisa and I at the same time holler out "What?!"

Aunt Lucille looks as if she just said a bad word and replies. "Hey, where I come from the only people I know who can afford something like that are drug dealers."

"And just how many drug dealers do you personally know with planes?" Momma wants to know.

Aunt Dot replies for her. "None! The woman watches too many re-runs of *CSI*."

Lisa defends Billy. "Billy's a pilot for the company where Faith works. He loves the Lord and despises drugs. He flew for U.S. Airlines for 15 years in New York, and did charter flights on his days off, saving every dime he made. Years before U.S. Air went into bankruptcy, he cashed in his stock and invested it in Google, the internet company.

"He sounds like a smart fellow to me, and I especially like the part about him loving the Lord," Momma says.

"It's been one long day and I think I'm going to call it a night. I'm doing a double shift tomorrow at work, so I can have Thanksgiving off," Lisa informs everyone as she stops to kiss Momma and the aunties before heading to her bedroom.

They each take turns saying good night to Lisa. "I think I'm going to call it a night, too. I feel a little jet lagged," Aunt Dot tells us.

"I'm going to sit out on the veranda, sip me a glass of wine and look out at the nighttime view." I follow Aunt Lucille out on the veranda.

"Would you look at that town? All those lights! Faith, it looks like there's another island out there? Look, across the water. Once it got dark, it lit up?"

"Yes, you're looking at St. Croix."

"Remind me to pick up a pair of binoculars tomorrow when we go into town," she says.

"There should be a pair in the sideboard," I say.

I look in one of the drawers and hand Aunt Lucille the binoculars. She settles in her chair with her glass of wine and the binoculars. I sit in a chaise next to her and pour myself a glass of wine, too.

"Girl, life doesn't get any better than this!" I smile and second that emotion.

Momma stays in the living room watching the rest of *Wheel of Fortune* and then *Jeopardy* as Aunt Lucille and I enjoy sipping our wine and talking out on the veranda.

"So, you really like these islands?" Aunt Lucille wants to know.

"Yes, I do. It's so peaceful and no one really rushes to do anything. It's so different from the states. When I lived in Los Angeles, I had to rush all the time, use all the right buzz words, have lunch with the right people, power dress, and even drive the right car, just to stay on top of the game. Here, you just relax, be yourself and everything falls into place."

"What about crime on these islands?" Aunt Lucille asks.

I think of Janna and I'm sad. "There is some crime, but nothing like at home. St. Thomas has drugs and with drugs comes crime. St. John, where we are building our house, is the safest. Nothing much happens over there. The people really look out for each other, and they don't want drugs on their island. I even heard of a father turning his son in to the police when he suspected him of selling drugs. However, you do find a high rate of domestic violence, especially when there's a full moon."

"Didn't I hear one of your co-workers got killed right upstairs from where you were living?" Aunt Lucille says this as if it was something that happened a long time ago.

"Yes, Janna was her name. She was a good friend. You would have liked her. That case is still under investigation," I sadly state.

"I can tell talking about that is making you sad, so let's talk about something else...what are the men like around here?"

I laugh, amazed that my auntie at age fifty-something, would ask me a question like that.

"Oh, you laugh. I might be 53 years young, but the girl still has desires! As a matter of fact, I'm just reaching my prime time I'll have you to know. So, you think you and Lisa can hook a sister up with a nice brother while I'm down here? Now, I like my men a little bit younger than myself. Older men tend to have too many health problems."

"Aunt Lucille, you're scaring me. You're my aunt, for God's sakes!"

"And? Look here, Faith, let me break it down for you. The way I see it, you're going to be my age before you can say, 'Terrence Howard sure is fine,' three times." We both laugh and take another sip of our wine.

Momma comes out onto the veranda to see what all the cackling is about. "Lucille, I certainly hope you aren't trying to turn my Faith into a dirty old woman like you!" Momma says very lovingly.

"Look, Miss Polly Pure Bred, I'm having a conversation with my niece, who, may I remind you, is over twenty-one years old...I've been waiting for the day when I could share grown woman stuff with her. Stuff I know you and my brother-in-law, who I miss dearly, God rest his soul, would never talk about." Aunt Lucille gives Momma a 'three-snapper'.

"Faith, don't listen to a word she says, until you check with me first," Momma admonishes.

Momma pulls up a chair and joins us. I don't bother to offer her a glass of wine because Momma only drinks wine at communion time.

"It sure is pretty out here. God certainly has blessed you, Faith," Momma says.

"Oh, Lord! Gloria, now you know I love God, but Faith and I were sitting out here talking about men. I'm trying to get hooked up while I'm here. So if you're ready to preach a sermon, save it for Thanksgiving or next Sunday!"

As Momma and Aunt Lucille lovingly exchange words, I excuse myself and say good night.

"Girl, don't leave me hanging!" Aunt Lucille hollers as I stand up to leave.

"I got you covered, Auntie," I reply. I leave her and Momma outside enjoying the view.

As I head down the hallway leading to my bedroom, I pass Lisa's room and I can hear her sobbing. I gently knock on her door and the sobbing stops. I press my face to the door and quietly say, "Are you alright?" Lisa opens the door wearing a colorful island rap tied snugly around her thin frame. I can tell she just came out of the shower because her hair is still wet.

"What's up?" I ask?

"I'm in deep trouble," she sadly says.

I walk past her and enter the room, sitting on her bed, where she joins me. About a thousand things run through my head of what might be her problem, including HIV and pregnancy. I immediately ask if it's any of these so I can relax and find out what the real problem is. Lisa blasts out at me.

"No I'm not HIV positive!" She says.

"Praise God...what about pregnant?" Lisa doesn't answer.

"Oh, hell no!" comes flying out of my mouth before I can catch it. Lisa falls across the bed bawling.

"I'm sorry, Lisa, I didn't mean to come off so hard," I say as I pat her back to comfort her. She finally stops crying, sits up and looks me in the eye.

"What on earth am I going to do, Faith?"

I'm stunned by her question. "Do you have an option," I say? We both are quiet for what seems like eternity. Finally I break the silence. "I thought you were practicing celibacy?" I say.

"I was, I mean I am," she replies.

"Then is this some kind of immaculate conception?" I ask.

"Don't be funny!" Lisa says as she ribs me in the side with her elbow.

"Does Billy know he's going to be a daddy yet?"

Lisa looks at me like I'm crazy and says, "What?"

"You didn't tell him yet?" I respond.

Then it gets real quiet and Lisa drops the bomb and says, "It's Trevor's baby." The tears start flowing again. I even cry with her.

"Ok ok. We're going to get through this. I mean, we're strong, we got our right mind, well at least one of us does...most of all, we got God on our side!"

"Faith, I'm thinking about going up to the states and getting an abortion."

"Lord, help me!" I say to myself. I'm about to cuss this girl out! "So now you're going to be a murderer?" I continued aloud.

"Why the hell would you say something like that, Faith?" If looks could kill, I would be in jail right now. "Faith, I don't want to mess up my relationship with Billy...even though it may already be too late," Lisa says.

"And what does *that* mean?" I say.

"Well, you know how small these islands are, especially when you're doing something you shouldn't be doing. Well, last week, I met Trevor at Hibiscus Point for dinner."

"You what!" I scream. Now, I'm standing up, pacing around the room fuming mad.

"Calm down Faith, you're not making it easy to tell this...Anyway, we had dinner. Trevor had been begging me to meet him so he could show me some tiles for my kitchen he wants to give me as a house-warming gift. There were some tiles I saw on the floor in one of the houses he built on St. John, and he knew how much I liked them."

"So, you sold yourself out for some tiles?" I say in a bitter tone.

"No Faith, it wasn't like that. I didn't think there would be any harm in going to see him. We needed to bring our relationship to closure. The way we left each other was not that good, and after all he did for me when I first moved here, I at least owed him one last visit."

"Lisa, you are stuck on stupid! That man broke your arm, you slept with him every night, for "free," if I might go there, and we paid rent for staying in Chocolate Hole, not to mention that the man is living with another woman. Now what exactly do you owe him?" I say.

"Faith, I don't want to talk about it...obviously, it's something you don't understand. So I'll just take care of my problem by myself," Lisa says.

"I can't believe I'm hearing you. Lisa, you've gotten down here in these islands and gone crazy. How in the world can you say I don't understand! I was the one who was there for you when you went through your last mess up. And may I remind you that's why you came to St. John, to grow up and make better choices."

"Well, I have a few choices and I'm going to do what works best for me." Lisa sounds like a teenager.

"And what choices are those?" I ask.

"Well... the abortion," she says.

"Not!" I say. Lisa continues.

"Trevor told me he would leave that woman if I would come back to him."

"Lie!" I say. Lisa continues.

"I could go away and put the baby up for adoption, come back and be with Billy," she says.

"Wishful thinking... but at least there is no murder involved," I reply. "And what reason for leaving the islands would you give Billy?"

"Well, that's what I was talking about when I said the island is small. You see, when I met Trevor at Hibiscus Point, after we ate at the restaurant, Trevor had reserved a hotel room for us to spend the night, and when we checked out the next morning, Billy's friend turned out to be the hotel manager who thanked us for coming and offered us a free stay on our next visit."

"You spent the night with Trevor! I don't remember you staying over on St. John?" I say.

"That's another thing...I lied and told you I was working a double...I'm so sorry, Faith."

I stare her down and roll my eyes!

"What? It was just a little lie, so I wouldn't have to hear your mouth."

"That's why your behind is in the trouble you're in. You only want my help after you've made dumb choices! Don't worry, because I'm going to send your butt a bill for all my counseling services. Then maybe you'll take my advice," I say.

"Whatever! Would you let me finish my story?"

I sit down on the bed again as Lisa continues.

"When I met Billy this morning at the plane, he told me a friend of his and his wife would be joining us on our trip to Tortola. Faith, I was rubbing and admiring Billy's new plane, and I looked up when I heard Billy holler out to someone heading towards us, and there was the man from the hotel with his wife. I felt like a real slut.

"No!" I sarcastically say.

"Faith this is serious, please don't joke," Lisa says, almost in tears again.

"I think you should call Billy, let him know you need to talk with him about something very important. Tell him before his friend does!"

"His friend is not going to tell," Lisa says.

"How can you be sure of that?" I ask.

"Well, let's just say I wasn't the only one some place where I shouldn't have been that night!" Lisa slyly says.

"And what does that mean?" I ask.

"Now, I know you're not going to believe this, but Trevor and I didn't have sex that night at Hibiscus Point."

"Girl, now I don't know what to believe when it comes to you. After all we've been through, I never thought you would lie to me," I say.

"Faith, get over it! Now where was I? Oh... I told Trevor I would only stay if he understood I wasn't going to have sex. He said he just wanted to talk."

"And you believed that?" I say.

"Well, sort of. You see, the last few times we were together, even when I wanted to do it, he couldn't get an erection...Faith, the man needs Viagra, but he's too ashamed to go to the doctor and ask for it."

I fall on the floor laughing.

"So you're trying to tell me y'all made this baby with a limp one? Girl you are so crazy!"

"No, but I think it may have been his last hurrah." We both fall out laughing!

"Lisa, get back to the part about Billy's friend!" I say.

"Oh, Trevor couldn't get it up just like I thought, so we lay in bed, with our clothes on, just hugging and talking. I told him about Billy and what a nice guy he was, and how he and I go to Bible study together and I didn't want to jeopardize that by seeing him."

"You couldn't tell him that on the phone? You had to go out to dinner and lay up in a five star hotel to tell your ex you're in love with someone else?" I ask.

"Faith, would you let me tell the story? Besides, everybody isn't like you."

"I'm glad everyone isn't like me! And just what does that mean?" I say.

"All strong and holy!"

"Don't go there, Lisa. You know I made stupid mistakes, too. I'm just not a glutton for punishment. And if I remember correctly we serve the same God, so what's with the holy thing? You just need to decide to "walk the talk.""

"Whatever! Anyway, as I was saying, Trevor and I were talking in the room and the people next door to us were "bumping and grinding" like nobody's business. Their bed shared a wall with ours. Honey, homeboy was laying it on her. The chick was moaning and hollering like somebody was killing her."

"Maybe someone was hurting her," I say.

"Yeah, right! Sister girl was saying, "please don't stop" in between all the hollering. Faith, this went on for two hours straight, and you know it was killing Trevor, especially since his big boy wasn't cooperating. Finally, Trevor decided he was going to go and knock on the door and tell them to keep it down."

"You must be kidding," I say.

"Girl, it was torture listening to them. When Trevor got up to knock on their door, I followed him. He told me to stay, but I had to see who this sex machine was. Faith, that man needed to be in the Sexual Hall of Fame! I'm talking two hours and counting non-stop until we knocked on his door! We knocked for a good five minutes before he opened the door. Hell, I wanted to ask him for his autograph. He apologized, and before he could close the door, I saw a white woman with a sheet wrapped around her, walk towards the bathroom. This man's wife who went to Tortola with us, is midnight dark and from Uganda."

"Lisa you guys could have gotten shot, knocking on someone's door while they're taking care of business," I say.

"The man should have been downstairs running the hotel instead of up in the guest room getting his 'swerve on.'" Lisa says.

"You're not kidding, these islands are small. You never know who you might run in to. I still think you need to tell Billy everything. He will respect you for it. Besides, other than your poor judgment of meeting Trevor at Hibiscus Point, the pregnancy happened before you and he started going out. Billy knew you weren't a virgin when he met you," I say.

"Wow, Faith, you sure do know how to make things sound so simple. I only wish they were. I sit here with a baby growing inside me by a man who's living with someone else, and the godly man I'm dating is not the father. How's that for a scene from a soap opera?"

"I think Billy will be a fantastic father to your baby. You just need to pray and ask God to help you through this one. Call Billy and tell him everything. He might even find some of it funny, just like I did."

We hug and kiss as I exit Lisa's room to check on Aunt Lucille and Momma before calling it a night.

Aunt Lucille had fallen asleep on the veranda. I covered her with a throw to keep her comfortable from the night air, in case she didn't wake up to go inside before morning. Momma had already gone to her bedroom, where I found her lying in bed reading her Bible. I came in the room and joined her in bed.

"I'm so happy to be here with you, Faith," she said.

I could see love in Momma's eyes as she spoke to me.

"I'm so glad you came," I reply.

"I'm not going to lie; it's been rough for me since your father went home to be with God. Some days, I don't even leave the house. I sit around and wait to hear from him," Momma says.

"Hear from who?" I say.

"Your father, silly! He visits me often. It's such a wonderful feeling. I considered selling the house, because it's so big, but I thought if I sell it and move, he wouldn't know where to find me."

"Oh, Lord, Momma's lost it," I think to myself.

"Momma are you feeling alright?" I ask.

"Why would you ask me something like that, Faith?" she says.

"Well, it's kind of strange hearing you say Daddy visits you when we both know he's...he's..."

"Dead," Momma says.

"Well, yeah," I reply.

"His body might be dead, but his spirit is alive...and that's who visits me - your daddy's spirit."

"Well, does he say anything?" I ask.

"Sometimes I just feel his presence and a few times I've heard him laugh when I've done something stupid."

"Stupid like what?" I ask.

"Like the time I was ironing my church gloves... I went to the kitchen sink to put some water in the iron...when I finished ironing, I put the iron in the refrigerator. We both got a good laugh out of that! I thought the iron was a pitcher of water! Yes, my darling, your dad is with me all the time when I'm in our house," she says.

"Dad is with you everywhere, not only in the house. He lives in your heart and wherever you go, he will go with you," I say.

Momma smiles and nods her head.

"I only pray that one day I will be blessed with a marriage like you and Daddy," I say.

"It looks like you're on the right track. I really like Fitzroy, and I can see he loves you," Momma says smiling.

"Yeah, I'm just watching and praying," I say.

"Watching and praying for what... a big boulder to drop on your head and knock some sense into it? Now, you listen to me, sugar, you wasted all that time with that good-for-nothing boy in Los Angeles, and now God has sent a gentleman your way...don't mess around and miss your blessing. Besides, I want some grandchildren soon. I'm tired of Dot bragging and showing off Debbie's kid's pictures. You know she's having twin boys? And her husband is being installed as our new pastor next month. I know your daddy is proud."

I smile and kiss Momma goodnight. "See you in the morning, and welcome to paradise," I say.

"Good night, baby," Momma says.

Chapter 13

I wake up to the smell of bacon and coffee coming from the kitchen. I can hear Aunt Dot and our housekeeper, Zipporah, laughing. I'm still wearing my nightgown as my nose leads my hungry body to the kitchen. I find Momma sitting at the island counter reading the local newspaper and drinking a cup of coffee. Aunt Lucille enters the kitchen from outside, wearing her sneakers, long jogging pants, a t-shirt that reads "Experienced," a visor that matches her outfit to shade her from the sun, and a water bottle.

"Ooo, it's already hot out there and it's only eight o'clock," she says as she wipes the perspiration off her neck with a paper towel.

"You need to sit your old behind down... out there jogging like some teenager on this mountain. You're lucky a car didn't run you over. Don't you know there are no sidewalks out there?" Aunt Dot jokingly says to Aunt Lucille, who retorts,

"You should join me. It might help your gout and high blood pressure. Who knows, you might drop some of that extra baggage you're carrying around your waist, before we get back to Atlanta!"

"Now I'm not up for hearing the two of you this early in the morning. Can't we all just get along?" Momma breaks the fussing up.

"Momma, you sound like Rodney King," I say as I hug Zipporah and pour my coffee.

"I met a real nice man, who was out walking too. And you'd never believe it, but he lives next door. His name is Wally. You think this house is big, Lord, you should see the inside of his house. It could swallow this one up!" Lucille says.

"Lucille, you went inside of the man's house?" Momma says.

"You know she did Gloria, the woman has the sense of a goat," Aunt Dot says, while pointing a rolling pin at Lucille.

"For God's sakes, he's Faith and Lisa's neighbor!" Aunt Lucille comes back at them.

Zipporah laughs. "Ah you is so funny. Mr. Wally a good man. He's from Nevis...he lose he wife last yer to cancer. He's a big time nightclub owner on back street in town," Zipporah continues teaching Aunt Dot how to make johnnycakes.

"From Nevis...? My friend Fitzroy is from Nevis," I say to Zipporah.

"Me know dat. Fitzroy mudda an' fadda from Brown Hill like Mr. Wally. Me family from Mount Lilly. Fitzroy and he twin brudda use to play cricket wit me bruddas."

Aunt Dot serves us a fried johnnycake with cheese. "Looks like half of St. Thomas and St. John are from Nevis." "De other half is from Dominica!" Zipporah says and laughs. "Here, try dis with you coffee," she continues, "Ah you need to be drinking bush tea wit dey johnnycakes. Mr. Atkins had me to plant lemon grass, mint, thyme and bay leaf tea 'long the side of de house, so him and Mrs. Atkins could have fresh bush tea in the mornin'," Zipporah says as she pours each of us a cup of lemon grass tea.

Momma pushes her coffee cup aside and tastes the bush tea. "It's good!" Momma says and Aunt Dot agrees.

"I'll have a cup of your tea, but I'm going to pass on the fried dough. It's too early in the morning for fried food. I'll have a bowl of bran cereal with a banana and some low fat milk, if you don't mind," Aunt Lucille says.

Zipporah is a little disappointed that Aunt Lucille doesn't want to try her johnnycakes, but with a smile, she pours her a bowl of cereal and adds a banana along with low fat milk.

"So Zipporah, what else can you tell me about Mr. Wally?" says Aunt Lucille.

"There she goes!" says Aunt Dot.

"There she goes what?" Aunt Lucille defends herself.

"You know perfectly well what I'm talking about. You just have to have a man paying you attention! Can't we just enjoy our vacation without you acting like..."

Now Aunt Lucille has her hands on her hips. "Like what, Dot? A single woman who still has desires and needs? I'm 53 years old, look better than most 35 year olds and can't help it if men are attracted to me. Don't hate me because you married your high school sweetheart, gave him babies, and now both of you at 65 don't find things so sweet anymore!" Lucille says.

"How dare you!" Aunt Dot says with hurt feelings while taking off her apron. "I'm going to go and get dressed. What time did you say we'd go shopping, Faith?" she continues.

Everyone is quiet and sad. "We'll leave around ten o'clock."

Aunt Dot exits down the hall to her room.

"What's wrong with her?" Aunt Lucille says, as if Aunt Dot was overreacting. Momma has a stern look on her face.

"Sometimes you don't know when to stop," Momma admonishes.

"What? We always act like this, since we were kids," Aunt Lucille says.

"George served Dot with divorce papers and moved out the house last week," Momma says.

"What! Why didn't she tell me?" Aunt Lucille says.

"Maybe she was afraid you wouldn't have any compassion and say something smart," Momma sarcastically says.

"I'm that bad, huh?" Aunt Lucille asks.

"And then some," Momma adds.

"I am so sorry. Dot must be going through hell. Am I the only one who didn't know?"

"No, she hasn't told the kids yet. She's hoping this trip will help her relax, so she can sort things out, before she tries to explain it to anyone," Momma says.

Aunt Lucille is pacing the floor. "There must be a law against people who been together over 50 years getting a divorce. I mean who else will want you except each other after being together that long?"

Zipporah excuses herself from the kitchen to run a load of laundry.

"Momma, was Uncle George having an affair?" I ask.

"Yes dear, with Sadie Green. You remember her; she used to be the church secretary until I made your father get rid of her."

Aunt Lucille is outraged. "Sadie Green! She's been after George for what...20 years!" Aunt Lucille says.

"Oh, she's the reason Aunt Dot threw hot grits on Uncle George," I say.

"He told Dot he's loved Sadie for a long time and now that all their kids were grown and had started their own families, he wanted to be happy before he died," Momma tells us.

Aunt Lucille looks like she is about to cry. "Dot should have thrown some grits on the other side of his face! I never trusted that man. I don't care if he is a deacon in the church. I can't believe it; he's going to leave my sister for that *stank*..."

"Alright, Lucille!" Momma interjects before Lucille says anything else.

"I thought she got married. Doesn't she have twins in high school?" I ask.

"No Faith, those were bastard kids!" Aunt Lucille is still hot.

"Woman, you better repent right now! God don't make bastards! Dogs have bastards!" Momma is shocked at Lucille's response.

"I'm sorry, it's just that I'm so mad, I could kill that fat belly, spineless ..."

"That's enough, Lucille!" Momma pauses for a moment, then continues. "Well, the two of you might as well know the whole story, so you can get all your anger out and we can help Dot during these trying times."

"There's more?" I say.

"Yes, Sadie's twins are George's kids."

"What?!"

"Oh, *hell* no!" Aunt Lucille and I holler at the same time.

Aunt Dot enters the kitchen. "So Gloria, I guess you told them everything," she says.

Aunt Lucille and I hug Aunt Dot and we all cry together. "I feel like hurting that fool! How dare he take all your good years and then leave you for that nasty woman!" Aunt Lucille cries.

"They deserve each other Lucille. It's not all George's fault...I should have left him thirty years ago, but I thought God wanted me to stay. George was never faithful to me and I knew it, but I didn't want to raise the kids without a father, I wanted to be at home when they got off the school bus, and there was no way I could afford the lifestyle me and the kids had become accustomed to with just a high school education."

"So what are you going to do now?" I ask.

"I'm going to take some time to get over the shock and then I'm going to *live.* Don't worry, the good Lord is going to take care of me. Besides, I'm entitled to half George's pension, the house is paid for, and he won't get a dime out of that, my lawyer says, since he committed adultery. I'm going to sell the house and buy something just big enough to have room for the grandchildren when they come to visit. It's time to purge, Faith. Sadie just may have done me a favor, taking George off my hands. It's sad to say, and I can finally admit it but, some days, I couldn't stand to look at him. The way he ate got on my nerves. The man chewed with his mouth open and smacked. Not to mention all those years I endured his stinking farts. I know they had to be toxic. It's a wonder I don't have cancer. Ten years ago I moved into the guest room, and dared him to cross the threshold. George and Sadie are two sorry individuals...may God bless them...or not!"

We all laugh.

Momma gasps, while continuing to read the newspaper. "Faith, look here, isn't that Fitzroy arresting someone?"

I rush over to take a look. The caption reads "Local Arrested for Murder of Wife." The picture shows Fitzroy leading handcuffed Eric into the Justice Building. I take the paper from Momma and read the article. "Eric's been arrested for Janna and Junnis's murder," I say.

"Janna...that was your girlfriend from work, wasn't she honey?" Aunt Dot asks.

"Yes, she was," I sadly say.

I want to call Fitzroy, but decide to wait until I hear from him.

"I'm sorry," Momma says.

"I pray the Lord will work this out soon for the sake of everyone concerned. And I especially pray for those children. You'll get to meet the children tomorrow, when we go over to St. Croix for Thanksgiving dinner. The Atkins family has practically adopted those girls," I say.

Zipporah enters the kitchen and wants to know if she should prepare lunch for us or just concentrate on dinner. "Don't bother with either. We're going to hang out all day and go to North Star Hotel for dinner and Lisa won't be home until late because she's working a double shift," I tell her.

Zipporah smiles and continues with her housework. My mind reflects back on the conversation I had with Lisa last night. "Lord, please give that girl wisdom to do what is right," I say a quick prayer.

"To do what's right?" I hear Momma say.

I didn't realize I was praying out loud. "Oh, I was just saying a prayer for a friend," I say.

Momma kisses me and then goes down the hall to get dressed.

The telephone rings and Zipporah answers it. "Miss Lucille, de phone fa you."

Momma stops in her tracks, Aunt Dot freezes with her hands on her hips, I sit down at the counter and Zipporah pretends to be cleaning the kitchen sink for the second time.

"Good morning, this is Lucille...Oh, hi Wally...no, it's ok, you didn't catch me at a bad time." Lucille turns around and finds everyone, including Zipporah, is eavesdropping on her conversation with Wally. "Excuse me a second, Wally." Aunt Lucille covers the mouthpiece of the phone. "I know y'all nosey cows got something better to do than to listen to my conversation!" Aunt Lucille takes the cordless phone out to the veranda to continue her chat with Wally.

"I can't believe her!" Aunt Dot says in disgust.

"Yes you can. Lucille is just being herself. You know that woman is a magnet for men. She's been that way since she started wearing a training bra," Momma jokingly says.

I was beginning to wonder why Aunt Lucille thought she needed me to introduce her to anyone. "Auntie got skills!"

"Well, I'm going to get dressed. Knock on my door if there are any new developments in the 'Hot Life of Lucille Summers'," Momma says as she heads down the hallway to her room. Following behind her, I excuse myself to get dressed, leaving Aunt Dot and Zipporah in the kitchen.

"Look like Mr. Wally interested in Miss Lucille. Me ain't never know him to call 'ere before. Day say he been lock up in dat house since he wife die. He Rastafarian son been runnin' de business for he. Some say he robbin' he fadda blind. I tink Mr. Wally got so much money him don't care. Maybe Miss Lucille might be de one to bring him out of he loneliness," Zipporah says to Aunt Dot as she puts our breakfast dishes in the dishwasher.

"Trust me, if anybody can do that, it's Lucille. She can charm King Tut back to life and get him to he bring all his treasures out of the tomb!" Aunt Dot says.

"Miss Lucille, she a gold digger?" Zipporah asks as she slams the door to the dishwasher.

"No, I'm probably painting a terrible picture of my baby sister. Now, don't get me wrong, I've never known her to fall in love with a poor man, but one thing she isn't is a gold digger. Lucille probably got just as much money as Mr. Wally. The girl owns more real estate in Atlanta than any black or white person I know."

"Den why she ain't got no husband?" Zipporah asks with a puzzled look on her face.

"To put it simple, Lucille is a hard woman to please. She's had her share of suitors, doctors, lawyers, bankers, stock brokers, even pastors... but none could tame her," Aunt Dot shakes her head in amazement. "One came close though...his name was Dr. Bedford Jennings. He came from old southern money and every woman in Atlanta would have given anything they had to be with that man. He was high yellow, had nice wavy hair, dressed to the hilt, drove a fancy car, and had a lucrative practice in Dunwoody, not to mention the mansion he lived in...but Dr. Jennings only had eyes for Lucille. That woman couldn't do any wrong. They were scheduled to marry two years ago on the 4th of July on a yacht. Everybody who was anybody, and everybody who was nobody was invited to their wedding," Aunt Dot is sad. She stops telling the story.

"Me son, wha' happen?" Zipporah is captivated with the story. Aunt Dot continues.

"The night before the wedding, Dr. Jennings' fraternity brothers gave him a big party. All kinds of famous people were there like the mayor, football players, exotic dancers...you get the picture. Anyway, one of the women who everyone thought was with the dancers, pushed her way up to Doc and fired four shots into his head before anyone could restrain her."

"Oh me God! Why she do someting crazy like dat?"

"The woman said the Lord told her in a dream Dr. Jennings was supposed to marry her, not Lucille. The sad part is Dr. Jennings didn't even know the woman. She read in the society section of the newspaper about his engagement to Lucille and started sending him crazy letters. Doc reported it to the police; they checked it out, and concluded the woman was harmless. Actually, Doc was more concerned about the woman hurting Lucille and he wasn't taking any chances, so he hired a bodyguard to protect her until after the wedding. No one thought the woman would hurt *him*. Lucille was devastated and had to be medicated for months. We're just now starting to see the old flirtatious Lucille again. Zipporah, the sad part is, if the police had done a more extensive background check on the woman, they would have found out that she's been in and out of mental hospitals for the past fifteen years. Apparently, she claimed that the Lord told her she was going to marry Michael Jackson in 1999, and she got arrested for trying to break into Never Land."

"Wow, what a story...well, me dear, I pray Miss Lucille finds happiness."

Lucille enters the kitchen from the veranda, smiling. "Change in plans for me, big sister...I'm going on a boat ride over to St. John with Wally. He wants to show me Trunk Bay and take me snorkeling," Aunt Lucille says.

Momma walks into the kitchen and I follow just as Aunt Dot and Lucille start another round of disagreements.

"Dot, I'm fifty-three years old and I don't need your permission to go to the beach with Faith and Lisa's neighbor. Hell, I'd rather hang out with Wally than go shopping with a bunch of women anyway."

"I can dig it," I hear myself say.

"Faith!" Aunt Dot cuts into me. "Lucille doesn't know this man and neither do you," Aunt Dot says, like we all have lost our minds except her.

"He's a good mon," Zipporah injects.

"Dot, let the woman go...all of us came down here to unwind from one thing or another. Give her your blessings and let's go shopping!" Momma says.

No one else said a thing after Momma spoke; well, except Aunt Dot who gave Aunt Lucille a final warning as we walked out the door to get into the jeep. "Don't make us have to come and identify your body in some morgue!"

Aunt Lucille smiles as she walks down the hall to freshen up and pack her beach gear for her first date with an island man.

Chapter 14

The public parking lot was full. After circling around for more than ten minutes, I decided to park in the vendors' parking lot next to Emancipation Park. It was closer to the stores on Main Street anyway. The temperature was nearly ninety degrees. There were five cruise ships in town and what looked like thousands of people gathered throughout the makeshift vendors' village purchasing T-shirts, sun hats, beach wraps, knock-off Louis Vuitton bags and every kind of trinket with 'St. Thomas' written on it. Oprah, the donkey, who wore giant-size sunglasses, a straw hat and lipstick was even out today, waiting for tourists to pay a fee to sit on her back and take a picture. Momma got a big laugh out of meeting Oprah and her over six-foot tall owner who was dressed in a long African robe, carried a tall stick, and sported buzzard-nest style dreadlocks that hung well below his backside. He almost looked like he'd been wandering around the desert and was on his way to the Promised Land with Oprah in tow. Momma wasn't sure if she wanted to take a picture with Oprah or the dreadlocks man because both of them were an equally unusual sight to her.

Aunt Dot paid to stand between the man and the donkey as I took her picture. Afterwards, she and I talked Momma into stepping on a stool that was provided by Oprah's owner, and climbing on the donkey's back so we could take a picture. Momma looked so funny straddling the donkey. I wanted to ask her if this was one of those times she could hear Daddy laughing. Aunt Dot made sure she got a picture with her camera of Momma, so she could get her daughter Debbie to print it in the church bulletin when they got back home to Atlanta. Momma threatened to wring her neck if she showed it to anybody. After we paid the man, who we found out is named "One Love," we decided to continue towards Main Street after Aunt Dot and Momma bought a sun hat, and I picked up a few T-shirts for my cousin Debbie's girls. Momma wanted to look for a linen tablecloth to give to Mrs. Atkins as a gift tomorrow when we visit them for Thanksgiving dinner. Main Street was just the place for linen tablecloths. It was so hard to decide which one to buy for her. Momma decided to purchase several table cloths. She would make up her mind later which one to give to Mrs. Atkins, and the rest she would take back to Atlanta for the sisters who served with her on the Altar Guild.

The sidewalks on Main Street are so narrow we were constantly bumping into tourists loaded down with cartons of duty-free liquor. When there was simply no more room on the sidewalk, we opted to walk in the street and compete with the tour buses picking up and dropping off cruise ship passengers. Momma and Aunt Dot loved all the hubbub and excitement of walking down Main Street. Aunt Dot said she felt like she was in a foreign country with all the Danish-style buildings made from stone, and the double-arch doors that were anchored to the wall with metal braces. We stop at Cardow Jewelers and Momma falls in love with their gold bracelets. She tells me to pick one.

"I want to buy you a gift for being such a sweet daughter," she says.

"Momma, you don't have to buy me anything," I say.

"Don't look a gift horse in the mouth. Besides, it's an early birthday gift."

I was going to remind her that my birthday isn't until July 16th, but I decided November 27th is close enough, since it seems she was determined to shower me with love by buying this $2,000 bracelet. It's was a gorgeous gold hook bracelet with rubies and diamonds. The sales clerk hooked it on my arm. Momma, Aunt Dot and I at the same time said, "Ooo!" I couldn't stop looking at my arm. Momma was beaming all over. I kissed her and told her it was the best gift I had ever received other than having her and Daddy as my parents. A tear of joy rolled down her face.

"Y'all need to save all this mushy stuff for Dr. Phil," Aunt Dot says, as she smiles and acknowledges that the bracelet is beautiful.

My cell phone rings and it's Lisa. I excuse myself to go outside and talk, leaving Momma and Aunt Dot shopping. Lisa tells me she's been praying non-stop since we talked last night and she's going to keep the baby. "Praise God," I say. She called Billy and told him she needed to talk to him about something important tonight. He tried to get her to tell him what it was about on the phone, but she told him it was something she needed to talk about face to face. Lisa said he sounded real nervous. She told him to come by the house around seven o'clock when she got off. I told her that I was taking Momma and the aunties out to dinner at North Star Hotel, so that would work out well. She would have her privacy and we probably wouldn't get back home until eleven o'clock. Lisa was scared, but was doing what God was leading her to do. In the middle of all the busyness of Main Street, I snuggled up against the building with my cell phone and prayed with my friend before hanging up. Lisa said if things didn't go well tonight with her and Billy, she would not join us tomorrow in St. Croix for Thanksgiving dinner. "Don't worry," I tell her, "God's got this."

As I turn to go back into Cardow to join Momma and Aunt Dot, my cell rings again. This time it's Fitzroy. "I miss you, Faith."

I almost melt at the sound of his voice. "Ditto." I say.

"So, what are we going to do about it"? Fitzroy replies with his sexy British voice.

I tell him that I'm on Main Street shopping with Momma and Aunt Dot and how Aunt Lucille met our neighbor and decided to go to Trunk Bay with him. Fitzroy laughs.

"Your Aunt Lucille has good taste. Wally's a good man. He's from my village in Nevis. What are you doing for dinner tonight?"

I tell him our plans.

"Is it ok to join you?"

"Of course," I say, smiling from ear to ear.

"Faith, would it be alright if I spent the night at your house tonight? It doesn't make sense to go back to St. John after dinner and then turn around and come right back tomorrow to fly over to the Atkins' for Thanksgiving, and I'm sure I'd miss the last boat to St. John if I try to go home tonight after dinner."

I pause for a moment.

"Faith, are you there? If you feel uncomfortable with it, I'll just get a hotel room."

"No! No! It will be fine. You can take my room and I'll sleep with Momma. I look forward to seeing you at seven." He hangs up and I walk back into the store, smiling like I just hit the lottery.

Aunt Dot is about to purchase five pair of West Indian gold bangles for her granddaughters Faith, Faren, Farrah, Freda and Fuisha. "These will be a gift for the girls from their wayward grandfather." Aunt Dot pulls out an American Express card. "Stupid fool served me with divorce papers but forgot to take my name off his credit cards."

"Aunt Dot!" I say.

"Aunt Dot what? George is going to pay for every bit of this trip to St. Thomas. We'll call it 'divorce therapy'."

Momma and I both laugh.

"Now, where do they sell those linen table cloths? Oh, I also want to get some crystal for Debbie and maybe a Rolex watch for her husband Byron, our new pastor."

Aunt Dot has a gleam in her eye that scares Momma and me. "Alright, Dot, don't go crazy. The man is already giving you the house and half his pension," Momma reprimands her sister.

"He's not giving me anything I didn't work for!" Aunt Dot cuts Momma off.

"Well, you've got a point there, but let's not spend all his money in one store," Momma says.

"Don't worry, I brought all the plastic with me. We can spread the wealth around town." Aunt Dot opens her billfold and at least ten credit cards unfold. "Oh, and by the way, they all have a zero balance...George and I never went anywhere to use them."

"Lord, bless my sister!" Momma says.

"He already has!" Aunt Dot responds to Momma's prayer as she leads us out of the store.

"Where are we going next, Faith?" she says.

"To Mr. Table Cloth...it's just a few doors down on your left," I respond.

The Greenhouse is packed. The waitress finds a seat for us near the bar but Momma tells her, "We prefer not to be near cigarette smoking...so we'll wait for a table on the front with a view to become available."

"Girl, as bad as my feet hurt... and my gout is acting up... I might smoke a cigarette myself!" Aunt Dot hollers, just as a group near the window gets up to leave.

"God is good," Momma says.

And I reply, "All the time."

"Y'all can stand here giving praises, but I'm going to go sit down while they clean off the table, and I'll give my praises from my seat!" Aunt Dot leaves Momma and me standing next to the hostess podium, waiting to be seated formally.

"What's up with this gout thing?" I ask Momma.

"She's been having trouble with her big toe and her knees for the past year now...the doctor told her she has to stop eating rich foods with heavy sauces and to lose some of that weight...but you know how your aunt is; she loves her gravies."

The waitress escorts us over to Aunt Dot who has removed her sneakers and is massaging her feet.

"Dot, you know that's ghetto!"

"What's ghetto? My feet hurt and to hell with anybody that has a problem with it."

"I just better not smell your feet or you're going to have go and massage them in the ladies room! The last thing I need is to smell stinky feet while I'm trying to eat my lunch."

"Gloria, my feet don't stink!"

Our waiter walks up, looks at Aunt Dot's feet, and asks if we need a few more minutes, referring to Momma and Aunt Dot's conversation.

"No dear," Momma says. We all want virgin Pina Coloda's.

"If you need the ladies room it's straight back on your right and up a few stairs," the waiter informs Dot.

Then he walks away to get our drinks. Momma and I laugh.

"Smart behind, wait until he sees the penny I'm leaving for his tip!"

The view from where we are seated is spectacular. It's just a stone's throw from the water. You can see all the cruise ships lined up along the dock at Havensight Mall. One of the main taxi drop-off and pick-up points is located in front of the Green House. We enjoy our lunch and watch all the tourists being dropped off and then going in different directions.

"These taxi drivers must be rich! I just counted 16 people getting out of that last van," Aunt Dot gives her assessment.

"In season, I understand they make out pretty well. I only hope they have enough sense to save some for those slow months," I add my two cents.

"When are the slow months?" Momma wants to know.

"Between April and October, but once it starts to get cold on the mainland, that's when people start to flock down here. Aunt Dot are you up for anymore shopping or would you like to head home?" I say.

"My mind is willing but my body is saying we're not going another further!"

I tell her and Momma that I will walk back to the vendors' area, just a few blocks up, get the car and pull into the Green House parking lot. They both agree that's a good idea, and will be looking out for me. I leave them to finish their lunch. I pay the bill before I leave, at the protest of both Momma and Aunt Dot. I wanted to make sure there wasn't any drama with Aunt Dot giving the waiter a penny tip. This island is too small and when they leave to go back to Atlanta, I'll still be here and will have to look that man in the face, and there's no telling who he's related to.

God was gracious once again; I didn't have a ticket on my car. The temperature inside the jeep must have reached one hundred degrees. I stood outside the car and let the air conditioner run for a while. Oprah and One Love had a line of people waiting to pose with the famous donkey and dreadlock Rasta. The vendors' village was jam-packed with people and the vendors were smiling with delight as their money belts bulged with cash.

Aunt Dot and Momma were standing at the bottom of the Green House Restaurant stairs waiting when I pulled into the parking area. Aunt Dot suggested going home, unloading the bags and taking a nap before we go to dinner. My cell phone rings and its Linda Peters, my intern, calling from the office.

"Whaz's up?" I say, trying to sound cool to my young assistant.

"Miss Faith, Mista Lever is 'bout to get on me last nerve! Him tell me to have you call him." I ask her what's going on that she can't handle? "De satellite feed from de states is acting up, an' he want to make sure it's fix right now! Him afraid we won't be able to broadcast de Tank's givin' day parade from New York ta morrow. I tell him de engineer workin' on de ting fast as he can! Me ain't know what he tink you gon do dat me ain't done already!"

I ask her to transfer me to Frank Summers, our Chief Engineer, and tell her how proud I am of her, and not to let Bob Lever push her button. Linda tells me she's going into the ladies room for fifteen minutes to calm down before she says something to Bob he won't like to hear, and to gather some more strength to deal with his nonsense. I tell her I think that's a safe place to go without running into him. We both laugh.

Frank picks up on the first ring. "Hi, Faith. I thought you might be calling. Bob needs to take a chill pill or go and find something else to do with himself. We're back online now and I've run a test with our New York affiliate and everything's ready to go for tomorrow's Thanksgiving parade."

"So, what was the big deal?" I ask.

"I think Bob is having trouble with Linda doing your job while you're on holiday. The girl is too smart for his uppity behind...Faith, go and enjoy your time off. Everything is fine."

"Thanks, Frank," I say, and ask him if he would find Bob and let him know. After I hang up, I call Linda on her cell phone to let her know all is clear.

"Is everything OK at work?" Momma asks.

"Just fine," I assure her and myself. "My assistant Linda is having a little drama with our new boss."

"If they need you to come in Faith, you can just drop us at home. Don't let our visit cause problems at your job."

"Momma, everything is fine...besides, I'm glad Linda had a chance to deal with Bob and his foolishness. Situations like these will help her manage conflicts when she's elected Governor of the Virgin Islands," I say.

"Your intern is running for Governor?" Aunt Dot asks in amazement.

"She's only a senior in high school right now, but has her eyes fixed on that office, and I can't see any reason why she won't get it. Linda Peters is as sharp as they come...and the best thing that's ever happened to these Virgin Islands."

I smile as I think about her standing up to Bob Lever.

"Well, I look forward to meeting this young lady before we go back to Atlanta," Momma says with admiration.

"Oh, I forgot to tell you we all are invited to her family's pig roast on Saturday, on Water Island. It's that little island just over there." I point to Water Island.

"I certainly hope we don't have to swim to get over there!" Aunt Dot says with excitement and trepidation.

"No, we won't have to swim...there's a little boat that shuttles residents of that island and visitors back and forth." Aunt Dot is relieved.

"We certainly do have a busy social calendar planned for this weekend," Momma says with excitement.

"I just hope Lucille can pull herself away from that new man she met long enough to join us...You all know how blinded she gets when she meets a man," Aunt Dot says bitterly.

"Oh, let her enjoy herself, Dot! It's been two years since I've seen her acting like her old self. It's been hard on her losing her fiancé," Momma defends her baby sister.

"All that money and the big house he left her should have helped soften the blow! How many people do you know who prepare a will leaving everything to their wife before they actually have the ceremony?" Aunt Dot sarcastically says.

"Dot! You know all those worldly things weren't important to Lucille. She was in love and would have given anything to spend the rest of her life with Bedford Jennings. I'm shocked to hear you talk like that...you sound like the rest of those fools who can't believe Bedford left everything he owned to Lucille. The man didn't have a single living soul, so it made sense." Momma, upset, stares out of the window with her arms crossed.

You could have cut the tension in the air with a knife.

"I don't know why you're getting your panties in a bunch, Gloria, I'm the one whose shoulder she cried on for the past two years, not you. You were so busy being the First Lady at Solid Rock Baptist Church you hardly had time for your biological family. All your energy went to your church family and what was left over went to your husband. It's only now that Rev is gone home to be with the Lord and Debbie is now the First Lady of the church, that you have time for Lucille and me," Aunt Dot says.

If looks could kill, Aunt Dot would be dead. Momma turned her head to the back seat and gave Aunt Dot a look that said, "If you say one more word, you will be sorry!" I thought I would try to change the subject before the rest of the day turned out to be a horrible one.

"Fitzroy's going to join us for dinner tonight," I said as if we all were in for a great treat.

"That's wonderful honey...will Lisa be joining us too?" Momma says.

"No, her friend Billy is stopping by tonight," I say, trying not to give up too much detail.

"Well why don't the both of them join us?" Momma is starting to get suspicious now. I recognize that tone.

"We haven't seen much of Lisa since we got here. You know I feel like she's my daughter, too," Momma continues.

"I know Momma, it's just that she needs to talk with Billy about a few things," I say.

"She ain't pregnant is she?" Momma blurts out.

"Now Momma, you are going to have to talk to Lisa about that."

"Why, when I've got you right here?"

I can't believe she zeroed in on what's happening. Then Aunt Dot chimes in. "You might as well go ahead and tell it...you know how your Momma is...she isn't going to stop until you give up all the details of the situation...besides, I want to know too."

"Lord help me, I'm being interrogated by two women who won't take any prisoners!"

"Well?" Momma says in her parental voice.

"Yes, she's pregnant." I prayed they wouldn't ask me any more questions.

"Is it by that fine little half-breed man?" Aunt Dot asks.

"His name is Billy, Aunt Dot."

"Girl, don't get cute with me. I don't care if his name is 'silly'; just answer the question."

The jeep climbs up Mafolie Hill as fast as legally possible. I turn right onto Skyline Drive and pull into our driveway and turn the jeep off, ready to bail out.

"So, you want to turn the air conditioning back on and finish this conversation in the car, or you want to go inside and get something cold to drink and finish it on the veranda?" Momma says. I agree to the latter.

"Good, 'cause I got to use the bathroom...now y'all wait until I finish before you resume this conversation...I don't want to miss a thing!" Aunt Dot races into the house with her bags.

"Momma, don't you think it would be better if we had this conversation with Lisa?" I say.

"Oh, that's going to be part two. I first need you to give me a briefing so I'll now how to pray about this situation before I talk to 'Miss can't keep her panties up Lisa,'" she says and walks into the house leaving me standing next to the jeep in deep thought.

Why do I feel like I'm back in high school again, trying to cover up for Lisa's bad choices? I stand here in the driveway reflecting on the time Lisa decided to lie to her parents, telling them she was spending the night at my house. As divine intervention would have it, later that night, her daddy stopped by to drop off some legal papers he'd been working on for the church to my dad. Everyone found out that Lisa wasn't where she was supposed to be and had lied. Once again, I faced intense interrogation until I spilled the beans and told them she was with Stephen, her college boy friend, in his dorm room. Lisa's dad and my dad went over there with the police and they made me come to make sure they had the right room. I told them I'd never been there before, so there was no need in me going. My dad looked at me and said, "Faith, get in the car!" To make matters worse, when we got there Lisa's dad threatened to have the boy arrested because he was eighteen years old and Lisa was just seventeen! Lisa fainted when she opened the door and saw it was her daddy, the cops and me, the 'stool pigeon'. When she fell, she bumped her head on Stephen's iron bed rail, and conveniently didn't come to until morning. Of course, everyone was concerned about the knot on her head and her being unconscious. So, I got scolded like I was the one who got caught in a boy's dorm room, wearing sexy nightclothes. Before I went into the house to face Momma and Aunt Dot, I reminded myself that I'm a grown woman now and I will not be treated like a high school girl asked to snitch on her best friend.

Momma had grabbed a bottle of water from the refrigerator and was waiting on the veranda. Aunt Dot was walking briskly down the hall from the bathroom heading towards the veranda.

"Come on, Faith, this is better than *All My Children.*" I dropped my purse on the kitchen counter and walked out onto the veranda determined to take a stand and not to give up any more information about Lisa's situation. As soon as Momma gave me that authoritative look, my cool points went out the window, and I spilled *all* the beans!

Chapter 15

After our naps we showered and got dressed to go out for dinner. Aunt Lucille is racing to get ready because she not too long ago arrived home from her beach trip to St. John with our neighbor, Wally. I hear a car turn into the driveway. Thinking it's Fitzroy, I walk outside, excited and ready to embrace him. The last people I expect to see pull up to the house are Trevor and Lisa. Trevor is driving her car. I think to myself, "This is deep." Trevor runs around to open Lisa's door and she gets out of the car smiling like she doesn't have a care in the world. Both of them walk up to the front door holding hands like new lovers. As much as I want to play this off like everything is "hunky-dory," my face just won't cooperate.

"Don't look so shocked, Faith...Trevor and I are working things out." They both walk past me smiling and head into the house.

I stand there dumfounded and follow them into the family room where Momma and Aunt Dot are watching the news as they wait for Fitzroy to arrive and Aunt Lucille to finish getting dressed so we can leave. Lisa introduces Trevor to Momma and Aunt Dot. Momma invites them to join us for dinner. Trevor accepts. I think I'm going to vomit. Then I hear Fitzroy's van pull into the driveway. I walk outside to meet him and give him a quick heads-up. Fitzroy is just as puzzled as I am. We come back inside and Fitzroy greets everyone with a smile, including his homeboy, Trevor. I lead him with his duffle bag to my bedroom where I give him a clean towel and wash cloth, and leave him to shower and change. When I return to the family room I see grinning Lisa sitting so close to Trevor you'd need a crowbar to separate them. Aunt Lucille, sporting a golden tan, joins everyone in the family room. Lisa introduces Trevor to her as if he's the King of Glory. I really want to puke now. Momma gives me a signal to be nice. I can tell she also is repulsed. The only difference is she's more seasoned at handling these sorts of situations than I am. Being a former first lady of a church taught her a lot about people and life. I suddenly realize that God is teaching and confirming in my spirit a few things about my best friend of thirty years - that she is a stupid fool!

The hostess sat us on the balcony of the restaurant. The night view of beautiful Charlotte Amalie from where we were sitting was spectacular. I heard Momma say, "This is beautiful!" at least three times and each time Aunt Dot said, "It sure is, Gloria!" Momma, Fitzroy, Aunt Dot and I sat on one side of the table and Lisa, Trevor and Aunt Lucille sat on the other side. Our waitress introduced herself to us and proceeded to take our drink orders. She abruptly stopped when she got to Fitzroy.

"Is there a problem?" Fitzroy asks her.

"Yeah mon...officers who arrest the wrong people! Wa you wan ta drink?" She says this to Fitzroy with a nasty attitude.

"Honey you better get that chip off your shoulder or I'll smack it off for you!" Aunt Lucille cuts in.

"Sasha leave!" Fitzroy demands.

The waitress turns and walks to the kitchen. Fitzroy follows her.

"What's her problem?" Momma asks.

"Fitzroy arrested her brother yesterday for the murder of his wife, Janna." I say.

"You mean the woman who used to work with you at the television station, Faith?" Aunt Lucille whispers.

"Didn't you see it on the front page of the Daily News?" Momma adds.

"Oh my God, *she's* Eric's sister," Lisa says. All eyes turn to the kitchen door as we hear Sasha storm through it, carrying her purse. She gives the entire table the 'finger' as she exits the restaurant.

"I don't suppose that was the 'I love you' sign she just gave us," Momma says.

Fitzroy joins us at the table as if nothing ever happened.

"The cook says trout would be a good choice tonight," he says. We all laugh.

"So what was that all about, Fitzroy?" I ask.

"The owner is my friend. You know him, Trevor, Ethan Rogers, he's from St. Kitts," Fitzroy says.

"Yes, his family owns a restaurant in Basseterre," Trevor replies.

"Well, I told him I didn't feel comfortable with Sasha serving us. She called me a few choice names and Ethan told her to go home," he says.

"She did have a nasty attitude!" Aunt Dot says.

"I was also concerned she might put something in our food," Fitzroy says.

"Good thinking...of course I had already planned to start eating my food at least fifteen minutes after all of you, to see if anyone dropped dead!" Trevor jokes.

Lisa punches him in the arm.

"That's terrible, Trevor!" We all laugh.

Lisa excuses herself and heads to the ladies room. I get up to follow. "Don't you two be talking about me in the ladies room," Trevor says.

"Don't worry, we will," I quickly respond.

"Don't worry baby, it's all good," Lisa replies.

I really want to smack her now.

As soon as the bathroom door closes I light into Lisa.

"What the hell is going on, and where is Billy?" I say.

"He isn't here...I did a lot of praying and I'm going to stay with Trevor," Lisa says with confidence.

"Praying to whom?" I say with rage in my voice.

"Don't be silly, Faith, who do you think I pray to?"

"You have got to be the stupidest woman I have ever met. Why would you hook up with Trevor, the cheater, when God sent a wonderful man into your life like Billy?" I ask.

"Faith, Billy is not the man for me...sure he's nice and loves God, but I don't love him like I do Trevor...we're getting married."

"You are making another bad mistake, Lisa!" I say.

"Not this time...I know what I'm doing...trust me," Lisa says.

"And where have I heard that before, Lisa?"

Lisa is now getting angry and we are up close in each other's face. "I don't need your approval to marry the father of my child and the man I love!"

"Yeah, well when he knocks your behind down again and breaks your arm, don't come running to me. Oh, will you be inviting his wife and children to the wedding, too?" I ask.

"He's not married to her, for your information. Her name is Laurie Ann and I went to her house and she told me he used to stay with her from time to time but they were never married!" Lisa says.

"And your dumb behind believed her?"

"You need to stop calling me names, Faith!"

"I only call it as I see it!" I say.

"Besides, the woman is moving back to Nantucket," Lisa says, as if that is going to make everything right between her and Trevor.

"And what about his kids?"

"There are no 'kids', there is just one little girl...her name is Kamari. She's two years old and she's going to stay with us. Trevor says Laurie Ann's parents are racists and he doesn't want Kamari living in Nantucket around them."

"Well, it sounds like you've got it all worked out...what about Billy?"

"I told him Trevor was back in my life and I was sorry," Lisa says.

"You told him that on the telephone?" I ask.

Lisa hangs her head down in shame.

"I'm sorry, Faith...he wouldn't wait to talk about it in person...he kept pressuring me to tell him what was up. He said he wouldn't be able to meet with me tonight because Mr. Atkins needed him to fly him to Anguilla to pick up some lobsters for tomorrow's dinner...I feel so bad," she says.

"You should!" I reply. "Well, you made your bed, so lie in it!" I turn to leave and Lisa grabs me by the arm.

"Faith, don't do this to me." Lisa is crying now.

"Do what? It looks like whatever is being done, you're doing to yourself..."

Lisa raises her voice at me, "You are all I have, and you need to accept me as I am! I'm not you, Faith! I mess up, I fall down, I get back up and I try again! Let me mess up, maybe this time I might get it right!"

"What do you want me to say, Lisa?"

"Nothing, just continue to be my best friend and love me unconditionally...just like Jesus."

She sure got me on that; I mean what could I say?

"Look, Lisa, I'm upset right now, so let me have my moment," I turn to leave.

"Well, have your moment and then let's talk about planning my wedding!" I leave Lisa in the bathroom wiping the tears from her face.

"Where's Lisa?" Trevor asks, with concern showing on his face.

"In the ladies room handling her business," I flippantly reply.

"So I guess she told you everything?" Trevor continues.

"Yep, and then some."

Fitzroy pulls out my chair as I sit down. Lisa walks out of the ladies room smiling as if she didn't have a care in the world. Who knows, maybe she didn't. Trevor stands up as she approaches the table. I notice someone has ordered a bottle of champagne in our absence. Still standing, Trevor takes his glass in hand and clicks it with his knife.

"May I have your attention, please...I'm sure some of you know how much I love this Yankee lady and to those of you who don't, I'll tell you this: she is the very air I breathe and I want to make her my wife...so, if you would raise your glasses with me and give us your blessings, I would be grateful." Trevor grins from ear to ear.

Momma, Aunt Dot, Aunt Lucille and even Fitzroy are beaming with joy and happiness for the betrothed couple. Lisa locks eyes with me. She and I both know it doesn't matter who else in this room shares her joy, it's my endorsement she wants. I think about what she said in the ladies room: "I need you to love me unconditionally, like Jesus!" I pick up my glass, and for the first time I realize it's not about me and what I think is best for Lisa, but loving her categorically.

"To my best friend, Lisa, who I love like a sister, may God richly bless your marriage and keep you and your family in his loving arms always!" Lisa and I both cry tears of joy as our two men from Nevis, who truly love us, comfort us.

We stayed at the restaurant until it closed. The food was great and the fellowship was awesome! My family fell in love with Fitzroy and he with them. They were even fond of Trevor. And I was working real hard at forgiving him for hurting Lisa. I kept wondering how all this would play out. Then the Holy Spirit spoke to me and said, "Peace, be still." I realized then that I had no choice but to forgive Trevor. The Word clearly says we must forgive seventy times seven. I also needed to stop trying to provide a cushion for Lisa every time she falls.

When we got back to the house Momma made it clear there would be no men and women sleeping in the same bed unless they had the same last name and it was typed on an official wedding certificate. Fitzroy immediately seconded that. Trevor looked a little puzzled, but said he was cool with it as long as he didn't have to sleep with Fitzroy. Momma worked out the whole rooming arrangement. I would sleep with her, and Lisa would sleep with Aunt Lucille, since Aunt Dot farts in her sleep and we might find Lisa dead in the morning. Fitzroy would sleep in my room and Trevor would sleep in Lisa's room. Now that all the sleeping arrangements were worked out and everyone was in accord, Momma said goodnight and headed off to bed. Aunt Dot followed.

Aunt Lucille suggested we play cards - for money, of course. I'm sure she waited until Momma was in the bedroom before suggesting we gamble, knowing how much her big sister hated folk playing cards for money. Trevor was the first one to agree. I wanted to know what the stakes were before I decided to engage.

"One dollar a game, twenty-one Black Jack," Aunt Lucille said.

"Sounds like fun, I'm in," Fitzroy announces.

"Me too," do you all take checks?" says Lisa.

Everyone looks at her like she's crazy.

"Don't worry, baby, I got you covered," Trevor says. We decide to play on the veranda at the breakfast table.

"Looks like your neighbor's lights are still on, Faith," Fitzroy says with a plan behind his observation.

"Isn't that where Wally Nesbitt, from Brown Hill lives?" Trevor asks.

"The one and only," Fitzroy says.

"Aunt Lucille went to Trunk Bay with him," I say.

"What! I can't believe it. I heard he was a hermit," Lisa blurts out.

"Well those days must be over because he's taking me to Nevis before I go back to Atlanta," Aunt Lucille boasts.

"I guess you pulled him out of his shell, Auntie!" I tease her.

"As you say, 'Auntie got skills'," Lucille says. We all laugh.

"Why don't we give him a call and invite him over to play cards with us?" I say.

Aunt Lucille objects right away. "No...no...no. Doing that might make me appear desperate. We had a great time today and now, I need to let him marinate in the moment."

"Well, if it's any consolation to you, Lucille, us Nevis men are just plain guys...we don't really need to marinate...when we see something we like, we're all ready for the sweet pot," Fitzroy says as he arranges his cards in his hand.

Trevor deals the last card. "Well spoken, me boy!"

I look at Fitzroy and smile. Oh God, how I love this man!

"Quiet, I hear something." Fitzroy puts his cards down on the table and walks towards the end of the veranda.

"It's probably a wild donkey," Lisa says. Then we hear a voice.

"Hello inside!"

"That sounds like Mr. Wally from next door," I say.

"I can't let him see me looking like this...I need to freshen up...deal me out!" Aunt Lucille says, as she jumps up and runs into the house.

"Come on in Mr. Wally," I say.

"Wally, me boy...you're the last person I expected to see tonight. Come on in, have a seat and let me get you something to drink," Fitzroy says as he leads him to Aunt Lucille's chair.

"Good to see you, Wally, been a long time," Trevor says as he stands up and shakes Wally's hand.

"I hope I'm not intruding," Wally says.

"Of course not," Lisa says.

"I could hear you all laughing from my kitchen window...so I decided to come down and see if I was missing a party my neighbors forgot to invite me to."

"Lucille will be out in just a moment, she went to freshen up."

I give Fitzroy a look that says he just gave up too much information. "T.M.I," I say.

"What?" he whispers.

"Too Much Information!" Lisa interjects.

"Oh, I thought the marinating was over and the pot was already sweet enough." We all laugh.

"Did I miss something?" Wally wants to know.

"Not a thing, Wally...the game is Black Jack, a dollar a game," Trevor says as he deals the cards.

"Do you all accept Visa or Master Card?" Wally asks. We all look at him and everyone says, "Cash!"

Aunt Lucille walks out onto the veranda. She has freshened up her make-up, sprayed on a little perfume and changed into a floor length caftan. "Don't worry Wally, I've got you covered," Aunt Lucille says in a sexy voice. Mr. Wally grins from ear to ear.

"How in the world did she change so fast?" Fitzroy whispers to me.

"Auntie's got skills!" I say.

Chapter 16

I can hear a phone ringing, but I think it's in my dream until I hear Momma, who's already up and cooking breakfast in the kitchen with Aunt Dot, saying to me, Faith, it's Mrs. Atkins on the phone."

"Hello...no, it's alright...no, Billy isn't here...He never came back from Anguilla?"

Rosalinda sounds very nervous. She tells me Billy is not answering his cell phone and the plane never arrived back in St. Croix. She thought maybe Lisa was with him and they might have called me. I sit up in bed, trying to focus and sound coherent.

"Lisa is here asleep. The last we both heard, Billy was on his way to Anguilla to pick up lobster for today's Thanksgiving dinner," I tell Rosalinda.

"My husband is on the other phone talking to Harvey; he's our lobster man. Honey, what did he say?" Rosalinda calls out to her husband. I can hear Mr. Atkins ending his conversation with the lobster man, and asking Rosalinda to let him talk to me.

Faith, I just got off the phone with our lobster guy and he says Billy is there with him."

"Praise God!" I say.

"Yes, yes...however, Harvey says Billy was drinking last night and got so drunk he couldn't see, let alone fly a plane back to St. Croix, so he got him a hotel room at Rawlins Plantation and took his keys to the plane...Faith, I need to know what's going on...Billy doesn't drink!"

"Well sir, Lisa broke up with Billy yesterday and that may have had something to do with it."

I can hear Rosalinda in the background.

"What happened, honey?" she cries.

"I'll fill you in when I get off the phone... That's not good," Mr. Atkins says.

"What's not good?" I hear Rosalinda say.

"Honey, grab the extension phone so I won't have to repeat this," Mr. Atkins says.

I hear her pick up the extension. "Faith says that Billy and Lisa broke up...and Harvey said Billy is still in Anguilla. He got a room for him last night at the Rawlins Plantation because he was drunk!"

"But Billy doesn't drink," Rosalinda interrupts.

"Well apparently he was drinking last night," Mr. Atkins continues.

"Faith, I'm sorry to have bothered you. It looks like this is something Billy and Lisa are going to have to work out. The only problem is I'm not sure if he will be in any shape to pick you and the family up and fly you all over ... Let's do this, call and get reservations on the Sea Plane and I'll have my driver pick all of you up when you land. Now, don't forget to tell them to bill our account. I'm not sure who's working the desk over there today since it's a holiday. It might be someone who ain't happy because they'd rather be home eating turkey with their family. So, if you have any problems call me immediately and I'll get them straight...We are looking forward to seeing you and your family around three o'clock."

"I'm so sorry this happened Mr. and Mrs. Atkins," I say.

"It's not your fault. Love happens," Mr. Atkins says.

"We're just glad he's safe," Rosalinda says.

"Faith, not to worry. Billy is in good hands with Harvey. If I ever met a man who's been through hell and back and became stronger through it all, it's Harvey. I'll give him a call back and tell him what's going on. He'll help strengthen Billy's spine. See you soon, dear." Mr. Atkins hangs up.

Momma is standing in the doorway with a perplexed look on her face. She closes the door and sits on the bed. "Is that young man Billy alright?"

I see so much concern for him on her face. This causes me to remember as a child and teenager how my mother always carried the burdens of her church members. Mom was truly coming back to herself, using the gifts again that made her so well-loved as a First Lady.

"Lisa told him she wanted to be with Trevor and he's taking it a little hard...The Atkins didn't know where he was and they were concerned."

"Well, did they find him?" Momma asks.

"Yes, he's still in Anguilla where they sent him on an errand yesterday...Mr. Atkins says he's in good hands," I reassure my mother.

"Good! Now, it looks like everyone in this house except Dot and I are still asleep and it's well past seven-thirty...I thought the smell of breakfast would wake you folks up."

"I'm sure everyone is tired. Lisa and I went to bed around three-thirty and left Aunt Lucille, Trevor, Fitzroy and Wally out on the veranda laughing and playing cards. The men were telling stories about their home."

"Wally? When did *he* come over?" Momma is surprised.

"Oh, he dropped by shortly after you and Aunt Dot went to bed. He said he could hear us laughing out on the veranda from his kitchen window, so he ventured out to see if we were having a party and forgot to invite him."

"A party? I thought the man was mourning the loss of his wife," Momma says.

"I guess you can credit your baby sister for bringing him out of his sorrow. Fitzroy and Trevor say they haven't seen him out socially since his wife died."

"Well, if anybody can bring someone out of their sorrow it's my sister," Momma says, smiling and shaking her head in admiration.

"Momma, I think we should let Fitzroy sleep as long as his body wants. He's been working so hard, I know he needs it."

"Sounds good to me, baby...so, what time are we going over to St. Croix?"

"Oh, my gosh, thanks for reminding me...I need to make reservations on the Sea Plane."

"What's a Sea Plane?" Momma asks like it's something that might bite you.

"Didn't you see the Sea Planes taking off and landing on the water near the Greenhouse yesterday when we had lunch?"

"Oh, my Father! Faith, you can't be talking about those little planes that make all that noise and have water skis attached to them!" Momma said with distress in her voice.

"Yes, those are the ones. I thought you might have seen them."

"When you went to get the car and left Dot and me waiting for you, Dot's the one who heard all that noise coming from the water and when it got closer to the dock, she said, and I quote, 'Hell will freeze over before I get on one of those things!'... So, who's going to tell her hell might freeze over around two-thirty today?" Momma asks.

"Why don't we tell her just before its time to board the plane?" I say.

"That's not going to happen. My sister would have a heart attack."

"Well, what would you suggest?" I ask, sounding desperate.

"Hmm, we are going to have to take a very different approach. You remember how much trouble we had in Puerto Rico getting her on that little plane that brought us here to St. Thomas?"

"Yes," I say.

"Well, I don't know if you noticed, but these first two days on St. Thomas have done something to Dot."

"Something like what?" I say, very puzzled.

"First of all, just getting her here...Dot had never left Atlanta much less been on a plane. She's taken a big giant step coming here. And look at how well she's handling the fact that your Uncle George served her with divorce papers."

"Momma, can you get to the point? I don't see how this is going to help get Aunt Dot on the Sea Plane."

"Hold your horses, honey! The point I'm making here is since we arrived this island has been affecting *all* of us. It's like we are seeing things new, for the first time."

"Well, that's true, especially since you've never been here before."

"Faith, if you'll stop cutting me off, you'll hear what I'm saying."

"Now, what I'm trying to tell you is Dot came here looking and hoping to find clarification on how to start a new life. So far she realizes that every one of her family members had a piece of her life all these years except her. George kept her pregnant almost every other year from the time they got married, until she secretly went and got her tubes tied. After the seventh child and no help with the children from him, she knew something had to change. You see, Faith, my sister has lived a miserable life for a long time. Now don't get me wrong, she loves her children and grandchildren. It's just that she never had time to find out who she is or do any of the things she dreamed of doing...until now. Riding on a plane, big or small, or with a plane with jet skis is all part of Dot learning that there are new challenges coming with her name written all over them. What we need to do is look at this as an adventure not only for her but also for all of us. Look at your Aunt Lucille who tragically lost the love of her life, and me, who lost the man who rocked my world for over 40 years, and Dot, who's just learning to love herself. Faith, God has led us here to encounter new experiences that are part of our healing process. It's like being a virgin again and I can't think of a better place to be right now than the Virgin Islands!"

"Wow, Momma, you put that so nicely...now I know how to approach Aunt Dot. I'll tell her we're going on an adventure."

I feel so good after talking to Momma. Just like old times. "So, Momma, how did Daddy rock your world?" I loving ask.

"I'll share those secrets with you when you get married...no need in me telling you things that might get you all hot and bothered...now, let me get back in the kitchen and help Dot with breakfast since Zipporah has the day off."

"I love you, Momma." Momma smiles and heads back to the kitchen. "Lord, let me have a marriage like my parents and I will praise you forever!"

I call the Sea Plane office and make reservations for their two o'clock flight. Praise God there are enough seats. The reservationist tells me that our party will take up the entire plane. This is good, so if Aunt Dot or anyone else including myself gets scared, we can holler, scream or cry and won't have to worry about strangers on the plane thinking we've lost our minds.

After I shower and dress, I join Momma and Aunt Dot in the kitchen, where they are cooking a first-class southern breakfast complete with grits, gravy, sausage, biscuits, fried chicken and waffles, along with homemade scrapple and jam brought straight from Aunt Dot's kitchen in Atlanta.

"Looks like you all got it going on in here!" I say.

"I just hope those who are diabetic brought their insulin," Momma says jokingly. I wonder to myself if all this rich food is the reason Aunt Dot suffers with gout.

Fitzroy is the next person to come into the kitchen. He looks so good, better than all the food on the table. "Lord, hurry up and let me marry this man before I sin!" Fitzroy greets us with a big smile, stopping to kiss me, Momma and Aunt Dot, too.

"Everything looks so good! Is there anything I can do to help?" Fitzroy asks.

"You and Faith can set the table and get the drinks out of the refrigerator," Momma says.

"When do you think the rest of them will be getting up?" says Aunt Dot.

"I heard Trevor getting out of the shower a little while ago. I'm not sure about Lucille and Lisa...I haven't heard a sound come from that room," Fitzroy gives his report to Aunt Dot, just as Trevor enters the kitchen.

"Good morning, everyone. Mmm-mmm-mmm, it sure smells good in here!"

"I trust you slept well?" Momma asks.

"Yes, ma'am, even though it was difficult knowing my sugar cane was in the next room and I couldn't taste it."

"Looks like you and Lisa's done enough tasting to last until you get married," Momma says. Fitzroy laughs.

"Sounds like a 'three–snapper' to me," I say.

"Yes ma'am, Mrs. Gloria," Trevor respectfully answers.

Fitzroy and I continue setting the table as Aunt Lucille enters the house through the kitchen door wearing the same caftan she had on last night when we were playing cards. Aunt Dot is shocked to see Lucille come in the door. Her mouth is wide open and her eyes are bulging out. Momma is shaking her head, appalled. The rest of us give her a big "Good morning."

"Well, would you look at what the cat dragged in?" Aunt Dot says with ferocity in her voice.

"It isn't what it looks like, Dot, so you can just shut up and, Gloria, save it for the 700 Club! I'm going to shower and if any of you care to hear the reason I stayed the night over at Wally's, I'll fill you in when I get back." Aunt Lucille, with her head held high, walks down the hall leading to her room.

"Can you believe that woman? I bet the neighbors are talking about her already and we've only been in town three days!" Dot says.

"Let's not be so quick to condemn her...she said she would fill us in after her shower...so, let's give her the benefit of the doubt," Momma says, as she continues putting breakfast on the table.

"Lisa certainly is sleeping late...maybe I should go and wake her up," Trevor says with concern.

"I think she's tired from pulling a double shift and staying up until three-thirty playing cards," I say.

"You're right, she's probably worn out," Trevor acknowledges.

"Let's bless the food, and whoever is not here can join us when they are ready," Momma suggests.

"Now that sounds like a splendid suggestion...I'm hungry," Trevor says.

We all take a seat around the breakfast table. "Trevor would you or Fitzroy please bless the food?" Momma asks.

"Let Fitzroy have the honors...he used to be an altar boy back home at his daddy's church," Trevor smiles.

"Whatever, man...let's bow our heads...Most gracious Father, we thank You for this beautiful day that You have made...we thank You for waking us up in our right mind this morning...we thank You for this time to fellowship with friends and family and we pray on this Thanksgiving morning that You will bless those who are in need...thank You Father, for this food and the hands that prepared it for the nourishment of our bodies, in Christ Jesus, Your Son's name we pray...Amen."

All of us say "Amen," and start to serve our plates.

"Mother and Mrs. Dot, you all really outdid yourselves...everything looks so good, I don't know where to start," Fitzroy says.

"Well, just start to your right and work your way around," Aunt Dot says.

"Sounds like a good strategy," Fitzroy agrees.

I decide I'm not going to pig out on food this morning, especially knowing Mrs. Atkins is preparing a large spread this afternoon. Besides, I want to be able to fit into that cute outfit I got at the Tutu Park Mall. As we eat, my mind wanders and I think about Billy. I wonder how he's doing and if he will be back to St. Croix today to join us for Thanksgiving dinner. I look over at Trevor, stuffing his face with food like there will be no tomorrow and I wonder how Lisa could choose him over Billy. Lord, forgive me...I know...You didn't put me in charge of judging people. I smile at Trevor and he smiles back. I find Fitzroy staring at me with a smirk on his face.

"What's up?" I say in a sweet voice.

"I love you more today than yesterday...and I didn't think it could be possible."

I smile so hard my face hurts. Momma, who is sitting next to me, hears what Fitzroy says.

"Faith, that's a rock your world statement," she whispers into my ear and we both laugh.

Aunt Lucille joins us in the kitchen and takes a seat next to Trevor. "You sure you don't need another plate to put your overflow on, Trevor? You have so much food on your plate it's sliding onto the table."

"Mrs. Lucille, I got this under control...ain't nothing here on this plate going to get away from me...You just worry about your plate, because this food is so good I might eat yours and mine."

Trevor and Fitzroy give each other a high five.

"So, Lucille, where you been all night?" Aunt Dot goes for the jugular.

Momma puts her fork down and takes an arbitrator's position, giving Aunt Lucille all her attention.

"First of all, it wasn't all night. We didn't leave here until after 4 A.M. Wally was feeling a little light-headed from drinking wine on an empty stomach, so Fitzroy and I walked him home. When we got there, he still wasn't feeling good, so I told Fitzroy I would stay with him until he was feeling better and I would call him on his cell phone to come and pick me up...I'm surprised Fitzroy didn't say where I was."

Aunt Lucille looks at Fitzroy who throws his hands up in a surrender position. "Mrs. Lucille, there was no way I could tell the story the way you just did. I thought of saying something this morning but I decided it would be better to keep my mouth shut for fear that these two women would have me on trial and then henpeck me to death." Everyone laughs so hard it takes us a few minutes to gather our composure.

"I hope he's feeling better," Momma says with concern.

"I found some club soda and crackers and gave it to him and it seemed to give him some relief."

"Did you fix him any breakfast before you left? The poor man is probably hungry and doesn't have anyone to cook a decent meal for him," Aunt Dot says.

"There isn't any food in his house," Lucille sadly says.

"You can't be telling the truth. Wally has so much money, he can afford to buy Giant and Pueblo supermarkets!"

"I wish I were telling a lie, Trevor. It's a sad situation over there. Sometimes all that glitters ain't gold."

"The man has three sons, surely one of them must be checking on their father," Fitzroy says with concern.

"What I'm about to tell all of you must not go any further than this room...does everyone agree?" All of us, with worried looks on our faces, agree not to repeat to anyone what Aunt Lucille is about to tell us.

"Wally has contemplated suicide...Yesterday when I was out for my walk on Skyline Drive, I met him walking down the road...He said my saying 'hello' to him, saved his life...He had been walking for some time that morning asking God to help him find peace from all the pain he had been suffering...He was looking for a reason to live...When he turned to go into his driveway if I hadn't asked to see the layout of his house, he was going inside to shoot himself."

"Oh my God! He could have shot you, too!" Aunt Dot says with anxiety in her voice.

"Relax, Dot, Wally wouldn't hurt anyone," Aunt Lucille says.

"So how did your looking around his house keep him from committing suicide?" Fitzroy asks, as if interrogating a witness.

"He said he felt a kindred spirit between us."

"She has that kind of affect on people," Momma says matter-of-factly.

"When we spent time at Trunk Bay yesterday, he said he knew God had sent me."

"Wow, that's deep," I say.

"Now, Lucille, you didn't come to St. Thomas to get involved with some crazy suicidal man...you need to cut this relationship off before it goes any further!" Aunt Dot says with forcefulness.

"Hold up, Mrs. Dot. Wally isn't just some crazy man. I've known him all my life. He's a Nevisian," Trevor says.

"I don't care if he's a Georgian...the man obviously has problems and I don't need my sister around him!"

" Dot, I appreciate your concern. However, you are forgetting one small thing."

"And what is that, Lucille?"

"It was not that long ago that I was in the same boat as Wally. When my fiancé, Bedford, was shot the day before our wedding, living was the last thing I wanted to do. I didn't eat for weeks. You and Gloria had me committed to St. Elizabeth and they placed me on suicide watch. I was fed through tubes for two months. The only reason I didn't shoot myself was I'm afraid of guns."

Everyone is quiet, then Momma speaks. "We need to be careful not to judge or turn our backs on someone who is in need. Jesus made it very clear when He said, 'When you did it to one of the least of these, you were doing it to me.'"

"I truly believe that God placed me in this place at this time to help Wally," Aunt Lucille says with optimism.

"I can't think of a better person He would use than you," Momma interjects.

"Maybe that's why Wally called us kindred spirits," Aunt Lucille says.

"We need to ask Wally to come with us to the Atkins' for Thanksgiving...holidays are a horrible time to be alone," I say.

"Oh, I already invited him. I hope that was ok," Lucille smiling says. We all laugh.

"Wally can take Lisa's seat on the plane and at the dinner table," I say to Aunt Lucille.

"Yeah, he can take my baby's place because she won't be going to St. Croix," Trevor says in his authoritative voice.

"So, what are you two going to do today?" I ask.

"Lisa and I are going to have Thanksgiving dinner with my two-year old daughter, Kamari."

"Is Kamari doing the cooking?" I sarcastically ask.

"No, her mother is," Trevor, says casually.

"Sounds like a real family affair," Fitzroy interjects.

"Does Lisa know about this?" Momma asks.

"Sure, it was her idea...she wants Kamari to get accustomed to her since she's going to be her new mother...and she thinks the best way to do that is in Kamari's home."

"What a wonderful *adventure* this is going to be!" Momma says and looks directly at me, giving me my cue.

"Yes it is...Aunt Dot, we need to talk!" I say.

Chapter 17

Lisa finally woke up as we were preparing to leave to catch the Sea Plane. I wanted to tell my best friend to be careful when she went to Laurie Ann's for dinner and not to eat until well after everyone else had eaten, but she couldn't let go of the toilet long enough for me to talk to her. Lisa had a bad case of morning sickness and Trevor wouldn't let anyone else into the bathroom to help. He had already prepared mint tea for her and planned to give her some ginger once she stopped vomiting. Trevor told us to go and have a good time. He would take care of Lisa. Momma made him promise to call us once she was feeling better and he said he would.

Everyone left the house and got into the van except Aunt Lucille who was at Wally's house making sure he ate some of our leftover breakfast she had taken up to him earlier so he wouldn't get sick on the ride over to St. Croix. She told us to blow the horn when we were ready to leave and they would walk down. Aunt Dot said that was "ghetto" and told her we would call on the phone like civilized people and let her know when we were about to leave. I wasn't quite ready to relinquish my guardian angel position just yet, so I asked Fitzroy to give me a second and I ran back into the house just as he was about to pull out of the driveway. Lisa was still regurgitating. Trevor looked at me and said, "You need to stop worrying, Faith. Lisa has a real man now, just like you do."

My mouth opened and I stuttered. "I just wanted to tell you not to let her eat any of Laurie Ann's food until fifteen minutes after everyone else had eaten." Trevor and I burst out laughing. Lisa holds her head up from the toilet bowl and tries to laugh with us only to find she quickly has to resume her position.

"You learn fast, Faith. Don't worry, I almost lost this little Yankee girl once because of my foolishness...trust me, I'm not going to let nothing happen to her or my child she's carrying."

I hugged Trevor and finally realized I was no longer on duty when it came to my sister-friend. Lisa had finally met a real man who truly cared about her. Thank you, Lord!

When I got back into the van, Fitzroy wanted to know if everything was ok. I told him I went back into the house to relinquish my title as Lisa's protector to Trevor. He smiled and said, "Good. I believe Trevor will do what is right by Lisa...and if he doesn't, I'm sure he knows he'll have to deal with me."

Momma, seated on the next row in the van says, "And me!" Aunt Dot sitting next to her says, "And me!" Aunt Lucille sitting next to Wally, who looks better than ever, says,

"And me, and a few of my friends from Atlanta who won't think twice about hurting the brother. All I need to do is make a phone call!"

"Well, it looks like God, all of us, and a few gangsters from Atlanta got this covered... so what do you say we go and catch the Sea Plane?" I say.

Aunt Dot lets out a big sigh. I get a little nervous. It took me all morning to convince her to get on the plane. The "it's an adventure" approach seems to have worked. Now the rubber is about to meet the road and I'm praying she doesn't jump out of this van and make a bee line back to the house. Lucille senses her apprehension and says, "Dot, I got a little something to settle your nerves...anybody got some water?"

"Wally, there's a small cooler under your seat...reach in there and give Mrs. Dot a bottle of water," Fitzroy says.

Lucille hands Dot a small pill along with the bottle of water.

"Lucille, what in the blazing hell is this?" Aunt Dot says, looking at the pill like it might kill her.

"Girl, don't look at me like I just gave you some dope! It's a nerve pill. It will keep you from being so stressed out on the plane. I got it from Dr. Goldman. He prescribed it for me after I got out of the hospital...Woman, take the darn thing!"

"Alright, but you all are my witness to 'Exhibit A' so if I die, just let the authorities know that my baby sister was to blame!" Dot holds the pill up in the air flashing it in front of everyone as an exhibit.

"Don't worry Mrs. Dot, I got your back. If anything happens to you, I'll bring Miss Lucille to justice," Fitzroy says.

"Where's that official business sign you keep in your window?" Aunt Dot wants to know.

Fitzroy flips the sun visor down and hands it to Aunt Dot. She holds the sign up in front of Lucille. "Remember, the man is always on official business so you'd better not be trying to give me something that will kill me so you can claim my assets!"

"Only assets you got are those beautiful grandbabies and you don't have to worry about me taking them. I enjoy having them over, spoiling them reckless and sending them home!"

Dot swallows the pill with the entire bottle of water. Momma pats her leg. "You don't have a 'ting' to worry about, as Zipporah would say. You are blessed."

Aunt Dot is the first one to board the Sea Plane; she is laughing and acting a bit strange. Fitzroy and I look at each other. "I'm beginning to wonder what's in that pill your Aunt Lucille gave her."

Wally helps Lucille up the stairs of the small plane. They take a seat together. Fitzroy helps Momma who has taken her pocket Bible out and has it in her hands. I climb the few steps behind them. I ask Fitzroy to sit with Aunt Dot and I'll sit with Momma, just in case Aunt Dot freaks out. He agrees.

"Now, Lucille if you feel frightened, just squeeze my hand," Wally says to her. Lucille smiles as the plane door closes, sounding like we've just been sealed in a vacuum chamber.

"Thank you, Wally, I think I'll do just that!"

Lucille holds Wally's hand. He wraps his arm around her opposite shoulder, shielding her from any unexpected danger. Momma takes my hand and begins reciting the Lord's Prayer. The engine starts, sounding like a hundred lawnmowers running at the same time; then the plane maneuvers from the ramp towards the open sea. It slowly taxies past the smaller boats in the harbor. When we pass Water Island I can see people on the beach. I smile knowing Linda Peters' family is enjoying the start of their Thanksgiving weekend. The plane picks up speed at an amazing rate.

"Oh, Lord, help us!" I hear Aunt Lucille holler.

Wally comforts her. "Don't worry, Lucille, the Lord didn't cross our paths for it to end so quickly."

"Oh really, and how do you know that?" Lucille says with a sweet spirit.

"Well, He sent you to save my life and I haven't had time to show you how truly grateful I am," Wally sincerely says.

The Sea Plane bumps and skids on the water like a speedboat determined to win a race before its nose is hoisted upward toward the beautiful Caribbean sky. Aunt Dot lets out a big laugh, "Whee! Look at all those little boats down there!"

"Lucille, you don't think that medicine was too strong for Dot, do you?" Momma asks.

"Don't worry; give her about ten minutes and she will be out like a light!"

"Out like a light? We're going to dinner at my boss's house, not to bed," I say with admonishment under my breath so Aunt Dot can't hear us.

"I certainly hope you're not talking about me over there Lucille! Don't let me have to tell Wally one of your boobies is bigger than the other!" Dot's sounding like she's drunk or over-medicated.

"Where the hell did she get that from?" Lucille says dumbfounded.

"Don't worry about it, Lucille, I'd think you're a wonderful person even if you didn't have any...you know."

"Thank you, Wally, but both of my 'girls' are fine and well proportioned."

Wally looks at Aunt Lucille's chest. "Yes, I agree."

"Dot, hush up talking like that! All of y'all need to change the subject right now!" Momma says in a stern tone.

"Oh, don't let me start on you Gloria, Mrs. High and..." Aunt Dot conks out with the weight of her body leaning against Fitzroy.

"I told you she'd be out in ten minutes...and not a second too soon, huh, Gloria?" Aunt Lucille says teasingly.

I notice Fitzroy staring. He can see the stress on my face. I try to smile but he's not buying it. I can't blame him; it was fake to me too. He knows I'm worried about Aunt Dot making a fool of herself and embarrassing all of us when we get to the Atkins' house.

"Faith, remember what I told you at the airport?" Fitzroy tenderly says.

"Yes... let you do your job."

"Good. Besides, can't you see I'm trying to make a good impression for your mother?" We both smile.

"You don't have to impress me, Fitzroy. You're the son I always prayed for. Besides, I checked you out the first day I met you, and saw it was all good!" Momma affirms.

"Amen!" Aunt Lucille concurs. Fitzroy has a strange look on his face.

"What's wrong honey?" I ask.

"What Momma just said means a lot to me... She feels like a mother to me more than any of you will ever know!"

Momma and I both smile.

The plane starts its descent. Momma and I recite the Lord's Prayer together. Wally pulls Lucille closer to him while she clutches his hand. "It's a beautiful day, not a cloud in the sky," Wally says.

"I'll take your word for it, Wally. Right now I'm not trying to look out the window. I'm just going to sit here and pray for a smooth landing."

And that's just what we had...a smooth landing. Only problem was Aunt Dot was still knocked out when we touched down. Fitzroy and Wally agreed they would carry her to the limousine. But Momma said that would not be necessary. She has something in her purse that could wake up the dead.

"I can't believe it!" I say to Momma.

"Believe it," she says.

"Momma, I thought they stopped selling that stuff!"

"Faith, you can find just about anything on that internet."

Everyone looks puzzled and wonders what secret weapon Momma has to wake up Aunt Dot. Momma opens her purse and pulls out a small packet.

"They don't sell it in the bottle anymore, but it works just as good!" Momma places her secret weapon, ammonium carbonicum, also known as smelling salts, under Aunt Dot's nose.

Aunt Dot jumps so high she hits her head on the bulkhead of the plane. "Gloria, what the hell are you doing?"

"Trying to wake your big behind up so Fitzroy and Wally won't have to carry you off this plane and embarrass all of us," Momma retorts.

"I wasn't asleep, I heard every word you all said," Aunt Dot protests.

"Um hmm... well, there's going to be a test after we get in the limo," Momma says.

Fitzroy steadies Aunt Dot down the stairs of the plane and into the limousine.

"Momma, is that stuff legal? Didn't they stop selling smelling salts in the drug stores?" I ask.

"And it's a shame. I had to go to www.cpr-savers.com to find it. It cost me $19.99 for a hundred. I remember I used to get a bottle of it at the corner store for fifty-nine cents. Faith, back in the day, when a woman in church would fall out in the spirit everybody pulled out their smelling salts. Now, they just make sure your dress isn't up in the air and your wig hasn't flipped. Then they leave you on the floor covered up with a little cloth until you come to."

Momma zips her purse and grabs the bag with the linen tablecloths for Rosalinda. Aunt Lucille and Wally walk past us. "Gloria, if you ever put something like that up my nose, we're going to have a few words," Aunt Lucille says sternly.

"And what makes you think I haven't already?" Momma replies.

Aunt Lucille smiles. "Well, if you did it when I wasn't in my right mind, then I forgive you." Lucille and Wally exit the plane.

"Momma, have you used it on Aunt Lucille before?" I ask.

"Sure did. I had to give her a double dose. Those people at St. Elizabeth Hospital had my sister so sedated, she didn't know who I was...I needed her to wake up and tell me what was going on at that hospital because it looked like they were trying to keep her crazy a little bit too long, as far as I was concerned. You know they charged $3,000 a day for a private room and Lucille was paying cash. Those vultures were miserable when their meal ticket checked out."

I took Momma's gift bag from her as we exited the plane. I felt so proud to be Gloria Davis' daughter.

Mr. Atkins' limousine driver, Emmaus, was waiting for us, just as Mr. Atkins had said. Momma told him she was very grateful that he would leave his family on Thanksgiving Day to come and pick us up. Emmaus told her it wasn't a problem at all. He and his wife both worked for the Atkins'. He was their driver and his wife, Solange, was their housekeeper. We learned that they both were originally from Granada and live on the grounds of the Atkins estate. Emmaus recognized Fitzroy from the Daily News, the St. Thomas newspaper.

"I saw you on the front page of the paper!" Emmaus exclaims.

"Yes, that was me," Fitzroy humbly says.

"Mrs. Janna's two girls are at the house. They are spending the holiday with us...we all feel so miserable 'bout what happened to Mrs. Janna."

"Yes, that's a hard one to swallow...I'm looking forward to seeing Chloe and Nyla. They were my neighbors."

"Yes, I know that, Miss Faith...now you and your Yankee friend live in the Atkins house on Skyline."

I'm beginning to accept the fact that people on these islands are going to know your story. So, what I discovered is to make sure it's the story you want everybody to know, because they are going to tell it. Just like Janna said, "Island people love 'melee'."

Fitzroy pours Aunt Dot a cup of black coffee from the mini-bar in the back. "Drink this; it should help keep you awake."

"Thank you, Fitzroy...I'm going to kill that crazy sister of mine for giving me that knock-out drug...I just hope it wasn't one of those sex pills you hear about on the news. You know, the one people slip into your drink and the next morning you wake up violated in some man's bed."

"Don't worry, Dot. If it's one of those kinds of pills, you're in good company...no one here will violate you," Fitzroy pats her hands.

"She should be thankful I gave her something for the plane ride over that knocked her out. Sugar darling, you might not realize it but I saved you from having a heart attack. That Sea Plane ride was deep!" Lucille says over dramatically.

"So was that tranquilizer you gave me! On the return trip back to St. Thomas, I think I'll take my chances of having a heart attack before I let you drug me again! If *you* managed the flight in one piece then I know I can do it too, because I'm a stronger person!"

"OK, 'Super Woman', just don't be begging me for a pill at take-off!" Everyone laughs. Aunt Dot holds her aching head as the limousine pulls away from the Sea Plane's parking lot.

The ride to the east end of St. Croix is uneventful until Fitzroy's cell phone rings. He looks at the number and decides not to answer it. Then it rings three more times. Finally, I say, "It must be important. Maybe you should answer it."

"Not today," he unequivocally says. Then my cell phone rings and I answer it. It's Lucinda yelling in my ear.

"Put Fitzroy on the phone! His child had an accident!"

I hand the phone to Fitzroy. "It's for you; your *nephew* had an accident." I say this in the phone, letting Lucinda know that I'm aware of the blood test results.
Fitzroy, very concerned, takes the phone from me. "Calm down, Lucinda, and tell me what happened...did you take him to the hospital...and what did they say...well, it sounds like everything is under control...you can buy another car...well, put him on the phone...Hey, buddy, I hear you and your mommy had a little accident...that's right, someone needs to do something about those cows...so how are you feeling...yeah, it's going to itch for a few days...you're watching the Thanksgiving Day parade...O.K., well go back to that and I'll call you tomorrow and check on you...yes, put your mother on the phone...Lucinda, the boy is fine, so stop ringing my phone with all your unnecessary drama...that's none of your business...I'm hanging up and if you ever call Faith's phone again, you'll have to deal with me...um hmm, you have a nice day too."

"What was that about?" I ask bitterly.

"Did someone get hurt?" Aunt Dot chimes in.

"Thank God everyone's alright... My twin nephews and their mother were driving to Coral Bay to visit her sister. Just past the clinic there's a blind spot in the road where Lucinda hit one of Abraham Bivens' cows.

"Jesus!" Momma hollers.

"One of the twins broke his arm."

"My Lord! Isn't it against the law to let your animals graze on the public road where the cars drive?" Momma wants to know.

"One would think so...we've had the owner of those cows in court before and he says the cows were walking on that road before there was a paved road. He argued that the road the cars drive on was part of his grandfather's land... it cuts straight through their pasture. He says the cows were there first and everyone else can go directly to hell without stopping because he ain't moving them."

"Can he get away with that?" I ask.

"So far he has. It seems like his grandfather donated the land to the government with that caveat in place...The government has been dragging its feet about putting up bold neon signs that glow at night and marking the road to read 'Cow Crossing' to alert the drivers," Wally interrupts. "It's not only the cows... Abraham's boars are a nuisance too. I think all of those animals, just like their owners, have a few screws loose. Once I was driving very slowly past his farm, being extra careful around the curves so that a cow's butt didn't become a hood ornament on my car, and I saw a baby pig nursing on the cow's udder along with two calves."

"No way!" Aunt Lucille says.

"It's true. I even have a picture of it."

"Oh, you just happened to have a camera in your car?" Fitzroy inquires.

"Actually, my son and his fiancé were visiting from Miami, and I let them use the car a few days earlier. One of them left a disposable camera in the car. Remind me to show you the picture when we get back to my house," Wally boasts.

"I'd certainly like to see that. I'm sure if you submit it to a magazine it would get national recognition. You can call it 'Pig Got Milk'!" says Lucille. Everyone laughs.

Our limousine continues winding its way around several mountains and climbing a few hills. The land on this side of the island is very dry and badly in need of water. Giant cactus is abundant all over the rocky hillside. A humongous iguana scurries across the road and into the brush just short of becoming road kill.

"Tell me that pill I took doesn't have me hallucinating! I just saw something run across the road that looked like a creature from the movie *Rodan Meets Godzilla,*" Aunt Dot says, petrified.

"It's just an iguana. They're quite harmless. Many people have them for pets," Fitzroy says trying to comfort Aunt Dot.

"They don't come into your house do they? Lord, I'd die if I woke up and found that dinosaur-looking thing in my bedroom."

"No...they're just as afraid of you as you are of them. Iguanas enjoy hiding in bushes and near cactus, where they can camouflage themselves and blend in with their elements far away from people," Fitzroy continues.

"In many places like Puerto Rico, green iguanas are nicknamed "gallinas de palo." Their meat is used for cooking. People say the taste and feel of the cooked iguana is similar to chicken," Wally enlightens us.

"Chicken gets blamed for tasting like every kind of weird food from frog legs to turtle," Aunt Lucille rejoins.

"Yes, iguana does taste like chicken. My brother is a chef at a hotel where he cooks 'sopi di yuana', also known as iguana soup. The meat is very soft and tender. But if you use a very large, old iguana it will be like using a large, old chicken: tough. The locals in my village believe that 'sopi di yuana' and 'yuana stoba', iguana stew, are good for the health."

"Excuse me, but how can something that rough and ugly be tender and good for your health?" I ask Emmaus.

"We encourage sick and old people to drink the soup or eat the stew to get stronger."

"In this area the green iguanas are listed as endangered species. In Puerto Rico it's created headaches for many people. The last time I was at the airport, for example, our flight could not take off and had to be delayed because a green iguana was spotted basking in the sun right on the runway," Fitzroy informs us.

"Too bad my brother wasn't on that flight...because if he had, that iguana would be stew the next day for his hotel guests!" Emmaus laughingly says.

"You all wouldn't be serving any of that today, now would you?" Momma inquisitively asks.

"No! They are serving lobster and I can't wait to 'throw down'!" Aunt Lucille challenges.

"Now, Mrs. Gloria, if you'd like to try some, I can have my wife Solange fix a little iguana stew for you."

"I'd like that very much," Momma says gratefully.

"Gloria, that's nasty. Why on earth would you come all the way down here to these islands to eat Godzilla?" Aunt Dot says with repugnance.

"God is doing a new thing in all of our lives. So, I'm leaving myself open to experience new adventures."

"You go, Momma! Let us know if it really tastes like chicken because I'm going to pass on the iguana adventure," I say with love.

"Ditto!" says Aunt Dot.

"I might give it a taste," Fitzroy says.

"How disgusting! Just make sure you brush your teeth before you kiss me," I scream.

"Oh, it's like that, huh?" Fitzroy teases me.

"You can kiss my hand but that's about it," I give him his options.

"How much longer before we get there? I'm starving!" Aunt Lucille says.

"Not much longer...there's some snacks and drinks to the left of the bar. Please help yourselves," Emmaus replies.

"Between that ecstasy pill Lucille gave me and all this talking about eating road kill, I think I've lost my appetite," Aunt Dot says miserably.

We continue along the deserted road, passing a few houses intermittently. Most of the homes are gated and situated on large plots, assuring privacy.

"I feel like I'm in the desert," Momma says.

"It's pretty dry out here, madam. We've been praying for God to send rain without the hurricane, for some time now," Emmaus says.

"Please don't let any hurricanes come while we're visiting or I might really have a heart attack," Aunt Dot begs.

"Well, madam, it is hurricane season so you never know when one might come this way. My poor village was hit this season very badly."

"What did you say the name of your island is?" Aunt Lucille asks.

"Granada...one of the loveliest islands in the Caribbean."

"He means next to Nevis!" Wally defends his native land.

"That's right!" Fitzroy adds.

"Granada speaks for itself. We have rolling mountains covered with fragrant spice trees and tropical flowers, stunning beaches...I believe you Nevis boys only have one good beach and that's Penny's Beach...and no industry. In

Granada, we supply most of the world with nutmeg, cloves, ginger, cinnamon, and cocoa. We also have cascading rivers, waterfalls, lush rainforests, and one of the most breathtakingly beautiful mountain lakes imaginable. You owe it to yourself to visit Granada," Emmaus says pompously.

"Just make sure you don't go when their volcano is spitting lava all over the place or you might arrive back home looking like a bar-b-cued spare rib," Wally humorously says.

"Oh my, I guess these beautiful islands come with their share of problems just like the United States," Aunt Lucille butts in.

"Emmaus, have any other guests arrived?" I ask.

"Oh yes, this is my third trip to pick our guests up...the first to arrive was Mr. Lever and he brought a friend. The second guest I picked up was Mr. Jay, his wife, and their little boy... the Mrs.' belly is so big, I thought she might give birth on the way to the house in the limousine."

"Why on earth would someone that close to delivery travel all the way out here to 'no-man's-land' so far away from their doctor?" Momma asks in amazement.

"If I know Barbara, she's not going to let Jay miss an opportunity to 'brown nose', especially if there's a chance to position himself for a raise," I say.

"Well, couldn't she send her husband and stay home close to the phone with her doctor's number on speed dial?" Fitzroy says like it's the most logical thing to do.

"Not on your life...she's the one who spoon-feeds Jay his lines," I say.

"I can't stand a man who doesn't have a backbone!" Aunt Lucille angrily says.

"I heard that!" Wally seconds.

"Has Billy come back from Anguilla?"

"No, Mr. Billy is going to stay a little while longer. He says he needs to work a few things out. Mr. Atkins sent Calvin down to Anguilla this morning to pick up the plane...don't worry none, Billy will be alright, he's in good hands with Mr. Harvey."

"What about the lobster?" Lucille loudly asks.

"Not to worry, Harvey put it on the commercial plane this morning...I picked it up when I got Mr. Lever from the airport."

"Good 'ting'!" Aunt Lucille says.

We turn off the main road onto a smoothly paved road that runs about a mile before we reach a secured gate. Emmaus punches in a code and the double gate opens. We continue another quarter of a mile before we reach the castle.

"It is beautiful!" "Wow!" "Ooh," "enchanting," "charming!" are words that are spoken by Momma, Aunt Lucille and me.

The castle looks like something out of a fairy tale book complete with a moat. Mr. Atkins and Mrs. Rosalinda come out to greet us as the limousine pulls up to the front door. Emmaus opens the limousine doors and we exit. Fitzroy takes my hand. Suddenly, I feel like I'm living out a scene from *The Batchelor* television show. Only difference in my mind is there better only be one rose inside that castle with my name on it. We step inside and the "Ooh, ah, and how beautiful," start all over again. I introduce the Atkins' to momma and the aunties. Everyone knows Fitzroy, of course, and to my surprise the Atkins know Wally. They've been to his club on several occasions when he's had well-known guest artists perform.

Momma presents Rosalinda with the small token of appreciation from her and the aunties for having them for dinner. Rosalinda gives each of the aunties a hug along with a humble thank you. Mr. Atkins leads us into the enormous family room where we find Jay, Bob Lever, a man I don't know and, of all people, Eric, Janna's ex-husband, having cocktails. Fitzroy is taken aback when he sees Eric.

"Faith, I think I should leave."

Eric looks just as uncomfortable when he sees Fitzroy.

Chloe and Nyla come running down a pair of grand stairways hollering my name. Before I know it, I'm being kissed and hugged by the girls, and Nyla won't let me loose.

"One second, honey," I say to Nyla. All I can think about is going outside and talking with Fitzroy. I, too, feel very uncomfortable."

"Girls, give Miss Faith a few minutes to catch her breath." Rosalinda begs.

"But we miss her!" Nyla says.

"Don't worry, she's not leaving for a while...why don't you girls help me show Faith's mother and aunties around the house?"

"Yeah! We get to give a tour!" Nyla says.

"Don't follow her, you might get lost...follow me," Chloe says in her big sister voice.

The aunties leave, following Rosalinda and the girls. Wally joins the men where cocktails are being served. Fitzroy and I stand at the door, planning our next move.

"I'll just ask Emmaus to give us a ride back to the Sea Plane...Momma and the aunties can come back later."

"No, Faith, you stay...you don't have a dog in this fight," Fitzroy says.

"Like hell I don't! That man killed my friend and left two little girls I happen to love very much without a mother!"

Fitzroy is shocked at my anger.

"I'm so sorry, Faith. I was so consumed with my job and the fact that I just arrested this man yesterday. And now he's standing a few feet from me out here in the middle of nowhere on Thanksgiving Day...please forgive me for being so insensitive."

I smile to let him know I understand his frustrations.

We continue standing not too far from the front door as if our feet are set in cement. I see Mr. Atkins speak to Eric who shakes his head but remains in the room drinking with the other men. Mr. Atkins walks over to join us.

"Fitzroy, may I have a word with you in my study?" Fitzroy doesn't answer and I feel so awkward but I don't say a word.

"I completely understand your apprehension.... Fitzroy, if you come with me into my study, I will be able to clear up any misunderstanding you may have about this situation."

"Please, because right now I'm feeling very angry and ready to swim back to St. Thomas." Fitzroy follows Mr. Atkins and I follow him. Mr. Atkins turns to face me.

"Faith, this is something I need to share with Fitzroy first."

"Oh," I say, very surprised.

"It's OK, baby, I'll join you in a few minutes," Fitzroy tells me as he kisses me on the lips.

Mr. Atkins and Fitzroy continue across the grand foyer until they reach his study, where they close the floor-to-ceiling double doors behind them. I stand in the three-story foyer looking like a lost puppy. I don't want to go into the family room where the men are drinking, so I decide to venture around the castle and find the little tour guides, Rosalinda, Momma and the aunties.

Chapter 18

I climbed the double stairway to the second floor expecting to find my family along with their tour guides, but no one was in sight. I decided to just look around hoping to run into them. The first room I wandered into was designed for a little princess. The four-poster canopy bed had beautiful lacy curtains that were draped back and tied to each of the posts, anchored with pink satin ribbons. Out of the turret window you could see a breathtaking view of the Caribbean Sea. A plush pillow seat made out of the same material as the bedspread was incorporated into the design of the window. Stuffed animals were positioned on the window seat looking out towards the sea. In a corner of the room stood a playhouse replica of the castle standing about five feet high. Next to the mini-castle was a standing wardrobe trunk, complete with princess clothes. A medieval mission-style table with two children's-size benches dominated the other corner of the room. On the table were a miniature sterling silver tea set and a place setting of tiny china. The wide floorboards were made of mahogany and were so well polished you could see your reflection as you walked around the room. There was a dresser in the room that matched the canopy bed. Attached to the dresser was an ornate mirror that looked like the one in the movie "Snow White." I was amazed at the huge walk-in closet, the size of a standard bedroom. The clothes hung on mahogany poles that were attached to a concealed metal carrousel like the ones you see in a dry cleaner's shop that move the clothes around.

Once back in the hall I ventured past an area that reminded me of a hotel lobby seating area. On the credenza was a pitcher of limeade and cookies. I wondered if it was there in case someone got lost and was hungry. I helped myself to a cookie and continued down the hall. The next room I wandered into was clearly their gym and dance studio. This room made Bally's look like a home gym. Every type of equipment you could think of was in this room including machines whose function I can't tell you. The walls were covered with mirrors so you could see yourself plié, relevé, or pump iron, or you could see whether your tutu was on straight. I spotted a passageway in the far corner of the gym that led to another room. Excited that I might find a masseuse on duty waiting to relieve me of these knots in my neck and shoulder, I walked briskly in that direction. "Wow!" is all I can say. Mr. Atkins and Sister Rosalinda got it going on in here! My next discovery was a room you may never want to leave. There was a swimming pool-size whirlpool, Jacuzzi, steam room, sauna and a red clay mud pit. Double glass doors led out to a sun deck, which was built on top of one of the bell towers of the castle. Lord, I just wanted to take off my clothes, lock the door and jump in! The whirlpool was so big there was enough room to throw an arthritis pool party.

Just as I'm about to walk out onto the deck, I hear a strange woman's voice with a heavy West Indian accent announce on the intercom, "Dinner will be served in the main dining room in fifteen minutes." I'll have to show Fitzroy this room...that is, if we're still staying for dinner. I can't believe Mr. Atkins would bring Eric here. What was he thinking? I close the door to the sun deck and notice a sign that reads "Elevator." I stand in front of the sign looking to my right and left for an elevator, but all I see is a beautiful door also made out of mahogany, like the floor in the child's bedroom. The door is handcrafted with elaborate carvings. I pull the handle to the door expecting to find a dressing room...instead it's an elevator. I decide to get in and take it to the first floor. This is the quietest elevator ride I've ever taken. I can barely feel it moving. I nearly freak out, thinking I'm stuck. Then the door opens not a second too soon. I'm on the first floor in a section of the castle that appears to be near Mr. Atkins' office.

One of the double doors is slightly ajar. I can hear Fitzroy and Mr. Atkins having a heated discussion.

"Sir, I'm just not going to do that. I'm an officer of the law and I took an oath."

"I'm not asking you to compromise your integrity...all I'm saying is just let the chips fall where they may!" Mr. Atkins pleads with Fitzroy.

"Look Mr. Atkins, I respect you and I understand your position with the child...but if she's the one who shot Janna and Junnis then we need to let the court decide what her fate will be...I'm sure she won't be prosecuted...look at the situation...from what you're saying Junnis repeatedly molested her, and was touching her little sister in inappropriate ways. Hell, any one of us would probably have shot him too."

"Fitzroy, the girl is a basket case already. How do you think she's going to feel if this story hits the newspapers? Every man, woman and child on these islands will be talking about it for the rest of her life...Let this case go to court as is. Eric is willing to stand trial because he knows his fingerprints were not on the gun. Everyone will believe it was Junnis who shot Janna and then killed himself."

"That is not going to fly, Mr. Atkins. Forensics knows the gun was only fired once. And the autopsy confirmed that the bullet went in through Janna and came out through Junnis. Mr. Atkins, we know either Janna jumped in front of Junnis or he pulled her in front of him to shield himself from the bullet."

I can't believe what I'm hearing. I suddenly become sick and start hyperventilating. Mr. Atkins and Fitzroy leave the study to find me sitting in a chair just around the corner from the elevator, struggling to breath.

"Faith, are you alright?" Fitzroy sits beside me.

"Faith, let me get some water for you," Mr. Atkins says.

He goes back into his study, returning with a glass of water with a slice of lime floating on the top. Again the woman's voice comes on the intercom.

"Please join us in the dining room in five minutes."

"You heard our conversation didn't you, Faith?" Mr. Atkins asks.

"Yes sir. I was lost and when I got off the elevator, I heard you and Fitzroy talking."

"I wasn't going to invite Eric here but the girls were so lonely for their father and he for them."

"If what you said is true then they should be together."

As I start to cry, Mr. Atkins asks Fitzroy to bring me into his study where they close the doors.

"Faith, we all loved Janna and this is a tragic thing that happened to her...but right now, I'm concerned about Chloe. Janna's in heaven with God and who knows where Junnis ended up...but this child is here, and there is not a day that goes by that she doesn't relive what happened...her nightmares are so bad, she has to take medication to sleep...Poor Nyla was getting sick with worry for her sister. She had to tell somebody what happened so they could help Chloe. Against her sister's threats, Nyla told Rosalinda the whole story."

"This is a hard one, Mr. Atkins, but my gut feelings say we need to tell the truth and everything will be alright," Fitzroy sadly says.

"Oh my God, what will happen to Chloe? We can't let her go to jail!"

"Calm down, Faith," Fitzroy says.

"Don't tell me to calm down!"

"Listen...we're not going to solve this today. Why don't we go and join the rest of the guests and try to salvage what's left of this Thanksgiving Day? We'll talk about it some more before you leave...OK?" Mr. Atkins implores. Fitzroy leads me out of the office. Mr. Atkins follows behind.

"You'd better let me show you where the dining room is or you might be walking around this house for hours trying to find it.

When we entered the beautiful dining room, Rosalinda was directing everyone to his or her assigned seat. Aunt Lucille and Wally were seated next to Bob Lever, and Eric was seated on the other side of Bob's friend. Aunt Dot was seated next to Brenda and Jay Steward. Fitzroy and I were seated near the head of the table next to Mr. Atkins, and Momma was seated at the far end of the enormous table next to Rosalinda. The children were seated at a kids' table nearby. A beautiful West Indian woman with flawless dark skin and pearly white teeth, who I assumed was Solange, Emmaus' wife, gave serving orders to five helpers who were busy making sure every command was followed to a T. Aunt Lucille smiled and waved to me from across the table. I could tell she was having a great time. I managed a smile and waved back.

Fitzroy and I both sat quietly through the first course, and then he finally spoke. He whispered softly in my ear.

"Let's try and make the best of this day. If not for us, let's do it for your family."
I was so mad at him. His rationale didn't make sense. Why didn't he feel the same way Mr. Atkins and I felt? I found it hard to talk to him, so I didn't answer. Momma, who was sitting at the far end of the table, leaned forward to get my attention. We made eye contact and I knew she was wondering if I was OK. I gave her the same fake smile that I gave Aunt Lucille, but she wasn't buying it. I decided to focus in another direction to avoid her intense look.

My eyes wandered over to the children's table where Chloe was staring at me. She had a look on her face that confirmed in my spirit that she knew I had found out what happened. I smiled and threw her a kiss. Her contorted face relaxed and she gave me the same smile I'd given to Aunt Lucille and Momma. I made a mental note to go somewhere quiet and talk to her after dinner. Mr. Atkins took his fork and tapped his water glass to get everyone's attention. Even the children stopped what they were doing and obediently listened.

"Rosalinda and I would like to thank each of you for coming to our home to share Thanksgiving dinner with us. It is our prayer that you are enjoying yourselves and if there is anything we can do to make your visit more comfortable, just let us know. I see some of you have already finished your first course, which is OK. However, I'd like to take this time to offer a prayer of thanks to our Lord. After I finish praying, I'd like to go around the table and have each of you say one thing you are thankful for.... Most gracious Father, we come before You with humble hearts and praises in our mouths...thank You for this time to come together and celebrate this Thanksgiving Day. I am truly thankful to you for giving me a wife who truly loves You and for blessing the work of my hands. Amen." Fitzroy speaks next.

"God, I thank You for the Atkins family opening their home and their hearts to all of us on this Thanksgiving Day." I speak next.

"Lord I thank You for this time that You have allowed me to spend with my mother and aunties...I thank You for bringing them here safely."

"I'm Jay Steward and Lord, I thank You for my job. Amen."

How dumb. Like the Lord doesn't know who he is. Surely he could have said something more intelligent than that. I wonder what Botox Barbie is going to say.

"Lord, I'm Brenda, Jay's wife, and I thank You for giving my husband a job that he truly loves."

Oh my God, 'Dumb and Dumber'. Aunt Dot is next.

"Lord, I thank You for delivering me from the power of fear that has been holding me hostage."

Wow, how profound. I'm touched by what Aunt Dot says. Eric speaks.

"God I'm truly thankful for a second chance to be a father to my children. I thank You for being a God of second chances."

I cut my eye over to the children's table and I see Nyla and Chloe smiling.

Well, it's going to be interesting to hear what Bob Lever has to say, with his mean-behind self! Forgive me Lord, I'm judging again. Bob speaks.

"Well, I'm Jewish so I'm not sure if I should say anything."

Now that was the stupidest thing I've heard yet. Momma speaks.

"Don't worry, our Lord and Savior Jesus was a Jew." Bob Lever continues.

"Well, this is hard. I'm not used to giving thanks...I guess you can say...I'm thankful for being here. Yes, that's what I'm thankful for."

Bob's friend talks next.

"Wow, I'm an atheist so I'm going to pass for real." Out of respect for the Atkins and not wanting to insult their guests no one says anything.

Then Rosalinda speaks.

"Lord, I thank You for your Word that is a lamp unto my feet and a light unto my path. I thank You for our guests who are here today and it is my prayer that those who don't have a personal relationship with You will seek Your face and learn that You are truly their strength and redeemer. Amen"

Aunt Lucille pauses to collect her thoughts before she speaks.

"Lord, I thank You for waking me up in my right mind this morning and I thank You for removing sadness and depression from my heart."

Wow, it sounds like Auntie is healing. Wally clears his throat.

"God, I am truly thankful to You for sending this lady sitting next to me to save me from the curse of death. I thank You for life and a chance to start over."

Aunt Lucille kisses Wally on the cheek. Next we hear from Momma.

"Father God, I am truly thankful for Your Word that says, 'You will never leave me nor forsake me.' I thank You for being with me during the dark times in my life when I wondered if I would ever find my way back to the light."

I know losing Daddy was deep for Momma.

Mr. Atkins speaks to the children.

"Kids, I want you to tell us what you are thankful for." Little Jay speaks.

"I'm thankful for all my toys." Everyone laughs because they think it's cute. Then Nyla speaks.

"I'm thankful for my daddy, godfather, godmommy and Miss Faith being in my life." Everyone says, "Aw!" Chloe is a little shy, but speaks.

"I'm thankful to God for forgiving me of my sins." Now that was the best one yet, I say to myself. It's apparent that every person in the room thinks so too, because everyone is clapping including Fitzroy.

Mr. Atkins summonses Emmaus and Solange over to where he is sitting.

"All of you have met Emmaus...and I'd like to introduce you to his lovely wife, Solange. Emmaus, would you and Solange please join us for dinner? Solange and Emmaus are as close as it gets to family for Rosalinda and me." Emmaus sits next to me and Solange sits closer to Momma and Rosalinda. Mr. Atkins continues.

"For those of you who are wondering where Billy is...well, he's in Anguilla working out a few issues of the heart. But as you can see, even though *he* didn't make it back, the lobsters did!"

We all laugh and continue eating until our bellies scream, "no more!"

After dinner Bob finds his way over to me. Fitzroy discovers that I'm suddenly a woman of few words and decides not to press me. He wanders over to where Eric is talking to Wally and Aunt Lucille. I see Eric and Fitzroy shake hands and embrace like brothers. Again, I'm puzzled and can't understand how Fitzroy can believe the best way to handle this situation is to turn Chloe in to the authorities.

"Hello Faith, you look stunning," Bob Lever says. I suddenly feel cheap and dirty.

"Thank you, Bob," I manage to say, hoping he will go away.

"So, Faith, are you enjoying your vacation?" Bob continues.

"Yes, it's been nice."

"We certainly do miss you at the office...it must be great being able to take a week off after only being employed with the company four months."

Lord, help me to keep my tongue!

"Actually Bob, it's not one week of vacation I'm taking, it's two."

"I see...do you think that's wise...I mean leaving a juvenile to run your department?"

God please help me, my patience is running thin. And I'm about to say something to this fool that I know won't be a sweet sound in Your ear.

Mr. Atkins joins us.

"I'm really glad you brought your family, Faith."

"Thank you for having us."

"So how long will we have the pleasure of their company? I'd like to take them out on our boat before they leave."

"Well, Momma and the aunties planned to stay two weeks but I might have to send them home early." Mr. Atkins is surprised.

"Why? Aren't they enjoying our beautiful islands?"

"Oh yes! It's just that I think Bob wants me back at work. He was just asking me if I thought it was a good idea to leave a *juvenile* running my department."

Bob turns a bright shade of red.

"Bob, are you talking about Linda Peters? Linda is a bright girl and very capable of handling things in Faith's absence. Didn't Faith give you a detailed copy of the duties Linda would perform while she was on vacation? I know I got a copy of it and it didn't sound like anything she and the production team couldn't handle. Would you like me to fax a copy of it over to you Bob?" Mr. Atkins says.

"No, no. I think Faith may have misunderstood me," Bob tries to cover his blunder.

"Bob, I'm only going to say this once...there are three people I truly value who work at our station. One of them has gone home to be with God. The second is Linda Peters and the third one is standing next to me."

"I clearly understand, sir. I didn't get to meet Janna but I've heard nothing but good things about her. And I agree that Linda and Faith are very valuable to our company."

I spot Jay Steward making his way over. I'm sure he thinks he's missing an opportunity to suck up.

I excuse myself to join Rosalinda, Momma and Aunt Dot who are laughing together like college buddies. Fitzroy and I lock eyes from across the room. I coldly turn away from his gaze.

"Faith, where were you? You missed the tour of the third floor!" Aunt Dot exclaims.

"I tried to catch up and ended up lost on the second floor," I reply.

"How did you like the gym?" Rosalinda asks smiling. "You have a gym?" Aunt Dot asks in awe.

"It's more like a health club," I say.

"With us being so far out here in the middle of nowhere, it was important to us to have a place where we could work out and relax."

"I'd love to check out that Olympic-size Jacuzzi," I say, almost salivating.

"Well, why don't we do just that?" Rosalinda says.

"We didn't bring any bathing suits," Momma says.

"As bad as my knees hurt, I'll go in naked!" Aunt Dot says.

"Oh no, you won't!" Momma chastises her.

"You don't have to do that, Dot," Rosalinda laughs.

"There are plenty of bathing suits upstairs...Let's see if any of the other women want to join us."

Solange declines saying she needs to supervise the workers. Brenda declines because she thinks the heat might send her into labor. And Lucille, excited, has only one concern. She wants to know if the bathing suits are one-piece or two.

Rosalinda takes us upstairs and shows us where the bathing suits, towels and robes are located. Momma and the aunties are in a daze. They can't believe their eyes. As Rosalinda is leaving us to change, she promises to join us shortly, after taking Brenda and all the kids down to the dungeon where there's a bowling alley and movie theater.

"A bowling alley and movie theater?" Aunt Lucille replies.

"I love movies. Especially old love stories, and Georgie is an avid bowler. I'm sure he's probably looking for someone to beat as we speak. There's a duckpin lane for the children, so they won't be in the way. I'll be right back." Rosalinda leaves.

"Girl friend, I'm selling my houses and I'm moving down here! Just let me be close to these people so whatever they have will rub off on me!" Aunt Lucille says as she slips into a sexy two-piece bathing suit.

After Momma, Aunt Dot and I change we spend the next ten minutes taking pictures before we get in the Jacuzzi.

"Lord, have mercy! This is just what the doctor ordered!" Aunt Dot hollers as she lowers her aching body into the water.

"Ooo wee...it's hot!" Momma whines.

"But it feels so good!" I say submerging my body up to my head under water.

"Lucille, aren't you coming in?" Momma asks.

"Yeah, soon as I find a swimming cap. My weave is allergic to water."

"Well how on earth did you go snorkeling at Trunk Bay without getting your hair wet?" My voice vibrating from the Jacuzzi jets sings out.

"Honey child, I had on three very expensive caps. The kind Olympic divers wear."

"Just get in, Lucille, you don't have to put your head under the water," Momma admonishes.

"Miss girl, I can work with the water part. It's the steam I'm worrying about wrecking this weave," Lucille barks.

"And you know she can't have that happen...what would Wally think if he didn't find every strand of her hair in place?" Aunt Dot says sarcastically.

"Please, Dot. I'm not worried about Wally. On the plane didn't you hear him say he would still like me, even without breasts? So I know he's not tripping about a little bit of fake hair. I just don't want to look at myself with a buzzard nest on top of my head!"

Rosalinda returns and gives Aunt Lucille two swimming caps.

"Did Mr. Atkins find anyone brave enough to challenge him to a game?" I ask.

"No, Georgie, Eric and Fitzroy are locked up in his office. Jay, Bob and Bob's friend, the atheist, are down in the dungeon bowling, and Brenda is keeping an eye on the children while they duckpin bowl."

"I never did get Bob's guest's name," I say, hoping Rosalinda might shed some light on who this guy is.

"Oh, I'm sorry, Georgie and I didn't introduce you to him. We just assumed you knew him, Faith. His name is Lander. He says he's from Trinidad and has been living in St. Thomas for two years now. It wasn't clear what type of work he does or what his relationship with Bob is." Rosalinda is putting her bathing suit on as she talks.

Lord, please don't let Aunt Lucille give her opinion. Too late, her mouth is opening.

"Humph... I think the man has a little 'sugar in his tank'," Aunt Lucille matter-of-factly says.

"Lucille you need to hush your mouth and repent!" Momma scolds, flabbergasted at her sister's comment.

"There she goes! Can't you just keep your opinion to yourself just this once!" Aunt Dot says.

Rosalinda, laughing, joins us in the Jacuzzi.

"Don't worry, Lucille; what you say in this room will stay in this room. Besides, I...well..."

"Spill it, girl!" Lucille prompts Rosalinda.

Momma gives her a stern look.

"Gloria, that look used to scare me when I was a child, but it ain't working today. Rosalinda said what we say in this room will stay in this room."

"That might be true but what I want to know is what is God going to say about your gossiping? You know He's in this room too." Momma informs all of us.

"Girl, you sure do know how to spoil a moment," Aunt Lucille blurts out.

"Gloria's right, it's bad manners to talk about our guest and it is gossiping," Rosalinda replies.

"Changing the subject, how come you all built such a large Jacuzzi when there's only two of you who live here?" Aunt Dot wants to know.

"Everything else in this castle is large, so why stop at the Jacuzzi?" I lovingly add my two cents.

"Georgie and I do a lot of fundraising for worthy causes. We not only use this castle as our residence but it serves as a vehicle to bless other people."

"I heard that, I'm being blessed right now!" Aunt Dot hollers as the whirlpool jets pulsate against her aching kneecaps.

"One of the organizations we support locally as well as internationally is the Arthritis Foundation. Once a year we hold a fundraiser, inviting donors as well as people afflicted by that debilitating disease to our home. We share this area of the castle with those who want to rejuvenate their tired bones. Occasionally this whirlpool is so crowded people have to wait to get in. In the spring, we host a charity performance for the St. Croix Ballet in the dance studio next door. You must come back in May. The benefit is usually the Saturday before Mother's Day."

"Include me in. I'm a big supporter of the arts," Aunt Lucille says.

"Great, leave me your email and snail mail address and our chairperson will make sure you receive an invitation...and if you like, you are more than welcome to stay here with us."

"Thank you, Rosalinda." Aunt Lucille is touched by Rosalinda's genuine hospitality.

"Well I'm going to get out, take a quick shower and then go into the sauna," I say.

"My body begs for more. This feels sooo good I can't get out just yet," Aunt Dot says.

"I'm going to try the red clay mud. I understand it pulls impurities out of your body," Momma says.

I leave Momma, Rosalinda and Lucille covering each other with red clay before they leave to go out onto the nearby deck to bask in the sun. Inside the steam room I hear relaxing music playing through a recessed speaker in the ceiling. I climb to the upper tier of the sauna, spread my bath towel on the tiled bench, and lie flat on my back, reflecting on the conversation between Fitzroy, Mr. Atkins and me, regarding Chloe's fate. As the steam fills the room, my mind is filled with deep questions about my relationship with Fitzroy. I begin to doubt myself, wondering just how well I really do know him. Today I saw a side of him I didn't like. He was stubborn and uncompromising. Lord, I thank you for conflict in a relationship. It certainly does have a way of illuminating our true character.

Chapter 19

I did get to talk to Chloe before it was time for us to go back to St. Thomas. I asked her if there was somewhere we could go and talk and she led me to her room. It turned out to be the princess room with the miniature playhouse castle. I shared with her how I had found out what happened so she wouldn't think someone had snitched on her. Surprisingly, she was glad the truth was out. I asked her what she thought should happen next.

"My daddy should not have to go to jail for what I did. God knows I didn't mean to kill my mother. She jumped in front of Junnis when I fired the shotgun... I did want Junnis dead though, so he would stop hurting Nyla and me...he just wouldn't go away and leave our mother alone." Chloe holds her head down.

I can tell this is hard for her.

"I remember when you used to take us to church and Nyla and I would cry at the altar asking God to help our family...I still talk to God and in my spirit I know what Junnis did was wrong...but I was wrong, too. The Bible says, 'Thou shall not kill'. Faith, I want to confess my sins to the judge and ask him to forgive me just like God has."

I cry like a baby. Chloe holds me in her arms and rocks me through my tears.

The plane ride back to St. Thomas was quiet. Momma, Aunt Dot and Aunt Lucille slept all the way. Our spa treatments left them so relaxed they couldn't keep their eyes open. Aunt Dot stayed true to her prayer asking God to deliver her from fear. She stepped boldly onto the plane, took a seat and went out like a light. I, on the other hand, had issues. Fitzroy and I were not speaking. I was restless, and as hard as I tried, I could not go to sleep. My brain would not shut down. I was still processing my conversation with Chloe and trying to make sense out of why she must be made to suffer at the hands of the system. Suppose the judge decided to put her away in a juvenile detention center until she turned eighteen? Suppose her lawyer forgot to stress the fact that Junnis molested her and Nyla? Suppose...suppose...suppose!

Fitzroy's van with the "On Official Business" sign was still parked in the loading zone of the Sea Plane office as we got off the plane. Wally helped Lucille and Aunt Dot into the back seat of the van. I climbed in behind them. Everyone was surprised. I didn't care. Momma sat up front with Fitzroy who shook his head in response to my behavior.
Thank God the ride home was quiet and short. I didn't feel like talking to anyone. I just wanted to go into my room, close the door and sort things out. Wally thanked us for inviting him and told us what a good time he had. He kissed Aunt Lucille goodnight before walking up the driveway toward his house. He asked her if she would like to go out to breakfast with him in the morning. She giddily accepted. Sleepy Aunt Dot waived to everyone and went directly into the house and straight to bed. Momma kissed Fitzroy on the cheek and whispered something in his ear. He nodded and got back into the van, never looking in my direction.

When I stepped into the kitchen from the parking lot, Momma was standing on the other side of the door waiting for me.

"I hope it's because you have your 'monthly' you're acting like an emotional fool!" Momma says in irritation.

I dismissively answer her, "I am not an emotional fool! And what makes you think I have my period?"

"It's either that or someone painted the back of your pants red." I look back and see my pants are saturated in blood. Momma walks down the hall, leaving her observation of me echoing in my ear. She closes her bedroom door firmly behind her as a sign that she doesn't want to talk any more. Momma is unmistakably disgusted with my behavior, and I can't blame her. Right now I can barely stand myself. The only redeeming factor is I'm grown; because there was a time she would have slapped the taste out of my mouth if I had spoken to her the way I just did.

Needless to say, I didn't sleep well at all. I tossed and turned all night, finally drifting off to sleep around five o'clock only to be awakened by the telephone ringing at six-thirty. It was Lisa, excited and talking non-stop. She was telling me what a wonderful Thanksgiving she had and how beautiful Trevor's daughter Kamari is. After I hollered her name three times into the phone, she finally stopped talking.

"Girl I don't want to hear about no half-breed child and your adulterous 'wanna be' husband at six-thirty in the morning!"

"Call me when you get off the rag!" Lisa says, and hangs up.

I instantly sit up in the bed, feeling guilty and without delay I call her back.

"I'm sorry," I pathetically say.

"You ought to be...so, what's got you so malicious this morning?" Lisa says with interest.

"I fell out with Fitzroy. Momma thinks I'm an emotional basket case, I've got the period from hell and I'm sure when I get up I'll be eaten alive by the piranhas."

"Girl, what piranhas? Are you still asleep?" Lisa yells.

"Aunt Dot and Aunt Lucille," I answered.

"I treated Fitzroy like he had the bubonic plague last night. No one except Momma said anything. Everybody else was too tired. So I know they're going let me have it when I get up.

Where are you?" I ask Lisa hoping she wasn't at the other woman's house.

"I'm at the old house. Trevor hasn't rented it yet.

"Oh," I say.

"I know you didn't care to hear about my Thanksgiving but is it safe for me to ask you how yours went, or will you bite my head off?"

"I said I was sorry...Momma and the aunties had so much fun you'd think they died and went to heaven," I report.

"And what about you 'miss thing'?"

"It was very different. Look girl, we need to get together and talk and I don't want to do it on the phone."

"You want to meet me at Trunk Bay?" Lisa asks.

"Didn't I just say I had the period from hell? I'd probably be a beacon to every shark in the area."

"Faith, meet me in Red Hook at the Cyber Café for lunch at noon. I'm finished talking to your crazy butt...Oh, look in my closet and bring me a couple of outfits and some underwear." Lisa hangs up.

I go back to sleep for a few more hours until the phone rings again. It's probably Fitzroy calling to apologize. I pick up the phone and it's Mr. Atkins.

"Hi Faith, it's George Atkins...How are you doing? I hope I didn't wake you."

"No, no, it's OK...I was just about to get up," I say, wondering why he's calling.

"Listen, I didn't get to talk with you yesterday and I know you were upset and rightfully so. Rosalinda and I know how much Nyla and Chloe mean to you. So I just wanted to share our strategy and let you know everything is going to be all right. I've hired two of the best lawyers from the states to represent our little girl. I put in a call to my good friend, Judge Drew; he's in charge of the Juvenile Division of the Virgin Islands Court. He's agreed to make sure it's an open and shut case," Mr. Atkins confidently says.

"How can you be so sure?" I ask.

"Judge Drew and his wife dine at our house often, Faith. His wife and Rosalinda chair several fundraisers together throughout the year. I gave his oldest son his first job. Beside that, I saved his marriage of 30 years and his career when word got out he was having an affair with an 18-year-old illegal alien from Santa Domingo who claimed she was pregnant. And most importantly, Judge Drew detests pedophiles. Junnis was raping these children. No one in his or her right mind would make Chloe pay twice for what happened."

"What about Fitzroy? What about the press?" I ask like a scared child.

"What do you mean 'what about Fitzroy'? It was he and I that came up with this plan. Faith, I don't know if you're aware of it, but Fitzroy is very well connected and well respected in the law enforcement community. And trust me, he earned that respect. Many officers in these islands will forget right from wrong especially if you wave a few dollars in their faces. But as you've learned first hand, if it's not right he won't have anything to do with it. And as far as the media is concerned, you've forgotten I own all the television stations, except one and both of the newspapers," Mr. Atkins says with authority.

"True," I reply.

"Faith, I'm not going to lie. This unfortunate incident is going to get out. We cannot totally control that. But what we can control is what part and how much of the story we want people to know. I'm having a meeting with our media specialist on Monday morning, and Monday afternoon, Eric, Fitzroy, Chloe, Rosalinda and I are going to meet with Judge Drew. That is the time when Chloe will confess to the murders. You are welcome to join us."

"Will they arrest her and put her in jail?" I say with panic in my voice.

"Absolutely not! If there is any bail that needs to be posted we will have our checkbook with us. Eric has agreed to let the girls remain in our custody and Rosalinda is going to homeschool them until this thing blows over. She says she's prepared to homeschool them through college if necessary."

We both laugh.

"Thank you so much for calling me Mr. Atkins," I say with comfort in my voice.

"Listen, on Monday, after this is over, everyone is coming by the house to celebrate. I already called Zipporah and asked her to fix us a big West Indian dinner. Zipporah knows how much I enjoy eating her salt fish, curried chicken, and stewed goat. I look forward to seeing you on Monday...Have a good day, Faith, and tell Fitzroy I said 'thank you'."

"I'll do that, sir." We hang up.

It's amazing what a hot shower can do for a body early in the morning. After I got dressed and gathered courage, I decided it was time for me to go into the kitchen and face the music, only to find Zipporah alone singing while soaking a big slab of salt fish in the sink.

"Morning, Miss Faith. I trust you sleep good? Can I get ya some bush tea?"

"Yes, thank you. Where's Momma and the aunties?" I ask.

"Dey gon to town. Your mudda want to get some postcards an tings." Zipporah pours a large cup of tea and sets the honey in front of me.

"Did Wally take them?

"No, me son. Miss Lucille and Mr. Wally leave well before your mudda and Dot."

"Well, how did they get to town?"

"Me ain't no how you sleep troo all de bat-tree charging 'n tings...Mr. Wally take yar kar up by he and jump start he kar 'cause it been sittin' so long. Den he bring yar kar back down an jump start de kar for de house cause no body drive it for so long. Your mudda and Dot dey gone in de kar for de house." Zipporah continues cooking.

"Oh my God, Momma might kill herself. She's never driven on the left before."

"Don't trouble your head none. Most people dat come down ear from de States say its easy cause de steering wheel on de left. De problem comes when dey go back home and forget to keep right." Zipporah lets out a big hearty laugh.

"Besides, it ain't your mudda driving. She didn't want no part of it me son. Your Aunt Dot, she de brave one!

I decided to be the better person and call Fitzroy. I would give him a chance to say he was sorry. My call went straight to voice mail. That's never happened. Maybe he's on another call. I'll try him later. Before I left to meet Lisa at the Cyber Café for lunch I call Fitzroy again and it immediately went to voice mail. Suppose he's blocked my calls, I think. I dismiss the thought, grab a few outfits out of Lisa's closets along with some personal items and head out to meet her at Red Hook.

Many islanders took the Friday after Thanksgiving off from work and were probably at home eating Thanksgiving leftovers because the café was deserted. It was exactly 12 o'clock noon and Lisa had not arrived yet. I wasn't sure if she was coming on the barge or by way of the local ferry boat. In any event, I decided to use the computer at the restaurant to check my e-mail. I had not been online since I left work last week. The first e-mail was from Linda Peters.

"Caught you...what you doing reading e-mail? You're supposed to be enjoying your vacation! See you on Saturday at the pig roast."

That Linda is a mess. I say to myself smiling.

My next e-mail is from Allison, the girl who's renting my townhouse in Los Angeles.

"Faith I pray all is well with you in the beautiful Virgin Islands. Faith, there is no easy way to say this so I'm just going to say it from my heart and pray that you will accept it and not hold any malice toward me. Your friend Daemon asked me to marry him, and I accepted. Daemon started coming to our church looking for you shortly after you moved to the Virgin Islands, and he found Jesus. A few months ago he got baptized. Since joining the church, he's become very active in our youth ministry, Wednesday night Bible Study, and Soup Kitchen Outreach Ministry. Last weekend, he took me home to Texas to meet his parents and they gave us their blessings. I pray that you will do the same. I spoke to our pastor and shared with him my concerns. I told him it was important that you know I did not mean to disrespect you in any way. He said I should write you and he was sure you would understand that 'love happens'."

I wondered if he talked to Mr. Atkins because that's the same thing *he* had said about Lisa and Billy. I continue to read Allison's e-mail.

"Daemon and I have set our wedding date for July 16th. If he had his way, we would get married tomorrow. I know it's because being celibate is a struggle for him. I, on the other hand, told him we need to work on clearing up his credit and paying off his debt so that we can enter into our new life together free to do ministry work and not have to worry about bills. Daemon has been so faithful with his finances ever since I presented him with a six-month debt-free budget. He knows I'm a virgin and he is willing to wait and do things God's way. I'm sorry if I'm giving you too much information. I just want you to know that we love each other and I pray that you will understand. PS... If you want me to move out of your townhouse, please let me know, and I will respect your wishes. Your Sister in Christ Jesus,
Allison Dean.

"Lord, have mercy!" I say out loud.

"Lord have mercy, what?" Lisa says standing behind my chair.

"Girl, Daemon is getting married to Allison," I say, still in shock.

"You mean that homey woman who rents your town-house...the spinster looking woman who runs the children's church...the one who dresses like the Virgin Mary?"

"That's the one." Lisa takes a seat next to me in front of another computer.

"Keep reading maybe Jason's going to be her flower girl!" We both laugh.

"Lisa, you know you're not right," I say, lovingly punching her in the arm.

"Did I tell you that fool had the nerve to e-mail me a couple of months ago asking if he could borrow a thousand dollars until he got his check? He wanted to know if we had Money Gram down here."

"Girl you know you didn't tell me that!" We laugh again.

"Did you send it to him?" This time she punches me in the arm and we laugh some more.

We order sandwiches and take a seat in the far corner of the café. I tell Lisa everything that happened yesterday at the Atkins and make her swear to secrecy. Lisa cries when I tell her about Chloe but finds some relief when I tell her Mr. Atkins and Fitzroy's plan. Lisa asks if it's a good time to tell me about her Thanksgiving. I apologize once again for the way I acted this morning.

"Faith, that little Kamari is a doll baby. She's drop-dead gorgeous and so loveable. I don't know how this woman can just walk away and leave this child!" Lisa says incredulously.

"I guess if she can't have the man, she doesn't want the child.

"What kind of woman is she?" I eagerly ask.

"You met her. She was the woman who served us drinks that night at Fred's!"

"That's why she was so rude to us. I wondered why she acted like her panties were in a bunch!" I say.

"Laurie Ann and I spent quite a bit of the day talking about Trevor while he and Kamari watched the parade until both of them fell asleep. She told me the only reason she planned to have a baby was in hopes of she and Trevor becoming closer...I told her that's the oldest trick in the book. It used to work in our parents' days but these days, it only makes a brother mad and turns him off. She agreed, saying Trevor only comes by to spend time with Kamari.

He told her he was moving on with his life and she should do the same. Faith, all this was before I moved to St. John."

"Wow, I guess she thought he might change his mind if she dangled the baby in front of him."

"Well, she finally realized it wasn't working and decided to pack up and go home. The sad part is her parents told her if she came home with her 'little brown mistake' they would disown her."

"How stupid! Pretty soon half the world is going to be mixed. Just like the slave children were. Only difference is now it's by choice," I say.

"Laurie Ann is leaving for Nantucket in two weeks. She wants to be home for Christmas. Trevor and I are going to enroll Kamari in the daycare at the Baptist church. They offer before–and-after school care."

"What's going to happen when you work a double shift?"

"Then it's on daddy to make sure she's picked up and fed. He can handle it," Lisa confidently says.

"So, I guess this means you're moving back to St. John?" I say sadly.

"It's just an 18 minute ferry ride, Faith," Lisa pleads.

"I guess I'll manage without my best friend especially knowing we're going to be neighbors soon." Lisa lowers her head. I continue,

"We *are* going to be neighbors soon, right?" I ask with trepidation in my voice, hoping she will soothe my fears.

"Faith, so much is happening so fast."

"And?" I say.

"You know Trevor had a problem with my purchasing the land and building the house in Bordeaux without including him."

"And?" I repeat.

"Faith, when we get married he doesn't want to live in the Bordeaux house." I can see it took a lot for Lisa to tell me this.

"Wow! That's deep. So, what are you going to do, sell it?"

"I haven't thought that far ahead yet. But I do have some good news," Lisa says, bubbling.

"Trevor is going to buy the Chocolate Hole house! The judge who owns it is not getting any better. He told Trevor he would give him the first choice of purchasing it since he was the builder. Faith, this makes so much sense...It's close to the daycare for Kamari. And it's closer to the ferryboat. That way my commute won't be so arduous," Lisa says matter-of-factly.

"Oh," is all I can say.

"Faith, don't worry, its going to be fine! And if it makes you feel any better, the Chocolate Hole house is going to be in both of our names."

"That does make me feel better, Lisa." I say sadly.

"Faith, I love him. Please be happy for me," Lisa begs.

"I am. Like you said, so much is happening so fast. Just give me a minute to catch up."

I take a bite of my sandwich and chase it down with a Brow Banana Soda.

"So when is the wedding, or are you going to wait until the new baby is old enough to be the ring bearer or flower girl?" I sarcastically ask.

"On Monday when we enroll Kamari at the Baptist daycare we're going to meet with the pastor. Trevor spoke to him on the phone and he said we have to counsel with him first before he will marry us."

"That makes sense," I say, still in shock.

"Faith we've set our date for December 31st," Lisa animatedly shares.

"Whoa, you guys are moving fast! Will that give you enough time to plan a wedding?"

"Don't worry. *You* and I will have enough time to plan the wedding."

"Oh, it's like that!" I say.

"Yeah. Now this is the plan. I want us to have our ceremony at the Baptist Church and have the reception at Ellington's. The only problem is we're getting married on New Year's Eve and they generally host a big New Year's Eve celebration that night for the public."

"That sounds like a big problem. Why don't you get married the week after New Years Eve?" I say.

"No, Trevor wants us to get married on a day when the whole world will be celebrating."

I don't say what I want to say because it might sound crass.

"OK then, why don't we purchase a block of tickets to the New Year's Eve celebration at Ellington's. That way you will have the people you want celebrating your wedding as well as people from the rest of the world." Lisa kisses me on the cheek.

"Faith, you are a genius. I'm going to call Ellington's today and see how many tickets are left and buy them all! Oh, Faith, there's an immense fireworks show at midnight on the water. I hear it's second to none and we will have a bird's eye view of it from Ellington's. It's going to be spectacular. Our guests will think it was staged just for us!" I get excited for Lisa.

"Girl, I'm so happy for you." We embrace.

I tell her about Momma, Aunt Dot and Aunt Lucille venturing out without me today and I invite her to Linda Peters' pig roast tomorrow. She accepts and says she's going to bring Kamari. Laurie Ann wants her to spend as much time as possible with the child so the transition will be smooth. However, Trevor won't be able to come. He has to work this Saturday. We chat a little more and I find out that Lisa's car is in the parking lot for the barge. She walked over and plans to take her car over to St. John. We leave the café and I drop her across the street to catch the barge.

There are a lot of cars coming off the barge. Lisa and I talk a little more before she gets into her car and lines up to drive it onto the boat. As I'm leaving the parking lot to head home, happy for Lisa and Trevor I see Fitzroy's van come off the barge with Lucinda in the passenger seat and each of the twins' heads sticking out of the window. I think I'm having a heart attack. Fitzroy turns in my direction and notices my car. He attempts to get out of the van and come towards me. I take off almost running over him and a few other people. I hear him calling my name. I don't stop. Tears are running down my cheek, blurring my vision. I use the back of my hands to wipe my face. The tears keep coming. My jeep speeds past Sapphire Beach Hotel and down the steep hill. I hit a winding curve just before Smith Bay. The jeep veers off the road a little. I continue speeding up the hill and pray no buses or trucks are coming as I make the sharp turn onto Mahogany Run. I suddenly hear sirens blaring coming up the Smith Bay hill behind me. Nervous, I pull over. My heart is pounding and I'm still crying. Just when I didn't think things could get any worse, I see there are three police cars behind me with lights flashing. I look in my rearview mirror past the three cars and see Fitzroy's "official" van. I can't find any tissue in the car. Not even one from the fast food joint. My mascara has run down my face and my rubbing it only makes it smear all the worse. It looked like I had two black eyes. I held my head down when the first officer approached my jeep.

"You're moving kind of fast I'd say, miss." I hear Fitzroy's voice next.

"Thanks, fellows!"

Suddenly all the police cars pull off. Fitzroy opens the door and climbs into the passenger seat. He sees my face and takes a handkerchief from his pocket and hands it to me. I look in my rearview mirror to see if Lucinda and the boys are waiting for him. Fitzroy catches on.

"They're not there, Faith. I was trying to stop you to tell you I was only giving them a ride on the barge because they missed the ferry. Lucinda was only going as far as Red Hook to the chiropractor. I'm sorry if I hurt you. It wasn't what it looked like."

I really start to cry. Fitzroy rocks me in his arms. Suddenly horns are blowing. A public bus going to Anna's Retreat is trying to turn the narrow corner at the top of Smith Bay and a concrete truck is trying to turn the corner in the opposite direction to go down the hill. Traffic from Tutu is backed up because of the two commercial vehicles.

"Darling, I'll follow you home before we both get arrested for tying up traffic."

I smile, as he gets out of my car and back into his. We both head towards Skyline Drive.

Chapter 20

I thanked God no one was home when I got back to the house. Fitzroy pulled into the driveway behind me. I raced inside ahead of him, leaving the door open. I went directly to the bathroom to wash my face and compose myself. I'd still been crying all the way home. What a fool I've been. Momma said I'd been acting like an emotional basket case, and she was right. Maybe it was because I had my period. Or it could be because my life was changing so fast?

Recounting the litany is enough to make me dizzy. Barely having time to adjust to the fact that my daddy went home to be with the Lord. My face being on the front cover of a newspaper with a man professing he loves me. Working crazy hours in a job I never dreamed I'd be doing in a million years. Dotting all my 'i's and crossing all my 't's to make sure I don't disappoint Mr. Atkins, my family, God or myself; not necessarily in that order. Losing a friend to a violent killing, just a few feet from where I live. Finding out it was my friend's daughter whom I love very much, that did it. Exacerbating my craziness even further, my best friend tells me she's pregnant by someone *other* than the person I think is the best thing that's ever happened to her. She plans to marry her baby's daddy in four weeks and adopt his two-year-old daughter by a white woman, who, by the way, is leaving town and wants *her* to mother the child. In the same breath my friend tells me we won't be neighbors once the houses we are having built next door to each other are finished because her future husband doesn't want to live there. He has a problem with the fact that he didn't build it, so he doesn't feel comfortable. Oh, I can't forget Lucinda, the crazy jealous woman stealing my car and leaving me a threatening note. I guess the only blessing in that situation is finding out that Fitzroy is not her twins' father. Lord, have mercy! It's no wonder I'm a basket case!

"Faith, are you alright?" Fitzroy is knocking on the bathroom door.

"Yes, I'll be right out," I say, trying to sound normal.

"OK, I'm going to get something to drink out of the refrigerator...would you like something?"

"I'll have a bottle of spring water," I holler to him. After freshening my makeup I enter the kitchen where Fitzroy is sitting at the island drinking a glass of maube that Zipporah made from scratch.

"Let's go out on the veranda and talk." Fitzroy grabs his drink and I follow.

I stretch out on one of chaises and he sits at the foot of it, looking directly into my eyes. His stare is penetrating straight to my heart.

"Faith, I unequivocally love you. You know that, don't you?"

"I do," I say.

"Good. That's what I need you to know about me, and to never forget; I'm not a player. I leave that to all the hustlers, pimps and school children. I'm a very serious man especially when it comes to my woman and my work."

I nod my head.

"Now, I'm not sure what was going on with you yesterday. I know you were shocked and upset about finding out about Chloe. I was surprised myself. But what I need you to understand is that as long as we are together, and I pray that will be a long time, there are going to be situations that will arise in my line of business that will shock both of us.

Police work is not a pleasant profession all the time. And as my lady and, hopefully, wife soon...." I smile and he smiles. "I need to know that you have my back."

I cut him off, "Of course I do."

"Wait Faith, let me finish. Having my back means not only when you agree with my decisions but also when you don't.

Again I cut him off. "So you're saying I have to agree with everything you do and say... That's crazy and chauvinistic!"

"Hold your horses. I'm not saying I want you to be a puppet. I wouldn't love you if you were. What I'm saying is if I'm taking care of police business and you disagree with my tactic there is a way to say so and what you did yesterday was not the way."

"You were talking about turning Chloe in for murder, Fitzroy," I plead my case.

"Calm down, darling, and hear what I'm saying. I know how much you love Chloe. None of us wants to see any more suffering come to that child. The point I'm trying to make is that you didn't trust me to handle the situation. And it's times like those that I need you to agree to disagree with me, but at the same time have enough confidence in me to know I will do my best to be fair and just. Sure, it would have been easy to let Eric stand trial knowing there wasn't any strong evidence against him. But how could we live with ourselves knowing that all of us were holding a lie in our hearts. Faith, when the day is over, the sun has set and I climb into my bed, I thank God for keeping me safe another day. Blessings and praises should not come out of the same mouth as lies."

I think about what he's saying and I reflect on my conversation with Mr. Atkins this morning. It's suddenly becoming clear to me why everyone respects Fitzroy, even when they don't like his choices. I think about the waitress Sasha, Eric's sister, who was mad at Fitzroy for arresting her brother. Even with her bad attitude when Fitzroy told her to leave, she left without any back talk. And now only a few days later Fitzroy along with Mr. Atkins has come up with a plan not only to exonerate her brother but also to pardon her niece for her crime. This man not only talks the talk but he walks it.

"Thank you for being a light in a dark world," I say and kiss him on the lips.

I so badly want to make love to this man. Well, not today with my little issue. Just kidding, Lord. I'm holding to the promise I made with You, because I know the rewards will be greater than what I already see.

"Yoo-hoo! Is anybody home?" I hear Aunt Lucille call out.

"We're on the veranda Aunt Lucille."

Aunt Lucille looks stunning as ever in her pink and white sundress with matching sun hat and sandals. She joins us on the veranda.

"Now I know you're a good man Fitzroy because I would have dropped Faith like a hot potato the way she acted yesterday."

"Aunt Lucille!" I can't believe she said that.

"Girl, don't 'Aunt Lucille' me. Because I'm going to tell you what nobody else will tell you...You acted like a spoiled brat and if you keep that foolishness up, somebody's going to move in and snatch that man up from your ugly-acting behind."

Now, I'm wondering if Aunt Lucille's been drinking. Fitzroy once again saves the day.

"Don't worry, Lucille, Faith has repented and I've accepted her apology."

"Hmm. I hope you made her beg."

"That's it!" I say to myself.

"Aunt Lucille can I see you in the house for a second?"

"Why, you want to talk about Fitzroy behind his back?"

Fitzroy thinks the whole situation is hilarious. I leave him on the veranda laughing and sipping his maube.

"No Auntie, I want to tell you something about Lisa," I lie.

Aunt Lucille looks very interested and heads towards the door.

"Oh hell, you want to gossip. Why didn't you say so?"

I follow her inside. She tries to sit at the kitchen counter but has trouble climbing up on the high chair. I suggest we go to her room where it's comfortable. I follow her down the hall to the bedroom. Thank God she doesn't have to pass a sobriety test because right now I don't think she could see a straight line, let alone walk one. Aunt Lucille falls out across the bed. She has one leg in the air. Reaching up she tries to unbuckle her sandal.

"Faith, can you help your poor old aunt out of these sandals?"

"Sure. So, how was your date with Wally?" I pry.

"Wally? Wally who?" I can smell alcohol on her breath.

"Aunt Lucille...I'm talking about Wally who lives next door. The man who took you to brunch."

"Oh! Girl, I know who you're talking about. He's fine. I sent him to the store to buy some groceries. We're having a dinner party tonight. Faith, can you unzip my sundress and put my hat up? I'm going to take a nap. I think I had too many mimosas."

I help Aunt Lucille out of her sundress. Before I can finish hanging it up, she falls asleep wearing her bra and panties. I cover her up with a sheet, close the bedroom door and join Fitzroy out on the veranda.

Fitzroy is lounging on the chaise. I sit in between his legs and rest my head on his chest.

"I hope you weren't listening to a word Aunt Lucille said," I tease him.

"*Every* word," he teases me back. It feels so nice just being in one another's company. We sit quietly enjoying the view of the harbor and the gentle trade wind breeze that relaxes our tired bodies to sleep.

Aunt Dot and Momma return home. They find Aunt Lucille asleep in her room and Fitzroy and me asleep on the veranda. Wally who enters the driveway and calls out for Aunt Lucille awakens us.

"Lucille, I'm back with the groceries." Aunt Dot runs to the kitchen door trying to silence him. She's too late. We both wake up from a deep peaceful sleep and join everyone in the kitchen. Momma and Aunt Dot greet Fitzroy and cut their eyes at me. I just smile, knowing it's a new day and I've been redeemed. I hug Wally.

"So I hear you're having a dinner party tonight," I say. Momma cuts in.

"A dinner party? Where?"

"Lucille and I are going to cook for all of you. I used to cook every night at my supper club that I let my son run since I lost my wife. I realized how much I missed cooking. Lucille suggested we have a dinner party. So, dinner is at my place at six o'clock," Wally proudly says.

"I hope you're not looking for Lucille to help you cook because she's out like a light. I think she had a few too many mimosas at brunch," I say.

"A few might be an understatement," Fitzroy says.

"Wally, you got my sister drunk!" Aunt Dot says in disbelief. Wally sheepishly replies.

"Guilty as charged. And for your information, we had a wonderful time!" Wally turns to leave and continues, "Don't forget, six o'clock is dinner. And by the way, if that sweet sister of yours wakes up anytime soon, please tell her 'Prince Charming' is waiting for her." Wally exits and we all laugh until our sides hurt.

Momma and Aunt Dot tell us about their day's adventure. Aunt Dot boasts of being a Virgin Islands driver now. She brags about taking on the hills and curves with only one hand on the steering wheel. Momma gives her version.

"Make sure you tell them how you were on the wrong side of the road when we left Cost-U-Less," Momma teases her sister.

"Honey, I was just having a 'senior moment'. I got this driving on the left down to a T," Aunt Dot brags again.

"Fitzroy and Faith, Dot made me get out of the car and take a picture of her driving on the left side of the road," Momma said. "She wouldn't just settle for a picture behind the wheel. She made me walk a block up and take the picture of her in traffic so everybody she shows the picture to can see she's driving on the left." We all laugh.

"Don't laugh. When I scrapbook that picture it's going to look like a postcard."

"Momma how in the world did you all find Cost-u-Less? That store is off the beaten path."

"When Dot and I went into Pueblo we thought we would have a heart attack when we saw the price for food. I simply went to the manager's booth and met a rude woman who sucked her teeth when I asked her if they had a Costco on this island. I told her when she finished clearing the food out of her teeth I would appreciate an answer. I'm not sure if that helped because I didn't understand a darn thing she said. So I asked her to write the directions down. She continued to suck her teeth while she wrote the directions. Dot asked her what her name was so we could pray for her nasty attitude tonight."

I can't believe my mother and aunt. I shake my head.

"That must have been Mora. She's the day manager," Fitzroy replies,

"I told you, Gloria, that's what she said her name was. You thought she said Dora. You're going to have us praying for the wrong person."

"If we called her 'Eviline', God would know who we were talking about!" Momma replies.

"You ladies are too much. And as much as I'm enjoying your company, I'm going to have to check on a few things at the station. I'll be back in time for Wally's dinner party," Fitzroy says.

We kiss; he says good-bye to Momma and Aunt Dot and leaves.

"You're blessed, Faith, and I hope you know it," Aunt Dot says.

"We're both blessed," I reply.

"Amen!" Momma says.

We spend the next couple of hours talking about Lisa. I fill them in on her wedding plans and tell them about Kamari. Momma and Aunt Dot are just as surprised as I was when I tell them about Lisa not moving into the house she's having built because Trevor doesn't want to live there.

"Well, I think I would do the same thing...I respect that," Momma says.

"Momma, Daddy wouldn't trip over something as stupid as that," I say.

"The Rev has been known to trip over stupid stuff, child," Aunt Dot says. Momma cuts her eye at Aunt Dot.

"I can talk about my late husband without your help," Momma jokingly says.

"Honey child, you might leave something out. Tell Faith about the time he flipped out when Lucille talked you into getting your hair weaved."

Momma and Aunt Dot both laugh.

"What? Tell me," I beg.

"Well, your daddy loathed fake hair," Momma says.

"If you knew that then why did you get your hair weaved?" I ask.

"That's the point, I didn't know it. Reverend was always telling me how nice this sister's hair looked and how nice Lucille's hair looked. So one day I told Lucille I wanted her beautician to do my hair. It was our third anniversary and I was going to surprise him with long hair. Well, my dear, that turned out to be the worst anniversary we ever had," Momma says reflecting and smiling.

"What happened, did you get a bad weave?" I ask.

"Tell the child the whole story, Gloria," Aunt Dot urges Momma on.

"Dot, let me tell this story please! Anyway, your daddy had a meeting at the church that evening with the trustees. He told me he would be home no later than eight o'clock. I cooked all his favorites and mine."

"You cooked on your anniversary! Why didn't Daddy take you out to a nice restaurant?" I exclaim.

"Because Dot's kids had the chicken pox and Lucille had a date herself. So we didn't have a babysitter. Are you going to let me finish this story?"

"I'm sorry, Momma."

"Hold all questions until the end. Now where was I? Oh yes, I fixed all this food, knocked you out with some chamomile tea, put on a sexy nightgown Lucille brought me for a gift and lit some candles. Then I positioned myself in a sexy pose on the couch near the door. When he walked in I wanted him to think I was Josephine Baker."

"And?" I say.

"The man called her 'Jezebel' and walked straight to the bedroom putting the candles out along the way!" Aunt Dot says.

"Now why did you think you needed to tell the ending to my story?" Momma asks.

"Because you were taking too long to get to the good part!" Aunt Dot says.

"I can't believe Daddy would say or do something like that. I'm stunned."

"All men are born with a stupid side to them," Aunt Dot says.

"Faith, your father was not stupid. He just wasn't in his right mind *that* night. We finally talked about it and we were able to settle our differences."

"Gloria, Faith is grown. You don't have to sugarcoat the story."

"Since you seem to know more than I do about it then why don't you tell it?" Momma retorts.

"The short and sweet of it is this: Your father thought all those women he was complimenting were sporting their own hair. He even thought your Aunt Lucille's hair was hers. 'The Rev.' didn't have a clue those women wore fake hair until my bald headed sister, your mother, came home with tresses," Aunt Dot exclaims.

"So, did you take the hair out, Momma?" I eagerly ask.

"I did nothing of the sort," Momma proudly says. Aunt Dot butts in.

"It took your daddy five days to come to his senses. I remember it distinctly, like it was yesterday. Your mother was so mad she came and stayed at my house. Remember, you said you didn't care if Faith caught the chicken pox. Better sooner than later anyway. And as fate would have it, Faith, you caught the chickenpox from Debbie. When it was getting close to Sunday morning rolling around, Rev. finally came and got you all. He was willing to do whatever it took to get his First Lady into her position on the front row at Solid Rock Baptist before he had to answer questions his congregants were sure to ask if that seat was vacant," Aunt Dot recounts the story.

"Oh, is that how you remember it?" Momma sarcastically says.

"That's how it was!" We all laugh.

"Momma did you take the weave out after daddy came and got us?" I ask.

"Of course not. I kept it in until the top track got so loose it slipped down and matted with the bottom track." Laughter brings tears to my eyes.

"Faith, I loved your daddy but I was not going to allow him to talk to me any old kind of way. And most of all, I had to let him know I was a woman of many faces. And if I wanted my hair short one day and long the next day the best thing he could do was to tell me how nice I look. And if he didn't like the way I looked then he should keep his mouth shut."

"You go, Momma!" I say.

"Why are you all in here making all this noise?" Aunt Lucille enters the kitchen holding her head. "Can somebody get me some Motrin please? I have a headache bigger than this room."

"Good for your drunk butt," Aunt Dot playfully says.

"Momma and Aunt Dot were just telling me the story about Momma getting her hair weaved and Daddy going off," I inform her.

"Turning your mother on to my beautician was the worst thing I could have ever done!" Aunt Lucille pops four pills in her mouth.

"Why is that?" I ask.

"After a month, your mother's head looked like a buzzard's nest. I offered to pay to have her get it done or take it out. She refused. I think she was mad at your daddy or something. I finally told her if she didn't take that thing out I was going to call animal rescue on her." Momma chases Lucille around the kitchen to hit her.

"You need to stop lying!" Momma hollers.

"Gloria, you were giving us 'thread heads' a bad reputation."

"Lucille, 'Prince Charming' stopped by to let you know he got the groceries. I hear we're invited to dinner tonight at six o'clock," Aunt Dot says teasing.

"Great. That man has been talking so much about back in the day when he used to cook at his supper club; the one he's letting his son run. I asked him if he missed cooking at the club then why doesn't he get off this mountain and go back to work?"

"What did he say?" Momma asks.

"He said there's a different crowd that comes into the supper club now. Mostly young people who like to listen to rap and hip-hop music and drink beer. Those kids eat burgers and fries, not Seafood Mornay, Chicken Cordon Bleu or Steak Tartar. He says his son makes him feel out of place when he comes to the club, always rushing him out and telling him he's got things under control."

"Well, does he have things under control?" I ask.

"You know it's hard to tell people about their children, especially when the friendship is so new. If you want my opinion, I think his son is up to no good and robbing his daddy blind."

"Lucille you've been on this island less than a week and already you're analyzing this man's life," Aunt Dot scolds.

"That may be true but I can recognize foolishness. I don't care if it's in Atlanta or St. Thomas. Foolishness is the same everywhere. I'm willing to bet you that child is running a second business out of that club," Aunt Lucille conjectures.

"So what, you're clairvoyant now?" Aunt Dot interjects.

"It all adds up. Wally was going through a stack of mail when I was up there the other night. He opened a few bills and discovered the taxes haven't been paid on the club. And the liquor license expired last month. He said those are things he told his son months ago would come due and he needed to make sure they were taken care of."

"Wow," I say.

"Well, Lucille, you're on vacation so don't start acting like Mother Teresa. Let these people work out their problems," Aunt Dot says like a mother protecting her child from danger.

"Dot, don't start! Wally's a great guy and if there is anything I can do to help him, I'm going to do it. I just don't want to overstep my boundaries."

"And when have you ever worried about overstepping any boundaries?" Momma asks.

"You're right. I'm going to straight up tell him: your son's a loser and he's pimping you...how does that sound?"

"Sounds good to me," I say.

"Try and use a little more finesse," Momma says.

"Mind your own business!" Aunt Dot says.

"Thanks for the advice," Aunt Lucille says and exits through the door to meet with 'Prince Charming'.

Chapter 21

Fitzroy called and said he was running late. He said we should start the dinner party without him. Something had come up at work that he needed to investigate. He promised he would join us soon. I said a quick prayer that God would keep him safe from hurt, harm or danger, and surround Fitzroy with His angels of mercy, before we left the house to walk up the driveway to Wally's for dinner. Momma saw concern in my face.

"He'll be fine," she said.

I smiled and felt comforted. Lucille greeted us at the door as if it was her house. She was wearing a colorful caftan that matched Wally's furniture. That had to be a coincidence. Then, maybe not, knowing my auntie, the fashion queen.

Wally and Lucille had set a table fit for royalty complete with china, sterling silver and crystal goblets. Wally came out of the kitchen carrying a tray of hors d'oeuvres.

"Welcome to my humble home," he said, with a heartwarming smile.

We each took a napkin and helped ourselves to some of the exquisite appetizers; they were delicious. Lucille followed with a tray of sparkling champagne. A few of the glasses had beaded charms around the stem of the glass.

"For you straight folks, the glasses with the beaded charms are non-alcoholic." Momma picked up one of those glasses.

To my surprise, Aunt Dot grabbed the alcoholic beverage. Momma was surprised.

"Dot, Lucille said the glasses with the beaded charms on them are non-alcoholic. You picked up the wrong one." Aunt Dot rolls her eyes at Momma.

"No I didn't," she says and then walks off to Wally's gigantic picture window to enjoy the fantastic view.

"Darling why don't you put on some music?" I heard Aunt Lucille say. Wally sets his tray down and crosses over to the entertainment center; it is second to none. He has a plethora of CDs that are stored alphabetically in an electronic CD holder.

"Now I have to warn you, ladies. I'm old school when it comes to my music."

"I didn't know there was any other kind of school," Momma says laughing.

"What you got over there?" Aunt Dot says while walking over to look. Lucille hollers from the kitchen.

"The man has a complete record store inside that fancy entertainment center."

"You have any Motown?" Aunt Dot asks.

"Does a chicken lay eggs?" Wally playfully says.

"Well *'Let's Get It On',* as Marvin Gaye would say," Aunt Dot shouts.

Wally pushes a button and types in the title and out pops Marvin Gaye's CD. Wally places it in the disc player.

"Now Faith, if we get a little too old school for you, let me know. I've got a little bit of young stuff somewhere around here," Wally jokingly says.

"Hey, I can hang. I listen to the 'Oldies but Goodies' station all the time. That's real music. Artists back then were actually singing about real issues. True love between a man and a woman. You know, stuff that made sense. Nobody was hollering at you, calling you or your momma nasty names," I say. We all toast to that.

"That is the truth. I feel violated every time I listen to music on the radio. Some of these songwriters and singers need to be arrested for the filth that comes out of their mouths!" Momma says in disgust.

"Wally, what's a boy from Nevis doing listening to our Yankee music?" Aunt Dot asks.

"Good music finds its way to the most remote corners of the world. When I was a teenager, I used to spin records at the only club in Nevis at that time, called Dick's Bar. People came from all over to dance. People called me 'The Mighty Spinner'." Lucille comes out of the kitchen.

"Say what?!" We all laugh.

"'The Mighty Spinner'...Nobody on Nevis could spin records better then me," Wally brags.

"Well get to spinnin', 'Mr. Mighty'!" Aunt Lucille teases Wally.

All of us dance to the beat and try to out-sing Marvin Gaye as his passionate voice wails "Let's Get It On" from Wally's surround-sound speakers. There is a knock at the door and Fitzroy enters.

"About time, man. My lobster bisque is getting cold," Wally teases.

"Better late than never," Fitzroy retorts.

"I second that!" I say as we embrace.

Aunt Lucille presents us with hot hand towels on a silver tray.

"I'm impressed." Fitzroy jokingly says.

"I can tell you don't get out much," Aunt Lucille comes back at him.

The song ends and Wally puts on some soft jazz to dine by.

"Please, join us in the dining room. There's no reserved seating so sit wherever you'd like."

He really sounds like we're at a supper club.

"I'll be starting you off tonight with our lobster bisque. It's one of my favorites."

Waitress Lucille helps Wally serve.

"This is good!" Aunt Dot says.

"It certainly is. So creamy and chunks of succulent lobster," Momma piggybacks.

"Well, I realized how fond of lobster Lucille is so I though I'd make something special for her." Lucille smiles.

"That's so thoughtful of you, Wally.

"My pleasure, pudding," Wally responds.

"Oh please don't make me lose my lobster bisque. You two are mighty lovey-dovey!" Aunt Dot says alluding to the possibility that something more than cooking together might be going on.

"Don't hate the player, Miss Fossil Butt!"
Even Momma laughs.

"May I continue...our entrée this evening will be a selection of surf and turf. I've prepared a pepper petite filet chevré cooked medium-well in brandy and peppered cream sauce topped with grilled tomatoes and mushrooms served on a bed of jasmine rice. Complementing the chevré will be a grilled halibut cooked in white wine and capers. To cleanse your palate after you've finished the chevré and halibut, I will present you with a serving of watercress salad topped with cranberries and pine nuts."

Wow, Wally, it sounds so scrumptious and elegant." I'm fascinated by his presentation.

"I'm sure your taste buds will agree," Wally responds.

"Sounds like we might get drunk from the brandy and white wine," Aunt Dot says. Lucille gives Aunt Dot a look that says, 'shut up!'

"I can't wait to try it, Wally," Aunt Dot utters, sounding more appreciative.
Wally and Lucille serve us our entrées on beautiful china. The plate looks as gorgeous as the food.

"Wally, you've outdone yourself," Momma says as she puts a piece of tender chevré in her mouth.

"I've died and gone to heaven," Fitzroy says as he slowly chews the halibut while making a moaning sound of appreciation."

"Gloria this chevré sure does taste good, but do you have any idea what we're eating?" Aunt Dot whispers to Momma with concern.

"Just enjoy it, Dot," Momma cuts her short so she can continue to enjoy her mouth-watering meal.

"One more thing, Gloria. What if it's iguana?" Aunt Dot says fearfully.

"If it's iguana then it sure does taste good. Now leave me alone so I can enjoy my food," Momma begs.

"Wally you are doing the people of the Virgin Islands a disservice by not serving them this great food!" I say.

"It's not only the people in the Virgin Islands being neglected. You need to pack up and come to Atlanta and open up a supper club," Momma says.

"Sounds good to me," Lucille seconds it.

"I just might do that if I can't talk this beautiful woman into moving down here," Wally says surprising all of us including Aunt Lucille.

"Well, we'll just have to see about that," Aunt Lucille says as she and Wally join us at the table after serving each of us.

We all are soon official members of the clean plate club. There wasn't a morsel to be found on any of our plates. And just when we thought it couldn't get any better, Wally places some homemade Tiramisu in front of us. Lucille follows behind him with café latte.

"Wally I've never heard of chevré before. What cut of steak is it?" I ask.

Fitzroy and Wally chuckle. Wally replies, "Faith, chevré is goat meat."

Aunt Dot sprays coffee from her mouth across the table. "I'm so sorry. Please forgive me," she apologizes.

"I trust you've never eaten goat before, Dot?" Wally says.

"No I haven't," Aunt Dot says in a sickly sweet voice.

"Wally it was good no matter what you call it," Momma says while laughing at Aunt Dot.

"Why didn't you just call it goat instead of chevré?" Aunt Dot says as if she had been misled.

"That's a good question, Dot. Actually there's a good reason why some people call goat chevré. You see a very long time ago, around 1920, goat herders realized that people like you, Dot, would not eat goat because of its name and their unfamiliarity with the animal. So, a very smart man who at that time was the President of the Sheep and Goat Raisers Association came up with a plan. He initiated a contest to come up with a name for goat meat. A name was selected from all the entries and he announced it at the Association's annual convention.

"You're making this up, right?" I say.

"No. I read this in one of my cook magazines. The name "c*hevon*" had been chosen as the official name. It is alleged that the reason for adopting that name is that it, like beef, mutton and pork, is of French origin, being a contraction of the French word, chevon, *chevre* means goat.

"Makes sense to me. I suppose if people thought they were eating "dead cow," they might hesitate. But calling it "beef" sounds better and probably contributes to its good taste.

It's all in the name," Aunt Lucille says.

"It's strange, but people have a peculiar attitude over eating goat. I think calling it by something different definitely makes those who are leery more willing to try it. Right, Dot?" Fitzroy teases.

After dinner we relax on the couch and listen to more of Wally's vast collection of music. Wally and Fitzroy talk about Nevis and days gone by with a pleasant sadness in their heart.

"When's the last time you guys been home?" I ask.

"Whoa, it's been ten years for me. I went home for Culturama," Wally says.

"Is that like carnival?" Aunt Dot asks.

"Yes. It happens in late August. It's a time when Nevisians who have moved away return to party with friends and family. There's music every night, food festivals and concerts." Wally smiles as he boasts of good times on his little island.

"When was the last time you went home, Fitzroy?" I ask. Fitzroy sadly answers.

"Last year. We buried Mother."

"I'm sorry, Fitzroy," Momma says.

"She struggled with diabetes for so long...I tried many times to persuade her to let me take her to the states so she could get treatment. But each time she refused. Mother said she didn't want any doctors putting a shunt in her body, hooking her up to a dialysis machine or cutting off her legs...She just wanted to stay home on her farm as long as she could until God called her home. And that's just what she did.

"I need to go home and check on my father. There's only the two of us left now. And I know he gets pretty lonely being there by himself. I thank God that his health is good. He attributes it to hard work. I think I told you, Faith, he pastors a small church and runs a honey farm."

"The best honey on Nevis!" Wally says. "I have a great idea! Why don't we take the ladies to Nevis before they leave? It will be so much fun," Wally says as if he was sharing a recipe for happiness.

Everyone is excited; even Aunt Dot, who was petrified of small planes. Fitzroy lights up at the idea.

"Capital suggestion! I need a few days off, and I'd love for my father to meet Faith and her family before they go back to the states."

"Then it's settled. I'll take care of the flights and make reservations for the ladies to stay at the Four Seasons Hotel."

"The Four Seasons! Isn't that a five star hotel?" Aunt Lucille asks.

"Yes it is. Only the best for you, my dear."

"I know that's right!" Aunt Lucille replies.

"Well, I don't know about you all, but I need to go lie down and think about all these exciting things that are happening. I don't know when I've had so much adventure in my life. The castle, the pig roast on a private island tomorrow, eating goat for the first time; excuse me, I mean chevré. And now a trip to Nevis," Momma says as she rises to leave.

"I'm out of here, too. I just pray this old body doesn't have trouble digesting goat herder's meat! Gloria and I will leave you lovebirds to your business. Just remember to keep your skirt down Lucille!" Aunt Dot says as she opens the door to leave.

"We have got to find a man for her!" Lucille yells.

"Not until the divorce is final," Momma says.

"Honey, that marriage was final a long time ago," Aunt Dot snaps.

"I'll walk the two of you down the driveway. It's pretty dark out there," Fitzroy says. Wally gives him a flashlight. They leave and Lucille fills our glasses with more champagne.

I ask Wally where the rest room is and he directs me down a long hall to a showroom bathroom suite. The bathroom sports a sunken whirlpool tub, a seamless glass steam shower, and a sitting area with a chaise lounge adjoining a round-skirted end table. A bookshelf lines one of the walls laden with cookbooks, health books, books about cancer and home decorating. Not only are there his and hers sinks, but his and hers water closets. Travertine tiles cover the floor and walls. The dual sinks are composed of an antique mahogany cabinet with a crystal bowl sitting on top of it that serves as the face basin. A gold gooseneck waterspout hangs over the bowl. There are no handles to turn the water on, you just pass your hand under the faucet and the water comes out.

Just as I exit the water closet about to wash my hands in Wally's beautiful sink I hear a strange voice coming from the living room. The person is yelling at Wally. I've only been gone five minutes. What could have changed? We were just having a wonderful evening. Who is this angry person and why is he here in Wally's living room trying to wreck our beautiful dinner party? So many questions are racing through my head. I cautiously walk down the hall and I see a man about 25 years old shouting to the top of his lungs at Wally. I ease closer with caution being extra careful that this person doesn't catch sight of me.

"Daddy you need to give me the money for the taxes or they are going to close the club down! And why didn't you renew the liquor license!"

"Honey why don't you calm down. All this yelling is not good for your father or yourself," Aunt Lucille says.

"Who is this slut you have in my mother's house!" the angry man screams.

"Junior, you better leave," Wally says.

"I ain't going nowhere until this whore leaves my mother's house and you write me a check for the taxes and the liquor license!"

Oh Lord, I know Aunt Lucille isn't going to take that. He's gone too far. I remain hidden, praying Fitzroy will come back soon and take control of this ugly situation.

"Honey, there aren't any whores or sluts in here. Only a nasty foul mouth crack head whose back is up against the wall and he's trying to take advantage of his daddy!" Aunt Lucille says with a vengeance.

Finally, I hear Fitzroy open the door.

"What's up, Junior?" he calmly says.

"Oh, so you called the police on me huh, Daddy?"

"Junior, leave now before I take Fitzroy's gun and shoot you dead!"

Junior weighs the situation and quickly decides it would be in his best interest to leave. He slams the door behind him like a spoiled child. Bewildered, I join everyone in the living room, not ashamed at all of being a coward.

"What in the world was that about?" I ask.

"Lucille hit the nail on the head," Wally says.

"You mean your son is on crack?" I ask, wishing I hadn't, after I see how sad it makes Wally.

Wally sits down on the couch looking defeated. Aunt Lucille sits besides him and comforts him, just as she did through his depression only a few days ago.

"I'm sorry he talked to you like that, Lucille."

"Don't worry about it, Wally. I can handle him. Besides, the boy is not in his right mind."

"How long has he been like this?" I ask.

"Probably longer than I'm willing to admit," Wally says.

"Do you think he would be willing to go to a rehabilitation center?" I ask Wally.

"He's not on his knees yet. Something would have to scare the hell out of him first. Then he might be ready for rehab," Fitzroy says.

"I am so sorry you all had to witness this calamity," Wally says embarrassed.

"Hey man, you and I go way back. You don't have to apologize for Junior. Besides, the way I understand it, you were almost my brother. And still might be according to some of the people in our village. We're family, Wally." Fitzroy and Wally shake hands and embrace. Fitzroy continues, "On a serious note, Wally, you've got to make some tough decisions without delay. We had a meeting this evening at the station and the word is out that Junior is selling rock cocaine for Mario Maynard out of the supper club."

Wally stands up and paces the floor. "Holy Father! My worst fears are true. I thought Mario Maynard was in jail! I just read in the newspaper that he got caught with a couple pounds of cocaine."

"Someone on the force helped botch that up. So they had to let him go."

"Someone botched it up? What exactly does that mean?" Aunt Lucille asks Fitzroy.

"The evidence is missing," Fitzroy sadly says.

"Internal Affairs thinks they know who it is. There's a dirty cop who's making a lot of money working from the inside for Mario."

"What do you think we should do?" Wally respectfully asks Fitzroy.

"I could have some of my boys go in and arrest Junior. I'd have them do it early before the crowd comes. Let him sit in jail for a couple of days and while he's locked up, you can close the club down," Fitzroy says.

"Man, you're talking about putting my son in jail," Wally nervously says.

"From what I've learned about the amount of drugs coming through that place, jail doesn't seem like a bad idea. Mario Maynard will not think twice about killing Junior if he's not paying him."

Aunt Lucille, Wally and I are now pacing the floor trying to come up with a solution to help Junior out of the mess he's gotten himself into, for Wally's sake.

"What if there are guns and someone gets hurt when they go to arrest him?" Lucille asks.

"I'll send my undercover cops in. They will disguise themselves as telephone repairmen. The night before, someone will cut the phone lines. When Junior calls the telephone company our special unit will be on alert. They will schedule an appointment to come out and make the repairs between eight and nine in the morning. Not exactly prime time for dope dealers. The arrest will be swift and quiet."

Wally is doubtful.

"Why don't I just talk to him about the dangers of drugs and let him know I'm on to him?"

All three of us holler at the same time, "You must be crazy!"

"Bad idea!" I add.

Aunt Lucille continues, "Junior doesn't want to hear about the dangers of drugs, Wally!"

"You're all right. My son Phillip who lives in the states tried to tell me what was going on when he and his girl were here visiting. Why don't we do this...deep down inside Junior is a chicken. I know the thought of jail will make him pee in his pants. Fitzroy, have your boys arrest him and take him to the airport. I'll be there when they arrive and we will give him a choice. He can either board an awaiting plane to the states or he can go to jail. I won't send him to his brother Phillip. Junior might ruin his brother's life with that mess. But I will send him to his mother's brother who happens to be a drug counselor in Virginia. I know Junior will take that option," Wally says with conviction.

"I'll have my people cut the phone lines tonight and tomorrow when Junior calls for emergency repair the ball will start rolling," Fitzroy says just like a skilled cop.

"I'll call my brother-in-law and alert him to what's happening and let him know his nephew should reach him in the next couple of days," Wally says with relief in his voice.

"Won't it be dangerous closing the club if Junior owes people money? They might get mad and burn it down or even worse, come looking for you," I say.

"I'll talk to my cousin Myra. She's the Director of Finance. I'll ask her to have her people board up the place and paste Taxes Due notices around the building. And if someone decides to burn the club down then so be it. The building is paid for and the insurance is up to date. I refuse to live in fear and be held hostage by a thug. If Mario or any of his boys come looking for me then they're going to have to come to Nevis. Because we're going on our trip come hell or high water," Wally says with vigor.

"What about the house? Will things here be safe?" Aunt Lucille asks.

I'll call Windward Security. When I'm off island they always look after the place. I don't know if you noticed but I have small web cameras positioned all around this property. I can watch my house from any computer all over the world 24 hours a day, 7 days a week, and so can Windward Security. If someone tries to break in, they might just meet their Maker."

It was late and everyone was tired but most importantly there was a plan in place to get Junior some help. It was time to bring my adventurous day to an end. It was only this afternoon that I found out my ex-boy friend who I'd been trying to get to marry me for four years was engaged to marry my tenant. And then there was that high-speed chase where three police cars and a man in a van who loves me were pursuing me. And now I find out that my neighbor's son has a drug problem. Yes, it was time for this day to come to a close.

I thanked Wally and Lucille for a wonderful dinner. Fitzroy said good-bye to our host and hostess after assuring them that everything would be alright. Wally was relieved and Aunt Lucille was merely happy to help Wally through another hurdle. Lucille said she would be down after she helped Wally with the dishes. Wally looked a little disappointed.

"Why don't you stay sweetheart. I need to be held," he said.

"So do I," Lucille smiled and said.

On that note, Fitzroy and I walked out into the star-filled night smiling. I was happy for Aunt Lucille and Wally. God had delivered both of them from depression and grief after losing a loved one. And now He's allowed two people from different parts of the world to meet under Caribbean skies and be a blessing to one other.

Momma and Aunt Dot were sound asleep when we entered the house. There was no way I was going to have Fitzroy racing over Skyline Drive trying to catch the last boat for St. John which was scheduled to leave in 10 minutes. He boasted that he's made it in eight minutes. I tell him he can't do that anymore. He has me to think about. Besides, it doesn't make sense to go to St. John and then have to come back the first thing in the morning to work. He agrees and asks me to walk with him to his official police van to get his uniform to change into tomorrow. After he takes the uniform, which is on a hanger, out of the van, I turn to go back inside. Fitzroy pulls me into his arms and passionately kisses me. I don't want to stop. Fitzroy then reaches inside the pocket of his uniform and pulls out a box. Oh, my God. It's a ring! He leads me to the veranda where I sit down. Fitzroy gets down on one knee, opens the ring box, and pulls out a white gold ring with a huge marquis diamond. The diamond was so big it might weigh my whole hand down.

"Faith, you are my morning star. From the first time I saw you I knew you were the woman I had been praying for God to send me. I would be honored if you would be my wife."

"Nothing would give me more pleasure than to be *Mrs.* Fitzroy Brown," I sincerely say.

Chapter 22

Lisa and her beautiful, newly-acquired two-year-old daughter Kamari met us at the boat shuttle to take us to Water Island. I greeted Lisa with a queen's wave, making sure my ring would not be missed. She was ecstatic. We hugged and jumped up and down with joy. However, beautiful Kamari quickly upstaged the news of my engagement. All attention was diverted to this gorgeous child. Momma and Aunt Dot raced to see who would be first to hold the little doll. Lisa and Kamari both looked so adorable. They were dressed alike. Each wore white shorts, a pink Indian gauze top, straw hat and sunglasses. Momma and Aunt Dot immediately fell in love with the child. Just looking at her made you want to hold her and kiss her. Kamari's skin color, if I had to give it a name, would be called golden sunset and her hair was thick, long, bushy and blonde. Her eyes were a beautiful shade of green. And she had a personality that could capture the heart of the 'Wicked Witch of the West'. Kamari went from arm to arm hugging and kissing all of us. Momma insisted the baby call her 'Grammy' and Aunt Dot wouldn't settle for anything less than 'Auntie'.

I look at my best friend as the little tugboat takes off from the dock headed for Water Island and I smile because I've never seen this motherly side of her before. And I must say, she is glowing and wearing it well. I praise God, because only He could have known that Lisa and I would leave Los Angeles, move to the Caribbean and get engaged to two wonderful men. Who could imagine that He would bless Lisa with a daughter given to her by a woman who didn't want to mother her any more because the color of the child's skin would bring embarrassment to her family in the states to whom she was returning. Lisa is also blessed that God is allowing her to bring life into the world with the baby on the way.

"Faith...girl that ring is the bomb! Brother Fitzroy didn't cut any cost! Did you'all set a date yet?" Lisa asks.

"No. There is so much going on. We need to clear a few things off our plate before we set a date. But one thing that I do know is I'm going to have my wedding in Atlanta at my Daddy's church," I proudly say.

Momma, busy tickling Kamari, smiles pleasingly at me. "I hear you and Trevor are getting married on New Years Eve," Momma says to Lisa.

"Yes. Will you come back for the wedding?" Lisa pleads.

"Of course, I wouldn't miss it for anything in the world. Besides, won't you and Trevor need Grammy to watch Kamari while you go on your honeymoon?"

Lisa kisses Momma. "You're the best, Mother Gloria."

"Well, I guess I must be wearing my invisible suit because I haven't heard you ask me if I was coming back for the wedding," Aunt Dot says with hurt feelings.

"Mrs. Dot, you, Miss Lucille and Mother Gloria are all the family I have, and I would be one sad bride if all of you were not there," Lisa affectionately says.

"Then it's settled. I'm buying my ticket tomorrow. Gloria I'm going to buy yours and Lucille's too, that is if she doesn't decide to just stay down here. Like I said before, I need to break in all these credit cards George and I never used, especially before the fool realizes he forgot to cancel them," Aunt Dot proudly says.

"Dot, George is going to kill you when he gets the bill," Momma warns her.

"Now you know better than that, Gloria. I wish he would try to put his hands on me. I've got a black skillet that would fit his head size perfectly. Besides, until our divorce is final, what's his is mine...Now can you think of anybody else I should purchase a ticket for?"

All of us laugh as the little tugboat pulls up to the dock at Water Island. Linda Peters is standing on the dock waving to us with a big smile on her face. The sound of steel pan music is heard in the distance as we step onto the dock. Linda greets each of us with a warm hug and a kiss on the cheek. I introduce her to Momma, Aunt Dot and little Kamari. Linda already knows Lisa. Aunt Dot is swaying to the steel pan music. "Yeah, mon! Dis is nice," she tries to say like the locals. We thank our boat captains and Linda leads us down a flagstone path towards the beach.

"Miss Faith, I so happy you and your fam-lee could come. It's been one big partee going on round ear from Ters-day."

When we reach the beach we see so many people. Children are running about chasing each other into the water. A full steel pan group plays for couples dancing on a stone patio which leads to the inside of the beautiful Danish-style house. Tables with umbrellas line the patio and beach area. Linda introduces us to everyone we pass including her mother and father, who insist we not act like strangers and make ourselves at home. Linda leads us to a table on the patio where we join a few of her family members. Linda's uncle Marlin walks over carrying a platter of fried fish, just out of the deep fryer. Uncle Marlin sets the fish down on the table, gives me the biggest smile, walks over and hugs me. Momma and Aunt Dot both have a puzzled look on their faces. I know they are wondering who is this older man greeting me like an old boyfriend. I introduce Marlin to Momma, Aunt Dot and Lisa.

"Me little darling I thought me lost you. Would you look at how good de Lawd is. Him sent you here ta me dis day...I com'in right back! I got some ting real sweet far ya, Miss Faith." Marlin runs off.

"So, is this Fitzroy's competition?" Lisa teases.

"So Miss Faith, you does know me Uncle Marlin? Him a real Romeo, you know."

"So I see!" Aunt Dot says.

"Honey, where did you meet Marlin?" Momma asks as she bumps Kamari up and down on her lap.

"Lisa you know Marlin," I say.

"No I don't!" She replies as if I was trying to incriminate her in some wrong doings.

"Girl, Marlin is the Mango Man on St. John. You know the one I told you would leave mangos on the porch for me every morning."

A light turns on in Lisa's head. "Oh! I thought he didn't have any teeth?" she says.

"Well, he has teeth today, OK?"

Sometimes I could strangle my best friend. Why would she say that in front of Linda?

Linda laughs. "Me Uncle is quite a character. De man has outlived seven wives. Uncle Marlin has twenty-tree chiren, forty-nine grand chiren and forty-tree great-grand chiren." All of us are shocked at those statistics. Linda continues. "Miss Faith is dat a rock on your finger?" Linda examines my ring. "Me son, you best get a bodyguard to protect you and dat finger! Da ting is nice!

Uncle Marlin walks up carrying two of the largest mangoes I've ever seen in my life. He stops short when he sees Linda examining my ring. A sad look temporarily crosses his face. "So, me sweetness, you dump me for another man?"

"Uncle Marlin, Miss Faith has been dating Officer Brown for several months now. You remember their picture was on the front of de paper?" Linda counters. Uncle Marlin smiles and walks over to Aunt Dot with the two mangoes.

"Hello darling. I'd be honored if you would taste me mangoes. Now, dey won't be as sweet as you, but I tink dey might come close." Aunt Dot is tickled by the attention. We all laugh.

"If ah you want to change into yah bath suits, ders a changing room just off de kitchen." Linda points inside.

"If it's OK with you, Lisa, I'd like to take Kamari in the water," Momma says.

"Of course. She'll love it." Lisa hands Momma Kamari's beach bag and they exit to change. Marlin talks Aunt Dot into dancing with him. Lisa and I send Linda to find some hot sauce to go with our just-out-of-the-fryer hot fish. Linda returns with the hot sauce and excuses herself. She's needed inside to help make johnnycakes. Aunt Dot and Marlin are busy dancing up a storm. Who would have ever thought, my Mango Man and Aunt Dot would be on Water Island dancing calypso?

Lisa and I spot two empty beach chairs under an umbrella and head for them with our large cups of maube in hand. From where we are sitting, we have a bird's eye view of Momma and Kamari having fun in the water.

"It looks like I've been depriving my mother of having a granddaughter," I say sadly.

"Don't worry about it. Mother Gloria is about to get a plethora of grandbabies!" Lisa brags.

"It must be from your fertile myrtle behind. I am not having a whole bunch of babies. Two will be enough for me, thank you!"

"Well, Trevor's made it clear he wants a lot of kids." Lisa comes back.

"And just how is that going to happen? I mean with his little or should I say big issue!" I tease Lisa.

"Girl, big boy is up and running better than ever! I told him there was no way I was marrying him if he didn't get on Viagra," Lisa says with resolve.

"You know you're crazy don't you?" I make fun of her.

I tell Lisa about Wally's son, Junior, and their plan to get him off the island. I also tell her about our upcoming trip to Nevis which she wants to go on, but can't because of her work schedule. Momma and Kamari, against her wishes, come out of the water to get some sunscreen.

"Mommy me want de wa-ta! Mommy me want de wa-ta!" Kamari repeats as Lisa rubs sun block on her body.

"Just one second, honey. Mommy doesn't want you to burn."

"Where's Dot?" Momma asks.

I point to the patio area where Marlin is teaching Aunt Dot to reggae dance. Momma laughs then runs after Kamari who has headed back to the water.

"Any word from Billy?" I ask. Lisa, a little surprised, answers.

"Yeah, I've talked to him every day since the break up." She calmly says.

"What? How is he doing?"

"He's healing," Lisa replies.

"What the hell does that mean?" Again, I want to choke her.

"It means that he's working at getting over the shock of me being pregnant and marrying Trevor," Lisa matter-of-factly says.

"You know you sound like we're talking about a recipe. And not a man who loved you and you claimed you loved less than a week ago," I scold her.

"Get over it, Faith. I told you Billy is not the man for me. I just thank God that we both found out before it was too late. Billy is going to be fine. He's just a little embarrassed. He says he's going to hang out in Anguilla for a while. He and a friend of Mr. Atkins are thinking about starting a business down there. They're going to run charter flights from Anguilla to a few of the neighboring islands. Don't worry, Faith. It's all-good. Billy is sad, but at the same time, he's happy for me to be marrying my baby's daddy."

"Don't you miss him?" I ask.

"Yeah. But..." Lisa pauses.

"But what?" I prod.

"Billy was fine as all get-out and he definitely has the spiritual aspect, but there wasn't any romance. You know, lust, passion!"

I look at her, shake my head and laugh.

"Lisa, the man was celibate! How much lust and passion could you expect? He was saving it for when you all got married."

"Girl, that's too scary for me. Suppose it wasn't good. I'd be stuck with it until 'death does us part'. Honey, sister girl needs a little sample. I don't care how holy the man was. Remember, I'm Lisa Walker, not the Virgin Mary," Lisa says.

"You know you have issues, don't you?" I tease her.

"Girl, we all have issues. Some of us are just a little more honest about it than others, because I know you're concerned about what Fitzroy has down there." Lisa points between her legs. I punch her in the arm.

"Girl you could go to jail for hitting a pregnant woman!" Lisa lovingly scolds.

"I'm not worried. You forgot I'm marrying the law!"

"All jokes aside. Billy sometimes scares me when we talk," Lisa says with concern.

"How?" I ask.

"Well, he keeps saying that the Lord told him we would be together again."

"The boy isn't giving up is he?" I say.

"I told him the Lord hasn't told me that," Lisa says.

"What did he say?" I ask.

"He said in time God would speak to me as well."

"That is some spooky stuff." I say.

"Girl, I don't even want to talk about it. I've made my choice."

Momma and Kamari are heading toward us. Lisa pulls a hooded beach towel out of her bag and wraps it around her.

"Hey, Momma!" I say.

"Hey, sugar. Kamari you ready to eat?" Momma says.

"Eat, Grammy. Mommy, me eat." We all laugh at her cute response. Momma dries herself off and puts her beach dress over her bathing suit.

"Come on, Kamari. Let's go find your Auntie Dot. We need to make sure she doesn't get into trouble."

"Get into trouble," Kamari parrots as they head toward the main house.

"Faith, I thank God for your mother. You think we could talk her into moving down here? You know both of us are going to need a grandmother like her to help with our kids."

"Not only do we need Momma down here to help with the kids but I think she needs us too. Since my Dad died and my cousin Debbie took over as the First Lady of our church, Momma doesn't really have any official duties at Solid Rock. It must be very lonely and hard for her," I say sadly.

"I have a great idea!" Lisa sits up from the beach lounge chair.

"What? I'm not moving back to Atlanta with Fitzroy, so you can forget it." I knocked out any notions of that.

"Chill out, Faith! Who would ever propose something like that? Why don't I ask your mother if she would like to buy my house, at a cheap price of course. Hell, I'll just about give it to her. We need a Momma down here!"

I almost want to cry. This is the most intelligent thing Lisa has ever said since I've known her.

"Lisa that is brilliant! Why didn't I think of that?" Lisa is beaming with pride.

"Because you're not the only one with sense. Let's go ask her."

My cell phone rings and it's Chloe.

"Hi baby. What's going on?" Lisa cuts in.

"Tell Fitzroy I said 'hi'."

"It's not Fitzroy, it's Chloe," I respond.

"Let me tell her hello." Lisa snatches the phone out of my hand. "Hey Sugar Pie! This is Auntie Lisa. I miss you and Nyla so much....OK, honey...Well, I'm living back in St. John now...OK, we can go to Trunk Bay. You just call me and let me know when you two want to come over. Oh, I have a surprise. Well actually two surprises....I'm not going to tell you until I see you or it won't be a surprise...OK, I'll give you a little hint...it's cute and has a lot of energy....No, I don't have a puppy. No, Chloe, it's not a goat...I'm not going to tell you until I see you...Chloe, you are too funny...I love you too...here's Faith. Faith I'm going to go talk to Mother Gloria and to get some more food." Lisa leaves while I stay and talk to Chloe.

"I'm back. Of course I'm going to be there...Yes, Mr. Atkins told me the plan....I think it's a great one. All of us love you, Chloe, and we're not going to let anything bad happen to you...He is? Momma is going to be shocked. Did you taste any of it? Oh, my gosh! You tasted iguana? Emmaus and Solange have been cooking it all day...they are bringing it over when you all come on Monday? Well I won't tell Momma...Don't worry I can keep a secret...No, I'm not eating any iguana...Girl, I don't care if it tastes like prime rib...I don't do road kill...I love you, too. Tell Mr. Atkins, Rosalinda and Nyla I say 'hi' and I'll see all of you on Monday. Bye, sugar...and don't forget to keep praying...I love you!"

After hanging up from talking to Chloe I lay there thinking about all that is going on in my life. I want to worry but my spirit won't let it happen. I relax, listening to the peaceful sound of the waves washing ashore. I watch a flock of pelicans gliding high in the beautiful blue Caribbean sky with their keen eyes sharply focused on the sea below. Once their prey is spotted they dive down like a speeding bullet and capture the struggling fish in their oversized mouth that resembles a fisherman's pouch. Watching this ritual brings to my remembrance the scripture in the Bible where God says: 'Look at the birds in the air for they neither sow nor reap nor gather into barns; yet your heavenly Father feeds them. Are you not of more value than they? Which of you, by worrying, can add one cubit to his stature?' I find peace in reciting that passage. It confirms in my spirit that everything will be all right. "Thank you Lord," I say.

The sound of Linda Peters' voice breaks me out of my reflection of how awesome God is.

"Miss Faith, girl you just gon look at de wa'ter or you gon get in? You bath suit still dry." Linda sits on the beach chair next to me.

"Girl I'm just sitting here marveling at God's handiwork and having a little conversation with my Heavenly Father," I say.

"Me just love dis place. It's so peaceful. Some days I go out on me little boat over der and just ride all around de island. Me mudder and fadder get married right over der." Linda points to a section of the beach adjacent to a cave. The little cave was carved out from the water beating against the rocks over a long period of time.

"How romantic," I say.

"And every one of us was baptized right ear on dis beach," Linda brags.

"Linda you are so blessed! Being here among your family reminds me of when all of my aunties, uncles, cousins and friends would get together for cookouts during the summer. Of course, we didn't have this beautiful beach. I miss them so much," I sadly say.

"So, when's de big weddin day?" Linda excitedly asks.

"We haven't set a date yet. However, I'm thinking February 14th sounds like a good date. And I want to get married in the church I grew up in where my daddy used to pastor."

What bedder date fa Romeo and Juliet to get married den Valentine's Day?" Linda says.

"I agree." We laugh and embrace.

"Listen, me couzin just get she massage license and she giv'in massages cheap, cheap on de beach over der under de tent. She husben won't let she massage any men. He a little jealous. Uncle Marlin talk your Auntie into get'tin one. She under de tent now."

I look down the beach where I see the white tent and spot Marlin with a drink in his hand, sitting on a fold-up chair waiting for Aunt Dot to finish her massage. How cute, I think. Just as I'm about to tell Linda to count me in for a massage we hear a scream. It's Aunt Dot. Next we see her running naked down the beach with her hands flapping in the air. Marlin is running behind her. Everyone young and old stops what they are doing and walks towards the tent. Aunt Dot turns and sees the crowd coming towards her. She jumps in the water screaming. "Get it off me! Get it off me!"

"She can't swim! She can't swim!" I holler down the beach.

Marlin throws his drink in the air and jumps in the water to save Aunt Dot who grabs on to him for dear life.

"Just relax my little sugar plum...daddy's here and he's not going to let anything happen to you, sweetie!"

I see Momma running towards the edge of the water with a beach robe and towel to cover Aunt Dot up. Linda pushes the crowd back.

"Me son, can't ya see de woman needs she privacy! I you go back!" The crowd moves back towards the house.

The steel pans start playing again and the children resume running back and forth on the beach. Linda's cousin is so nervous.

"Me didn't do a ting! A scorpion craw up she arm while she had dem dangling down. She get so excited flapping she arms de ting landed in she hair. I sorry, mon. Me ain't mean no harm," the masseuse says almost in tears.

"Don't worry, Aunt Dot is tough. She'll be all right," I hug her and say.

Momma follows Aunt Dot and Marlin down the beach.

"I'm OK, Gloria. Just a little embarrassed. If you would get my clothes for me, I'd appreciate it," Aunt Dot says.

"No need to be embarrassed, me darling. Don't trouble your head with what dees people tink! You wit me and me ain't going to let nutting ever frighten ya again." Marlin leads Aunt Dot to the little cave where they sit on a rock waiting for Momma to bring her clothes.

I attempt to walk over to where Aunt Dot and Marlin are sitting but Momma stops me in my tracks.

"She's all right. Let's just leave them alone," Momma says.

"Oh, ok." I walk over to the tent and sign up for a massage. Linda's cousin and I both comb the area for scorpion and any other creatures before I take off my clothes.

We later say good-bye to Linda and her family and climb into the little tugboat. Marlin and Aunt Dot linger at the dock like two teenage lovers. Marlin kisses Aunt Dot's hand and helps her into the boat. Aunt Dot is grinning like a schoolgirl. In one hand she holds a giant mango and in the other her beach bag.

"I'll see you on St. John tomorrow, my little sugar apple," Marlin says as the boat pulls away from the dock. He stands waving until we are almost across the sea.

"Well it looks like both you and Lucille came down to these beautiful islands and got love struck! Just remember the divorce isn't final yet," Momma lovingly reprimands.

"Gloria, right now I can't even remember what my ex-husband's name is. Honey, I haven't ever had anyone talk so sweet to me like Marlin. Lord, thank you that you are a God of second chances!" Aunt Dot looks up to the sky and hollers out.

"Hallelujah! I heard that! Thank you, Jesus!" Lisa seconds it.

Kamari is peacefully resting on her new mommy's lap as we pull up to the dock at Charlotte Amalie. Just as we are about to get off the boat several police cars with their sirens blasting and lights swirling rush past us. Following the police cars is an ambulance.

"What in the world is going on?" I say. Linda's cousin, our boat captain, speaks.

"Me just heard on de radio der was a shooting at Wally's Supper Club. Dey saying a man get shot."

I fall back down in the boat. Momma rushes over to comfort me as tears stream down my face and I start crying uncontrollably.

"Faith, honey, calm down. I'm sure Fitzroy is fine."

"Let me call him on your cell," Lisa says as she goes through my purse looking for my phone.

Aunt Dot takes sleeping Kamari from Lisa while she calls Fitzroy. He must have noticed my number on his caller ID because Lisa didn't get to say hello or anything.

"I'm fine, sweetheart," was all we heard him say, and then the phone cut off. My tears of fear turned into tears of joy. I continued to sob and was reminded of what God revealed to me earlier with the birds in the sky. "Just as He takes care of the birds, He will take care of us and we don't need to worry."

Chapter 23

I decided to drive Lisa and the baby to catch the ferryboat at Red Hook. Lisa insisted on taking the boat from Charlotte Amalie, only a few yards up the dock from where we got on the little shuttle boat. I objected. The town boat, as it's referred to, only runs four times a day and the next boat would not be leaving for another two hours. Momma, and Aunt Dot, who was still in lovers' heaven, both agreed that Lisa and the baby should not wait in the hot sun for two hours especially when we could drop them at Red Hook in time to catch the next boat that ran every hour on the hour. Lisa agrees with us and offers to drive. I was glad so that I could be still for a moment and thank God for keeping Fitzroy safe.

Once we were all in the jeep and situated, Momma insisted we stop and purchase a car seat for Kamari right away. She was not having her grandchild riding in any car without being properly strapped in. Momma reprimanded Lisa for not having one.

"Mother Gloria, it's not required when riding on the ferry," Lisa replied.

"Well, it's required in this jeep. So you just find a place right now where we can buy one before all of us go to jail," Momma scolds.

"Speak for yourself, child. I have a date tomorrow and jail isn't in the plan," Aunt Dot jokingly says.

"Mrs. Dot, I think you had too many mangoes!" Lisa teases.

"Honey child, I'm looking forward to checking out that 'big mango', if you know what I mean." Momma is appalled.

"Jesus! Have mercy! Dot, what has gotten into you? Both you and Lucille have gotten down here in these islands and forgotten your morals and your Christian upbringing!"

"Mother Gloria, I figured this thing out. It's a combination of the sun, the beautiful Caribbean Sea, the hot weather and all that sweet talk coming out of these men's mouths. It will make the strongest of us weak and forget about our religion!" Lisa says laughing.

"Relax, Gloria. God willing, you might even meet somebody before we head back home," Aunt Dot teases.

"Bite your wicked tongue. I just buried my darling husband of over 30 years," Momma proudly says.

"And?" Aunt Dot replies.

"And what?" Momma says.

"And the man is gone to heaven and you're here. So don't be afraid to live. You're not dead, he is. I bet if the tables were turned, he'd be looking as we speak for another First Lady to sit on the front row at Solid Rock while he delivers his Sunday morning sermon. Then again, the Rev might not have to look because I know at least 10 women who probably prayed every night you would die first so they could make a move on him. I won't name any names, but a few of them used to grin in your face and tell you how lovely you look every Sunday," Aunt Dot says.

Momma's feelings are hurt.

"Lisa, pull over by that K-Mart. I'm sure they sell car seats. And let me out of this car before I smack my sister silly."

Momma climbs out of the jeep and briskly walks into the little K-Mart store.

"You want me to come with you?" Aunt Dot hollers out of the window. Momma waves her hand, dismissing Aunt Dot.

"I think you hit a nerve," I say.

"She'll get over it. One thing about your momma, she's not petty and she's very forgiving. Let me out, I'm going in to apologize to her." Aunt Dot walks quickly to catch up with Momma.

My cell phone rings. It's Fitzroy and I quickly answer it.

"Hi, is everything alright?" I say in one breath. Lisa intently listens. I continue, "Oh my God! Are you all right...what about Wally and Aunt Lucille? Good. Is Junior safe? Unbelievable... They are... Wow. Sure, I understand... I love you too." I hang up.

"So what's up?" Lisa asks.

"Girl this sounds like something out of the movies. Mario Maynard is dead."

"You mean that guy who got caught with a couple pounds of cocaine? It was in the newspaper. I thought he was in jail?" Lisa says puzzled.

"That's another story. Anyway, Fitzroy's undercover cops disguised as telephone repair men went into Wally's to get Junior out and put him on a plane to Virginia, but instead, they caught Mario Maynard in the process of making a drug deal with some men from St. Croix. The two men surrendered without a struggle. But Mario refused to give up without a fight. He shot one of the cops in the arm before they killed him. And get this: Mario had sent Junior to the Crazy Cow to get them some breakfast. He wasn't even there when the bust went down," I tell Lisa.

"So now, Mario is going to think Junior sold him out." Lisa blurts out.

"Hello! Didn't you hear me say the man is dead? Any grievance he has with Junior he'll have to file in hell."

"Faith, we didn't have this much excitement in our lives in Los Angeles. Aren't you glad we moved here?" Lisa excitedly says.

"Well, one of us did. I'm sure there was never a dull moment for you with your 'sugar pie' Jason," I tease.

"Now, that's cold! Sometimes we need to let sleeping dogs lie, as the expression goes," Lisa comes back.

"Anyway, Lucille and Wally are at the airport with Junior. They are putting him on a plane to Virginia. To answer your question, yes, I'm glad we moved here or I never would have met the man God had in His plan for me."

"Nor would I have met Trevor," Lisa interjects.

"Nor would Mrs. Lucille have met Wally and neither would Mrs. Dot have met 'The Mango Man'," Lisa says in a sexy voice.

"Girl you are so crazy!" I tease.

Our laughing wakes Kamari up.

"Mommy boo-boo. Get boo-boo off me." We both laugh.

"Now if she can say all that then she should be able to say 'Mommy I got to potty'," I say.

"Mommy I got to potty." Kamari repeats. We laugh again.

"Well, I don't do doo-doo, so climb your pregnant butt in the back seat and take care of your daughter's business," I tease.

"Auntie Faith, now is a good time to learn how to change a diaper!" Lisa says.

"I don't think so. When you have your baby I'll give it a try. Besides, the baby boo-boo won't be so big and stinking!" We fall out laughing as Momma and Aunt Dot open the car door carrying Kamari's new car seat.

"What's that smell?" Aunt Dot asks.

"It's your beautiful little niece. Don't you want to change her?" I ask.

"I think I'll follow the chain of command. Grammies get the pleasure before Aunties," Aunt Dot jokingly says.

"Move out of the way, Dot, and let me change the baby. Lisa, hand me her changing pad and some wipes out of the bag."

Lisa obeys. "See Faith, I told you we need her down here with us," she says.

"Sooner rather than later!" I respond.

After we dropped Lisa and Kamari off to catch the ferryboat we headed home. Zipporah the housekeeper had been there and left some more food in the freezer for Monday's dinner party. It looks like we are not the only ones looking forward to seeing Mr. Atkins, Mrs. Rosalinda, Chloe, Nyla, Emmaus and Solange. I think Zipporah has fixed everyone's favorite food. She even left us a pot of stewed chicken, fungi, fresh vegetables and johnnycakes on the stove. Momma went straight to the shower and I followed right behind her. Aunt Dot got a phone call from Marlin just as we entered the house. "The man must have radar," I thought. I could hear her giggling on the telephone as I stepped into the shower.

Fitzroy called around seven o'clock and asked if I would meet him at Red Hook. He wanted me to spend the night at his house on St. John and go to church with him tomorrow over there. I told him I would meet him at the eight o'clock ferry and we could ride over together. He sounded so tired and was probably hungry. There wasn't enough time for me cook him one of my specialties that I used to serve to ungrateful Daemon. So, I decided to put some of the dinner Zipporah had prepared into a few containers and take it to St. John. Fitzroy and I could enjoy Zipporah's 'West Indian pot' together. I was looking forward to visiting his home again. I reflected back on the day I got sick on the barge and he took me home and gave me bush tea and I slept until the next morning. Fitzroy's house was so tranquil and orderly. It felt safe. I wondered if he'd given any thought to where we would live once we got married. The Lord certainly has blessed me. Some people don't have a house to live in at all and here I am about to have two houses. I'm sure Fitzroy is not going to want to sell his house. I can tell he's put so much into making it his little refuge. I could see myself being comfortable there. It's close to town and will make an easier commute for me. Lord, have mercy. Looks like Lisa and I might be living close to each other again if she and Trevor purchase the house they are living in from the judge who lives in the states. What will I do with my house that's being built in Bordeaux? Lisa mentioned selling her house to Momma who surprised me when she sounded interested. After church tomorrow Fitzroy and I will sit down, plan our wedding and most importantly, decide where we will live.

I kiss Momma, tell her my plans and ask her if she wants to join us at church tomorrow. Aunt Dot volunteers to drive the guest car to the ferry tomorrow. She says she and Momma can ride over to St. John together when she goes to visit Marlin. I tell her I'm not sure if Marlin has a car so Fitzroy and I will pick them up at the nine o'clock boat. Aunt Dot makes it clear she isn't going to church with us. She and Marlin have made plans to go swimming at Jumbie Beach. Marlin is going to give her swimming lessons. I don't bother to tell her that Jumbie Beach is a nude beach where mostly state-siders swim naked. I'm sure Marlin must have mentioned it. Lord, Aunt Dot is about to get buck wild on St. John. I knew if I mentioned Jumbie Beach being a nude beach, Momma would read her the riot act.

As I open the door to leave and meet Fitzroy at the ferry Momma calls me back into the kitchen.

"Faith, Fitzroy will enjoy it better if you wait and give it to him on your wedding night."

"I'll remember that Momma," I say as I open the door to leave. Lord, Momma is keeping watch over all of our vaginas.

Fitzroy was waiting for me when I pulled into the parking lot. The boat was ready to depart but Fitzroy asked the captain to give me a minute to park the car. As we walked up the plank together all eyes were on us. Some people sucked their teeth, angry because the boat was leaving late. Fitzroy took me by the hand and led me into the captain's quarters. He introduced me to LaRon, the boat captain, who was busy maneuvering the boat away from the dock. I made myself comfortable on the plush leather seat and listened to the men talk. LaRon, a very handsome dark-skinned man, looked very regal in his white captain's uniform and white shoes. LaRon laughed and smiled a lot. He and Fitzroy talked politics and cracked jokes about a few of our government officials during most of the boat ride over.

I listened, smiled and even laughed at a few of their jokes until the girl who collects the tickets entered.

"You need to give me your ticket and get out me seat!" she said vehemently.

Both Fitzroy and LaRon stopped talking and turned in her direction.

"Asha! You must have lost your mind. Since when do you come in here talking to people like that?" LaRon scolds her.

"Me ain't know what da hell she doing up in here. She don't work here. Dis area is for workers!"

I get up to leave. "Hey, listen, I don't want any trouble. I'll just grab a seat outside with the rest of the passengers."

"Hold up, Faith." Fitzroy says as he takes my hand.

"What's the real problem, Asha?" Fitzroy continues. LaRon, trying to stay focused on driving the boat as the high waves take us up high and lower us down with a thump, turns slightly to hear what the girl has to say.

"Me ain't got no problem! It's all dees damn Yankee women come down here from de states and tink dey can have all we men," Asha angrily says.

"Like I said, I'll just go sit out with the rest of the passengers. I don't know what this girl's problem is but it isn't with me."

Again, I attempt to exit but Fitzroy holds my arm.

"Faith, this has nothing to do with you. Asha you better apologize or when this boat pulls up to the dock in St. John, you can get off and go find yourself another job. This is a professional company and we don't have rude people working on our crew."

Asha sits her ticket box down on the seat and leaves.

"I guess she made her choice," Captain LaRon says.

"What was that about?" Fitzroy asks.

"Man, you don't want to know," LaRon replies.

"Try me." Fitzroy says.

"I made a big, big mistake and took the girl out a couple of weeks ago. I realized there was no chemistry immediately. She was immature and so was her conversation. The girl has been literally stalking me. Last night when I got off work and went home I saw her car parked in my yard. I had to turn around and leave." LaRon shakes his head.

I take my seat again, hoping this girl doesn't come back. Lord knows I'm tired and not up for any drama.

"Wait, let me get his right. The girl was in your yard uninvited and you turned around and left. Something's wrong with that picture," Fitzroy says like a detective.

"Well...I had this girl with me who just moved down here from New Jersey and I didn't want any problem. So we just went to her house. The girl sort of favors you, Faith. Asha probably didn't see you come on the boat with Fitzroy because she was down below collecting tickets, and when she walked in she thought you were Candy," Captain LaRon explains.

"Candy?" Fitzroy asks.

"Yeah, Candy! And trust me, she's some kind of sweet!"

The men laugh while I just shake my head. It appears that Captain LaRon is quite a lover. I'm sure when he's driving this big boat and wearing that important looking uniform he needs a catcher's mitt to catch all the panties women drop when he flashes those pretty white teeth and invites them to sit in the captain's chambers.

The boat pulls up to the dock in St. John. We watch as LaRon maneuvers the boat into position along side the dock. Several of his crewmembers jump from the boat and quickly secure the ropes, steadying the boat so the passengers can disembark. Fitzroy and LaRon shake hands. I thank him for the ride and we exit the boat. Once on the dock Asha approaches us. Fitzroy shields me from her.

"I'm sorry. I tink you was somebody else. And no disrespect to you, Officer Fitzroy," Asha apologizes.

"No problem," I say. With Fitzroy's arm around my neck and my arm around his waist we continue walking toward the police station where Fitzroy left his car.

"Do you think I should have said something else to her?"

"Like what, Faith?" Fitzroy says with a puzzled expression.

"I don't know, I just felt in my spirit I should tell her to wait for the man God has for her," I say.

"I'm not sure if she would hear you," Fitzroy replies.

Once at Fitzroy's house, I immediately fall in love with the place all over again. After locking his gun in the cabinet Fitzroy excuses himself. He goes to take a shower. I busy myself by setting the table and heating up the food I brought from home. The telephone rings. Fitzroy hollers out of the shower for me to get it. I feel a little uncomfortable about answering his telephone. It takes me a few seconds to realize that this man is about to be my husband and soon this will be my phone too. I boldly answer.

"Hello...Lucinda, Fitzroy's in the shower. I see...Well that's mighty kind of you...I'm lost for words...well, thank you...you too...goodnight."

Well that's a shocker. The bathroom door is open and Fitzroy again hollers out of the shower.

"Who was it, Faith?"

I walk closer to the bathroom. "It was Lucinda," I casually say.

With soap on his body Fitzroy open the seamless glass shower door so I can hear him. He steps half-way out with one foot on the bath mat and the other inside the shower. He thinks I'm still in the kitchen. "She didn't say anything stupid to you, did she?"

I'm speechless. My eyes are locked on Fitzroy's genitalia. Oh my God. The thing is so long it's half way down to his knees and it's fat. Lord, please have mercy on me. I have never seen anything so big. Fear and pleasure race up and down my body. I briskly walk back into the kitchen. I hear Fitzroy calling my name.

"Faith, did she say anything offensive?"

No, as a matter of fact, she wanted to congratulate me on our engagement," I holler back at him, distracted with visions of joy to come dancing through my head.

"Humph!" Fitzroy says and closes the door to the shower. I decide against going in the bathroom and asking him what 'humph' means. I think it would be safer if I wait until he's dressed, or I might do something I'll enjoy immensely, but regret tomorrow.

Fitzroy joins me at the table. He's wearing a pajama bottom and no top. The man smells good.

"Wow, Faith, you must be a magician. How'd you cook all this food while I was in the shower? God knows I'm hungry!"

"The meal is compliments of Zipporah. However, don't get used to it because this might be the last time I'll allow you to eat another woman's cooking," I lovingly say.

"That's fine by me. Let's bless. Father God, we thank You for the food we are about to receive for the nourishment of our bodies. We thank You for Sister Zipporah preparing it for us, and I look forward to my beautiful bride being my only chef. Amen." We laugh.

"So what does 'humph' mean when I told you Lucinda called to congratulate us?"

"It means don't trust her as far as you can spit! The woman is wicked, conniving, manipulative and a liar," Fitzroy says as he enjoys his food.

"All of that, huh?" I jokingly say.

"And then some. But don't worry baby, I already told her I will be her worst nightmare if she ever tries to do anything mean to you again," Fitzroy proudly says.

I smile and watch as my fiancé enjoys his meal. We talk about Wally and Lucille putting Junior on the plane.

Fitzroy says Junior was so scared he kissed his father and thanked him for saving him from going to jail. We didn't talk about Mario Maynard or the officer that got shot. Fitzroy avoided those details. It suddenly dawned on me what being the wife of a cop will be like. You do a lot of praying when your husband is at work and a lot of rejoicing when he comes home.

After I loaded the dishes in the dishwasher I changed into my nightgown, kissed my fiancé and turned in for the night in the guest room. Just as Fitzroy turns to go into his room he calls out to me, "Faith, I saw you looking at 'Mister'," and then he laughs.

"Mr. who?" I naively say.

"Your Mister," he says looking down towards his groin area.

Embarrassed, I laugh. "Well tell 'Mister' that '*Missis'* can't wait to make his acquaintance on our wedding night." I smile and climb into bed. "Lord, I'm so proud of myself!" I could scream.

The next morning we park in a no parking zone and walk a few steps onto the dock to meet Momma and Aunt Dot who are just getting off the ferry. Once again, LaRon is at the helm. Fitzroy and I waved to him. He opens the door to the captain's quarters and hollers down to Fitzroy.

"Officer Fitzroy! Man, I need your help!" A large white gauze is taped to the side of LaRon's face.

I continued walking to meet Momma and Aunt Dot leaving Fitzroy to help LaRon with his dilemma. I'm sure the gauze on the side of his face has Asha, his jealous lover's name, written all over it. LaRon climbs down from the boat so he can talk to Fitzroy up close and personal.

I kiss Momma who is a bit overdressed for church. I forgot to tell her that people on the island rarely wear hat and gloves to church unless it's a special occasion like 'Women in Hats Day' or a funeral. Aunt Dot on the other hand looks like 'Bahama Momma.' She's wearing a big floppy sun hat with fruit all around it. A yellow bathing suit and a red, yellow, blue and green floral beach wrap tied around her waist along with hot yellow beach flip flop sandals adorned with a giant green flower. Aunt Dot is also carrying a big straw beach bag in the shape of a banana.

"Well, aren't we the colorful one," I say to her.

"Don't hate. I know I look good. Besides, I didn't want Marlin to miss me in the crowd," Dot says.

"A blind man could spot you from St. Croix," Momma says in disgust. I can't help but laugh out loud.

"I refused to sit with her on the boat, Faith. Your Aunt Dot looks like a giant bag of skittles! Let's keep walking. Let her find her Mango Man before someone thinks she's with us." Momma walks ahead of us in true 'First Lady' form.

"Alright Mrs. High and Mighty. I hope you burn up in that hot behind hat and that suit!" Aunt Dot says loudly.

Momma, holding her head up high, ignores Aunt Dot and keeps walking. Aunt Dot notices Fitzroy. Momma doesn't.

"Looks like Brother Fitzroy is on 'official duty' again," Aunt Dot teases.

"Isn't he always?" I reply. Fitzroy spots us and excuses himself from LaRon.

"I'll get with you later, man," Fitzroy promises.

Momma turns to see if we are following her. She stops so we can catch up. "You look very festive, Mrs. Dot," Fitzroy says.

"Thank you, dear," Aunt Dot replies. Not sure if it was a compliment or just a statement, she smiles. At the entrance to the dock we hear the sound of a loud muffler backfiring. We see Marlin driving an old sky blue and white convertible Volkswagen 'Thing'. The Volkswagen Thing was hot in the early 70's. The doors were designed to come off and windows were designed to flip down, all of which were flipped down and taken off.

"What kind of military contraption is that Marlin's driving?" Momma asks.

"I like it! See ya later. My chariot awaits me." Aunt Dot sashays to the car where grinning Marlin gets out to help her in. We watch as they drive off in the direction of Jumbie Beach with their muffler sounding like it's about to explode.

"All the money that man has, I don't know why he doesn't buy a new car," Fitzroy says.

"Money? He looks like a vagabond," Momma says as Fitzroy opens our car door.

Fitzroy continues talking as he drives in the direction of Cruz Bay Baptist Church. "Marlin is one of the richest men on St. John. The Coconut Palm Resort is built on land he sold them."

"Stop lying!" I say.

"I'm not lying. He lives right next door to the hotel in a little shack right on the beach. The hotel planted a bunch of mango trees at Marlin's request to buffer his shanty from the five star hotel. They recently offered him double what they paid for the 50 acres he sold them 20 years ago, to purchase the land his little shanty is on. See, you never know who's rich around here. People don't flaunt their worldly goods like they do in the states," Fitzroy informs us.

"Is there anything *you* want to tell us?" I ask.

"About being rich?" he asks.

"Yes. Are you rich too?" I ask.

"Beyond measure! I'm about to marry a beautiful, godly woman who loves me. Now, how much richer can I get?" Fitzroy brags.

"Good answer!" Momma says. We all laugh.

Fitzroy pulls into the courtyard of the little Baptist church, parks, and opens the doors to let us out. The pastor and his wife are standing at the entrance, greeting people as they arrive. Fitzroy introduces Momma and me. I have never been to this church before. Fitzroy and I had been going to a Pentecostal church in St. Thomas. Fitzroy enjoyed the message but he didn't like the people falling on the floor when the pastor touched their heads and said, 'Be healed'. He thought some of them were fake and playing with God. He finally refused to go back to worship when a few of the members who praised God on Sundays showed up on Mondays at the courthouse fussing and cussing about some crime they claim they didn't commit although the evidence showed they did. I told him he shouldn't look down on the people. Church is like a hospital. People are sick and they come there for healing. He agreed and then said we would try the 'Baptist Church Hospital'. At least no one would be falling out in the aisles. He wanted a little less drama and more Word. I told him I was willing to give it a try. This is the church where Lisa says she and Trevor are counseling with the pastor and will be married. Kamari will also be attending their pre-school.

"Hello, Pastor. My best friend Lisa Walker and her fiancé Trevor Libard are getting married in your church," I say as we are greeted at the front door of the church.

"Yes, yes. Brother Trevor, Sister Lisa and their lovely little girl are here with us this morning."

"What a surprise," I say and spot them sitting towards the front as soon as I step into the little church. Momma stays behind chatting with the pastor's wife before following Fitzroy and me inside. Lisa and Trevor are surprised to see us.

"Girl, why didn't you tell me you were coming here to church?" Lisa says.

"I didn't know until after I dropped you at the boat. Move over." We all slide on the same row. Fitzroy and Trevor shake hands.

"Where's Mrs. Gloria?" Lisa asks.

"She's back there doing her 'First Lady' thing. Talking to the pastor's wife," I reply.

"I guess Mrs. Dot hooked up with her 'Mango Man." We laugh.

"He's taking her to Jumbie Beach as we speak." Fitzroy, shocked, turns around. "Jumbie Beach?! Faith, why would you let him take her there? That's not a place you take a lady on a date," he scolds.

I'm lost for words. I still don't say anything.

Momma enters the church and greets Lisa and Trevor.

"Where's Kamari?" She asks.

"She's in children's church," Lisa says.

"Oh. Well, the First Lady invited me to sit next to her. I'll talk to you after service." Momma walks to the front row taking a seat next to the pastor's wife.

"Look at Mrs. Gloria. She's found her seat on 'First Ladies Row'." Lisa giggles.

Fitzroy is quiet. I know he's angry about Aunt Dot being at Jumbie Beach. I avoid discussing it.

"Let's all stand and turn to Hymn number 162 "Pass Me Not, Oh Gentle Savior. Hymn 162," Pastor says. We all stand and sing.

The pastor's sermon is about taking a stand for what is right even when everyone else is doing wrong. A couple of times during the service I think Fitzroy was looking at me. I felt so stupid. The next time he asks me about it I'm just going to tell him I just assumed Marlin told Aunt Dot Jumbie Beach was a nude beach. I mean with all that hot talk about checking out the 'big mango' I didn't think it would be a problem. I mean it's not like Marlin didn't see her running naked with her breasts flapping up and down on the beach at Water Island yesterday. Maybe the pastor is talking to me. I should have taken a stand for what's right. But then who am I to say anything with all my skeletons in the closet. Less than a year ago if Daemon had asked me to jump naked from the Santa Monica pier I probably would not have given it a second thought. I thank God He saved me from my indiscretion. Besides, my mind was so consumed with Fitzroy's safety during the drug bust, I didn't care who swam naked on Jumbie Beach.

"Lord, please forgive me," I say.

Service is over and I hear Lisa calling my name.

"Faith! What are you thinking about?" Lisa says.

"I'm sure it's about letting Marlin take her aunt to a nude beach," Fitzroy says as he excuses himself to go and talk to the pastor.

"Look, I'm going to go and get the baby from children's church. Don't leave." Lisa exits.

"Don't worry, little sister. You know your man wouldn't be himself if he weren't trying to protect everybody from evil. Look, Lisa cooked a pot of food. Why don't you all come over for lunch?" Trevor says as he hugs me trying to make me feel better.

"Sounds good to me. Let me see what Brother Fitzroy wants to do."

Lisa returns with Kamari who is wearing a beautiful white sailor dress with blue and white hair boggles in the shape of a ship. As soon as Kamari sees Momma she runs into her arms.

"I think I've been 'dissed'!" I say.

"Next time change her diaper and she might show you some love," Lisa says laughing.

We all exit into the courtyard of the church making small talk with church members. A safari bus stops in front of the church on the other side of a tall wall that separates the yard from the street. I hear Aunt Dot's voice.

"You sure this is the only Baptist church in Cruz Bay? They said they were going to the Baptist Church."

"Trust me, madam; this is the only Baptist Church in Cruz Bay."

"Well how much do I owe you?"

"That will be fifteen dollars, madam."

"Fifteen Dollars?! Cabs in Atlanta don't cost that much money!"

Fitzroy walks around the other side of the wall and rescues the driver from Aunt Dot by offering to pay. We all agree to go over to Lisa and Trevor's for lunch. They get into their car and leave the courtyard. Momma is saying good-bye to pastor and his wife as she looks up and sees Dot coming into the courtyard with Fitzroy. Momma, embarrassed at the way Dot looks, quickly walks past me on her way to the car as if she doesn't know her sister.

"Faith, tell Fitzroy to hurry up and throw her in the car before she embarrasses us."

When the pastor and his wife go back into the church to lock up, Fitzroy, Aunt Dot and I are the only ones left in front of the church.

"That nasty man had the nerve to take me to a naked beach! It was bad enough we had to climb down a steep hill to get to the water but when we got there he proceeded to take off his clothes," Aunt Dot says with disgust.

This was the moment when I thought I could redeem myself. "I thought you wanted to check out his 'Big Mango'," I say.

"Not outside on a beach in front of God and everybody! Those sorts of things you do in the privacy of your home. He had the nerve to tell me I was overacting, and attempted to untie my beach wrap. I smacked him so hard his teeth flew out his mouth and landed in the water. I left that nasty fool on the beach diving, trying to find his teeth." Aunt Dot is truly upset.

"I'll have to have a few words with Marlin. I don't know what's gotten into him. He's usually quite a gentleman." Fitzroy says, leading us to the car where we join Momma. Before we get in the car Aunt Dot stops us.

"Please do me a favor and don't mention this to my sister. She'll condemn me to hell right here in front of this church."

"I thought you said Momma wasn't petty," I say.

"She's not. But trying to get her to understand why I would go to a nude beach with a man I only met yesterday might be stretching it."

"Got yah," I say.

As we pull out onto the road headed to Lisa and Trevor's we climb the steep hill known as Jacob's Ladder. Behind us we hear the sound of a loud muffler backfiring. Fitzroy looks out his rear view window and smiles. We continue toward Chocolate Hole.

Chapter 24

We ate until our bellies were well past full. Lisa has really learned to cook like a true West Indian and I can see Trevor loves every bite of it. I watch him finish his third plate of stewed goat, plantain, peas and rice, dumb bread and ginger beer. I can't help wondering if eating like this might be the reason his blood pressure is high, which necessitates the use of Viagara to aid him in managing his manly obligations. Trevor kisses Lisa and thanks her for the wonderful dinner as he and Fitzroy make their way onto the deck to listen to a cricket game on the radio. Their favorite team is playing. The stakes are high. It's the final game of the Eastern Caribbean League playoffs. Their boys from St. Kitts are presently winning.

Momma is in 'Grammy heaven' singing all the nursery rhymes she used to entertain me with in between playing peek-a-boo with Kamari. I help Lisa with the dishes while we laugh about Aunt Dot, who just went out on the deck to talk to Fitzroy and Trevor about Marlin sitting outside in the driveway in his 'Thing'. Marlin followed us to Lisa's house after church and refuses to leave until Aunt Dot allows him to apologize. Aunt Dot asks Fitzroy if she could borrow his gun and put Marlin out of his misery. She's tired of seeing him sitting out in the driveway in the hot sun looking like a sick, pitiful dog. Fitzroy tells her he can't give her his gun but he will go out and have a few words with Marlin on her behalf. Aunt Dot settles for that and gives up on shooting Marlin. Of course, Momma wants to know why the sudden change in the way she feels about the Mango Man.

"He lost his manners and needs to be taught a lesson," Aunt Dot says.

"I'm sure the whole story will come out sooner or later; it always does," Momma replies.

Fitzroy goes out to the driveway and joins Marlin in the car, ready to listen to his testimony. We can't hear what they're talking about but Marlin is doing some serious explaining. His hands are constantly flapping in the air and pointing towards the house. Lisa, Aunt Dot and I have a ringside seat at the front window. I find it very amusing seeing this man who is twice Fitzroy's age explaining his dilemma like a kid trying to prove his point to a scolding parent. Aunt Dot on the other hand found nothing amusing about it. Even though she was mad and her feelings were hurt, deep down inside I could tell she loved all the attention.

"Lord, I think the old man is crying!" Lisa yells. Aunt Dot pushes us out of the way so she can get a closer view from the window.

Lisa and I run to the front door and crack it, trying not to appear too conspicuous. "Looks like tears to me," I say. Then we see Marlin lay his head on Fitzroy's shoulder while Fitzroy pats his back and comforts him like a child.

"Oh Lord! Now all the man's cool points have gone out the window! I know Mrs. Dot doesn't want a crying man!" Lisa exclaims. We close the door and walk over to where teary-eyed Dot continues to stare out of the window.

"Isn't that sweet?" she says.

"Isn't what sweet?" Lisa interrogates.

"Marlin," Aunt Dot sobs.

Momma crosses over to the window from the couch to observe. "Looks like a grown fool out there crying like a baby to me," she says and walks back over to the couch.

"That's not what I see. I see a sensitive, caring man," Aunt Dot says.

"Why don't you go out there and talk to him, Aunt Dot? Give him a chance," I say.

"I think I will," she says. Aunt Dot checks her hair in the hall mirror and then exits to talk to Marlin.

Trevor runs from the deck and hollers out the window, "Fitzroy man, the Bajans are killing us!" We see Fitzroy heading back to the house. Aunt Dot stops him in the driveway and kisses him on the cheek. She continues walking to the 'Thing' where Marlin quickly gets out of the car, runs around and respectfully opens the passenger door for Aunt Dot to get in.

"What's the score?" Fitzroy asks Trevor, who stopped in the kitchen to take a Guinness out of the refrigerator for him and Fitzroy.

"The Bajans have 116 runs. That Brown fellow is good." The men return to the deck and continue listening to the game.

After we finish cleaning the kitchen we join Momma in the living room holding sleeping Kamari on her lap.

"Mother Gloria let me put her in her bed," Lisa says as she attempts to take Kamari out of her arms.

"No, no. I don't mind holding her."

"Mother, are you trying to spoil my child?" Lisa teases.

"Yes! Now do you have a problem with that? Don't you know it's a Grammy's job to spoil her grandchildren reckless and then send them home to their parents?"

We all laugh.

"When will Kamari permanently come to live with you and Trevor?" I ask.

"Laurie Ann is leaving next week. You might get to meet her before you leave. She said she would pick the baby up around 4:30," Lisa says.

"I still can't understand how she could let this beautiful child go. It just doesn't make sense," Momma says sadly.

"Her loss, my gain," Lisa says boldly.

Aunt Dot peeps her head in the door smiling. "What boat are we taking back over to St. Thomas?"

"The six o'clock boat." I reply.

"Great. Marlin wants to show me where he lives. He says it's not too far from here. I'll be back shortly."

Momma shakes her head. "Remind me to avoid the water, stay out the sun and most of all not to listen to a thing that comes out of these men's mouths because it looks like my sisters have gotten smitten by island men just like you girls." Momma continues shaking her head smiling.

"See you shortly," Aunt Dot says.

"Just don't make a fool out of yourself!" Momma hollers as Aunt Dot closes the door.

We hear the sound of the 'Thing' starting up. The loud backfiring muffler startles Kamari who begins to whimper. Momma rocks and calms her back to a restful sleep.

Lisa shows us a picture of the wedding gown she's purchasing from a bridal shop in Los Angeles and the sexy maid of honor gown she's expecting me to wear exposing ninety-eight percent of my breast, and the back of the dress drapes down exposing the whole of my back, stopping just before it reaches the top of my butt.

"Lisa, are you trying to get my daughter arrested for indecent exposure? That looks like something those women wear to the Academy Awards," Momma rebukes.

"With Faith's shape this gown will look stunning," Lisa replies.

I realize how serious Lisa is about me wearing this 'Whore-Rena' gown. I don't want to hurt her feelings but at the same time I know there is absolutely no way I am going to wear it.

"Girl, you know you don't want me to wear that gown on *your* wedding day. If I put that on I'll steal the show. People will say, 'Lisa who?' No girlfriend, this is your day and all eyes should be focused on you, not me. Now if you really want me to upstage you, like you said, with this shape, I can work that gown," I say, praying she will pick something else.

"You have a point. On my wedding day, it's about me. What was I thinking?" Lisa shows us another choice.

"That's nice!" Momma and I say at the same time.

I remind Momma that Aunt Lucille doesn't have a key to the house and maybe we should give her a call and let her know there's a hide-a-key on the ledge of the gazebo at the far end of the property in case she needs to get something out of the house. Momma tells us Lucille and Wally stopped by this morning and moved most of her things up to Wally's house at his request. I was surprised Momma was able to tell us this with ease.

"I knew it was just a matter of time before it would happen. That's why in each of the compartments of her luggage I placed a copy of scripture dealing with fornication. And I handed brother Wally a letter as he was taking the last suitcase up the hill," Momma proudly says.

"What did the letter say, Mother Gloria?" Lisa asks, dying to know all the details.

"All I can say is either he will do right by her or flee like Daemon did when Rev flew out to Los Angeles to get him straight about violating his daughter!" We all laugh.

"Oh, Momma I forgot to tell you. Daemon is getting married to the Sunday school teacher I rented my house to. And get this...their wedding date is on my birthday," I say.

"Lord, have mercy! What a wonderful birthday gift. Now you have been totally saved from that man. I had no idea your Daddy would have such an impact," Momma says.

"So are they going to stay in your house? That might be weird for Daemon, making love to his new wife in the same room he used to..." I punch Lisa in the arm.

"We get the point!" I boldly say.

"Ouch!" Lisa cries.

"I'm not sure if they will move or not. I called Allison and told her she is welcome to stay there as long as she wants. I have no problem with her and Daemon living there. As a matter of fact, she was so happy to hear I'm engaged too."

"I bet she was. As homely as that chick is, she's probably scared you might come back to Los Angeles, kick her behind out of your house and take Daemon back!" Lisa says.

"You know sometimes I question why I call you my best friend. You say some of the most 'off the wall' stuff."

"It's the truth." Lisa points her finger at me.

The St. Kitts Cricket Team lost big time to the Barbados team. Trevor and Fitzroy blamed it on one of the bowlers. Trevor went so far as to denounce the man's citizenship saying he was born in St. Lucia and wasn't a Kittitian. Trevor said the bowler made the people from St. Kitts and Nevis look bad. Fitzroy just laughed and shook his head as he reminded Trevor that the man moved to St. Kitts when he was ten months old and both his parents are Kittitians.

Laurie Ann came to pick up Kamari. Lisa introduced Momma and me to her. She turned out to be the woman I thought she was, who worked at the club where Lisa and I went on 'girls' night out'. She had a bad attitude then. Now realizing she knew about Lisa all along, I understand why.

Laurie Ann stayed a while and talked with Momma, Lisa and Trevor. Lisa even offered her leftovers.
Fitzroy and I went out on the deck to discuss wedding plans and what to do with all these houses we would collectively own. Fitzroy was excited about having the wedding in Atlanta. He was looking forward to meeting all his new stateside relatives. We both thought it was a great idea to have the wedding in the church where I grew up. Fitzroy prayed that when we went to Nevis he would be able to talk his dad into coming to the wedding. He remembers how unsuccessful he was at getting his mother to the states to get help with her diabetes. I assured him this would be different. His father would be coming to celebrate our new life as husband and wife and not for medical reasons. He smiled and acknowledged I had a point.

We then talked about the townhouse in Los Angeles. Fitzroy laughed when I told him the girl I was renting it to is engaged to my old boyfriend. He confirmed that God works in mysterious ways. I thought we should sell the townhouse since I had no desire to return to Los Angeles. It was settled that we would give Allison the first option to purchase and if she passed on the opportunity we would list it with a realtor.

"I'll sell my house and move to Bordeaux if you think you'll be happier there." Tears form in my eyes and I start to cry. "Did I say something wrong?" Fitzroy says as he comforts me.

"No darling. I just love you so much and I would be very comfortable with your home becoming our home."

We kiss and hug as Lisa enters.

"Faith, your old room is still available if you two need some privacy, or I can call and see if they have a room at the Coconut Palm Resort," she says joking.

"Group hug!" I say. Lisa, Fitzroy and I are embracing as Trevor enters.

"What???" Trevor says.

"Come on and join us, baby," Lisa says.

"I'll hug you and Faith but I ain't hugging no big ugly man!" We all laugh and individually thank God for all he is doing in our lives.

Aunt Dot met us at the six o'clock boat just as it was pulling away from the dock. Marlin whistled to the female captain and she pulled back to the dock to let Aunt Dot on board. Momma was relieved to see she had changed out of her Bahama Momma clothes and into a pair of jeans and a T-shirt that must have belonged to Marlin. The shirt read, 'No Problem Mon' on the front. And on the back it read, 'Sex is a misdemeanor. The more you miss the meaner you get'. Thank God Momma didn't see the back of her shirt until Aunt Dot got out of the guest car she was driving and walked into the house ahead of her. Had she seen the back of the shirt earlier, I'm sure she would have sat far away from Aunt Dot on the boat. Momma just shook her head and decided to pick her battles. She was glad her sister had made the boat and had decided not to stay the night with Marlin on their first date.

Lucille came down as soon as she heard the two cars pull into the parking lot. She was excited and grinning from ear to ear. I was so happy to see her. I had not seen her since the night we had dinner at Wally's. There was so much to talk about. Aunt Lucille waived airline tickets in the air.

"It's on! We are leaving for Nevis the day after tomorrow!" Lucille does a little dance. Excited, I join in. We lock arms turning left and then right.

"All right! Nevis, here we come!" Aunt Lucille and I sing.

"The day after tomorrow? That's too soon. Marlin is giving me swimming lessons tomorrow. He swears he's going to have me snorkeling before I leave to go back to Atlanta." Aunt Dot cries.

"Who is Marlin?" Aunt Lucille wants to know.

"You'll be happy to know you're not alone. There's a new fool in town and it's your sister. Dot has met a Bush Man. Excuse me, I mean a Mango Man and now she's acting giddy and gullible just like you. Dot, tell Lucille about you running up and down the beach naked on Water Island with your titties flapping in the sea breeze and Marlin in high pursuit," Momma teases Aunt Dot.

"Oh my Lord! Let me sit down and hear this story. Please tell, Dot, and don't leave out a single detail." Aunt Lucille takes a seat at the kitchen island.

"Trust me, Gloria is exaggerating! Faith introduced me to a wonderful man named Marlin when we arrived on Water Island. Marlin has a thing for mangoes and that's why they call him the Mango Man. He's very poetic and romantic," Aunt Dot says.

"I'm waiting to hear the part about you running on the beach naked with your breasts flapping in the wind!" Aunt Lucille says.

"Yeah, tell the scandalous part!" I holler.

"Faith you need to stop. It wasn't at all like that. Anyway, Linda's cousin was giving me a massage under the cabaña on the beach. The girl was good, too. She was working all my muscles until I happened to look down at my arm that was dangling at the side of the table close to the sand and I spotted a scorpion crawling up my arm. I freaked out and ran out of the cabaña. I jumped in the water hoping to drown the thing."

"Yeah and the crazy woman almost drowned herself. She forgot she doesn't know how to swim." Momma interjects.

"Anyway, Marlin jumped in and saved me," Aunt Dot brags.

"Were you still naked?" Aunt Lucille asks.

"As naked as the day she was born!" I say.

"It was quite embarrassing I must say," Momma adds.

"Was everybody looking at you? You must have scared some folks with that body," Aunt Lucille says. Aunt Dot punches her in the arm.

"I beg your pardon! I was so scared I didn't care if Jesus saw me naked on the beach," Aunt Dot says.

"Trust me, He and all the heavenly hosts were looking. They had a front row seat," Momma jokes.

"Actually, my assistant Linda Peters asked everyone not to come down on the beach. Other than the little children who were swimming in the water, no one else saw her up close," I say.

"Poor little children. I'm sure they will have a lot of questions for their parents, like was that the ladies stomach, or was that her butt turned backwards?" Aunt Lucille jokes. We all laugh.

"May I finish my story? Anyway, Marlin saved me and the rest is history," Aunt Dot says.

"You're not going to get off that easy. Lucille the man has the world's most ugliest car and it backfires. When they took off from the dock in St. John on their way to some beach for swimming lessons, the car backfired so loud people hit the deck. They thought it was a terrorist attack," Momma says. Even Aunt Dot gets a good laugh out of Momma's description of Marlin's car.

"And the sad part is the man is a millionaire. He can afford to buy a new car," I say.

"Hold up. A millionaire? Where did you hear that?" Aunt Dot asks.

"From brother Fitzroy. Marlin didn't tell you he's loaded?" I say.

"No. As a matter of fact, I felt a little sorry for the brother. He lives in a little shack on the water right next to that five star resort," puzzled Aunt Dot says.

"It's alleged that the developers paid Marlin a lot of money to build that resort on his property," Momma states.

"See, Aunt Dot, you can't judge a book by the cover. You thought Marlin was just a poor Mango Man," I say.

"Wow, I'm stunned," Aunt Dot says.

"Well, I'm not sure if this is a good time to tell you, but George, your husband in Atlanta, called this morning. You remember him don't you?" Aunt Lucille says.

"Vaguely," Aunt Dot says laughing.

"Well, he wanted me to inform you that he's coming back home and he misses you very much. It appears the grass wasn't greener on the other side.

Chapter 25

Juvenile Court was packed - standing room only. Every member of Janna's as well as Eric's families was present and accounted for. Mr. Atkins, Rosalinda, Nyla, Chloe, Solange, Emmaus and three attorneys were the last to enter the courtroom. When Chloe saw all the people who came out to support her, tears of joy streamed down her face. Family members and friends clapped and cheered as they took their seats. Chloe's attorneys approached the judge's bench. Lisa and I sat next to Fitzroy and cried like little babies as he comforted us. When everyone finally quieted down, the weirdest thing happened. Three young ladies stood up in the back of the courtroom crying out one at a time.

"He was my father and he repeatedly raped me!"

"He was my uncle and he raped me!"

"I am fourteen years old. He was my neighbor and he raped me many times over!"

All heads turn to the back of the courtroom. Everyone is trying to understand what is going on.

"Order in the court! Order in the court!" The judge pounds his gavel.

The three women continue talking, ignoring the judge. "He gave me drugs then took advantage of me!"

"He told me not to tell!"

"He said he loved me and wanted to marry me."

The judge continues pounding the gavel. "I want this courtroom cleared out. The only people to remain are the three women in the back who seem to have trouble understanding what 'order in the court' means! I also want the attorneys and their client to remain."

Everyone slowly clears the courtroom, but not before they kiss Chloe or pat her on the hand. Mr. Atkins and Eric stay. As we exit the courtroom I see Mr. Atkins approach the bench talking very casually to the judge. Then it hits me. This is Judge Drew, the judge whose marriage of 30 years and career Mr. Atkins helped save, by the grace of God, when word got out he was having an affair with a supposed 18-year-old illegal alien from Santa Domingo. The girl turned out to be 17 years old and claimed she was pregnant. Not only had she lied about her age but she had nearly managed to talk him into divorcing his wife.

Apparently I didn't give Mr. Atkins enough credit. Looks like his plan to free Chloe was in full affect and working. I wondered if he had anything to do with the testimonies of the three victims who stood up at the back of the courtroom. I'm willing to bet the two who came from Dominica were flown here to St. Thomas on his private plane. Mr. Atkins was truly a man of his word. He is not going to stop until this wrong is made right and it looks as if things are moving in that direction. For Fitzroy's benefit as an officer of the law, everything was being done through the court system and in perfect order, just as he requested. I smile as I wait with the rest of the crowd outside the courtroom. We make small talk, laughing about happy moments we shared with Janna and the girls. Even though I'd only known her a short while, I felt privileged to be able to share at least one story where she had touched my life and made me laugh.

It seems like an eternity before we are allowed back into the courtroom. As soon as we enter, we see Chloe smiling and hugging her father. Nyla runs up and joins them. The judge assembles everyone.

"I must say this is a very unusual case. This young woman represents the many children who are victims of child molestation and incest on our islands. My heart cries out in pain and sadness. We Virgin Islanders must stand together to help stop this terrible injustice that is happening to our children. Two of the young ladies who were yelling at the back of my courtroom traveled all the way from Dominica to have their voices heard. It appears the deceased Mr. Junnis Mantu took advantage of a lot of young women before he met his demise. As God is my witness, I will make a pledge to each of you young ladies that I will punish anyone found guilty of child molestation in my court to the fullest extent of the law. Chloe and Nyla, I'm very sorry that you had to lose your mother because of a bad choice she made. We can't bring her back. But I urge you to hold on to the positive memories you have of her. And remember that none of us are perfect people. Chloe I know you are carrying a heavy burden for what you did and it is my prayer that time will help to ease the pain. There are a lot of people here today who love you and each and every one of us, including myself, are here for you. I ask all of you family members and friends to continue to pray for this child and the other victims as they go through their healing process. Bail has been set and paid by Mr. Atkins on your behalf, Chloe. You are free to go and I will see you back in court in a couple of months. At that time we will bring resolution to this case. God bless you, my child."

The judge strikes his mallet.

Mr. Atkins invited everyone to join us on Skyline Drive to continue celebrating. Thank God, Solange, Emmaus and Momma were there to help Zipporah serve all those people. Zipporah must have cooked everything she knew how to. There was so much food it seemed we could have fed the entire island. Emmaus and Solange came through on their promise to prepare stewed iguana for Momma. I was shocked when I saw her scoop up a second helping. Momma said it tasted like smothered steak. Aunt Lucille and Wally prepared a few of their gourmet dishes to add to the long buffet table already heavily laden with food. Wally even ran a few of his speakers down the hill from his house so people could dance on the patio and under the gazebo. Aunt Dot and Marlin showed up later in the day after her swimming lesson at Hawks Nest Beach. Marlin says he might be able to make a swimmer out of her after all. I had never seen my Aunt Dot so happy. Marlin brought a box of giant mangoes for everyone to share. Surprisingly, the mangoes were just as much a hit as the goat and conch. Island people love their mangoes. It was so good to see Chloe and Nyla laughing smiling and running around playing tag with the other children like they didn't have a care in the world. Fitzroy and I vowed to help watch over the girls. I know Janna would like that.

Rosalinda and I found time to talk. God bless her for her willingness to homeschool Chloe and Nyla until this whole thing blows over and they are strong enough to answer the barrage of questions that will surely come their way. Fitzroy and Mr. Atkins have apparently been spending time on the phone lately. Rosalinda knew about the engagement, not that I could hide it with this big rock on my finger. She said she would be honored to host my bridal shower at their castle. "Wow!" was all I could say. I introduced Lisa to Rosalinda who joined us on the patio with a plate full of food including stewed iguana.

"Girl, I don't know what this stuff here is, but I can't stop eating it! I think it's some kind of smothered steak."

Rosalinda and I both laughed. Lisa stopped with her fork in mid-air.

"Please don't tell me this is some kind of goat testicles or something nasty like that," Lisa says with her lips and nose frowned up.

"No, it's nothing like that," I said, trying to relieve her. Lisa continues eating. "If this is goat testis, it sure tastes good."

"No honey, that's stewed iguana." Rosalinda says matter-of-factly.

"Oh my God, Oh my God, I'm eating a baby Godzilla!" Lisa drops her plate on the nearby table and runs in the house headed towards the bathroom.

Rosalinda is concerned and suggests we go after her to make sure she's OK. I tell her not to worry. My friend is a drama queen.

"Isn't she the woman who broke Billy's heart?" Rosalinda asks.

"That's her. How is Billy doing?" I ask.

"He and a good friend of ours, Harold, the lobster man, are starting a charter business. They'll be flying passengers and lobster between islands. He sounds like he's happy. With my cousin who knows, but time has a way of healing broken hearts." Rosalinda says with hope in her voice.

I notice Momma sitting in the gazebo talking to the two girls who came from Dominica. Their smiles tell me Momma is doing what she's been trained to do - comfort those who are lost and hurting. Fitzroy, Mr. Atkins, and Eric are sitting at one of the patio tables laughing and talking. Mr. Atkins calls me to join them.

"Well, Faith, looks like God worked everything out," he casually says.

"He sure did, with the help of Chloe and Nyla's earthly godfather, I must add," Eric says.

Mr. Atkins waves Eric's accolade away. "Janna would not have forgiven me if I didn't do everything in my power to help her girls," he sadly says.

"Now, now, now! This is a time for rejoicing," Fitzroy says. I slide into the seat next to him and kiss him.

"Hey, you two love birds, I hear congratulations are in order," Eric says.

Fitzroy grins from ear to ear. "Yeah, she gave me a hard time and even made me beg, but I finally got her to say yes," he jokingly says.

I laugh and kiss him again.

"Faith, if there is anything Rosalinda and I can do to help make your wedding a memorable one, please don't hesitate to ask. You and Fitzroy are like family to us," Mr. Atkins lovingly says.

"Thank you. That's so sweet. Rosalinda has already offered to host my bridal shower at the castle. However, I really don't have a lot of friends in the Virgin Islands to invite other than Linda Peters from work and my best friend Lisa so I'm not sure if it makes sense," I say with concern.

"Well, why don't you put together a wish list of all the people from near and far that you would like to come to your bridal shower and e-mail it to Rosalinda. What the heck, we'll fly them here. How's that for a wedding gift?" Mr. Atkins says smiling.

"Oh my God! Oh my God!" I say as I run from the table with my arms flapping to tell Momma.

"Is Faith OK?" Mr. Atkins asks, puzzled.

"I think that was an 'I'm overwhelmed with joy, and thank you very much'." Fitzroy says to Mr. Atkins as they watch me run towards the gazebo.

"Someone might have to pinch her so she'll know she's not dreaming!" Eric adds.

Rosalinda, Aunt Dot, Aunt Lucille, Solange and Lisa were in the gazebo with Momma. They had just finished praying with the three young women who had been victimized by Junnis and were saying good-bye. Emmaus was waiting to take two of them to the airport to go back to Dominica and the third one to the market place to meet her parents. I excitedly shared the news with every one about Mr. Atkins offering to fly my friends to the Virgin Islands to attend my bridal shower. All you could hear was a group of women screaming with excitement and delight.

The last people to leave the celebration were Marlin, Eric and his sister Sasha, who had a much better attitude than she had when she was our waitress at North Star Restaurant. That was the night Lisa dumped Billy and announced she was marrying Trevor. I'm glad I got to meet her in a less stressful situation. We exchanged phone numbers and she invited me to work out with her at the Uptown Gym sometime. Zipporah and Momma packed up food for them and the other guests to take home and there was still a lot of food leftover. Wally suggested he and Lucille take it downtown to the senior citizens home and he would make a call to his cousin at the jail to see if they wanted some of it. Momma held on tight to the little bit of iguana that was left. She said she was having it with her grits in the morning. Marlin got the recipe from Emmaus and Solange and said he was going to make some for Aunt Dot who looked at him like he had lost his mind.

"No, baby, I don't do road kill!" she said as Marlin waved good-bye and took off in his 'Thing', which backfired louder than I'd remembered hearing before.

"I'm surprised they let him bring that car over on the barge," I say with amazement.

Fitzroy and Lisa had left together earlier. Lisa had to pick up Kamari from daycare and Fitzroy needed to tie up a few loose ends at the station in St. John before we took off for Nevis tomorrow. Aunt Dot announced she wasn't going to Nevis with us. She wanted to spend her last few days with Marlin before it was time to head back to Atlanta. Momma tried to back out of going. She said it looked like a "couples thing" with Lucille and Wally and Fitzroy and me going. I told her I needed her there to meet my future father-in-law and to make sure I was marrying into a nice family. She hemmed and hawed but finally relented.

Later that night while Momma and I were packing, Aunt Dot was eating leftovers and Lucille was with Wally, the telephone rang. Momma answered it, making small talk with George before giving the phone to Aunt Dot who didn't want to talk to him. Momma had to hit her with the phone before she would take it.

"What do you want, George...yes, Lucille told me you called...George I don't have to explain a darn thing to you...that is not going to work! Then start looking for a room to rent. Yes, I changed all the locks on the doors. George you made a choice: now you live with it...Call an exterminator and hire a housekeeper...Look man, work it out...I've moved on and I suggest you do the same!" Dot slams the phone down.

"Sounds like that went well," Momma sarcastically says.

"Don't start, Gloria. George thought leaving me for Sadie was going to make him happy and now he wants to come back home."

"That was quick," I say.

"Stupid fool. Everybody knew Sadie kept a nasty house except him. I guess by it being a 'wham, bam, thank you ma'am' kind of relationship with her, he never stopped long enough to see the filth in her house. Now he's complaining that her house is nasty and she's got roaches. I told him to hire a housekeeper and call an exterminator.

He says the kids are rude and want money all the time. I'm sorry, but I just don't want to hear George's sad story. Let him tell it to Oprah. I'm divorcing his ungrateful behind and moving on with my life. Faith, how much are you asking for your house in the mountains? I think I'll buy it."

"What?!" I say in shock.

"I'm not going to let that man harass me. I'll sell the house in Atlanta, which I had already planned to do, purchase a little condo for when I come up during the summer months to see my grandchildren and live down here in the winter months. Girl, I've realized that I've got to find happiness for myself. I can't depend on a man like George to make that happen for me. So give me a figure and I'll work on getting you the money," Aunt Dot boldly says.

"Well, looks like we're going to be neighbors," Momma says.

"What?!" Aunt Dot and I say in unison.

"It was going to be a surprise wedding gift to you, Faith. Every daughter needs her mother nearby when she plans a family. Lisa and I made arrangements for me to purchase her house for a price I couldn't refuse," Momma says with a big smile on her face.

"Please tell me how much that was so I can do a home market analysis and know how much to offer Faith."

We all laugh.

"That's between Lisa and me," Momma says as she continues packing.

"Gloria, don't make me hurt you before we get to be neighbors!"

"Don't worry, Aunt Dot, I'll offer you a price you can't refuse," I say as I hug her.

"Did I ever tell you you're my favorite niece?"

"Aunt Dot, I'm your only niece." We all laugh.

Chapter 26

Fitzroy was running late, so he decided to catch the boat directly into Charlotte Amalie from St. John and meet us at the airport. Lucinda had called and said she was having a problem with one of the twins. Apparently the older twin had stolen a cell phone out of the beach bag of a tourist that was snorkeling at Trunk Bay. Fitzroy said he needed to stop by to talk with the boy before we left to go to Nevis. I'd be telling a lie if I said it didn't bother me. Lucinda needed to find a daddy for those boys. Right now she was messing up my groove. I told myself to calm down. All I need to do is talk to Fitzroy, tell him my frustrations and he will probably do something about it. Momma could tell I was boiling hot as we went through customs and Fitzroy still had not arrived. Aunt Lucille was so excited about going to Nevis she picked up a guide to the Caribbean from the little bookstore in the terminal. She and Wally were marking off places he wanted to take us. Momma joined in and pointed out a few places that sounded interesting that she'd like to visit.

"Nesbitt Plantation. That looks exciting," she said.

"We'll go there for lunch and tour the grounds. The Plantation house is beautiful. You ladies will love the way it's decorated. It's very colonial. There are marble counters in the bathroom, fancy ceiling fans and original watercolor paintings by local artists. Oh, I forgot to mention the food. It's the best. The chef is a cousin of mine. He really does a nice job of blending local ingredients with international elements in his recipes. We must go to the beach BBQ on Thursday night. There's a 'jump up' band called Casanova. Those boys are so good they get everyone up and dancing on the beach deck," Wally says with pride.

"These old bones don't jump up so well anymore," Momma says.

"Well, just shuffle your feet, Gloria. It sounds like fun!" Aunt Lucille says.

"Maybe I'll book you guys at that hotel on Thursday. Then you can experience the Four Seasons *and* Nesbitt Plantation," Wally excitedly says.

"What a brilliant idea, darling," Aunt Lucille seconds.

I keep watching the customs area looking for Fitzroy. Momma pats me on the leg. "Don't worry honey. He'll be here." She gives me a reassuring smile.

A woman with a British accent announces the boarding of our flight. The four of us line up to board the plane. Besides us, there are no other people on this flight except the pilot and flight attendant. Now Wally, Lucille and even Momma are also looking towards the customs area for Fitzroy. I take out my cell phone and dial Fitzroy. It goes directly to his voice mail. A customs officer approaches the flight attendant who is collecting our boarding passes. He whispers in her ear. She acknowledges his message with a nod of the head. I can only assume that the stressful look on my face told her I was the person she needed to talk to.

"Madam, Officer Fitzroy is clearing customs now," she says as she rips my ticket.

Momma smiles, Wally breathes a sigh of relief and Aunt Lucille shakes her head and sucks her teeth, as if I should be ashamed of myself for thinking he wasn't coming.

"O, ye of little faith." She says and walks out onto the runway to board the small propeller plane.

If looks could kill, Fitzroy would be dead. As he raced to the gate to catch up with us, he saw the anger in my eyes. The smile on his face quickly turned upside down. I turned and walked away just as he was about to kiss me on the cheek. Here we go again! Déjà vu. This was a replay of how I felt a little over a week ago when we were in St. Croix and he didn't respect my feelings. Lord, I'm not going through this again! I stop just as I'm about to go up the stairs leading to the plane and turn toward Fitzroy who is walking behind me.

"Fitzroy, I will not allow you to disrespect me. If you think every time Lucinda calls with a problem you're going to run and solve it for her, you'd better look for another bride...I'm not having it!"

I didn't realize I was talking so loudly until I looked up the stairs and saw Wally, Lucille, Momma, the flight attendant and the pilot bunched in the doorway smiling at us.

"I will never disrespect you again. I told Lucinda she was going to have to call her father to help with the boys or pray for the Lord to send her a husband. Of course, I'll be there for them, I'm their uncle; but not if it means hurting you. I love you so much, Faith. Please forgive me." We embrace at the foot of the stairs.

"Excuse me...if you plan to go to Nevis you need to get on the plane," the flight attendant says. Everyone standing in the doorway whistles and cheers as we walk up the stairs.

Our flight to Nevis was quite bumpy. Momma and Aunt Lucille seemed to be handling the sudden drops in altitude better than I did. I found myself squeezing Fitzroy's hand each time we dropped and my stomach felt like we were on a roller coaster.

"Looks like we might get storm showers," Fitzroy says.

"As long as it's not a hurricane. Hurricane season did end last month, right?" I say with a bit of nervousness in my voice.

"Yes, but it has been known to linger on into December." Fitzroy pats my hand to comfort me. I begin to smile but it's cut short once we take another dip.

"How much longer before we arrive?" Aunt Lucille asks.

"About 15 more minutes," Wally says in a comforting voice.

"Good, cause I've repeated 'The Lord is my Shepherd' and 'The Lord is my light and my salvation' about 50 times; I need some more scriptures to recite!" Aunt Lucille says with anxiety.

"Just don't recite 'Now I lay me down to sleep'." Wally jokingly says.

I look over at Momma and I see her with her eyes closed. I know she's talking to the Lord.

The little propeller plane finally lands after skipping and skidding on the wet runway. The rain is coming down so hard you can barely see the small terminal. We are greeted by two customs agents with large umbrellas and led into the immigration building.

"Welcome to our beautiful island. I must apologize for this unseasonable weather we're having today. It seems to have come out of nowhere."

Fitzroy and Wally are soaked. There is only enough room under the umbrellas for Momma, Aunt Lucille and myself. The terminal looks like a ghost town. The customs officers inform us that we are the last flight to arrive for the evening. Apparently the storm is coming off the coast of South America not too far from Trinidad where flights have been cancelled. Momma, Lucille and I hand our customs forms and passports to the officer. Once our passports are stamped, we take a seat inside the terminal. There are no taxis outside waiting to take us to our hotel. When Fitzroy and Wally clear customs, they linger talking to one of the immigration officers who they know from their village. They are trying to get more information on the weather. Wally is upset that no one in St. Thomas knew about the storm; if they did know, they should have given us a heads up.

After Fitzroy tells the officer where we are going, the officer tells them that the road to the Four Seasons and Nesbitt Plantation is washed out. No cars are able to pass. It is agreed that we should head towards Brown Hill where the roads are somewhat passable. Fitzroy announces that we are going to his father's farm. The customs officer radios for a police vehicle with four-wheel drive to come and pick us up. There is a glimpse of daylight left and I can see the palm trees swaying ferociously. The flight attendant and pilot from our plane enter the terminal shaking out their umbrellas.

"Well, looks like we're stuck here in Nevis. I need to call my husband and tell him to find something for the kids to eat for dinner," the flight attendant says. She goes behind the airline counter to make a phone call, only to find out that the phone lines are down. "Hey mon, what's up with the phones?" she hollers across the small terminal to a customs officer.

"Current gone. Only a few villages on the island still have power. We're running on generator," the officer hollers back to her.

"Olivia, try my cell phone. You might be able to get through," the pilot says, handing her his cell phone.

"Man, this thing is dead as a door nail!" the flight attendant says.

Wally checks to see if his cell phone is working. His phone is on roam with a faint signal. "You might be able to get a call through on this." He hands her his cell phone.

"Thank you so much." The flight attendant dials her home. The signal is bad. Every other word is bleeping out.

"It's Mommy. I'm stuck in Nevis. There's a storm. It's Mommy. Yes, Mommy. Honey, get your daddy." The phone goes dead.

"Well, that was my four-year old daughter," the flight attendant says.

"Do you think she got your message? Aunt Lucille asks.

"I heard her say ok," she replies.

"The question is will she tell your husband? These children are terrible about giving messages," Wally says.

"If it was my 15-year old son, I'd be worried...but that little girl is a miniature woman. She's probably telling her daddy what to cook for dinner right now." We all laugh and nod our heads in agreement.

Two police cars pull up in front of the building.

"Olivia, the officers have made arrangements to take us to a guesthouse just up the road," the pilot informs the flight attendant who opens her umbrella and follows him to an awaiting police cruiser. The wind has really picked up and the rain is coming down in sheets. Once again, Momma, Aunt Lucille and I are escorted under a big umbrella to an awaiting car. Fitzroy and Wally wait until the men return and come on the second trip. I guess getting soaked once was enough. Fitzroy and Wally quickly load our suitcases into the back of the police cruiser. Wally sits up front with the officer while the four of us squeeze together tightly in the back seat.

"Man, this weather looks ominous," Wally, says as we continue down a dark paved road.

"Yeah, mon. Didn't you hear? We've just been upgraded to a category four," the officer says as he swerves to avoid hitting a fallen palm tree.

"Category four, as in hurricane?" I ask.

"Yes, madam. They've named her 'Lucille'."

All eyes turn to Aunt Lucille. We laugh.

"Lord, let's pray it's nothing like you or we all better start looking for a bomb shelter to take cover in!" Momma says.

"Thanks a lot, Gloria!" Lucille sarcastically replies.

"Don't worry dear, if it's anything like you, it will be a sweet sound in my ear," Wally interjects.

"It doesn't sound so sweet out there to me," I say with fear in my voice.

"Faith, I'm not going to let anything happen to you," Fitzroy whispers in my ear as he pulls me even closer to him.

"You'll be very safe at Fitzroy's father's place; it's an old fort where Lord Nelson himself fought off the French," the officer informs us.

"There's a fort on your dad's property Fitzroy?" I ask.

"Yes, and we all will be safe there just as the officer said."

"You told me your dad had a honey farm. You never said anything about living on the grounds of an historic fort."

"Yeah, mon, there's a lot of history there. The old cannons still line the fort wall," Wally cuts in.

"Just before Mum died, she and father decided to donate that portion of the property to the Historic Preservation Society. Needless to say, we are still waiting for them to accept the property and help with the restoration. Father wants to turn the old fort into a museum," Fitzroy tells us.

"It's a crying shame your father hasn't received any money yet to get the work started," the officer says.

"He better not hold his breath either. Our people are so slow at getting things done in Nevis. I just hope it happens in his lifetime," Wally says.

"Oh, it's going to happen! Father and I are prepared to do it ourselves if it comes down to that," Fitzroy informs us.

"Will I be dropping you further up the road at your brother's place in Brown Hill, Wally?" the officer asks.

"No, no. All of us will be going to Fitzroy's until the roads clear. Then we're headed to the Four Seasons and Nesbitt Plantation," Wally informs the officer.

"Say Wally, you know my sister would like to know you're in town. What do you say if I have her give you a call?"

Wally pauses for a second searching for words to say. Just as he is about to respond, Aunt Lucille speaks up. "What the hell would he want to hear from your sister for?"

Everyone is quiet. You can hear a pin drop. The officer clears his throat.

"No disrespect intended, madam. It's just that my sister and Wally were good friends at one time."

"Well that sounds like yesterday's news to me. What you can tell your sister is that Wally's in town and he brought Lucille with him and she isn't up for any crap! Let her know I'll huff and puff and blow her damn house down if she even thinks about calling my man!"

"Yes, madam," the officer responds.

"Lucille!" Momma scolds her.

"'Lucille, my foot! Y'all heard what I said. I didn't come down here in this hurricane to put up with no foolishness from some old flame. I'm nipping this in the bud! And you can tell her I'm a category 10!" Aunt Lucille crosses her arms and looks around daring anyone else to challenge her. Wally turns to face Lucille in the back seat.

"I can't see nobody but you, baby!" Wally winks at Lucille who smiles back with a wink of her own.

"Well, looks like we're here," the officer nervously announces.

"And not a moment too soon," Fitzroy says laughing.

We pull up into the driveway of a large stone house. One of the shutters on the house is flapping and knocking against the window. There is a large porch on the front of the house lined with several large rocking chairs. One of the chairs has turned over. You can hear the sound of the ocean pounding the shore, but it's too dark to actually see the water. Everyone thanks the officer for the ride except Aunt Lucille. We help Wally and Fitzroy roll our luggage to the front door, which we find wide open. Rain is blowing into the house.

"Father, Father!" Fitzroy yells out as he quickly searches the kitchen and parlor area.

"Mr. Brown?" Wally runs upstairs calling out. Fitzroy follows.

Both men return finding us standing in the same spot, clutching our purses. We're not sure if we should sit or run.

"What's going on Fitzroy?" I ask.

"I'm not sure. Sit down and relax. I'm going to check outside to see if Father is on the grounds trying to secure the bees." Just as Fitzroy is about to leave the power goes out. We find ourselves standing in the dark. Fitzroy goes into the parlor and lights two hurricane lamps on the mantle. We follow him into the parlor.

"There are a few more lamps in the kitchen. Faith, please look for them and light them. I need to go and look for Father."

"Don't worry, go, we will be fine."

Fitzroy kisses me and exits the house.

"Hold up buddy, I'm right behind you," Wally says as he runs to catch up with worried Fitzroy.

"This reminds me of an episode from *Tales of the Crypt*," Aunt Lucille eerily says.

Momma walks around the parlor checking out the pictures on the wall. "This must be Fitzroy and his twin brother when they were children."

Aunt Lucille and I walk over and join her. "Lord, that boy had some big teeth!" Aunt Lucille says.

"I think he looks cute!" I defend the picture.

"How can you tell which one is Fitzroy? They look just alike," Momma asks.

"The eyes. Fitzroy's eyes are smiling. The other boy's eyes look troubled," I say.

"You're right," Momma agrees.

"That must be a picture of Fitzroy's father. He sure is fine!" Aunt Lucille says.

"He's a very handsome man," Momma agrees.

"We'd better look for the other lamps before the men get back," I say.

"Well, I'm going to sit my butt right here. This house is a little too big for me to be roaming around in the dark," Aunt Lucille says as she takes a seat, clutching her purse.

"I'll go with you Faith," Momma says.

Aunt Lucille's eyes get big as silver dollars. She jumps up to follow us. "I'll be darned if you two are going to leave me here by myself."

I take a hurricane lamp off the mantle and lead us into the kitchen.

"What a beautiful country kitchen!" Momma says. We spot two more hurricane lamps on top of the cupboard. Aunt Lucille, who's the tallest, reaches up and takes them down. Momma finds a match on the stove and lights them.

"Why don't we leave one in here and take the other one upstairs?" Momma suggests.

"Take the other one upstairs? Why do we need to go upstairs? Can't we just go and sit our behinds in the parlor and wait for the men to come back? You two are a little too adventurous for me," Lucille says.

"Aunt Lucille, we need to find as many of these lamps as possible and place them in the rooms where we will be sleeping. Now are you coming or what?" I say.

"So I guess this means we won't be doing any five star hotels tonight?"

Momma and I ignore her and head up the stairs leaving Lucille standing there, trying to decide whether she's going to join us. Then, the loose shutter slams hard against the house and Aunt Lucille skips steps to catch up with us.

"I'm glad your brain decided to move out of the stupid position and get with the program!" Momma says.

The first bedroom we enter must be for Fitzroy's father. There is a giant four-poster mahogany bed with a matching velvet- cushioned seat at the foot of the bed. A large dresser with a hand-carved mahogany mirror is positioned in the center of the wall and a matching highboy dresser stands in the corner. The immaculately clean floorboards are made from thick pinewood. White sheer curtains with small flowered embroidery hang from the window. One of the windows is slightly opened. It's the window whose shutter is flapping back and forth.

"Let's secure that shutter," Momma says as she walks toward the window.

"Aren't we the brave one?" Lucille says sarcastically as she takes a seat on the bed. I hold the light as Momma reaches outside for the shutter, latching it in place.

"Now, that will help calm a few nerves."

We both turn to look at Aunt Lucille who seems to be enjoying Fitzroy's father's bed. "Ooo, this is one comfortable bed. I bet Poppa Brown and Momma Brown had some good times on this comfortable sucker!" Lucille jokingly says.

"You know you're nasty, don't you!" I say.

"Lucille, get your butt off that man's bed."

Momma lights the two hurricane lamps on the dresser in Fitzroy's dad's room. We continue down the hall to another room. The next room has two twin beds that mimic the same style as the king-size bed we found in Fitzroy's dad's room. In the corner of the room is an old wardrobe closet. I open it and find it's filled with bed linen and pillows. On each of the small nightstands we find hurricane lamps.

"I'm beginning to wonder if the power goes off around here often. I mean there is a hurricane lamp in each of these rooms. It's like folks are just sitting around waiting for the power to go off so they can light one," Lucille says.

"Looks to me like they are just prepared," I say.

We continue to the other four bedrooms and the bathroom lighting lamps. Just as we pass the bathroom, Aunt Lucille announces she has to go. Momma and I tell her we'll meet her downstairs when she's finished. Aunt Lucille looks at us like we just lost our minds.

"There is no way in hell y'all are leaving me in this bathroom alone! So don't even think about it. Now Faith, move a little closer so I can inspect the toilet before I sit my behind on it," Aunt Lucille says.

"Look, Lucille you don't need both of us in here with you while you take care of your business. You and Faith can handle this. I'm going downstairs to finish looking at the pictures," Momma says.

I block the door. "She's your sister. Why should I have to stay in here and suffer while she does her business?" I cry.

"Because I'm the momma and I say so. Now move out of the way! Good Lord, Lucille what did you eat? It smells like something dead up in there?"

Just as Momma is about to push me out of the way and escape to the parlor there is a loud knock at the front door. We hear Fitzroy and Wally's voices yelling,

"Open the door!"

"I know you're not going to leave me sitting here on this toilet with no light." Aunt Lucille cries anxiously as I turn to leave with the light.

"Come on, Aunt Lucille! Cut it short!" I say, opening the bathroom door to exit.

"I can't!" She cries out.

"Momma, hold the lamp and stay here with her. I've got to open the door for Fitzroy and Wally."

I race down the stairs in the dark. Fitzroy and Wally are pounding on the door and yelling,

"Open the door!"

"I'm coming!"

Something has happened, I thought. I say a prayer. When I open the door, I find Fitzroy and Wally holding an unconscious Mr. Brown whose forehead is bleeding.

"Faith, clear off the kitchen table!" Fitzroy yells.

I run as fast as I can with them close behind me. What happened?" I ask as I remove the sugar bowl and salt and pepper shakers from the center of the farm house style table.

"I'm not sure. We found him on the ground in the barn. I think he may have been hit with the barn door."

Fitzroy removes his father's soaking wet shirt. Wally finds a pot, lights the stove and starts to boil water.

"Where's Lucille?" Wally asks.

"She and Momma are upstairs in the bathroom," I say.

"Together?" Wally asks with a puzzled expression on his face.

"Yes, it's a girl thing...what can I do honey?" I ask.

"We're going to have to stitch his forehead up. It's bleeding pretty badly. There's a sewing kit in the second bedroom in the wardrobe closet. I need you to get it."

I race up the stairs as Aunt Lucille and Momma are heading down. "Momma, Fitzroy really needs your help. It's his father."

"Faith, there's a problem with the toilet. It won't flush and there's something wicked in there!" Aunt Lucille says, embarrassed.

"Aunt Lucille, right now there are more important problems at hand." I run up the stairs leaving Momma and Aunt Lucille rushing toward the kitchen.

"Is he breathing?" Aunt Lucille asks.

"Yes, but he's unconscious and bleeding," Fitzroy replies.

"Lucille, go in the parlor and get my purse."

Aunt Lucille hesitates but looks into Momma's eyes and realizes she'd better do it and she'd better do it quickly.

"My smelling salts should bring him around."

Lucille returns with Momma's purse just as I reach the kitchen with the sewing kit.

"Let me put some of my smelling salts under his nose." Momma opens a packet, placing it under Mr. Brown's nose. Within a few seconds he's sitting up like a lightning bolt hit him.

"Lord, have mercy, Hannah! What's that you put under my nose?"

"Dad, that's not Mum," Fitzroy says to his father who is still in a daze.

"Fitz, my boy, is that you? What are you doing here, and who are all these lovely people?"

"Dad, you need to lie back down. You got a terrible cut on your forehead. We need to stitch it up."

Mr. Brown obeys and lies down on the table. Wally, brings a pot of boiling water and places it on the table.

"Faith there is some gauze in the bathroom upstairs under the sink along with some peroxide. Would you be so kind to run up and get it?" Fitzroy asks with distress in his voice.

"Who's the doctor in this room?" Mr. Brown asks. Everyone is quiet.

"I've sewn up a few pheasants after I stuffed them with my famous guava berry stuffing." All of us look at Wally with disbelief.

Momma moves closer to the table and takes Mr. Brown's hand. "Don't worry, Mr. Brown, I have my nursing license. I'll take good care of you."

Our mouths hang open. I forgot Momma was a nurse before she married Daddy. All my life I've only thought of her as First Lady of my daddy's church and my mother.

"Hannah, you keep an eye on these young people," Mr. Brown says as he slips in and out of consciousness.

"Get some blankets. He's in shock. I'm going to need some monofilament line!" Momma yells her orders.

"And where the heck do you expect us to get some monofilament line from? I don't remember seeing a Home Depot on the way here from the airport." Aunt Lucille whispers in Momma's ear.

"Fitzroy, does your daddy have any fishing line around here?" Momma asks.

"Yes, his tackle box is on the back porch."

"Please get it as quickly as possible. I need you and Wally to clean the monofilament line in scalding hot water, and the needle as well. Lucille, keep the smelling salts nearby and when I tell you to put it under his nose, I need you to be ready."

"Got you, 'Nurse Ratched'."

Fitzroy returns with the monofilament line and I come with the blanket. Momma continues to clean the wound as she sews up the gash. The only sound that can be heard in the room is the wind howling outside and Momma praying.

Chapter 27

It was a long night for us. Mr. Brown kept slipping in and out of consciousness. Fitzroy and Wally were able to carry him up to his bedroom where 'Nurse Momma' sat in a chair at his bedside. The phones were down and even Wally's cell was not getting a signal. Fitzroy found an old transistor radio in the attic. We were able to listen to the weather report during the night. The only hospital on the island was being evacuated; apparently part of the roof had blown away. The government was calling for people with four-wheel drive cars to come to the hospital and help move the sick to nearby Sugar Bay Hotel.

Aunt Lucille suggested that we all sleep on the floor with blankets and pillows in Fitzroy's father's room. That way, we could take turns watching him. Even though that sounded thoughtful, I think Aunt Lucille was scared and wanted to remain with the group. However, Momma said no. She didn't need all those bodies robbing the room of air. Momma told Wally to find a room to sleep in and Lucille and I were to go and sleep in the room with the twin beds. We needed to get some rest because she was expecting Wally, Lucille and me up early to start breakfast. Mr. Brown would be hungry. Momma and Fitzroy agreed they would take turns sleeping in chairs at Mr. Brown's bedside. If I know Momma, she'll be doing more praying than sleeping. We all agreed to Momma's plan and left the room.

Of course, Aunt Lucille didn't listen to Momma's orders. No sooner than I was in the bed with the sheet over my head praying that the hurricane would pass, I heard her tiptoeing out of the room.

"And where exactly are you going 'Miss Hot Momma'?"

Aunt Lucille, looking like she just got caught with her hands in the cookie jar, approached my bed whispering, "Look, you know I love you and everything, but it's times like these that I need a strong chest to lay my head on. You understand." Aunt Lucille turned to leave the room.

"No, I don't understand! All I know is Momma said for us to sleep together in this room," I boldly say.

"Well, I'm not sure if you realize it, and I hate to go there on you, but...Gloria isn't my momma; she's yours. So, you better do what she says and I'll see you at breakfast in a few hours."

Just as Aunt Lucille was about to open the bedroom door the sound of thunder rolled through the room, followed by a bolt of lightening that lit up the room. Aunt Lucille raced to my bed. "Girl, move over!" She jumped under the covers with me. A few minutes later after things calmed down she asked, "Faith, would you be a dear and walk with me to Wally's room?" I rolled my eyes at her. "Fine, fine; I'll go by myself." She raced out of the room before the next round of thunder approached.

I wake up to the smell of bacon frying. The sun is shining and I can hear laughter coming from the kitchen. This can't possibly be the same house I went to sleep in only a few hours earlier. I jump out of bed and run to the window. The sea is a little choppy but the view is spectacular. A few small trees have fallen on the lawn, but for the most part, everything else appears to be intact. I race out of the room headed to Mr. Brown's room only to find it empty. I head for the steps following the sound of laughter in the kitchen. I stop short after realizing my breath is not fresh. I turn back for the bathroom where I remember seeing some mouthwash under the sink when I found the gauze and peroxide.

Someone must have flushed the toilet because Aunt Lucille's monster is gone. I look in the mirror and see bags under my eyes. I attempt to turn the water on to wash my face but nothing comes out. The current is still off and the pump isn't running. "Oh well, at least my breath is fresh." When I enter the kitchen, I want to cry. How could anyone not believe our God is a God of miracles! I see Mr. Brown sitting at the table drinking bush tea. Wally and Lucille are at the stove cooking bacon, oatmeal and eggs. Momma is setting the table and Fitzroy is sitting so close to his father it almost looks like he's protecting him.

"Well good morning, sleeping beauty!" Fitzroy says as he gets up to meet me.

Fitzroy takes me by the hand and leads me over to his father who is smiling. "Father, I'd like you to meet Faith, the woman I'm going to marry."

Mr. Brown attempts to stand, but sits back down. "Forgive me, my daughter. I'm going to need a little more time before I'm back on my feet again."

I bend down and kiss him on the cheek. "It's a pleasure to meet you, Mr. Brown."

"Mr. Brown! I'm not going to have any daughter of mine calling me Mr. Brown. Do you know how long I've been waiting for a daughter so I could love her and spoil her? I insist that you call me Father. You can even call me Dad or Daddy. I know that's what you Americans call your fathers."

I start to cry. Fitzroy hugs me.

"Did I say something wrong?" Mr. Brown asks.

"No, no! I'm just so happy." I look at Momma who looks as if she's going to cry but turns to help Wally and Lucille at the stove.

"Faith, you want some coffee?" Momma asks.

I take a seat on the other side of my new father.

"Sure. Where did you find water?" Everyone laughs.

"Did I miss something?" I say.

"Well, Lucille was having a fit about not being able to flush the toilet so I showed her how we get water when the pump is out," Wally lovingly says.

"Faith, you won't believe it. The man gave me a bucket and a rope and had me bailing water out of a hole in the floor they call the cistern. That's how I was able to flush the toilet and get water to cook with. And Wally made me break one of my nails!" Aunt Lucille punches him on the arm.

Wally kisses her broken fingernail. "Don't worry darling, as soon as the hotel opens I'll take you to the salon there and we'll get it fixed," Wally says.

"Mr. Brown, I mean Father, I love this house! I can't wait to go outside and look around."

"Good! Because after breakfast I'm going to need you to help me check on the bees," Fitzroy says.

"Check on the what?" I say, wondering whether he too had a head injury.

"On Father's bees," Fitzroy says, as if we were talking about baby chickens or something. Fitzroy continues.

"Father is very concerned about the bees, that's how he hurt himself," Fitzroy says.

"He was trying to move them into the barn when a strong wind gust came causing the barn door to knock him in the head," Momma says.

"Don't worry, Faith, you won't get stung. We have clothing to protect you," Fitzroy assures me.

"The main thing I need you two to do is make sure the queen bee is still alive. If she's alive everything will be OK." Father says with concern in his voice.

"Does she have any identifying marks? How will we know the queen bee?" I ask.

"Good question honey, no pun intended," Fitzroy says laughing. I stick out my tongue at him.

"The queen bee is larger than the drones and the worker bees. I've even put a spot of white paint on her back to make her easy to identify. Sometimes all these bees grow so large it's hard to tell who's who unless you're really familiar with them." Mr. Brown explains.

Wally and Lucille are finished cooking. We all gather at the table where Father leads us in a wonderful prayer. Momma is extremely quiet. I've never seen her like this. While we are eating, Fitzroy's cell phone rings.

"Hey, there is life! Hi Lisa, yes, we're fine. I think Faith turned her cell phone off because it wasn't working. We were surprised too...yes, she's right here." Fitzroy hands me the phone.

"Girl, guess what? I have a new dad!" Everyone smiles. I excuse myself and take the phone into the parlor. "Lisa, it was rough! I hope I don't experience another hurricane anytime soon. Yeah, I heard on the radio it skipped right over St. Thomas, but St. Croix got hit pretty hard. I need to call Mr. Atkins and Rosalinda. I hope Chloe and Nyla are alright. You're right; they do live in a castle...Get out of here! Billy called? What did he say? Stop lying! What is he, a fortuneteller or something? The Lord spoke to him in a dream and said you wouldn't marry Trevor, you would marry him and y'all would have three kids...Girl the man has gone completely crazy now. Are you sure he wasn't smoking one of those Jamaican blunts? I'm just kidding. I know he doesn't smoke weed. Why are you so upset? You know you're marrying Trevor, so that's that! Right? I'm just checking. You know you change your mind about things like you change drawers. Just kidding. Anyway, Fitzroy's father is the bomb! And the house is so beautiful. It's on the grounds of an old fort."

"Girl, before I forget, let me tell you how good God is! When we got here Fitzroy and Wally found Fitzroy's dad unconscious out in the barn. His head was split open. And get this - Momma sewed his head up. She and Fitzroy were up all night watching over him...The hospital's roof blew off and they had to evacuate folks to a hotel. Besides, we couldn't get out in that hurricane. Honey, we had our own hospital right here on the kitchen table. Look, I've got to go. Fitzroy and I have to go and make sure the queen bee survived the hurricane. The queen bee...it's a long story. I'll fill you in later. How's my beautiful niece Kamari doing? Give her a big kiss from Auntie Faith. Girl stop worrying about what Billy said. Go and enjoy that Mandingo warrior. I love you too."

As I get up off the couch in the parlor I notice the picture of Fitzroy's mother on the mantel for the second time. Only this time it's much lighter in the room so I can get a better look at her. Suddenly an eerie feeling overcomes me. I feel like I'm in an episode of *The Twilight Zone.* "Oh, my God! She favors Momma." I turn with the picture in my hand ready to go into the kitchen to show the others, and I see Fitzroy standing in the doorway.

"Isn't it strange?" he says.

"It's scary! How come you never mentioned how much my mother looks like your mother?"

"I don't know. When I first met your mother that day at the airport it was frightening. I had to go to the van and pull myself together. I took it as a sign that God was speaking to me. That he was saying, 'Momma's gone but I'm sending you a new family'."

Fitzroy walks over to me, takes the picture out of my hand, looks at his mother and starts to cry. "Faith, I feel so guilty. I should have insisted that she go to the states to get medical help. I let her down."

I take the picture from him and place it on the couch next to us. Honey, let's sit down. Fitzroy, you're a good man and a good son. Please don't beat yourself up. Your mother, from what you've told me, made a choice and there was nothing you or anyone could do about it. She wanted to live the rest of her life here on the farm without amputations and machines. Fitzroy, I feel so much peace in this house. I think I probably would have made the same choice." Fitzroy stares into my eyes, piercing my heart.

"I love you so much, Faith. Thank you for your kind words."

We hug as Momma enters the parlor. Her eyes focus on the picture lying on the couch next to us. Momma walks over and picks it up. "It was dark last night when I looked at this picture so I wasn't sure what I was seeing. Then when your father called me Hannah, all I could think about was coming back in this room at first light so I could get a closer look at that picture. I mean, other than the hair we look like twins," Momma says.

"I'm so sorry I didn't say anything before," Fitzroy apologizes.

"That's OK. Even if you did, who would have believed this? Folks are always saying stuff like you look like this person or that person. But there was no way you could explain something like this without having a picture to validate it."

Momma continues to stare at the picture. Then Aunt Lucille enters the parlor. "What, y'all having some sort of prayer meeting in here?" Lucille notices the picture in Momma's hand. "Gloria when did you take that picture? Girl, don't ever let your beautician style your hair like that again!" She jokingly says.

"That's not Momma, Aunt Lucille, it's Fitzroy's mother," I say.

"Oh, my Lord!" Lucille takes the picture and studies it. "I told you there was something eerie about this house! Look, Wally and I are going to borrow your daddy's truck. We want to see if the road to the Four Seasons is passable. I love it here but..."

"We know it's hard for you sleeping in the same room with Faith," Momma says.

"Now see, you got your mind in the gutter!" Aunt Lucille defends herself.

"She doesn't need to go to a hotel to sleep in the same room with Wally. Isn't that right, Aunt Lucille?" I sarcastically say.

"Thank God I'm grown and ain't none of y'all my mother or father!" Aunt Lucille sashays out of the parlor.

Momma yells at her, "You better be worried about answering to your Heavenly Father!"

Aunt Lucille turns with a sad look on her face then continues walking to the kitchen.

Before Wally and Aunt Lucille leave for the Four Seasons Hotel, the men help Father back upstairs to his bed at Momma's insistence. If Father had it his way, he would be outside helping us with the bees. Momma stayed with Father while Fitzroy and I checked on the colony. We lingered in the barn for some time before we went back into the house to give father the bad news. The queen bee had not survived. The few bees that were living were swarming around like they were in mourning. After we took off our bee clothes Fitzroy took me on a tour of the grounds.

We sat on the cannons and looked out onto the sea. "What a beautiful place this is. I don't think I ever want to leave here," I told Fitzroy.

"It's amazing, I never realized how much I missed this place until now," he said.

We both sat quietly for a moment; then I spoke. "You think Mr. Atkins would fly my friends and family down here for our wedding?"

Fitzroy walked over to the cannon I was sitting on, picked me up in his arms, and hugged me. "I don't see why not, Mrs. Brown."

THE END